DEATH OF A FLYING NIGHTINGALE

DEATH OF A FLYING NIGHTINGALE

A NIGHTINGALE MYSTERY

LAURA JENSEN WALKER

Author Photo Credit: Brian Baer

First edition

ISBN: 978-1-68512-559-2

Cover art by Level Best Designs

This book was professionally typeset on Reedsy.
Find out more at reedsy.com

For Edith "Titch" (Lord) Joyce

And in memory of Lydia Alford, Edna Birkbeck, Myra Roberts, Lilian (Bancroft) West, Elsie Beer, Gladys Florence Batch, Joan Crane, Margaret Wilson, Florence "Rita" (Marshall) Holt, Anne Mettam, Margaret Campbell, Margaret Walsh, and all The Flying Nightingales who served.

"At the going down of the sun, and in the morning, we will remember them."

— Laurence Binyon

Blue skies and fair winds…

Praise for Death of a Flying Nightingale

"Laura Jensen Walker honors The Flying Nightingales, the overlooked volunteer air ambulance nurses of World War II, in this riveting and affecting murder mystery. Walker deftly mixes the fear and terror of war with the humanity and courage of this remarkable Band of Sisters—creating a touching and heartfelt celebration of three 'ordinary' women—who achieved the extraordinary."—Susan Elia MacNeal, *New York Times* bestselling author of the Maggie Hope mysteries and *Mother Daughter Traitor Spy*

"A compelling tale of courageous young women in World War II, *Death of a Flying Nightingale* depicts the lives of nursing orderlies who escorted soldiers with horrific injuries home to England. Told through the eyes of three young women who risked their lives in their jobs and also at the hands of a murderer at home, the reader will soar and weep alike reading Walker's well-told story."—Edith Maxwell/Maddie Day, Agatha Award-winning author of historical and cozy mysteries

"Brimming with historical detail and layered with emotional depth, *Death of a Flying Nightingale* serves as both a cracking good mystery and tribute to the Flying Nightingales who risked their lives to bring the wounded boys of World War II safely home. I loved it!"—Melissa Amateis, WWII historian and author of *The Stranger from Berlin*

"With a gripping plot and a tender heart, *Death of a Flying Nightingale* transports the reader to Down Ampney Airfield in the throes of WWII and what a trip it is! Laugh and cry with these three splendid women, marvel at their bravery, cheer on their sleuthing, and simply luxuriate in the company of a writer who does both romantic and unflinching brilliantly."—Catriona McPherson, multi-award-winning author of *In Place of Fear*

"Laura Jensen Walker vividly captures the challenges of serving in WWII as air ambulance nurses for the Royal Air Force in this immersive fictional tribute. Here is a deserving novel of these wartime heroines that has been just waiting to be told."—Susan Meissner, USA TODAY bestselling author of *Only the Beautiful*

"*Death of a Flying Nightingale* by Laura Jensen Walker is a captivating story of courage and heartbreak as three disparate women find friendship and love during the last perilous year of the Second World War. Readers of historical fiction will revel in the period detail and atmosphere."—Marty Wingate, author of the London Ladies' Murder Club

"Walker does a splendid job of bringing the little-known Flying Nightingales to life in this novel. You'll applaud the grit and determination of the young women who risked their lives for the war effort. Bravo!"—Joyce St. Anthony, author of the Homefront News Mysteries (*Front Page Murder* and *Death on a Deadline*)

"Three cheers for *Death of a Flying Nightingale*, Laura Jensen Walker's captivating historical mystery, a tribute to the bravery and contributions of those who never picked up a rifle in WWII. With alternating and interwoven story lines, these three air ambulance nurses will keep you laughing, crying, and guessing as they solve two murders in their ranks. This book is full of heart and will remind you to never underestimate a woman. If you loved the smart, inspiring females in *Hidden Figures*, you'll love Death of a Flying Nightingale."—Tina deBellegarde, Agatha Award-nominated author of *Winter Witness* and *Dead Man's Leap*

"Brave beyond measure, those Flying Nightingales. Their service and sacrifices in the war forgotten all too soon. It is incredible to meet these young women now—to be there for their journey every step of the way. I didn't want to leave them when the story ended."—Major General Meri K. Eder, U.S. Army Retired, author of *The Girls Who Stepped Out of Line - Untold Stories of the Women who Changed the Course of World War II*

Chapter One

June 1944

Maeve

The drab-green Dakota with its identifying black-and-white invasion stripes on the fuselage shook from side to side as it flew over the English Channel. Maeve Fitzgerald tightened the straps of her Mae West life jacket and held her hamper of medical supplies in place to keep it from sliding across the floor of the bouncing plane.

Approaching the Normandy coast, she saw once again the indelible scene of the aftermath of the D-Day landings: barrage balloons, ships of every shape and size, and abandoned tanks and discarded equipment strewn across the blood-soaked beaches. Maeve crossed herself. *So many men lost.*

The RAF plane, ferrying urgent medical supplies and munitions from England, descended into Beny-Sur-Mer amidst intermittent shelling.

"Incoming!" the wireless operator yelled.

Shrapnel shot through the Dakota's windows, and Maeve ducked, clutching her St. Christopher medal. She exhaled when the pilot managed to land the plane safely. *That was a close one. Must crack on. Lots to do.*

The crew began unloading supplies amidst great clouds of dust wafting up from the French airstrip, a flattened-out cornfield. While the freight was being unloaded, twenty-one-year-old Maeve met with the field hospital nurse to get details of the various injuries. Moving amongst the wounded, the nursing orderly dispensed water, tea, chocolate, and a smile. She joked with the men, belying the horror she felt at their injuries, and made them as comfortable as possible while they waited to be evacuated.

With the help of the crew, she settled the injured onto the aircraft. The ones requiring special care or treatment Maeve loaded last so she could access them more quickly and easily during the flight. The Douglas Dakotas, the "heavy lifters" of the war, had been adapted for casualties with space for nine stretchers fitted on each side, in rows of three with the lowest on the floor. The remaining space squeezed in six sitting wounded.

Maeve never sat. As the lone medical person on board, she was far too busy. Moving from patient to patient, she dispensed oxygen, changed colostomy bags, and cleared out a tracheotomy tube. She handed out urine bottles, wedged sick bags against the necks of the nauseous, delivered tea, and provided care and comfort to twenty-four wounded men.

While at the rear of the cabin, tending to a man with a broken arm, she heard a couple of the lads call out, "Nurse, you're needed up front." They gestured to a soldier on a top stretcher who was holding a full urine bottle over the side. His arm had dropped, and the contents were trickling out. Maeve hurried over and discovered the liquid had been landing on the face of the unlucky lad beneath him.

Retrieving the bottle, she cleaned up the soldier on the floor stretcher. "Never you mind," she reassured him with a wink and a smile. "This will do wonders for your skin."

"I'll bet you say that to all the lads."

An hour later whilst delivering another round of tea to her patients, Maeve spotted the English coastline below. Over the roar of the engines, she announced, "It won't be long now before you're home."

The men cheered.

In the quiet, dark hours before daybreak, something awakened Maeve. She sat up in the bottom bunk, careful not to wake her bunkmate, and listened. Although all was silent, she sensed a disturbance in the air of the Cotswolds camp.

Sliding her feet into sheepskin-lined flying boots, she pulled on the coarse-wool "Hairy-Mary" uniform jacket over her pyjamas. Tiptoeing past her fellow sleeping WAAFs she slipped out the door of the Nissen hut into the night and made her way behind the women's quarters.

All was still, save a slight breeze in the June night air.

Maeve leaned against the back of the metal hut and gazed up at the stars. The same stars Seamus had once gazed upon. The ones her sister Briony back in Ballydavid stared at. Before Maeve left Ireland, eleven-year-old Briony made her sister promise to look up at the stars every evening and say goodnight to her, and she would do the same. That way, they would always be connected even though many miles and the Irish Sea separated them.

"Sleep tight, sweet Briony," Maeve murmured. Then she blew a kiss to the heavens and added, "Sleep tight, my love."

The elder Fitzgerald sister had been desperate to leave her small village of Ballydavid ever since her fiancé died fighting the Germans. Although most of the villagers were sympathetic at the loss of one of their own, some muttered that Seamus McCarthy shouldn't have been fighting at all. Ireland had chosen to remain neutral, a decision the young couple disagreed with, which is why Seamus joined the British Army, and Maeve emigrated to England to serve as a Women's Auxiliary Air Force nursing orderly in the RAF.

A "Flying Nightingale."

The newspapers assigned the nickname to the women who flew on air ambulances to pick up the D-Day wounded and tend to them on the flight home, and the romantic moniker had stuck. Not that there was anything romantic about what the nursing orderlies did. As one of the Flying Nightingales, Maeve made twice-daily flights to France in the noisy Dakotas since arriving at RAF Down Ampney in Gloucestershire three weeks earlier.

Her first flight would be forever seared on her brain.

Half a dozen of the injured men were burn cases, whose burns had been treated with butter—the smell was horrendous. Some of the wounded were missing arms and legs; others had severe head or facial injuries from bombs.

3

All the men clamored for tea. One young soldier with piercing blue eyes motioned to her for a cuppa, but he had no mouth to drink it. The bottom part of his face was gone.

Maeve shivered in the night air as she thought of the poor lad and wondered what had happened to him. Then she heard something. A rustle. She moved quietly in the direction of the sound. Approaching the back of the women's shower hut, she saw a flash of movement on the ground. Was it an animal? A dog? Injured perhaps? Maeve moved closer, peering at the shadows, and glimpsed pilot's wings in the moonlight. Her cheeks flamed as she realized she'd happened upon a lover's tryst.

She backed away from the intimate scene, putting distance between herself and the anonymous couple. Once she was out of hearing range, she scurried back to her billeting hut. Creeping indoors, Maeve continued her cautious retreat to her bunk, careful not to wake any of the other girls. Removing her jacket, she stepped out of her boots and slipped beneath the covers, breathing out a relieved sigh.

What if I'd actually seen who they were? I'd be scarlet.

Closing her eyes, she put the scene out of her head. Dawn was but a few hours away, and Maeve needed her sleep to face another grueling day. Drifting off, she heard the door of the hut squeak. Her eyes flew open, but she remained still. In the darkness, she could just make out a curvy shape tiptoeing to the bunk second from the end. Sally Roberts' bed.

Twenty-year-old Sally, with her blonde Victory roll and red lipstick, was the biggest flirt in camp. Sally loved men and wasn't shy about showing that love.

She wasn't the only one.

The war had changed things. After the Blitz killed thousands, Maeve saw traditional mores fall away. In the face of random potential death at any time, sex before marriage was no longer looked at askance by many young people. And not just the lads. The philosophy was, "If I don't do it now, I may never get another chance."

Maeve understood that and refused to sit in judgment. Life was too fleeting.

4

Sally liked to have a good time, but she was also a good nurse. The casualties on her flights all loved her. Sally flirted equally with the wounded—men with no legs, only one arm, horribly burned faces. Their injuries didn't matter; they were all her "boys." She'd change their bandages, joke as she passed out cups of tea, and soothe the men with her gentle ministrations. She never let her boys see the effect their injuries had on her. She saw some horrific things.

They all did.

Things they couldn't talk about with their families. They had to keep calm and carry on. Their job was to keep the men on the planes alive so they could receive the operations and procedures they needed once they returned to England. But it took its toll. More than one Nightingale collapsed in tears behind the communal hut at the end of her shift.

Maeve happened upon Sally behind the hut one evening, crying over one of her boys. In a right state herself, after encountering a flaxen-haired soldier missing both eyes on her last transport, she rounded the corner of the communal hut. The tears she'd been holding at bay in front of her patients trickled down her cheeks.

"You all right there, Irish?"

Maeve startled and swiped at her eyes as Sally approached.

Sally blew her nose, folded her handkerchief, and stuck it into her uniform trousers pocket. Pulling a robin's-egg-blue box out of that same pocket, she extended it to her fellow Nightingale. "Cigarette?"

Maeve shook her head, trying to get herself under control.

Removing a Woodbine from the pack, Sally stuck it between red lips vivid against a pale face, which usually displayed rosy cheeks, and struck a match. Lighting the cigarette with a shaking hand, she took a long drag.

"What a ruddy awful day." Sally released a gust of smoke. "I had an eighteen-year-old who lost his foot. Only one foot, mind you—not as bad as some of the other poor buggers—but this boy loved to take his girl dancing. He said they won a dance contest just before he shipped out. Now, he'll never dance again. Bloody Germans!" She took another long pull from her

5

Woodbine and glanced at Maeve. "What set off your tears then?"

"A lad who lost both his eyes," Maeve said in as calm a voice as she could muster.

Sally's eyes glistened. She stubbed her cigarette out against the metal hut and placed it back in the pack. "Right then." She slung her arm over Maeve's shoulder. "What you and I need is a drink and a man to distract us from our troubles. Shall we see what's on offer inside?"

Maeve stiffened. She still didn't want any man but Seamus. "You go ahead. I've some letters to write."

"Suit yourself." Sally fished out a compact and lipstick. Reapplying her signature scarlet shade, she smacked her lips at the mirror and smoothed her Victory roll. Snapping the compact shut, she sauntered to the entrance of the communal hut where everyone gathered between flights.

Maeve heard Sally say in a flirtatious tone, "Hello, boys. What's a girl got to do to get a drink around here?" Although drinking wasn't allowed in the huts, sometimes one of the wireless operators would sneak in a flask and pass it round. Returning to her barracks, Maeve put the soldier with the missing eyes out of her head and put on a brave face as she began her latest letter to her sister.

Dear Briony,

I'm happy to hear how well you're doing at school, sweetheart. Mam and Da must be bursting with pride at your high marks, especially in maths. You were always good with numbers, unlike me.

How are Patrick and Andrew getting on at the factory? Since neither of our brothers are letter writers, I rely on you to keep me informed. All's well here. They keep us busy so by the end of the day I'm fair done in, but I hope to go to the cinema soon with one of the girls. There's a new American film with Bing Crosby as a priest that sounds a right treat.

Is Seamus's mother still poorly? I haven't heard from her in a while. Please give her my best.

It's lovely now with the roses in bloom. I'm glad they weren't all removed for vegetable gardens. The rolling green hills remind me so much of Ireland. When the war is over, I'll bring you here one day. You'll love it.

I'll send my goodnight to you later while looking up at the stars. The same stars you'll be looking at, sweet Briony. The stars that will always connect us.

Love,
Maeve

She set down her pen and sighed. Maeve couldn't tell her sister what her job was really like or where she was posted. She had to be circumspect for the censors. More importantly, though, she would never worry her family by letting them know the horrors she'd seen and how dangerous it was flying over to France and Belgium in the Dakotas.

On the outbound flights, the nursing orderlies were classified as air-crew and wore parachutes. The planes couldn't display the Red Cross insignia since they were "operational flights" ferrying supplies—sometimes munitions—which made them a target for the Luftwaffe. Maeve's Dakota had been hit more than once. Thankfully, the crew always made it safely to their destination.

Touch wood.

On the way home with the wounded, however, the Nightingales weren't permitted to wear parachutes. As the lone medical person on board, should the aircraft crash, their orders were to remain with the plane and their patients. They were forbidden to bail out.

Something Maeve would never tell her family.

Chapter Two

Betty

Betty Hall didn't think she'd ever get used to the noisy planes. The youngest Nightingale, whose mother referred to her as "a plain girl, but good and strong," grew up on a small farm in Herefordshire. The loudest sounds on Cherry Tree Farm were squealing pigs, squawking chickens, and her father's tractor, which sounded like the purr of a cat compared to the constant droning of the Dakota engines.

Seventeen-year-old Betty had arrived at Down Ampney two days earlier after finishing up six weeks of training. In addition to her medical training—how to cope with broken bones, missing limbs, head injuries, burns, and the like—she also underwent several hours of flying experience.

She would never forget the night she joined a Dakota crew on glider-towing exercises. The plane's cargo door had been removed, and Betty sat on her parachute, back pressed up against the bulkhead separating her from the cockpit. Brown eyes fixed on the open doorway in terror, Betty prayed she wouldn't slide out. When the glider was released, jolting the plane, she dug her nails deep into the parachute silk, determined not to show her fear. This was her big chance to earn her own money—an extra eightpence a day for flying pay—and serve her country.

She wasn't about to muck it up.

Betty wasn't bothered about blood and tending the wounded; growing up on a farm, blood and death were a part of daily life. She killed her first hen at eight and wolfed down her mum's roast chicken, veg, and mash for dinner that night. Nor was she bothered about going into an active war zone despite not being recognized as a nurse—in the RAF, you had to be an officer to be a nurse. Caring for injured soldiers as an enlisted nursing orderly and saving them from dying like her big brother Wilf, who'd been killed at Dunkirk, suited her just fine.

But Betty had never been on a plane before and was frightened to fly, a secret she kept to herself. Her first flight made her stomach turn inside out. Luckily, on the days they flew, as part of the aircrew, the nursing orderlies received the luxury of an orange, two packets of chewing gum, and a barley sugar. Chewing gum kept her nausea at bay.

After passing her training, Betty was posted to 46 Group, RAF Transport Command at Down Ampney in the Cotswolds, where she bunked with eleven other WAAF's in one of the women's billeting huts. She'd met a few of the girls in her hut—Maeve, Etta, Doreen, and the glamorous Sally who reminded Betty of a film star with her blonde hair and red lips—but the rest of the Nightingales were off on flights when she arrived.

Maeve, an Irish girl a few years older than her with lovely porcelain skin and raven-black hair, took the farm girl under her wing and showed her around the camp. Betty followed Maeve, wide-eyed as she pointed out the runways, Mess sites, hospital huts, and Navy, Army, and Air Force Institute (NAAFI) canteen.

It's like a proper town, Betty marveled. *The only thing missing is a church.*

Maeve jerked her head to one of the many metal Nissen huts dotting the camp. "That's the communal hut where the crews gather after flights for a cuppa."

The domed shape reminds me of Christmas pudding with the insides hollowed out, the young nursing orderly thought. As the pretty Irish girl chatted and continued to show her round the camp, Betty's nervousness abated.

"I know it's a bit overwhelming at first," Maeve said, "but you'll soon settle in. If you have any questions, just ask me or any of the other girls. They're a good lot." She indicated the barbed wire around the perimeter, installed to protect against intruders, and showed Betty the gaps in the wire where they took shortcuts during their rare off-duty times.

"It's a short walk to the village where there's a shop, post office, and church," Maeve said. "Cricklade is three miles away, and it's a bigger town with several pubs, and dances and cinema showings. A couple of girls I went through training with are based at RAF Blakehill Farm near Cricklade."

Then, she introduced Betty to the pilots, navigators, and wireless operators. After leaving the men, Maeve warned the newest Nightingale which ones to watch out for. "Some of the lads are all hands and think we're here for their personal pleasure. But a few well-chosen words, and if necessary, a knee in the right place always does the trick."

"I don't think I'll have to worry about that." Betty lifted her broad farm shoulders in a resigned shrug. "Men rarely give me a second glance." She pushed a stick-straight brown hair behind her ear.

"You might be surprised." Maeve regarded her kindly. "Men's heads may be easily turned by a pretty face, but in the end, you'll find most just want to settle down with a nice girl."

Ducking her head, Betty blushed. *I wonder if I'll meet someone who wants to settle down on a farm and raise a family. I'd like to have lots of children.*

The sky was overcast the next day when Betty made her first flight across the Channel. *Please don't let the weather turn,* she prayed. Chewing gum to keep her queasiness at bay, she ran through all the possible medical scenarios she might encounter to keep her mind off the rocking and jolting of the Dakota. Men's lives depended on her.

When they touched down, Betty helped the crew offload some of the supplies, before turning her full attention to the wounded on the ground. *The poor lads.* Wilf's face flashed before her as she dispensed tea to the casualties, many not much older than her.

"Here you go, soldier." She gave a cuppa to a sandy-haired corporal missing both his arms. "Here's a nice cup of tea." Betty held it to his lips.

"Ta, duck."

Grateful the weather had held and it wasn't raining, she made her way down the line of wounded waiting to be evacuated, offering a smile, a touch on a shoulder, and tea from the catering-sized urn she carried. A stray dog appeared and began to play with the injured men, bringing smiles to weary faces. One of the soldiers set his helmet on the ground and asked Betty to pour water into it for the thirsty pup.

Then, it was time to load the casualties on board. The crew lifted stretcher after stretcher onto the Dakota beneath a darkening sky, settling the men into the waiting slings on each side of the aircraft. As the plane took off, the novice nursing orderly found herself too busy to be nervous or afraid.

Betty administered oxygen to two soldiers with internal injuries that made it hard for them to breathe. "There now," she reassured them as she made sure their oxygen masks were fitted to their faces, "this will help you breathe properly. Just let the oxygen do its work." She cleaned sick off a queasy private, distributed urine bottles, and rebandaged an officer with a terrible head injury whose bandage had come undone.

The seventeen-year-old did whatever was needed for the men in her care. Noticing a white-knuckled corporal clutching the edge of his stretcher as the Dakota continued its ascent and recognizing his fear of flying, Betty sought to distract him. "Where are you from, soldier?"

"Poole. In Dorset," he said through gritted teeth.

"I've never been to the south. I imagine it would be a lovely place to go on holiday."

The corporal's jaw unclenched, and his eyes took on an animated gleam. "You'd love it—we've got the best beaches for swimming, fishing, and the like." He proceeded to regale her with all the things to see and do in his coastal town.

Next, Betty approached an older sergeant, missing a leg. "Would you like a cuppa, love?"

"Ta, nurse." Flashing her a grateful smile, he held out his enamel cup.

She continued moving down the line of stretchers offering tea and TLC. One lad stared up at her in a feverish delirium and asked, "Are you an angel?"

"No." She placed a cool hand on his warm brow. "I'm Betty."

A crack of thunder sounded, and the heavens opened up.

Betty's stomach churned as the plane lurched to and fro in the thunder and pounding rain. She squeezed her rabbit's foot and chewed her gum to prevent being sick. *Please, God, please, God, don't let me start vomiting now.*

Some of her patients weren't as lucky.

She wedged one sick bag after another beneath their chins.

"I dinnae know how fliers do it," a Scottish solder declared after retching. He swiped at his face, a bilious shade of green. "I'll not be goin' up in a plane again once we're back on land. I need solid ground beneath my feet."

"Not me." An injured pilot's eyes shone from the stretcher above. "I can't wait to get back up. Flying high as a bird beyond all earthly constraints, there's nothing like it."

"Ye and the birds can keep it." The Scotsman retched again.

Betty removed the close-to-overflowing sick bag, forcing herself not to gag as she dropped the smelly sick in the rubbish. Wiping her hands, she lifted the water urn and began dispensing drinks to the lads.

The Dakota juddered and dipped in the storm. One of the burned men who'd been unconscious when they'd loaded him in his stretcher sling bolted upright, crying, "We're going down, we're going down. Abandon ship!"

Betty hurried over to the patient whose upper torso, head, and half his face were swathed in bandages. "It's all right, Corporal," she soothed, patting his hand. "Everything's fine. We're not going down. We've just run into a bit of bad weather." She eased him back to a supine position as he drifted back into unconsciousness again.

Turning round, Betty noticed the discomfort of a bear of a man across the aisle. His thick right arm was encased in plaster, while his left arm ended above the elbow and was swathed in bandages. The young private, who couldn't have been much older than her, was red-faced and restless.

"Are you in pain, soldier?"

"No, miss." He squirmed in his stretcher.

"Can I get you some tea or water?"

"No thanks, Nurse." His tree-trunk-sized leg jiggled, his face a mask of misery.

Realization dawned. Noting the name on his uniform, Betty leaned in close and whispered, "Private Martin, is this what you need?" indicating the empty urine bottle in her hand.

He gave an imperceptible nod, turning a deeper shade of crimson, unable to meet her eyes.

How can I distract him? Betty wondered. *I have nothing to say to help this embarrassed lad.* Suddenly, the right words tumbled out—all about Cherry Hill farm.

She chattered about her family and the farm as she discreetly attached the bottle to the soldier's nether regions. "Dad remembered how things had been in the Great War and said we needed to make sure there was enough food to go round, so we planted rows and rows of spuds at the start of the war," Betty said. "We have a large victory garden, too—one of the first in our area. My brother Wilf was a right one for veg. He loved his carrots and sprouts."

She blinked back sudden tears. "We lost Wilf at Dunkirk."

Private Martin's face returned to a normal colour. He gave her a sympathetic look. "I'm sorry. We've lost too many good men." His blue eyes flicked to his stump. "I'm one of the lucky ones. I only lost part of my arm." He wriggled the fingertips of his remaining hand. "Once this cast comes off, I can get back to work with my brothers and dad."

Betty gave herself an internal shake. Her job was to take care of the men, not wallow in grief. She pushed aside thoughts of Wilf. "What kind of work do you do, Private?"

"We've got a dairy farm in Shropshire. As a farmer, I was exempt from joining up, but I didn't think it was right to stay at home whilst all the other lads were fighting."

"That's how my brother felt, too." Discreetly, Betty removed the urine bottle. "My father understood, but my mother wanted Wilf to stay at home where he'd be safe. Mum wanted me to do the same." She squared her shoulders. "But it was important for me to go where I was needed."

Betty retreated to the back of the Dakota and emptied the full bottle into the waste container. Then she checked on the men in the rear, who all wanted more tea. Moving from stretcher to stretcher, she poured tea from the large urn, trying her best not to spill.

13

The bouncing plane had other plans.

Tea sloshed out, dampening her blue uniform trousers. "My mum always said I was a messy eater. As a girl, I was forever spilling my tea and getting jam all over my face."

"Och, some jam and bread would go down a treat." A soldier with a missing leg gave her a hopeful look. "I don't suppose you have any?"

Betty shook her head. "But you'll be home soon and can have some then." *Although the bread will be horrid National Loaf*, she thought. Jam can disguise the taste, but not the terrible texture.

"I'm craving me mum's sausage and eggs." The lad in the stretcher above licked his lips. "Her breakfasts were a right treat: bacon, sausage, mushrooms, tomato, and black pudding." He sighed. "I can almost taste it now."

Across the aisle, another soldier groaned. "What I wouldn't 'alf give for a good fry up."

The Dakota lurched and tilted, sloshing out more tea, dropping blankets to the floor, and dislodging an oxygen mask from one of the men. Betty hurried to secure the mask onto the struggling-to-breathe soldier, calming him as she did so. Picking up the fallen blankets, she tucked them around the injured. While doing so, she heard a retching sound behind her. Spinning round just in time, she shoved a sick bag under the nauseous soldier.

Private Martin watched in admiration. "You're a regular Florence Nightingale, you are."

"A *Flying* Nightingale," the lieutenant beside him corrected. "That's what the newspapers call these girls. And I'd add angel of mercy to that." Earlier, Betty had acted fast to fashion a tourniquet to the lieutenant's leg, where a deep wound had opened up and begun bleeding. "I'd tip my hat to you, Aircraftwoman Hall," the officer said, "if my arm wasn't in this sling."

Betty's cheeks warmed. "Thank you, sir."

Another crack of thunder, followed by a flash of lightning, jolted the Dakota, highlighting anxious faces.

Private Martin began to sing in a deep bass, "Pack up your troubles in your old kit bag…" Betty joined in, and before long, the entire plane combined their voices in a rousing singsong that drowned out the bad weather and the noisy drone of the Dakota.

Chapter Three

Etta

E tta took a final drag from her cigarette before stubbing it out and placing it back inside its pack. She downed a couple of aspirin as she made her way to the Dakota, hoping the little white pills would do their magic before she was airborne.

No more closing the canteen for you again, Blackwood. What were you thinking?

Etta *hadn't* been thinking. That was the point. She'd had a miserable day yesterday and just wanted to forget everything: The shrapnel bursting a hole in the fuselage and some of the crew's parachutes falling out. The back-to-back flights with terrible injuries, including a shell-shocked lad who'd seen his best friend blown up and lost both his legs in the same bomb blast. The sniper fire whilst she was walking back to the airstrip after relieving herself behind a bush.

Topped off by the letters waiting for her upon her return.

One from Jack saying he'd met someone else and was getting married. The other from Mavis, her friend and former flatmate, whom Etta had worked with at the munitions factory. Mavis wrote that Helen, their third flatmate, had been killed in a factory accident.

Instead of heading straight to her bunk after her last flight like usual, Etta decided to drown her sorrows by going to the canteen with the aircrew and Sally from her hut. Sally was always up for drinks and a good time. She'd invited Etta to accompany her in the past, as had Harry Denton, the wireless operator on most of her flights. Handsome Harry, with the laughing eyes and roguish grin, had been pestering Etta for weeks to join them, but she had always declined.

Having grown up with a father who drank away his weekly wage at the pub, Etta wasn't much of a drinker. And there was Jack to consider. Nice, dependable Jack who'd grown up in the same London tenement as her. Although they weren't engaged, there had been an unspoken understanding between them that one day they would marry. Before settling down, though, Etta wanted adventure. She had always wanted something more. More than just being a housewife like her mother.

Once she'd come of age, Etta packed in her job at the dress factory her mum had pushed her into and went to work in a munitions factory on the other side of town. She was determined to help the war effort and get away from her family. Far, far away. Etta and two of the other munitions girls, Mavis and Helen, pooled their scant resources and shared a tiny flat.

Although Etta reveled in the freedom of being on her own, her work on the assembly line didn't provide her the kind of adventure she craved. When she heard the RAF was seeking women to join the WAAF and become air ambulance orderlies, Etta promptly joined up.

She'd arrived at the camp in March. To receive as much flying experience as possible, she went up in the air whenever her aircrew did, day or night, in the Dakotas. On her first operational flight to Normandy, Etta explored a concrete dugout the Germans had occupied mere days ago. Looking round the abandoned dugout, she envisioned the carnage the enemy had inflicted on the Allies as they stormed the beaches. Her mouth thinned to a grim line. Spying a German helmet and bayonet on the ground, Etta grabbed both as souvenirs.

Today's souvenir, an unwelcome hangover from last night, she vowed to do without in future. As she approached the plane with her parachute, medical hamper of equipment, and urns of hot tea, Etta recoiled at the sight of curly-headed Harry in the doorway. Recalling the too-close-for-comfort dance with the flirtatious wireless operator the night before, she felt the back of her neck flush.

"Hey, Red, how's the head today?"

"It's been better." She loaded her gear on board, her movements swift and focused. "Remind me never to mix beer and gin again."

"Will do." Harry winked. "I'll also remind you that you owe me a date to the dance on Saturday."

Definitely no more beer and gin for this girl.

"Sorry." Etta shoved her auburn hair behind her ears and busied herself with a stretcher sling. "I won't be able to make it. I—"

Harry held up his hand to cut off her fumbling excuse. "Right-o. I never hold a girl to a promise made when she's in her cups." He gave her another wink. "But never fear, I will ask again."

"Okay, Romeo," Flight Lieutenant Harkness ordered. "Let's finish getting this cargo loaded so we can be off."

"Yes, sir."

Etta's face flamed at the disapproving look the pilot directed her way. Lieutenant Harkness and his pilot pal Jock McCannell over at RAF Blakehill didn't approve of having women onboard the planes, Harry had informed her when she'd first arrived. Both men came from fishing families, and fishermen would never put out to sea with a woman onboard. It was bad luck. Etta thought back to that first week in June when the Nightingales were grounded from further training flights as all the planes took part in the D-Day landings.

And Warrant Officer Jock McCannell's plane never returned.

Determined to prove she wasn't bad luck and deserved her place on the plane, Etta became the hardest-working Nightingale in camp. She volunteered for extra shifts, took on duties none of the other nursing orderlies wanted, and picked up the slack if one of the other girls got sick. Etta worked harder and longer than most of the men.

She wasn't about to let her sex, or a centuries-old superstition, hold her back.

Etta jolted awake at the sound of screaming. "Bloody hell! What's going on?"

Across from her, Maeve bolted out of bed and hurried in the direction of the noise now reduced to loud weeping. She approached the new girl, Clemmie Brown, sitting up in her bunk at the front of the hut, shaking and crying with a face as white as the cliffs of Dover.

Maeve sat on the edge of the bunk and enfolded the weeping woman in her arms. "There, there, it's okay," she soothed, stroking the light-brown curls, damp with perspiration. Glancing over Clemmie's head, she saw Etta staring at them with an uncertain look. Maeve mouthed the word "water," and Etta scurried off.

Returning moments later with a glass of water, Etta remarked with a casual air, "I ran into Harry Denton. He said you had a bit of a scare, dodging the Luftwaffe and thinking your plane was going to wind up in the drink. Harry said the pilot did some fancy flying and saved the day."

Clutching the glass with both hands, Clemmie gulped down the water.

"Who was the pilot?" Maeve asked.

Clemmie grimaced. "Lieutenant Blake. The one who thinks he's God's gift to all the girls. After we landed, he could see I was shaken up and whispered he had just the thing to make me feel better. When I turned him down, you should have seen the nasty look he gave me."

"Some men just can't take rejection," Maeve said.

"Especially the ones who don't have a lot on offer," Etta said. She watched as Maeve pulled a hankie from her pocket, dried the newest Nightingale's tears, and handed her the square of white muslin.

"Go ahead, blow," Maeve ordered.

Clemmie blew her nose and released a last shuddering sigh. "Sorry." She glanced round the empty nut. "I'm glad none of the other girls were here to see me like this." Her cheeks pinked. "You both must think I'm an awful ninny. I don't usually have nightmares or break down like this."

"I don't think you're a ninny. We all have nightmares. Some of the injuries we encounter are pretty horrendous," Maeve said. "They stay with you. It's hard to erase them from your mind."

"I've never seen anything like it." Clemmie's voice broke. "I thought I was prepared, but it's so much worse than I expected."

Having grown up in the rough-and-tumble East End, Etta found she was better equipped to handle the casualties than many of the other girls.

23 June 1944

Dear Jack,

Congratulations on your upcoming marriage. I hope you and Florence will be very happy together. Flo's a great girl; she'll make a great wife. You deserve that.

I know everyone expected us to get married. You told me when I left to join the WAAFs that you would wait for me. I thought that's what I wanted, but since I've been here, things have changed. I've changed (as you could probably tell from my letters.) Truth is, I'm not sure how good a wife I'd have been to you. Or anyone, for that matter.

As you know from my dreadful shepherd's pie and the countless custards I've murdered over the years, I'm a terrible cook. I'm not a good seamstress either, and my knitting is abysmal. Like the scarf I made for you last Christmas. It looked like something the cat dragged in. Feel free to chuck it in the bin. (I doubt Flo would like you wearing it.)

I've said before how much I love being a nursing orderly and caring for the injured on the flights. When the war is over, I want to become a full-fledged nurse. Maybe in Oxford. There are several good hospitals there, and it's a lovely city full of books and learning. You know how I love books.

I'll not be returning to London. There's nothing for me there.

With all best wishes for your happiness,

Etta

She sealed the letter, knowing this would be the last letter between them. Etta felt a flicker of sadness. Jack was a good bloke. He'd been a good friend to her, providing a welcome refuge from her horrible family. Mostly, though, what she felt was an overwhelming sense of relief.

Freedom.

Being a Flying Nightingale had shown her a different world—a different way to *be* in the world—and Etta loved it. All of it. The flying. The beauty of England from the air. The friendship and camaraderie amongst the girls. The pay. And no hostile mother, drunken father, or sleazy brother.

She pushed the unwelcome memory down. Deep down.

Most of all, Etta loved caring for the wounded. She was fascinated by the human body and how it worked. She saw horrific injuries transporting the casualties, more terrible than anything she could have imagined. Rather than being sickened by what she'd seen, though, Etta found herself fascinated at what the human body could endure and still survive. She felt it was her sacred duty, her privilege, to keep her patients alive.

Thus far, touch wood, none of the Nightingales had lost a single man.

But Etta wanted to do more than give the wounded oxygen, cups of tea, and reassuring words. She wanted to aid in the actual healing process, be a part of the patient's recovery after he went on to hospital. She longed to work alongside doctors as a proper nurse in a proper hospital. Maybe someday, she scarce dared to hope, even be part of a surgical team.

With two, sometimes three flights a day and back again, Etta rarely had free time. But when she wasn't on duty, she could be found with her nose buried in *Gray's Anatomy*. She'd saved up for months for the classic, rather dear, medical tome until she had enough to buy a used copy from the bookshop in Cirencester. The medical Bible became her prized possession.

Growing up in the slums of the East End, Etta had never had anything of her own. When she'd finally fled home and got a job in the munitions factory across town, her wages went to her portion of the rent and the groceries she and her flatmates managed to cobble together.

Becoming a WAAF in the Royal Air Force changed all that.

For the first time in her twenty-four years, Etta had a sense of security and a place to belong. Even more than that, though, in nursing the wounded, she'd discovered her calling.

And nothing, and no one would take that away from her.

Chapter Four

Maeve

On the flight to France, Maeve sat on a box of supplies, daydreaming about Ballydavid and her lost love. She recalled the long walks she and Seamus would take through the countryside, sharing their hopes and dreams and planning their future together. She would pick wildflowers, and Seamus would read Yeats to her. Closing her eyes, Maeve remembered her fiancée jumping up and exclaiming,

"Come Fairies, take me out of this dull world, for I would ride with you upon the wind and dance upon the mountains like a flame!"

Seamus was now riding upon the wind.

Shaking her head, Maeve thought of happier things, remembering nights at the family pub when her da would play the fiddle, and she'd serve Seamus and his pal Padraig stew. Everyone loved Mam's Guinness stew. Maeve's mouth watered, thinking of the hearty meal of braised beef, onions, carrots, and potatoes in a thick Guinness broth. She could almost taste it…

Flak attacks punctured her food fantasies.

As the plane veered to escape the German gunfire, Maeve fell off the supply box and landed hard on the floor. Shrapnel pinged inside as the Dakota continued its defensive maneuvers. Pressing her elbows to her sides, she made her body as small as possible, her fingers tightening around her St. Christopher.

Across the plane, she saw the wireless operator wince. Grabbing her hamper, Maeve crouched low and scuttled to Harry's side. "Are you hit?"

Then she saw the blood.

"It's just a scratch."

Loosening his tie, Maeve unbuttoned Harry's collar and examined his neck. "It's not deep. You won't need stitches." She unscrewed the lid of her water urn, wet a cloth, and dabbed at the nicked flesh before bandaging it.

"I've not seen you up this close before, Maeve." Harry's eyes gleamed. "You're quite a beauty, aren't you, with that alabaster skin and those emerald eyes. A man could get lost in those eyes. What say you and I have drinks when we get back to camp?"

"Ah, Harry, you are a one, aren't you? But I'm afraid you're barking up the wrong tree."

"You can't blame a lad for trying."

The plane juddered as it began its descent. Shrapnel burst through the fuselage, and Maeve ducked and grabbed Harry's hand.

Sally Roberts blew a puff of smoke at the ceiling of the communal hut. "I miss our training days," she said. "Remember when the pilots would invent bogus problems so they could divert into RAF Northolt? They'd nip into London, and I'd tag along and buy lipstick. Once, early on, before nylon was heavily rationed, I even managed to get a pair of stockings. Cost me most of my wages, but it was worth it."

Sally cast a rueful glance down at her uniform trousers. "I haven't worn stockings in ages."

"Shame." Harry gave her a wolfish look. "Those legs should never be hidden. I'd be happy to take them out for a spin on the dance floor tomorrow night."

Sally pouted. "I'd love to, Harry, but I'm on duty."

"I'm not." Maeve cradled her cup of tea in her hands, grateful for its comfort after her earlier flight. "As long as the duty sergeant agrees, I'll switch with you. I'll work for you Saturday if you'll take my Sunday shift."

Sally's blue eyes lit up. "Thanks, Maeve. You're a peach."

"You are indeed." Fingering the bandage on his neck, Harry saluted the

Irish Nightingale. "Thanks, Maeve."

Frank Timmins scowled. "I was going to ask Sally to the dance, Denton. I didn't when I saw she was on the schedule to fly tomorrow."

"Sorry, old man. The early bird catches the worm."

"Now, now, fellas, I'm sure we can work something out." Sally batted her lashes at the two wireless operators. "You can *both* take me to the dance."

Betty watched the exchange wide-eyed. She turned to Maeve sitting beside her. "Isn't Sally something?"

"She is that."

"She's so pretty and glamorous she could be a film star." Betty stared admiringly at the blonde nursing orderly. "She looks like Lana Turner."

"Don't tell her that, or there'll be no living with her."

The door pushed open. "Any char? I'd murder for a cuppa." Wireless operator Dickie shoved his hand through his sandy hair.

Doreen, billeted in Maeve and Betty's hut and known as a confirmed teetotaler, sank into the nearest chair, white-faced. "I'd rather have something a bit stronger."

"What happened?" Maeve asked her fellow Nightingale.

Dickie answered. "Nothing much. Just a tyre bursting on landing that had us skid out of control and crash. But the pilots did a cracking job stopping us from running into two Dakotas."

Doreen grimaced. "A bit too close for comfort that."

Thinking of her own too-close-for-comfort flight and her next flight coming up, Maeve hurried to pour tea for the rattled crew members.

"Cheers," the group chorused, holding up their cups to Dickie and Doreen.

"I'm dead on my feet." A bedraggled Maeve pulled off her flying beret and headed straight to bed, sinking down on the bunk opposite Etta, who was engrossed in *Gray's Anatomy*. "I'm going to stay right here for the rest of the war," she said as her head hit the pillow. "Wake me when it's over."

Etta raised an eyebrow over her book. "Planning to sleep in your boots, Irish?"

Groaning, Maeve sat up. Swinging her legs off the bed, she reached down to remove her boots. As she set her footwear on the floor, she caught sight of the letter waiting to be posted. "Is that the final missive to Jack?"

Etta nodded. "But never mind about that." Her face took on an animated expression. "Did you know that the proximal and distal tibiofibular joints permit the fibula to adjust its position relative to the tibia, increasing the range of motion of the ankle?"

"I did not but thank you for telling me. Now I'll sleep well tonight."

Etta stuck out her tongue at her Irish pal and returned to her book.

Awake now, Maeve decided to catch up on her letters. She sat cross-legged on her bunk, pushed her dark hair behind her ears, and picked up her pen.

> *Dear Seamus,*
>
> *I know it's silly to keep writing you letters when you're dead, but you'll never be dead to me, my darling. You're my heart, my soul, my best friend. We always told each other everything, and I don't want to stop now.*
>
> *Today was quite the grueling day. I'd scarce got the wounded from my first flight offloaded onto the waiting blocks for the medical officers to examine, and I was enjoying a cuppa in the communal hut when the duty sergeant told me one of the girls was sick, and I needed to replace her ASAP on the next flight out. I ran to the loo (there are NO facilities for women at the French airstrips), grabbed my medical supplies, flasks of fresh tea and water, and we were off.*
>
> *Once we were over the Channel, the weather turned, and by the time we arrived in France, it was bucketing down. As you know, I've never been one to let a little rain stop me. Not Maeve Catherine Brigid Fitzgerald. What self-respecting Irish lass would?*
>
> *Flying back to Blighty was a bit dicey, though, and I instinctively crossed myself. Yes, I still do that even though I don't go to Mass these days or know if I even believe in God anymore. Hard to shake the habits of a lifetime.*

Maeve stopped writing as memories of her fiancé and growing up in

Ballydavid flooded her. Living next door to one another, she and Seamus had been childhood playmates. They'd loved going fishing together, tramping through the woods looking for fairies and leprechauns, and pretending to be Queen Maeve and the mighty warrior, Cú Chulainn. Maeve and Seamus went to Mass daily in the local Catholic school run by nuns, received their First Communion once they'd reached "the age of reason" at eight, and had their Confirmation at thirteen. They snickered together over Sister Fidelma's bad breath and droning voice during catechism that put the class to sleep.

As the playmates grew up, their childhood friendship blossomed into love, and on her fifteenth birthday, Seamus kissed Maeve for the first time. She had taken out the scraps for the pigs, and Seamus approached her in the back garden with a birthday present; a wooden dog whittled in honour of her beloved Blackie, who'd died the week before. As her eyes filled with tears, Seamus leaned in and kissed her.

Maeve touched her fingers to her lips, remembering.

There were many more kisses after that. The young couple fell head over heels and planned to marry once they were of age.

Then the war came.

With Ireland neutral, only two villagers from Ballydavid signed up. Most of the men—including Maeve's older brothers Patrick and Andrew—felt it wasn't their war. "Let the English fight the Germans," the Irishmen said.

Seamus felt differently, much to his mother's dismay and his father's anger. Father and son had several heated rows about it, but the son stood his ground. "What kind of man would I be if I didn't do what I know to be right?" Seamus said when he told Maeve he was enlisting in the British Army.

His friends and family were all against it. Most of the villagers were. No one could understand why Seamus McCarthy wanted to go off and fight in a war that wasn't even his. But Seamus, a voracious reader with a keen interest in history, didn't care what everyone thought. Listening to the news reports and reading about Nazi Germany's invasion of Europe and subsequent violence against Jews and others, he recognized that Hitler must

26

be stopped.

And Seamus was determined to do his part to stop the madman.

He had many impassioned discussions about it with Maeve. "Edmund Burke said, 'The only thing necessary for the triumph of evil is for good men to do nothing.' Even Scripture says it's a sin when someone knows the right thing to do and doesn't do it. Fighting the Nazis is the right thing to do," Seamus declared. "I can't stay here in Ballydavid and do nothing while the world is falling apart around me."

Maeve planted a big kiss on his lips, proud of the man she loved. The man she was going to marry. She believed in him even if the rest of the village didn't. Then she showed Seamus how much she loved him.

Even though it was a mortal sin.

She had wrestled with her decision to give herself to Seamus, body and soul. Raised in the church, Maeve knew it was wrong. Good Irish Catholic girls didn't do such things. Only hussies did. And she was no hussy. But Maeve also knew that the love of her life was going off to war. A war that was killing thousands. What if, God forbid, Seamus didn't come back? She crossed herself. *This may be our only chance, and besides, we're engaged.*

And so, before she sent her beloved off into battle, Maeve gave Seamus all of herself with all of her heart—never telling anyone they'd consummated their love.

A consummation that ended in pregnancy.

A pregnancy that ended in miscarriage.

The day Maeve received the shattering news that Seamus had been killed, she lost their baby. Something she kept secret from her family, his family, and the entire village. And one of the many reasons she fled Ballydavid and joined the WAAF.

When Seamus died, Maeve thought God was punishing her for their sin. As more and more men died in the war, though—legions of them—she knew God couldn't be punishing everyone. Or could he?

That's when she stopped going to church.

Maeve resumed her letter.

Our little boy or girl would be nearly three now, my love. I imagine your son frolicking up there with you—the two of you going fishing and catching a mass of salmon. Or playing conkers—do they have conkers in heaven?

She gazed upward as a new thought struck.

But what if we'd had a daughter instead? What would you be doing in heaven with our little girl? Having tea parties? Playing with dollies? Reading her fairy stories, perhaps? Aye, that's it. I can see you reading our daughter Rapunzel...

Falling asleep, Maeve dreamed of Seamus roaming the earth in search of her like the blind prince roamed the land for years in search of Rapunzel. Eventually, the prince found his beloved, and Rapunzel's tears falling on his eyes restored his vision. The reunited couple returned to the prince's kingdom, where they lived happily ever after.

Chapter Five

Maeve, Betty, and Sally were on their way to Cricklade for a dance—Maeve, under protest. She didn't want to dance with anyone other than Seamus, but Betty begged.

"Please, won't you come, Maeve?" the youngest Nightingale pleaded. "You don't have to dance, just keep me company while Sally's tripping the light fantastic. Likely, no one will ask me to dance—the boys back home never did. I didn't mind because the lads never asked my friend Josie either. Josie and I had a good natter while we enjoyed the music. Here, I'd be all on my own."

Looking into Betty's brown eyes, Maeve knew there was truth in what she said. With her blonde hair and curves, Sally never lacked for dance partners. She hoped the soldiers here wouldn't ignore Betty the way the men in her village had, but Maeve knew that wasn't a given, and the thought of her friend sitting alone on the sidelines hurt her heart. "Oh, all right then." She gave Betty a rueful smile. "I won't dance, but you and I will have fun watching Sally in her element."

Sally lifted her penciled eyebrows when Maeve donned her navy shirtwaist for the occasion. "That's not a dance frock."

"I don't intend to dance. I'm just after an evening out with the girls."

Sally got them a lift from Billy, one of the lads in transport, by promising him the first dance. Halfway to Cricklade, though, the motorcar broke down. Billy let out a curse when he checked under the bonnet. "Sorry, this will take a bit for me to set right. Go on without me, and I'll catch you up. Sally, be sure to save me a dance."

Sally kissed him on the cheek. "Of course I will." Linking arms with Maeve and Betty, she grinned. "Come on, girls." As they marched off beneath the summer sky, she began to sing the Army marching song, "We're Going to Hang Out the Washing on the Siegfried Line."

Half a mile later, Maeve stopped. "Hang on, I've got a stone in my shoe." Stooping to unlace her Oxford, she noticed an overturned bicycle in the ditch up ahead. "Looks like someone took a spill." Shaking out the stone, she urged Betty and Sally forward. "I hope no one's hurt."

Approaching the bicycle, Maeve noticed a bit of pink peeking from behind a hedge and pointed it out to the girls. As they rounded the hedge, the trio of Nightingales found a young woman in a party frock face down on the ground.

"She must have hit her head when she fell," Betty said. "I hope she's all right and has only got the wind knocked out of her."

Carefully, they turned the fallen woman over. Maeve gasped. "Oh, my goodness. That's Agnes Wilson from Blakehill Farm. We went through training together."

Agnes was decidedly not all right.

Checking the fallen Nightingale's wrist for a pulse, Sally shook her head. "I'm afraid she's gone."

"Her neck," Betty whispered. "Look at her neck."

Sally rocked back on her heels. "Oh my God. She's been strangled."

They never made it to the dance.

Word spread like measles that a nursing orderly at Blakehill Farm had been murdered. The Cricklade Police interviewed the three Nightingales from Down Ampney who'd found her, but the girls couldn't tell the detective much, apart from what time they had found the body: eight-fifteen.

No, they hadn't heard or seen anything, just the overturned bicycle and the girl in the pink dress.

No, they didn't know her, apart from Maeve.

"I didn't know Agnes well," Maeve told the police detective. "I haven't seen her since we trained together ages ago. Agnes was posted at RAF Blakehill and I'm at Down Ampney, so once we completed training, our paths didn't cross again."

"Not even at one of the dances?" the detective asked.

"I haven't been to any of the dances. This was my first."

"Right." He scribbled in his notebook. "When you knew her, did the deceased mention a boyfriend?"

Maeve scrunched up her eyes, thinking back. "She *may* have mentioned she had a lad back home, but I could be confusing her with another one of the girls. Sorry. As I said, I didn't know Agnes well. Some of the girls from training went on to Blakehill Farm with her, though. They would know better than me."

The dead Nightingale's colleagues at RAF Blakehill were questioned. One of her friends said Agnes used to have a boyfriend back home in Coventry, but they'd split up a while ago. Her bunkmate, Lil, said Agnes had been seeing someone the past couple months, but she didn't know more than that, not even his name.

"Agnes was very close-mouthed about her private life," Lil told the police. "I could tell she was crazy about him though as she was always humming "You Made Me Love You" before going to see him."

"And you have no idea where they would meet?"

"No, she never said."

Back at camp, Sally comforted Betty. "It's all right, love," she said, sitting beside the youngest Nightingale on her bunk and putting her arm around Betty's shoulder. "Don't you worry. The coppers will catch the blighter what did this."

Betty shuddered. "I've never seen anything like that before—those awful hand marks on that poor girl's throat. Who would do such a terrible thing and why?"

"Perhaps this Agnes wouldn't give him what he wanted, so he took it by force," Thelma, one of the older nursing orderlies, said primly. She sniffed. "Although, that's what girls get when they go meeting a man out in the middle of nowhere."

Etta squashed out her cigarette. "We don't know if she was meeting someone, Thelma. She could have just been out riding her bike, and some stranger attacked her."

Doreen gasped. "What if there's some madman out there running around and killing girls?" She looked wildly around the hut. "Are we safe?"

"As long as you stay close to camp and don't go out gallivanting alone at night, I'll wager." Thelma sent a pointed glance at Sally.

"I'm never alone," Sally said. "Unlike some who will *always* be."

Maeve waded into the sniping. "One of ours has been brutally murdered," she said. "A lovely young girl, a fellow Nightingale. We do her a disservice with our speculations. I think we should let the police do their job and honor Agnes by continuing to do ours."

A few days later, word spread through camp that the dead Agnes had been in the family way. When the news hit Down Ampney, Maeve and Betty were both off on flights, so the girls in their hut felt free to gossip.

"Some blighter got her preggers," Sally said as she flipped through an old copy of *Vogue*. "He probably scarpered once he found out. That's why the coppers haven't been able to find him."

"Either that," Doreen said, "or maybe he didn't want to be a dad. When Agnes told him, he might've exploded and gone crazy. Crazy enough to kill her."

"Or maybe he's *already* a dad," Sally speculated, "and a husband. Perhaps that's why Agnes kept his identity such a secret. She could've been seeing a man who'd already got a wife and kiddies at home."

Thelma pursed her lips. "I imagine her being in the family way would have been most unwelcome news to the adulterer she'd been fornicating with. News he would *not* have wanted to get back to his wife, and so he killed his bit on the side to prevent her from saying anything."

"A bit extreme, that, don't you think?" Sally said. "All he had to do was give her money to get her little problem taken care of. Happens all the time and would have been a much easier solution than murder."

Etta, who'd been trying to concentrate on *Gray's Anatomy* while the girls gossiped, interjected, "Unless, of course, Agnes refused the money and decided she wanted to keep the baby."

Returning from her flight that night, Maeve sat down and wrote to Seamus. Writing to her dead fiancée always helped her to sort out her feelings.

> *Dear Seamus,*
>
> *One of our Flying Nightingales has been killed. Her name was Agnes Wilson. I went through training with her. I didn't know Agnes well, so I'm not sure why I'm taking this so hard. Maybe it's because she wasn't killed in the line of duty. Something we're conditioned to expect in wartime.*
>
> *We live with the daily knowledge that our Dakotas could go down at any time—shot out of the sky by the Germans. I've told you that as the only medical person on board, nursing orderlies are not allowed to parachute out if such a thing was to happen. Our job is to stay with the wounded and care for them. I know that and fully accept it. (Although I've not told my family about that risk—Mam and Da would have never let me leave Ireland if they'd known.)*
>
> *But this poor girl was brutally murdered, and she was carrying a wee babby. Maybe that's why it has affected me so deeply. Now both Agnes and her poor babby are gone, their lives cruelly snuffed out before the wee one ever took a breath. Sometimes I despair of the evil in this world...*

Maeve wept thinking of her own wee babby who'd also never got to take a breath.

Chapter Six

August 1944

On a sunny August afternoon, Betty moved amongst her burn-injury patients outside, trying to keep their spirits up as they waited to be moved to hospital in Odstock. Throughout the day, flights and patients arrived continuously. Sometimes, like now, the Nightingales were held up from moving the wounded through to their next location as they waited for trains to get a clear run-through to the next hospital.

The waiting, now that they were back home on English soil, made some of the men anxious, worried about their families and futures. Betty did her best to reassure and distract her patients, talking about her farm or the weather. "Such a lovely day, isn't it?" She tilted her face up to the sun, basking in its warmth. "A welcome change after all the rain."

Two medics walked past carrying a stretcher. An invisible stretcher. The medics introduced their imaginary patient to the wounded awaiting transport. The pretend patient fell off the pretend stretcher. Picking up the fallen man, the comic duo tucked him back in to the imaginary stretcher and dropped him in an exaggerated Charlie Chaplin mime routine.

Everyone laughed.

"Titch, that man of yours is a right jokester." Betty smiled at the diminutive nursing orderly beside her.

Edith "Titch" Lord returned her smile. "Paddy's always got me laughing."

Sally, freshening her lipstick, gave Titch—so named for her small size—an approving nod. "Good for you finding a man who makes you laugh. Life with him will be fun and never boring." She wrinkled a pert nose above red lips. "If there's anything I can't stand, it's a boring man."

"Find your own funny man. This one's taken."

Sally gave Titch a mock salute.

The roar of a Dakota overhead made the Nightingales look up. Betty shaded her eyes against the sun. "Here comes Etta."

One of the ground crew approached Sally. "We're ready to move your lot on now."

The blonde Nightingale returned her attention to her waiting patients with head injuries. "This is where I leave you, lads. You'll be going on to hospital in Oxford, and the docs will take good care of you. Soon, you'll be home with your wives and sweethearts." She wagged a finger at the men, offering a coquettish smile. "Don't forget me." As she moved away, Sally murmured, "I won't forget you."

Betty saw her burn patients off. After saying goodbye to the last man, she hurried over to the admin office, having missed monthly mail call and yearning for word from home. Upon seeing the letter from Cherry Tree Farm, she bounced from foot to foot, longing to open her mum's missive then and there. Betty decided to wait though until she got to the communal hut, where she could settle in with a cuppa while she read.

Handed a second letter, a frown creased her forehead as she stared at the unfamiliar name and postmark—she didn't know anyone in Stoke Mandeville. Outside, Betty stepped onto the wooden planks laid down over the ever-present mud and carried on to the communal hut, pausing at the threshold to scrape mud off her boots. Inside, she nodded to Margaret, one of the older Nightingales, tucked away in a corner, her familiar fortune-telling cards splayed out on the table before her. Betty poured herself a cup of tea and ripped open the letter from her mum, eager to hear the latest from home.

Dear Betty,

You'll never believe what that silly goose Tillie's gone and done now. She was chattering away to Rose, gathering eggs, not paying attention, when she slipped on some chicken muck and fell, breaking FOUR eggs. Can you believe it? Then, spotting a mouse, she ran screaming from the henhouse straight into my washing, dropping my good Sunday knickers in the mud.

Betty giggled as her mother recounted the latest story of Tillie, the hapless Land Girl. Eighteen-year-old Tillie from Manchester had never been to the countryside before, her mum had written in an earlier letter. She said when the city girl first arrived in the Wye River Valley, Tillie had been stunned by the vision of the rolling green hills and dense forests. Tillie had never seen a pig, chicken, or cow before coming to Cherry Tree Farm. She hadn't seen many fresh vegetables either and had no idea how to pick them. Rose, the other Land Girl, from Sussex had spent summers at her grandparents' farm, so she knew the ins and outs of farm work. She helped Betty's dad teach Tillie how to work the land and take care of the animals.

Thank goodness for Rose. I don't know what we'd do without her. Your dad taught her how to drive the tractor, which will be a big help during harvest. John Thorpe stops by often—he really misses our Wilf, too. Rose caught his eye, and they've started stepping out together. I wouldn't be at all surprised if one of these days we heard wedding bells. John's always been a good lad, and Rose is a lovely girl. They get on well and make a fine pair.

You forgot to pack your jumper, so I'll send that along next month before the weather turns. We don't want you catching cold this winter.

I'm happy to hear you've made some friends among the other girls. Are their mothers as worried as I am about their daughters flying round in those big aeroplanes? I don't know how you do it. Personally, I don't intend to ever set foot on a plane. Do the Germans ever shoot at you? Silly question. Of course, they don't, seeing as how you're transporting the wounded and have Red Cross markings. It's just my mother's fretting, making my imagination run wild.

Betty stopped reading. She could never tell her parents that when the Dakotas left camp, they were loaded with supplies, often ammunition. As such, no Red Cross insignia appeared on the plane. Although the nursing orderlies had been issued Red Cross armbands, they'd been instructed not to wear them on the flights carrying supplies over the Channel.

A fact their families would never know.

Betty wasn't accustomed to keeping secrets from her mum and dad. Up until now, she'd never had to, but war changes things. Needs must. Rather than lie to her parents, though, she learned how to deflect those kinds of questions. She filled her letters home with stories about her patients, her fellow Nightingales, and the local flora and fauna, a subject close to her parents' heart.

Betty didn't tell her mum and dad about Agnes, either, the nursing orderly from Blakehill Farm who'd been strangled. She would never forget the sight of the poor girl and those awful marks on her neck. She still had nightmares about it and made sure never to leave camp alone—most of the other girls did the same. In her daily prayers, Betty prayed the police would catch the culprit soon and put him away before he could kill anyone else.

She returned to her mum's letter.

Please be careful, love. I couldn't bear it if I lost my girl too. Your dad and I are proper proud of you taking care of our injured lads. You were always good at nursing wounded creatures. Remember when you fixed up poor Pip after he got into a scrap with that German Shepherd? And that time you stayed up all night in the barn watching over Bessie after she had that rough calving? Your father said you never once left her side.

Dad sends his love and thanks for sending him your monthly sweets coupons. I'm off to make our tea now: Woolton Pie, again. Do you ever have that? I'd think not since the RAF will be keeping their troops well-fed. (Although I reckon there's not much in the way of homemade jams and puds.) Be sure to watch the post for a sweet surprise arriving soon.

Love,
Mum

Betty's mouth watered in anticipation of the surprise—likely her mum's famous blackberry jam. The best jam in the county, as evidenced by the multitude of blue ribbons hanging next to the cooker in the kitchen. Finishing her tea, she opened the letter from Stoke Mandeville.

Dear Aircraftwoman Hall,

You probably won't remember me, not with all the wounded men you see daily. I was a patient on one of your flights back from France. The one-armed Private Martin? (Although I suppose you've seen more than your share of one-armed privates amongst the wounded you care for.) Let me introduce myself. I'm Albert Martin, from a dairy farm in Shropshire. You talked to me about your farm in Herefordshire and your brother Wilf. Does that ring a bell?

We also had a singsong on the way home during some rather grim weather. If you don't mind my saying, you have a lovely voice.

I wanted to thank you for your kind care of me and the other patients. It made the rough flight home much easier. You're a good nurse. I'll bet a strong, strapping girl like you is a big help on the farm. We have a Land Girl at ours now, but Mum says she's a tiny slip of a thing who can barely lift a bale of hay. Not much use that. Dad says at least she's able to milk the cows.

I miss milking cows. I miss feeding them and breeding them too, but most of all I miss calving season. There are so many things about our farm I miss. You see, I haven't been home yet—I'm still in hospital having physiotherapy. I'm getting stronger every day, though, and learning how to manage things one-handed. The doctor says I should be home in time for Christmas.

I'm counting the days.

My mum and dad came to visit soon after I arrived. Mum said she needed to see with her own eyes her youngest was all right. She knew about my missing arm but still cried when she first saw my stump.

"Don't worry, Mum," I told her. "This won't stop me from playing the harmonica." That made her laugh. Mum hates my "screechy" harmonica—says it sounds like cats fighting. I used to play it just to get her goat.

Enough about me, I'd like to know about you. Whereabouts in Herefordshire do you live? Our farm is just outside Ludlow. We might be neighbors! Imagine that.

I would like to write to you if you don't mind. You aren't spoken for or engaged or anything, are you? And your Christian name is Betty? That's what I heard the wireless operator say.

I introduced myself as Albert earlier, but most people call me Bert (although my mum prefers Albert.) You only know me as Private Martin, but I hope you'll call me Bert, or Albert, if you like. I'll no longer be Private Martin once I finish up here; there's not much call for one-armed soldiers. As soon as I'm demobbed, I'll go back to being a dairy farmer and contribute to the war effort that way. There's plenty needing milk and cheese.

I hope you'll write back. But if you don't, I understand. You probably have lots of soldiers writing to you.

Yours sincerely,

Albert Martin

Betty stared at the letter, dumbfounded. She read it again, focusing on the part that said, "You aren't spoken for or engaged or anything?" She remembered the private, a bulky bear of a man who'd been embarrassed and bashful.

He certainly wasn't bashful in his writing.

She couldn't believe the soldier from a neighboring county wanted to write to *her. Ludlow's not far from us,* Betty mused. Perhaps after the war when I return home, Private Martin—Albert—and I can visit each other. Her face heated at the thought, a shy smile curving her lips.

"What's this?" Sally's voice cut through her romantic reverie. "Letter from your fella got you blushing?" She flashed a coy smile.

Betty's face turned a brighter shade of pink. "He's not my fella," she stammered. "Just one of my patients."

"Watch out," Sally teased. "Before you know it, he'll fall in love and ask you to marry him. They always do." She fluffed her hair. "I can't tell you the number of men I've had to say no to."

"And the number of men you haven't," Thelma muttered. "And I'm not talking about marriage." The religious teetotaler, fast approaching thirty, shot the popular blonde a disapproving look.

Sally tossed her head. "Marriage is the last thing on my mind. I'm having far too much fun playing the field."

Thelma's mouth thinned. "Not everyone's as indiscriminate as you."

Off duty for the rest of the day, Maeve decided to use the rare free time and escape camp for a bit. Careful not to snag her uniform, she slipped through the opening in the barbed wire fence and set off for the village shop to buy some sweets, enjoying the sound of birdsong and children's laughter as she walked.

Hearing the local children playing behind the houses she passed, she wondered what her little sister was doing right now. Was Briony tramping through the woods with her friends, looking for fairies and leprechauns as Maeve had done when she was young? Or was she helping Mum do the washing and cleaning? Maybe helping Da at the pub? Maeve smiled to herself. More than likely, her sister was squirreled away up in her room doing homework or reading her latest book down by the stream, nestled in her favourite spot at the base of a willow tree.

Ah, Briony, I miss ye lass. Don't grow up too much while I'm gone.

Maeve wondered just how long she would be gone. How long would the war go on? Next month would be five years since England declared war on Germany, and in that time, hundreds of thousands of British soldiers had died. It was unimaginable. How many more would die before the fighting ended? And it wasn't just soldiers losing their lives, either. She recalled reading in the newspaper that close to 40,000 civilians died in the Blitz.

How many had been children? Maeve's eyes filled with tears, her hand involuntarily touching her stomach. It didn't bear thinking about.

A girl darted past, tripping in her haste, and Maeve caught her before she fell. "Where are you off to in such a hurry then, lass?" She smiled at the scrawny child who couldn't have been more than six or seven.

"The shop to get sweets. I want to get some before they're all gone."

"Me too. May I walk with you?"

"If ya walk fast."

Maeve quickened her pace.

The girl stole a sideways glance at her. "You one of them typists over at the RAF base?"

"I'm a nursing orderly."

"A *Flying Nightingale*? I heard about you lot rescuing our lads. Must be excitin'". She gazed at Maeve with new eyes. "Is it scary flyin' up in the sky in those big planes?"

"It can be, although I'm usually too busy to be afraid."

"I reckon you see lotsa blood and such, huh?"

And such. The boy with no eyes flashed through Maeve's head. "That's part of our job. You get used to it." She would never get used to the burn victims, though. The awful smell of burnt flesh and butter...seeing the horrific pain the soldiers endured.... *Thank God for morphine.*

The girl looked at her wide-eyed. "Didja ever have to cut off someone's leg? My friend Hazel's brother Tom come home with only one leg. He'll be gettin' a wooden leg soon, though, so's he can walk proper again."

Maeve was used to the morbid curiosity of children, but usually, it came from boys. She smiled down at the girl. "What's your name then, love?"

"Nancy."

"Well, Nancy, to answer your question, nursing orderlies don't perform amputations." Thank goodness. "The doctors in the field hospitals are the ones who do that sort of thing."

Arriving at their destination, Nancy pushed open the door of the shop to reveal a queue inside. "Hiya Miz Walsh. I hope you still got some sweets left," she said. "We got a genuine hero here wantin' some—one of them Flyin' Nightingales from the camp. Seein' as how she's savin' our lads ev'ry day, I reckon she should go to the front of the queue, don't you?"

"I reckon you're right, Nancy." The shopkeeper bobbed her head at Maeve. "Miss, if you'd come up to the counter, please."

Maeve demurred. "I'm no hero. It's our fighting men who are the real heroes."

"I don't deny that, but I know for a fact how you lot help our wounded boys on the planes. My own son told me, and I'd like to thank you for bringin' him home safe to his mum."

Blinking back tears, Maeve nodded at the shopkeeper. She slung her arm around the young girl's neck. "In that case, may I bring Nancy?"

Chapter Seven

The Cricklade Police continued their investigation into the murder of Nursing Orderly Agnes Wilson with help from the MPs. Unfortunately, the dead Flying Nightingale had kept the identity of the man she'd been seeing such a closely guarded secret, the law enforcement agencies hit a dead end.

Etta told the girls she'd overheard one of the MPs say to a Cricklade copper, "Unless the killer walks into the local nick and confesses, I don't see as how we're ever going to find this bugger." The policeman agreed with him, she reported to her fellow Nightingales.

"And so the murderer of Agnes Wilson and her unborn child gets away with it," Maeve said.

Etta's eyes flashed. "Men get away with everything."

Etta pulled on her kit, bypassing the long, elasticized—and hideous—navy blue "passion killer" knickers all the girls hated in favor of her own. Not that she had any passion to worry about killing. She couldn't be bothered with men, apart from nursing them.

Nursing was her sole focus.

Maeve and Etta had volunteered to care for a group of bomb-happy boys who had to stay in camp overnight before being moved on to hospital the next day. The shell-shocked men couldn't be left alone and needed watching over. Always eager to undertake additional tasks to prove her nursing worth, Etta stepped up first to volunteer for the extra duty.

Maeve followed her lead.

As the two Nightingales entered the hut housing the anxious patients, they found men calling out for their wives, girlfriends, and mothers. One bolted upright in bed crying, "Mummy, Mummy!" and stretching out shaking hands to Maeve.

Etta watched as her Irish friend hurried to him and clasped her hands in his. "There, there. Everything's going to be all right," Maeve said.

"Oh, Mummy." The soldier threw himself into her arms, overcome by great racking sobs. Maeve cradled his head and rocked him like a baby. "It's okay," she soothed. "It's okay. I'm here."

Awkwardly, Etta approached a man who was trembling uncontrollably. He looked right through her, gazing at unseen demons in the distance, his mouth open in a rictus of horror.

"Can I get you anything, Corporal?" she asked. "Water? Tea?"

He stared at her, uncomprehending.

Etta pulled the blanket at the foot of the bed up over the shivering soldier. "That's better. Nice and warm." At a loss of what else to do, she clumsily patted his arm. "Sleep now."

The patient's mouth relaxed, and he closed his eyes.

Maeve moved on to the next bed, where a man was yelling, "Eileen, Eileen, get the children to the bomb shelter!" His head swiveled to and fro, scanning the room. "Where's Joey?" he cried. "It's not safe. We have to get Joey and Lizzie into the Anderson shelter. Hurry!" Suddenly, he thrust his arm up in front of his head. "It's going to hit! Take cover!" He ducked and curled into a fetal position, weeping. "It's not safe, it's not safe."

Two soldiers on the other side of the room jerked upright in their beds, yelling, "It's not safe!"

Etta hastened over to the two men while Maeve comforted the father in front of her. "Shh." She rubbed his back in a calming, circular motion. "You're safe now. There's no bombs. You're in hospital, safe and sound." Maeve hugged the agitated man, continuing to rub his back until he calmed down.

Etta positioned herself between the yelling soldiers' beds, extending a hand to each man. Grabbing her hands, they held on for dear life. She watched as Maeve moved on to the next bed, where a soldier was sitting up and furiously scrubbing at his hands with an imaginary cloth. "So much blood. It won't come off!" He scrubbed harder, growing frantic.

Maeve laid her hands gently atop his. "Shall I help you?" Etta watched as her Irish friend removed her handkerchief from her pocket and wiped the top of the man's hands. She turned his palms up and wiped them as well. "There. I've got it all now." Maeve stroked his hand and returned the hankie to her trouser pocket.

The soldier released a shuddering sigh and laid back down.

Desperate for a wee and a cigarette, Etta knew she couldn't leave her bunk mate to cope with the shell-shocked soldiers on her own. She carried on until it felt as though her bladder might burst, finally sending a desperate look to Maeve and mouthing the word "toilet."

Maeve nodded, and Etta scurried from the room. Escaping to the nearby latrine, she took a puff of a Woodbine. *What the bloody hell have I got myself into,* she wondered. *And must I go back?*

Quit your whinging, her conscience scolded. *You can't abandon Maeve and those lads.*

Sighing, Etta stubbed out her cigarette and hastened back to the hospital hut. The sound of bomb-happy boys calling out for their mums made her wince and come to a halt outside the door. *Buck up, Blackwood, you can do this.* Straightening her shoulders, she reentered the ward.

As another man called out in a plaintive voice for his mother, and another, his sweetheart, Maeve began to sing in a lilting soprano, "There'll be bluebirds over…"

The Irish Nightingale sweetly sang her patients to sleep.

The next morning, after the bomb-happy group were taken to transport Maeve hugged Etta and wept. "Those poor men." She swiped at her eyes.

Etta sank down hard on one of the beds, pushing her auburn hair away from her face with a shaky hand. "Cleaning up sick, bandaging bloody wounds, even dealing with blown away stomachs and colostomies is easier." *I'm never volunteering for this duty again,* she vowed.

"Those lads broke my heart. I wonder what's going to happen to them."
Maeve stared off into the distance. "The horrors they must have seen."

A tall, gray-haired woman in a blue dress and white veil stopped in the
doorway. "Well done, girls."

Maeve and Etta snapped to attention before Matron.

The camp nursing supervisor, who'd served in the Great War, gave them
a brisk nod. "It's a difficult task caring for shell-shocked men, and you did it
well. Not everyone can cope with those invisible injuries. It takes patience,
compassion, and a strong mental constitution. I shall recommend you both
for this duty again." Matron gave them a brief smile. "Now go and get some
sleep."

"Yes, ma'am."

Leaving the hospital, the girls ran into Will Nichols, one of the male
nursing orderlies. Will tipped his hat to them and smiled, his gaze lingering
on Maeve. "Well, if it isn't my two favourite Flying Nightingales. Where are
you off to in such a hurry?"

"To get some kip." Etta rubbed her eyes. "We spent the night watching
over a group of bomb-happy lads."

Will's smile faded. "Poor buggers. I can't imagine what they've been
through."

Maeve's eyes filled. "Hell." She turned away as fresh tears began to fall.

The girls headed to their hut, each caught up in her own contemplations.

Etta tried to sort through her conflicting emotions. Although she was
gratified by Matron's words of praise—something the nursing supervisor
doled out sparingly—she knew she wasn't cut out for last night's kind of
nursing. Mothering didn't come naturally to Etta as it did to Maeve. The
last thing she wanted was to be a mother. Or wife, for that matter. This set
her apart from the other Nightingales.

Most of the girls talked of getting married and settling down to have a
family after the war. Some were engaged to childhood sweethearts, some
had fallen for the wireless operators they flew with every day, and a handful
were being romanced by members of the air support ground staff.

More than a few of the Nightingales had a crush on handsome Doctor

Moore, one of the medical officers who examined patients upon their arrival. The dark-haired officer's more than passing resemblance to Clark Gable set several hearts aflutter.

Including Sally's.

"Doctor Moore can examine me any day," Sally pronounced with a smirk as the girls giggled in the hut one evening, chatting about the men they fancied.

"Any man who's *breathing* can examine you," Maeve teased.

Sally flipped her hair. "Variety is the spice of life."

Intent on the latest chapter of *Gray's Anatomy*, Etta turned on her side in a futile attempt to block out the girls' chatter.

"I think Doctor Moore would be immune to your charms," Doreen said primly.

"He's immune to most of our charms," Thelma declared. "And for good reason." Pausing to make sure she had everyone's attention, the resident gossip who prided herself on always having the inside scoop said, "Did you know Doctor Moore's wife and son were killed in the Blitz?"

The girls gasped.

Thelma leaned forward to recount the tragic tale. "Apparently, Doctor Moore had only just seen his family on leave. Before returning to camp, he made arrangements for his wife and two-year-old son to leave London and go to the country where they'd be safe." She paused before continuing in a hushed tone. "The night before they were to depart, the Germans bombed their bit of the city. All the flats on one side of the street were leveled, including the one with Doctor Moore's family."

Betty's hand flew to her mouth.

"No wonder he looks so haunted," Doreen murmured.

No wonder indeed, Etta thought.

As Maeve and Etta continued on to their hut after watching over the bomb-happy boys, Etta scowled and shoved her hand through her hair. She acknowledged to herself that she didn't want to be a nanny. Brutal as it was to admit—and she felt guilty for even thinking this—but tending to the shell-shocked lads last night had felt rather like minding children. Only these were men, not children.

Men who needed their mummies.

Etta wasn't a mummy. Or a nanny. She was a nursing orderly who wanted to become a full-fledged nurse in Princess Mary's Royal Air Force Nursing Service after the war. Hopefully, on a surgical ward, which would allow her to see inside the human body that so fascinated her. For months, she had worked hard to get Matron to notice her nursing skills—coping with colostomies, gangrene, tracheotomy tubes, and the like.

Etta didn't mind the smell of gangrene or colostomies; she had a strong stomach. Growing up in a tenement where a dozen families shared the same toilet—often broken—she was used to the smell of shit. More than once since arriving at Down Ampney, she had stepped in and taken over for a squeamish Nightingale who couldn't bear the stench.

Etta was hoping a recommendation from Matron would open doors for her to continue her RAF nursing training after the war. But now that Matron had finally noticed her, it was for something she didn't want to do. How was she to redirect her? Etta squared her shoulders. She would just have to redouble her efforts and gain a reputation amongst the doctors and nurses for being able to do the difficult tasks the other nursing orderlies struggled with.

Reaching their billeting hut, the girls tumbled into their cots, too spent to even remove their uniforms. Etta fell asleep instantly.

Maeve couldn't sleep. The face of the traumatized soldier trying to find his two children and get them safely to the bomb shelter haunted her. Her heart clenched as she thought of the patient who'd called her Mummy. And he wasn't the only one. Throughout the long night, soldier after soldier cried out for their mothers. Maeve hugged them and rocked them, thinking of the child she'd lost as she soothed them back to sleep.

Perhaps this is the mother I was meant to be, she thought.

Chapter Eight

September 1944

"Why does the pilot keep circling?" Betty asked wireless operator Dickie upon their return to camp after delivering patients to Oxford.

"Because we're going to crash land," he said. "Best prepare yourself."

Betty's heart lurched. *Crash?* She squeezed the lucky rabbit's foot in her pocket, then put her hands behind her head and curled into a ball to roll and take the impact as she'd been taught in flight training. Bracing herself, she prayed, repeating the Julian of Norwich saying she'd learned in church as a girl that never failed to calm her. *All shall be well, and all shall be well, and all manner of thing shall be well.*

The Dakota landed hard and skidded on the runway. When it stopped at last, Betty found herself at the tail of the plane. She looked up in surprise. "That wasn't too bad."

Dickie gave her a thumbs-up. "You're getting to be quite the pro at flying."

Betty smiled and stroked the rabbit's foot, proud of how far she'd come since her first flight. Her nightmares over Agnes had also stopped, much to her relief. It had been a couple months now since the nursing orderly at RAF Blakehill had been killed, and no other Nightingales had been assaulted, so Betty and the other nursing orderlies decided Agnes's death had been a one-off. Likely, her lover had killed her when she told him she was going to have a baby.

Something Betty didn't need to worry about.

Betty took another spoonful of porridge as she read over her response to Private Martin's letter. Mindful of the censors and respectful of her patients' privacy, she had to be careful what she wrote. She musn't say anything that might identify Down Ampney or the general area, or Admin would black it out. Someone in camp had mentioned Swindon in an outgoing letter recently, and everyone had been herded into barracks and reprimanded. Rather than risk such an offense, Betty decided it would be safest to write about her family and home.

> *Dear Albert (I like your full name),*
>
> *Thank you for your letter. I appreciate your kind words. It was such a surprise to hear from you. Yours is the first post I've received from any of my patients.*
>
> *I hope your physiotherapy is going well. Make sure you do what the doctor says, and before you know it, you'll be home on your farm once again. I confess I'm missing home and our farm. In answer to your question, Cherry Tree Farm is on the outskirts of Brampton Bryan, about ten miles west of Ludlow, so we are indeed neighbors. Fancy that!*
>
> *Brampton Bryan is a lovely little village known for its long, ancient yew hedge around the old castle and church. St. Barnabas is one of the few churches built during the Commonwealth. It isn't a grand church, rather plain and simple, like me, actually, but it has a lovely window with beautiful Easter scenes I never tire of looking at.*
>
> *You already know about my brother Wilf, and I believe I mentioned my mother as well. As I recall, I didn't say much about Mum apart from her worrying about me when I joined up. I think all mothers worry, don't you?*
>
> *You said there's a Land Girl helping out on your farm. Dad has two Land Girls, Tillie and Rose. Tillie's a city girl, and not used to working the land or being around animals. Apparently, she fainted the first time she saw Mum kill a hen. City sorts are funny, aren't they? Rose is a*

pip, though, and with her and dad's help, Tillie's coming along well. (Although she still can't eat chicken.)

Mum's quite active in the local WI. Her blackberry jam and Victoria sponge have won first place for as long as I can remember—even when she had to use carrots instead of sugar for sweetener. I've been going to Women's Institute meetings with Mum since I was a girl and have learned a lot from the speakers. I especially enjoy the games and quizzes. Is your mum in the WI?

Betty blushed as she read over the next bit.

I'm not spoken for or engaged or anything like that.

Was that too forward? Should she cross it out? After wrestling with herself, she decided to leave it. After all, he had asked the question, it would have been rude not to answer.

I look forward to hearing from you again.
Sincerely yours,
Betty Hall
p.s. Do you like films? I do, although it's been ages since I've been to the cinema. (I quite like harmonicas too.)

As she sealed the letter, Thelma plopped down on the Mess bench beside her. "I'm so sick of porridge every day." She pushed her spoon around the ubiquitous bowl of oatmeal. "I wish we could have eggs every now and then, like the rest of the crew."

"Haven't you heard?" Maeve said from across the table. "We're not aircrew. Aircrews are made up of *men*." She fanned herself with an imaginary fan and affected a Southern American accent. "Big, strong men who need the proper food to keep up their strength. We're just l'il ol' women. The weaker sex."

"Well, fiddle-dee-dee," Betty said, emulating the heroine of the film she adored. Wilf had taken her to see *Gone with the Wind* at the cinema when it first came out, and she had been mesmerized. Scarlett O'Hara went after what she wanted and didn't let anyone or anything get in her way. Betty had begged her older brother to see the film again and they'd stayed for the second showing.

Thelma poked at the offending gruel. "The weaker sex who fly in the same plane with the men, loading, unloading, and delivering the same supplies to the front as they do."

"The weaker sex who go into the same war zone as the men and get shot at by the same enemy." Etta finished her tea. "The difference is I can't see our male aircrew cleaning up sick from a load of wounded."

Maeve arched an eyebrow. "Now *that* I would pay to see."

Betty giggled. "Me, too."

Etta stood. "Meanwhile, best eat up, girls. Things are hotting up."

Chapter Nine

The camp had been a hive of activity of late, more so than usual. For the past few weeks, the flying squadrons had been doing training exercises towing Horsa gliders with airborne troops and practicing drops on Salisbury Plain. Something big was brewing. The Nightingales just didn't know what.

Until 17 September.

That's when the squadrons took off as part of the Allied assault on Arnhem, a German-occupied Dutch town on the Rhine River. The aim of the Allied military campaign dubbed Operation "Market Garden" was to seize key bridges in the Netherlands, outflank the German defenses of the Siegfried Line, and create an invasion route into Northern Germany.

Medical evacuation flights came to a halt in those first days of Operation Market Garden. Grounded, the Flying Nightingales spent hours winding bandages, cleaning the barracks, and scrubbing and readying the collection of Nissen hospital huts for the expected incoming wounded. When that was done, the girls caught up on their correspondence.

A couple of the nursing orderlies decided to use the time to iron and press the injured men's uniforms. Maeve enjoyed ironing; she found it relaxing. Back home, she'd always done the ironing. Every Saturday, she would iron her mother's best dress for church the next day, as well as hers and Briony's. Then she'd tackle her father's and brothers' suits. She also took on the task of ironing Seamus's clothes when his mother's arthritis made it impossible for her to hold an iron any longer. The night before Seamus shipped out,

Maeve ironed his Army uniform with great care.

Titch and Maeve ironed side-by-side, lost in their memories.

Maeve thought of home and Seamus. Lately, though, her beloved's face was no longer as sharp in her memory as it had once been. When she tried to picture her fiancé now, the image was fuzzy. She could still hear Seamus's voice, though, as if he were in the same room with her. His voice filled her head now. *It's time to let me go, darlin'. Past time. You've grieved long enough. Go on and live your life, love. Life is for the living, not the dead.*

The iron in her hand stilled as Maeve blinked back tears and gazed off into the distance.

Titch, finished with the soldier's uniform she'd been working on, returned the olive-drab wool serge to his bedside.

"Ta, love." The young corporal shifted in his bed. "Uh, Nurse, did you empty the pockets before ironing my trousers?"

Titch smiled and handed him the small, flat square containing the latex rubber preventive issued to British troops that the lads had dubbed a French letter. "Here you are. All safe."

The corporal's face flamed scarlet.

As Maeve and Titch exited the hospital ward, Titch smirked. "I've never seen a grown man blush so much." The two Nightingales burst out laughing.

Inside her hut, Maeve pulled out Seamus's picture and stared at it, memorizing the beloved features. Then she kissed the photo and tucked it away. "Goodbye, my love," she whispered.

She pulled out pen and paper.

Dear Briony,

Thank you for your recent letter, love. I'm sorry you had flu and felt so rotten, but I'm glad to hear you're feeling much better now. Mam's chicken soup and poultices always do the trick.

It's a lovely autumn day. The leaves are just starting to turn, and there's a brisk breeze. How's the weather there? Starting to feel a nip in the air, I'll wager.

Briony, I know how much you loved Seamus, and I also know how much he adored you—he always said you were the little sister he'd never had. Remember when I wrote and told you how I hear his voice clear as a bell in my head sometimes? I heard him again just now. Seamus came to me (when I was ironing, of all things) and told me to let him go. He said, "Life is for the living, not the dead."

He's right, Briony. It's been more than three years since he died. I will always love Seamus. He will always be in my heart and in my memories, but I have to move on now. I hope you'll understand, sweetheart, and not be upset or see this as a betrayal of the love Seamus and I shared. I don't.

With all my love,
Maeve

Whilst the other girls were busy with their letters, Etta followed the nursing sisters round the wards as they tended to the remaining patients waiting to be moved on to hospital for treatment. She recalled the first time she'd met a nurse when she'd gone to hospital as a child after breaking her arm. Etta had thought the nurse was a nun since she was called sister and wore a veil. The nurse explained to the curious eight-year-old that she wasn't Catholic but that nurses got their start from the Sisters of Mercy, who were Catholic nuns, and the title of "Sister" continued.

Eager-to-learn, Etta emptied bedpans and catheters to make herself useful. She watched as the nurses administered injections and oxygen, changed bandages, and provided all manner of care to the wounded. Afterwards, she peppered them with questions. "Sister, why did you turn that last man with the leg injury onto his side?"

"To prevent bed sores." The tall nurse's plummy vowels were clipped as she moved on to the next patient. "Lying supine in one position too long causes sores."

Etta scribbled in her notebook. "And why does the corporal in Bed Four have so many pillows propping him up?"

Annoyance flared across the face of the slender nurse in her mid-twenties, the nurse whose voice and whole being screamed that *she* hadn't left school at fourteen. "He has respiratory issues and needs to be able to breathe properly."

Etta scribbled some more. "The sitting up helps his lungs, then?"

"Yes, you stupid girl." Sister Agatha turned her back on the nursing orderly. "Now go and empty a bedpan or whatever it is that you do. I don't have time for this nonsense." Her voice dripped with disdain.

Etta tamped down the flash of anger that threatened to erupt. Talking back to an officer could be grounds for dismissal, or, at the very least, charges of insubordination. Something she didn't want on her record.

"Yes, Nurse. Sorry, Sister." Etta pasted a contrite expression on her face. *Bloody cow.* As she started to leave, one of the senior sisters stopped her—a small, nondescript woman of an indeterminate age bearing the rank of flight lieutenant and the surname of Collins.

"Leading Aircraftwoman Blackwood, would you please come with me?" *Bloody hell. I'm in for it now.* "Yes, ma'am."

Sister Agatha smirked as the senior sister with dishwater blonde hair below her nursing veil led Etta outside. Lieutenant Collins walked down the walkway between the row of Nissen huts. A walkway that felt interminable to Etta.

Finally, they stopped in front of the last hospital hut.

As the senior nurse turned round, Etta blurted, "Sorry, Sister. I didn't mean to interfere with Nurse Turner's work. I won't do it again. I—"

The lieutenant held up her hand. "Wait here, please." She opened the door and stepped inside, closing the door behind her.

Maybe I can make a run for it. Etta glanced round. There was no one about to see her flee. *And where exactly would you go, nincompoop,* her practical nature asked. *Just shut up and take it like a man. What's the worst that could happen? So, you'll get written up. Big deal. You've been through worse.*

Etta flashed back to her father's drunken beatings, her mother's hostility and neglect, her brother's thieving, brawling, and worse. And the constant, unrelenting hunger. Not just for food—always scarce—but for something more. Something different. Something better.

She'd finally found the something better, and she wasn't about to lose it now.

Etta had never fitted in with her family. Never belonged. Bright and clever, she loved to read and learn and did well at school. Her teacher had encouraged her to continue her education, but her parents weren't having it. When Etta broached the subject, her mother laughed and told her she was giving herself airs.

"School's not for the likes of us," her mum said. "You'll go to work in the dress factory, my girl, and start paying for your keep."

Etta left school at fourteen and started working in the factory down the street. And every Friday, she handed her meagre wages over to her mother. Her mum would buy potatoes and the cheapest cut of meat from the butcher, then spend the rest down at the pub with her husband. Once, Etta asked for a portion of her pay, and her mum cuffed her round the head. She never asked again. But the minute she was old enough, Etta left home, family, and her job at the dress factory and never looked back.

The nursing sister returned with a large book in her hands. She smiled. A smile that transformed her nondescript features. "It's Etta, isn't it?"

"Yes, ma'am."

"I'm Louise." The senior nurse extended the blue-leather-bound book to the bewildered nursing orderly. "You might find this helpful."

Etta read the title: *The Principles and Practice of Nursing.*

"This is one of my textbooks. I found it invaluable during my nursing training and still refer to it regularly. You can borrow it if you like."

Etta stared. Looking down at the thick book in her hands, she caressed the title. Speechless, she raised her eyes to the nursing sister in front of her.

"You do want to become a nurse, I take it?"

"More than *anything.*"

Louise smiled again. A smile that lit up her whole face. "I felt the same way."

"Nurse Collins?" A male voice thundered. "I need you."

"Coming, Doctor."

Etta watched as the nursing sister returned to the hospital ward. Beaming, she clasped the textbook to her breast.

Maeve's sweet tooth propelled her to the canteen. As she ordered tea and cake, she spied Clemmie at a nearby table, nose in a book. "Is that from your aunt?" she asked as she joined her hutmate.

"Yes, it just arrived. Aunt Phil's such a dear to keep me supplied with books."

Taking a bite of her cake, Maeve grimaced and washed it down with tea. "Do you suppose they replace the sultanas with sawdust?"

"Either that or straw to give it that lovely dry texture."

Maeve chuckled as a group of doctors walked by. The officers glanced at the two nursing orderlies. Maeve's eyes met Doctor Moore's, and heat flooded her face. She looked down, affecting an absorbed interest in her cake.

Clemmie released a wistful sigh. "Too bad there's no fraternization within the ranks."

Too bad indeed, Maeve thought.

The girls chatted over their tea, then stood to take their leave.

Approaching the canteen exit, Clemmie whispered, "Don't look now, but a certain doctor can't take his eyes off you."

Maeve blushed, and her insides went all wibbly-wobbly.

Saturday night, Betty and Sally donned their dress blues and hitched a ride with a lorry driver into Cricklade. Betty had been hesitant to go at first, recalling the last time they'd gone and found Agnes Wilson strangled in a ditch.

Sally reassured her, saying there was safety in numbers. "No man would be a match for the two of us." Opening her purse, she showed Betty the Swiss Army knife inside.

"I can't believe we're going to the cinema!" Betty bounced in her seat, eyes shining and cheeks flushed. "It's been ages since I've seen a film."

Opening her compact, Sally checked her lipstick. "We don't even know what's playing."

"It doesn't matter. I love all films—dramas, comedies, love stories..." Betty's voice trailed off. She got a dreamy look in her eyes.

"Who's your favourite actor then?"

"*Actors*, you mean," Betty emphasized the plural. "Too hard to choose just one." She raised her hand and ticked off on her fingers: "Errol Flynn, Ronald Colman, and Cary Grant. I saw Errol Flynn in a pirate film when I was young—he was so dashing—but I especially loved him as Robin Hood, where he stole from the rich to give to the poor peasants."

"I'd quite fancy a man who took from the toffs and gave to the poor," Sally said.

The lorry driver snorted and flicked his cigarette out the window.

"Maid Marian did too. Robin Hood fell in love with the beautiful Marian, played by Olivia de Havilland. Robin and his band of merry men rescued her from Nottingham Castle, where she was being held prisoner." Betty released a blissful sigh. "It was *so* romantic."

Sally gave her a playful nudge. "You do love your films, don't you?"

Betty bobbed her head up and down.

"I reckon you have more than one favourite actress too?"

"Yes. I love Greer Garson and Ingrid Bergman, but I also love Irene Dunne and Vivien Leigh."

The lorry driver dropped them off in front of the cinema and chugged away.

Lighting a cigarette, Sally read the marquee aloud. "*A Guy Named Joe* with Spencer Tracy and," she paused and smiled at her film fan pal, "Irene Dunne. Aren't you the lucky one?"

"Ooh, I love Spencer Tracy," Betty gushed. "He was such a good priest as Father Flannagan in *Boys Town*."

Sally blew out a puff of smoke. "I don't have much use for priests."

"How about pilots?" A tall, dark-haired officer tipped his hat to the blonde Nightingale as his shorter pal with an overbite scrutinized the two girls.

Sally offered a flirtatious smile. "I always have time for pilots."

Chapter Ten

Five days after Operation Market Garden began, the camp resumed its supply and evacuation flights, this time to the Netherlands. The Dakotas were loaded with stores of food, tents, and medical supplies. Approaching Holland for the first time, Maeve looked down to see a patchwork quilt dotted with rivers, windmills, and bombed-out cities. She wondered how many people, how many children, had lost their lives in the carnage. It didn't bear thinking about.

Betty's plane followed Maeve's to Holland. The two Dakotas landed on the airstrip, and the stores were unloaded in a flash. The weather closed in just as quickly though, forcing the aircrews to have to stay overnight.

Maeve and Betty looked round at the camp full of men, with no facilities for women. "Where can we sleep?" Maeve asked.

"Ye can sleep with me, lassie," a corporal teased, adopting a bad Irish accent. "I'll keep ye nice and warm."

"You couldn't keep an Eskimo warm," snorted a burly sergeant standing outside his tent. "You're far too skinny." He leered at Maeve. "We've plenty of room inside for you both." The sergeant flapped the tent invitingly. "But you won't get much sleep." He smacked his lips at Betty.

Betty stepped closer to Maeve, giving her an anxious look.

"That's enough, lads." A tall, distinguished-looking man with a chest full of medals frowned at the group of ogling soldiers as he strode up to the two Nightingales. "Mind your manners, men. Didn't your mothers teach you how to talk to ladies?"

Tipping his hat to the two girls, the commanding soldier with gray-flecked hair and a pencil mustache introduced himself as Sergeant Major Lance. "Please accept my apologies for my men's rude comments, ladies. I'm afraid these soldiers have been out in the field far too long and have forgotten how to act in polite company." He pinned a penetrating gaze on the offenders. "That's no excuse, however. Rest assured it won't happen again. Isn't that right, lads?"

They squirmed under his gaze. "Yes, sir."

"And do you have something you'd like to say to these ladies?" he prompted.

"Sorry, love," the corporal mumbled, red-faced.

The burly sergeant echoed the corporal's apology. "No offense meant. We were just having a bit of fun."

"That's all right, boys," Maeve said. "We know women are a rare, exotic species from another world that you're unaccustomed to handling."

As the soldiers hooted with laughter, Sergeant Major Lance gave Maeve a nod of approval, a smile tugging at the corners of his mouth. He scanned the camp. "As you can see, we're not set up for women, but I'm sure we can find somewhere for you ladies to bed down safely for the night." His eyes flicked to the two Dakotas. "What if you slept in one of your planes?"

"Aye, that'd be grand." Maeve delivered a dazzling smile. "Ta very much, Sergeant Major."

Eyes locking on hers, he quirked an eyebrow. "You're Irish."

"I am." Maeve tensed. *Was he going to be one of those who resented Ireland's neutrality and blamed her?* It had happened before. When she'd first joined up and was undergoing basic training, some of the other WAAFs heckled her and called the Irish cowards. It happened again when she first arrived at Down Ampney. One of the ground crew lads questioned her patriotism until she put him in his place. Was she going to have to do the same again now?

"The Emerald Isle. Beautiful country, great stout." Sergeant Lance's eyes crinkled at her. "Whereabouts in Ireland are you from?"

Maeve relaxed. "A small village just outside Dublin called Ballydavid."

The sergeant major gave her a thoughtful look. "You could have sat out the war safely there, but instead, here you are, risking your life to take care of our wounded." He delivered a slight bow. "On behalf of my countrymen, I thank you." He turned to Betty. "Thank you both."

As the sky darkened, the girls returned to Maeve's plane and busied themselves, making beds on two of the stretchers behind the cockpit. Betty gave the Irish Nightingale a wide-eyed look. "Do you think we'll be safe?"

"Safe as a babe on its mother's breast." Maeve held up a large rock she'd snagged. "Never you fear. If any of those Romeos come looking for love tonight, they'll get more than they bargained for."

Betty giggled. A dreamy haze settled over her face. "That sergeant major was certainly something. So handsome. He looks like Ronald Colman in *Random Harvest.*"

"I've not seen that film."

"Oh, it's *so* romantic. Ronald Colman is a shell-shocked soldier from the Great War who has amnesia. He doesn't know who he is or where he's from or anything." Betty threw her hands out dramatically. "Greer Garson, a dance hall girl, finds him wandering around and takes care of him. They fall in love and marry and are living happily ever after in a country cottage where she's about to have a baby. Ronald Colman goes off to the city on business, and guess what happens?" Betty leaned toward Maeve, her brown eyes snapping with excitement.

"He gets hit on the head, remembers who he is, and forgets all about his life with Greer Garson?"

Betty stared. "I thought you hadn't seen it."

"I haven't. That was a wild guess." Maeve cast an affectionate gaze at the film-loving farm girl. "But never mind Greer Garson and Ronald Colman—I want to hear about *you* and this dairy farmer you've been writing. What's his name? What's he like?"

Betty coloured to the roots of her hair. "He's called Albert," she said bashfully. "Albert's a nice lad from Ludlow, although he's not in Ludlow now. He's still recovering in hospital. He's doing well with his physiotherapy exercises and learning how to do everything one-handed. He says he's not going to let the lack of an arm stop him from *any*thing." She puffed up with pride.

"Good lad. And how old is Albert?"

"He'll be nineteen in January."

"And what does he look like?"

Betty blushed. "He's a fine strapping lad—tall like that Sergeant Major Lance, but not slim like the sergeant. Albert's not fat," she hastened to add, "just well-built and strong. He has lovely blue eyes and a sweet smile."

"And what do you talk about in your letters?

"Home, mostly. Can you believe our farms are only ten miles apart?"

"And you'd never met before?"

Betty shook her head. "Albert wrote that he came to the horse fair in Bron—that's what we call our village of Brampton Bryan—with his brothers a couple times. I used to go to the horse fair with Dad and Wilf when I was young, so we may have passed each other without knowing. Fancy that." She gazed at Maeve in wonder, trying and failing to suppress a yawn.

Maeve's yawn echoed Betty's. "We'd best get some kip. We've got an early start tomorrow." They settled into their stretcher beds, the rock on the floor beside Maeve.

The next morning, the Dakotas flew on to Eindhoven to pick up British casualties and return home. When they arrived in the Dutch city—gutted by German bombs killing hundreds and injuring countless others—the nursing orderlies discovered their casualties hadn't yet been assembled. Instead, they encountered masses of weary, starving Dutch refugees who'd lost everything and needed transport to Belgium. The aircrews loaded the refugees onto the planes and set off for Brussels.

Maeve's heart broke seeing the hungry, orphaned children who'd lost their families and their homes. She gave them tea and chocolate, which they devoured in a flash. Remembering the aircrew-issued orange in her pocket she'd been saving for the flight home, Maeve peeled the citrus fruit, splitting it between the littlest ones.

After landing in Brussels and bidding farewell to the homeless refugees, Betty and Maeve found a private spot to hug each other and cry.

"The poor weans." Maeve swiped at her eyes. "They fair broke my heart."

Betty wrung her hands, her face wet with tears. "I had a young brother and sister who'd lost their entire family—parents, grandparents, and older sisters. They were the only two left. Can you imagine?" She turned haunted eyes to Maeve. "The boy couldn't have been more than four or five, and he was taking such good care of his baby sister, who was still in nappies. Even though he was clearly starving, he gave her the bit of orange I'd given him."

Maeve raised a shaking hand to push her hair away from her face. "I had a mother whose husband and all four of her children, including her newborn babe, were killed." She slammed her hand into a stone wall. "I hate the bloody Germans, and I hate this bloody war!"

"I hate it too," Betty said. "I try to remember, though, that some of the German soldiers are young lads just like Albert and my brother Wilf. Some of them were probably forced into military service—they can't *all* be Nazis. Those German lads have mothers and fathers, and perhaps sisters like me, who love them and worry about them as well."

"You're right." Maeve exhaled a weary sigh. "It's been an emotional day, and I'm just ready to go home and sleep in my own bed."

Once again, though, the weather closed in, and the planes couldn't take off. The two Nightingales exchanged despairing looks.

"I don't think I can sleep another night in the plane," Betty declared. "My back is killing me."

"Never fear, duck," a member of the ground crew said, "we have WAAF accommodation for you." He pointed to a four-storey building in the main square.

"Thank goodness."

"Any port in a storm," Maeve said. "Or, in this case, any bed will do."

Issued bedding for the night, the worn-out WAAFs climbed the steep, narrow stairs to the fourth floor, wobbling under the weight of the heavy blankets. When Maeve and Betty finally reached the top previously billeted by German troops, a filthy room greeted them. The troops had obviously left in a hurry. Empty beer bottles, old newspapers, and empty chocolate boxes full of discarded wrappers littered the floor that was sticky with spilled beer and sick.

Betty wrinkled her nose at the cots that still bore the Germans' soiled bedding. Too tired to give the place a proper clean, the girls shoved the clutter to one side, stripped the cots, made up their beds, and fell across them, dead to the world.

The next day, they had a quick breakfast, eager to leave Brussels and get home. *I get to sleep in my own bed tonight,* Maeve thought. She vowed never to complain about her hard Army cot again. That's when the crews advised them that they were still grounded.

"No," Maeve and Betty groaned in unison.

A local woman took pity on the two nursing orderlies and shepherded them to a nearby beauty shop where they got their hair shampooed and set.

Reveling in the unexpected treat, Betty blew out a rapturous sigh. "For the first time in days, I feel human again."

"You look *more* than human." Maeve admired her friend's soft waves. "You look like one of your film stars—Ingrid Bergman in *Casablanca.*"

"Do you really think so?"

"It's a good thing Albert's not here; you'd have to fight him off with a stick."

"Oh, Maeve," Betty protested, but when she looked in the mirror, a shy smile curved her lips.

Maeve couldn't get over the blood. So much blood. *Jaysus, Mary, and Joseph.*

The field hospital nurse at the Dutch airstrip where they'd landed had sent her to the hospital tent to get more bandages. It was Maeve's first time inside a field tent. Usually, when they arrived to pick up casualties, the wounded were all waiting to be loaded onto the Dakota, but this time, they weren't quite ready yet, so she pitched in to help the nurses.

Maeve entered the tent to see a doctor sawing off a soldier's arm. Blood sprayed, and the surgical nurse quickly pressed a bandage to the stump while an orderly carried the discarded limb away. Bile rose in her throat as the man passed her with the arm dripping blood. Her eyes dropped to the ground. She swayed and swallowed back the vomit.

A pair of boots appeared in Maeve's line of sight. "For God's sake, don't faint," a female voice said.

Collecting herself, Maeve raised her eyes to see an older nurse looking at her with contempt. "I was sent to get more bandages," she said in the most professional tone of voice she could muster.

The nurse plucked a stack of bandages from a shelf and thrust them at Maeve. "Here. Now get out."

She scurried from the tent, her face flushed with shame. *Pull yourself together. You've got a job to do.* Maeve knew she was good at her job. But what she also knew now with absolute certainty—she never wanted to be a surgical nurse.

She would leave that to Etta.

Visions of Down Ampney filled Maeve's head as her Dakota crossed the Channel. Like the wounded men on her flight, she couldn't wait to get back home. These past months, the RAF camp in the Cotswolds had become home to her. The Mess hall. The communal hut. The canteen. The billeting hut with all her friends. The hospital huts…. The doctor who'd lost his wife and son just as she'd lost Seamus and their unborn babe….

Maeve's heart skipped as she thought of the kind doctor who resembled Clark Gable.

"Nurse, could I have a cuppa?"

She scolded herself for letting her mind wander. Returning her attention to her patients, Maeve dispensed tea, offered reassuring words, emptied urine bottles, and checked oxygen masks. After landing and seeing her casualties off to their respective hospitals, she returned to her hut to find two letters on her bunk—one from Briony and one addressed to *The Irish Nurse.*

She opened Briony's missive first.

Dear Maeve,

Your last letter made me so happy! I've been praying for this to happen. I'm glad Seamus spoke to you and that his words have set you free at last. He loved you so much. And you're right, I did adore him. Seamus was a great big brother who passed on his love of learning to me, for which I will always be grateful.

Thank you for telling me he thought of me as his little sister. That made me cry. (Happy tears.) Now that you've finally let him go, I will pray God brings another man into your life. Someone who will love you the way Seamus did.

You deserve that. (And besides, I want to be an Aunt!)

Love,

Briony

p.s. Liam Ryan called me four-eyes, and I punched him in the nose. Now, he won't stop following me around. Boys are stupid.

Placing her sister's letter back in its envelope, Maeve's lips curved up. *You won't always think, that, Briony.*

She opened the other letter.

Dear Nurse,

Sorry, I don't know your name. I hope this letter finds its way to the Irish nurse with the black hair and green eyes who recently kept watch over a group of bomb-happy lads.

I'm one of those lads.

I wanted to thank you for being so kind to me. I don't think I'd have made it through that night if not for your care and comfort. I'd heard of shell shock—me granddad had it from the Great War. Mum told me he came back from the war a different man from the happy-go-lucky father she knew. When I was little, we always had to keep quiet around Granddad and never make loud noises.

Now I understand why.

I joined up as soon as I was old enough, ready to kill as many Nazis as I could to keep Britain safe. No one tells you, though, what it's like to kill a man, another human being. Or to see your friends killed. Your best mate, blown to bits beside you.

It does something to you. All the blood. The dead. Men screaming in agony. All I could think about was how much I wanted my mum. To be back home again and safe in her arms. She always knew how to make me feel better.

Ta very much for being a mum to me that night and for singing me and the lads to sleep. It made us—well, me at least—feel safe. Mum always sang me lullabies.

With sincere gratitude,

Lance Corporal William Smith, Royal Marines

Chapter Eleven

Etta double-checked the contents of her hamper as the Dakota began its descent. She always checked her supplies before landing to make sure everything was in order. Bandages, check. Oxygen masks, check. Emergency morphine, check. Tourniquets, check. Splints, check. Colostomy bags, check. Sick bags, check. Urine bottles, check.

"Everything all present and accounted for?" Dickie grinned. "I wager you're the most proper organized of all the Nightingales."

"I like to be prepared. To know that everything's where it belongs, and I can access it easily."

"Unlike Thelma." Dickie's lip curled. "Her medical kit is always a right mess, but then so is she. That one fair likes her gossip. Always prattling on about someone or other."

"Thelma does tend to prattle."

"She should be careful. Folks don't like their dirty laundry spread about."

Etta flapped her hand in a dismissive wave. "I don't think people pay much attention to Thelma's chin wags. I know I don't. I've more important things on my mind." Like showing Flight Lieutenant Harkness he needn't worry about having a woman on board. Etta hadn't flown with the superstitious pilot in weeks, but each time she did, he kept his distance. He did the same with all the girls.

She was determined to show the pilot she wasn't like the other girls and that his fears of having a woman on board were groundless. *The only difference between you and me, Lieutenant Harkness, is some anatomy and your posh education.*

Approaching the makeshift runway cut out of a field in German-occupied Holland, the Dakota touched down, and Etta heard a loud boom. A boom that jolted her off her seat. The plane veered left and hurtled down the runway toward the forest, throwing her backwards. She glimpsed smoke and smelled burning rubber. "What happened?"

"A tyre exploded!" Dickie shouted over the roar of the engine. "Brace yourself."

Quickly wedging herself against the bulkhead, Etta placed her hands behind her head and curled into a ball as the plane continued careening forward. The brakes screeched, and something crunched beneath the belly of the Dakota. She heard yelling and cursing from the cockpit, followed by a deafening crash. Etta squeezed her eyes shut.

I don't want to die.

Finally shuddering to a stop, the plane tilted sideways, throwing her across the floor with tremendous force. Etta landed, disoriented, in front of the gray-faced wireless operator. "You okay, Dickie?"

He gave a dazed nod.

"Nurse," the co-pilot yelled, "up here."

Etta stood, head spinning. She reached out her hand to a stretcher mount to steady herself. Quickly, she searched for her medical hamper and found it shoved beneath a forward stretcher. Grabbing the hamper, she scrambled through the cockpit doorway, glass crunching beneath her boots.

The co-pilot, Lieutenant Dawkins, unstrapped himself and stood, swaying, bleeding from a gash on his forehead. He swiped his sleeve across his face to wipe away the blood and swayed again.

Etta made a mental note. *Possible concussion and shock.*

The navigator, Warrant Officer Lewis, was unstrapping himself from his harness. Blood dripped from his hand.

Cuts on hand, maybe elsewhere?

Lieutenant Harkness groaned, and Etta hurried over to him. Sprinkles of glass studded the pilot's face, polka-dotting it with blood. He cradled his left arm, and she noticed that his left foot was bent inward.

Broken arm, possible broken ankle.

70

"Dickie," she yelled, "Bring water." Etta reached into her hamper to pull out a splint and bandages.

"Get out!" Harkness cursed. "Don't you smell the petrol? You need to get out. Now."

Etta froze. She'd been so busy cataloguing the crew's injuries, she hadn't noticed anything else. Now, the unmistakable scent of aviation fuel filled her nostrils. But she knew her duty. A Nightingale never abandons her patients, and Etta was damned if she was going to lose Lieutenant Harkness and prove his superstition correct.

Not on her watch.

Her training kicked in, and she took charge. "Dickie, guide Dawkins out—careful; he may be concussed and in shock."

"Right-o." The wireless operator squeezed past her and grabbed the beefy copilot's arm, removing him from the cockpit.

"Blackwood, I gave you an order." Lieutenant Harkness grimaced in pain. "Get the hell off this plane."

"No, sir." Etta glared at him as she released him from his harness. "My job is to take care of my patients and bring them safely home. Now, are you going to help me so we can both get the hell out of here, or are you and I going to die together on this Dakota?"

He grunted, and she saw the assent in his eyes.

"There's no time to splint your arm, so keep it nestled in your lifejacket." With the navigator's aid, she helped the pilot stand. As Harkness's left foot touched the floor, he groaned.

"Sorry. I know that hurts like a bugger." Etta positioned herself snugly against the slim lieutenant's right side and draped his good arm over her shoulder. She nodded to Lewis to pick up her hamper of medical supplies. "Now hold tight," she said to Harkness, "and lean on me." As the trio exited the plane surrounded by trees, Etta saw the Dakota had slammed into an ancient oak.

"Over here," Dickie called.

Mindful that the plane could go up in flames at any moment, she increased her speed. Harkness winced, and Etta saw that his lips were pressed together

71

tightly. "Sorry, sir. We have to hurry." They advanced to a small clearing where Dickie crouched, tending to Dawkins, who sat with his back pressed against a tree.

"Looks like the landing gear sheared off, and the props were destroyed," the wireless operator said.

Gently, Etta and Lewis lowered the injured pilot to the ground, where she examined him. Luckily, his ankle wasn't broken, just badly sprained. She gave him a shot of morphine, splinted his broken arm, wrapped his ankle tightly with a bandage, and carefully removed the bits of glass from his face. As Etta daubed at the blood, she was relieved to see none of the cuts were deep.

All the while she was working on Harkness, Etta was vaguely aware of Dickie behind her mumbling on the radio. Out of the corner of her eye, she glimpsed Lewis, wrapping a bandage around his cut hand. Finished with the pilot, Etta moved swiftly over to Dawkins. The co-pilot was holding a hand to his bleeding forehead. She wiped away the blood, noting the deep gash. "I'll need to stitch that up." She was examining his pupils to check for concussion when an explosion rent the air.

Her eyes flew to what was left of their plane as flames scorched the sky, and the acrid scent of burning metal and plastic filled her nose. Etta glimpsed Dickie conferring with Harkness and Lewis and saw the wireless operator and the navigator help the pilot stand.

"We need to get out of here," Harkness said, "before the Germans arrive."

"But…" she began, as Dawkins leapt to his feet.

"Move!" he ordered. "And leave the hamper."

Etta quickly grabbed bandages, sulfa, and morphine and shoved the lot inside her jacket. She supported the still unsteady copilot as they followed their commanding officer, navigator, and Dickie away from the burning Dakota.

Their transport back home.

Hours later, deep in the forest and with dusk approaching, they finally stopped at a small clearing. Dickie eased Harkness down to a sitting position, and Dawkins and Lewis plopped down on the ground beside their pilot pal.

During their trek, Etta had managed to sprinkle sulfa powder on the co-pilot's wound and wrap a bandage around his head. A bandage now spotted with blood. She pulled another fresh bandage from her jacket along with a morphine syrette.

"What happened?" Dawkins asked Harkness. "Why was no one at the supply drop-off when we landed?"

"Apparently, they'd come under surprise attack from the Germans and had to flee the area."

"And no one thought to warn us?" Lewis said.

"It happened just before we arrived. Did I mention it was a *surprise* attack?" Harkness winced, and Etta saw that his face was beaded with sweat. She moved toward him, intending to give him another shot of morphine, but he waved her away. "No more. I need to keep my wits about me."

"Yes, sir." Etta knelt beside Dawkins and removed his bandage, pleased to see the wound appeared clean. Removing a fresh bandage from inside her jacket, she wrapped it round the co-pilot's head. She moved over to Lewis and replaced the bandage on the navigator's hand as well.

"So, what's the plan?" Dawkins asked.

Etta had been wondering the same thing.

Harkness shifted his leg, pain contorting his features. "Tomorrow, we're going to make our way to the nearest field hospital. From there, we'll get transport home."

Etta saw the relief in Dawkins' eyes and noted that his pupils were normal. *No concussion.*

"What about tonight?"

"We'll rest and bed down here." The lieutenant jerked his head to a hollowed tree nearby. "Blackwood, you can shelter there; the rest of us will sleep out here."

Spare me your chivalry. "Begging your pardon, sir, but from a medical standpoint, it's best we all sleep together," Etta said. "We'll need the body warmth."

The pilot frowned, considering.

"Good idea, Blackwood." The autumn breeze ruffled Dawkins' hair. "Although this Dutch air is a bit warmer than ours, temperatures drop at night, especially in a dense forest like this." He sent a sideways look to Harkness, the officer in charge. "I presume we'll not be building a fire in case there are Germans in the vicinity."

"Correct."

The co-pilot scanned the area. "We can rig up a lean-to against that hollowed tree using some of these branches on the ground and cover the branches with pine boughs—they'll provide the best shelter from the wind."

"That's right, sir." Dickie beamed. "I learned that in Scouts."

For the next twenty minutes, the group worked together as a team, constructing the hasty shelter while the injured pilot watched, frustration etching his features. *It must be killing him not to be able to do anything*, Etta thought. They finished up as darkness fell, and Etta realized she was hungry. She hadn't eaten anything since that morning's porridge—there'd been no time to think of food. She fingered the orange in her pocket.

Dropping down beside Lieutenant Harkness, the weary crew discovered the officer in charge hadn't been idle while they worked. The moon bathed the forest in light, and Etta saw the pilot's flight cap on the ground. Nestled inside was an orange and some chocolate. Pulling out her orange, Etta placed it inside the cap. Dickie added his barley sugar.

Lewis held up empty hands. "Sorry I've nothing to add to the feast—I ate mine on the flight over." He held up a water urn. "I managed to snag this, though." They split the chocolate and one orange, saving the other orange and barley sugar for breakfast.

Etta ate slowly, holding the square of chocolate in her mouth and letting it dissolve on her tongue, savoring the taste. She leaned back, palms on the ground behind her, gazing up. Her breath caught seeing the canopy of stars stretching across the sky. She'd never seen so many stars before.

Beside her, Dickie let out a low whistle. "Now, ain't that a pretty sight?"

"We'd best turn in so we can make an early start tomorrow," Harkness said.

The crew huddled together inside the lean-to, and within moments, everyone was asleep. Everyone except Etta. She could feel the stillness all around her, punctured only by the sound of the men's breathing and Dickie's soft snores. Then, an owl hooted, and the rustling began. The London-born-and-bred Nightingale wasn't used to nature. *No telling what kind of wild animals are out there. Bears, wolves, wild boar....*

She scooched closer to Dickie.

Just before dawn, Etta crept out of the lean-to and slipped away from the men, eyes darting round as she sought refuge behind a large tree and took care of business. *It would be just my luck to run into a pack of wolves or whatever the hell creatures live out here.* She was more afraid of animals than she was of the Germans. Buttoning up her trousers, she hurried back to the makeshift camp.

"Blackwood, what the hell were you doing?" Lieutenant Harkness snapped as the rest of the crew pulled the lean-to apart.

"Answering the call of nature, sir." Etta lifted her chin.

His eyes pinned hers. "Do *not* leave this group again. Is that clear? I'm responsible for you. For all of you. The last thing I need is some woman wandering off and getting herself lost or captured by Germans."

Her face burned. "Yes, sir. Sorry, sir. It won't happen again." *Next time, I'll just drop my trousers right in front of you.*

Dickie sent Etta a sympathetic glance as he and Dawkins scattered pine boughs randomly about to hide evidence of their camp.

After their spartan breakfast of barley sugar and the remaining orange, Etta checked the pilot's splint and tightened the bandage around his ankle before they set off. *You can't blame him, you know*, she told herself. He is the officer in charge, and his arm and leg must be hurting like a bugger, especially without morphine to dull the pain. She would be happy when they got to the field hospital today, and Harkness could be seen to properly.

Only they didn't make it to the field hospital.

As the crew headed west through the woods in the direction of the hospital, they heard the sound of gunfire. The sound increased as they drew near their destination. Dickie tried again, unsuccessfully, to reach the hospital on the radio. Approaching the edge of the forest, the three officers pulled out their pistols, crouching low and indicating that Etta and Dickie should do the same.

A bullet whizzed over Etta's head.

"Snipers," Harkness whispered. "Stay down."

Another bullet whizzed past, ricocheting off the tree behind Dickie. Etta flinched, and a sheen of sweat broke out on her forehead, her thoughts ping-ponging wildly. *Why don't I have a gun?* This might be the time to retreat. *Let me at those bloody Germans!* Let's get the hell out of here.

Harkness stabbed his finger in the air for them to fall back, but as they turned to retreat, a German soldier burst through the trees in front of them. The pilot felled him with one shot and collapsed.

Hours later, after they'd doubled up and taken turns carrying the unconscious Harkness through the forest, they stopped to rest. Etta unwrapped the pilot's bandage and saw that his ankle had swollen to twice its normal size. "The lieutenant can't move on this leg," she said. "We're going to have to make some kind of stretcher to carry him or find a place to rest until the swelling goes down."

Looking round to get his bearings, Dawkins pulled out the silk map all Allied pilots are provided, in case they're downed in enemy territory. "Looks like there's a small town east of here. Maybe we can find somewhere there to hide out for a couple days and get some food."

"Isn't this whole area occupied?" Dickie asked. "I thought the Germans had taken over all the cities and towns around here."

"My guess is they won't have as much of a presence in the smaller towns, especially with all the fighting at present," Dawkins said. "They need their men on the front lines. I'd imagine this town has only an officer and a small handful of soldiers at best." The co-pilot took a sip of water and passed the near-empty urn to Dickie. "Besides, we need food and water."

Picking up the pilot again, they headed east.

As they trudged through the forest, Etta wondered if they were going to make it out of this alive. *We'd better*, she thought. *I'm not bloody well ready to die. Not when I've finally discovered what I want to do for the rest of my life.* Her heart swelled, envisioning herself working in a hospital after the war and assisting in complicated surgeries wearing her crisp-white nursing veil. *Sister Etta has a nice ring to it*, she thought.

Two and a half hours later, Etta glimpsed a church steeple and caught a whiff of wood smoke. Her stomach growled. She and Dickie set the injured officer down beside a fallen tree trunk. Etta arched her back, flexing her aching arms and shoulders, and knelt down to check on the injured pilot as Dawkins sent Dickie and Lewis to reconnoiter the area and report back.

Harkness let out a groan. His eyes fluttered open, and Etta gave him the last of the water. "Here you go, sir. Drink this." When he finished, the pilot asked, "Where are we?"

I have no bloody idea, Etta thought. *Some forest in ruddy, bloomin' Holland.*

Dawkins crouched down beside them. "We're near a town called Velp. We're out of food and water and need to find somewhere to stay for a bit until you can walk again. I've sent Jones and Lewis ahead to scope out the area."

Harkness clenched his jaw. "Just leave me. I'm holding you back. You can move faster and easier without me."

"We're not leaving you, sir," Etta said, glancing at Dawkins. "At least *I'm* not. You're my patient, and a nursing orderly never leaves her patients."

The scouting duo returned. "Just outside the forest, there's a meadow and then the town," Lewis said. "I saw houses, several buildings, and a couple churches. I also saw a German soldier patrolling the edge of town."

"Only one?" Dawkins asked.

"Yessir," Dickie piped up, "but that doesn't mean there aren't more."

"Right." Dawkins looked at Harkness. "What do you think?"

"I think—" a slight rustling silenced him. Harkness tried to pull out his pistol, but he was too weak. Etta grabbed his gun as Dawkins and Lewis raised their pistols. All three trained their weapons in the direction of the sound. Etta cocked the pistol, heart racing, and readied herself to shoot. *At least we'll go down fighting,* she thought.

Dickie pulled a knife and crouched, ready to pounce.

A loud whisper wafted their way. "Hello? Are you British?" a girlish voice asked in accented English. "I will help."

They strained their ears for the sound of others. All was still, save for the sound of the breeze and birds twittering overhead.

"I am alone," the voice whispered. "May I come?"

Dawkins gestured for Dickie and Lewis to investigate, then nodded to Etta, crouched over Harkness, shielding the lieutenant. Dawkins mouthed to her, "Answer," as he aimed his gun in the direction of the voice.

Gripping her pistol, Etta swallowed hard, her throat dry. "Yes, but slowly."

More rustling. A skinny girl in a threadbare dress emerged from the woods, holding up her hands. "Don't shoot. There are Germans in town. I am here to help."

Dickie and Lewis reappeared. "It's okay," Lewis said, "she's alone."

Etta lowered her gun and stared at the waiflike teen with dark hair and enormous brown eyes. It was obvious the girl was malnourished, yet she held out a crust of bread to them. "Who are you?"

"My name is Audrey," she said shyly.

Chapter Twelve

Everyone at camp knew the aircrew was missing in action. No one had heard anything since Dickie had radioed the Netherlands field hospital four days ago, informing them their plane crashed on landing and they were heading to the hospital. The officer in charge informed the Down Ampney CO his hospital had come under heavy fire from German snipers, so it was likely the crew had retreated. Unfortunately, he didn't know their whereabouts. He'd dispatched a rescue group to find them, but so far, nothing.

Telegrams were sent to each aircrew member's family informing them their loved one was missing in action. All except for Etta, whose personnel records said she had no family.

Her Nightingale family rallied round Etta's distraught friends.

Sally hugged a crying Betty. "They'll find them, sweetie. If anyone can get through this, Etta can. She's a tough cookie, that one."

Betty continued to weep. So did Maeve.

Straightening, Maeve wiped her eyes and got hold of herself. "Etta's the best nursing orderly we have. That woman is a walking, talking medical encyclopedia."

"I'll say." Doreen grinned. "She's always going on about parts of the body I've never heard of—like sacrum and anterior this, proximal that. I never know what she's talking about."

Betty smiled through her tears. "Etta's one of the smartest people I've ever met. She's always reading that big anatomy book of hers." Her eyes slid to the thick book sitting on top of her friend's footlocker. Her lip trembled.

"But what good is a book against men with guns? What if they're all lying dead somewhere? Or have been captured by the Germans?" Her hand flew to her mouth. She whispered, "I've heard the Germans do awful things to women."

"Etta can handle herself," Sally said. "Besides, she's not alone. She's got Dickie and the others. They'll stick together."

"But what if the men were injured in the crash?"

"Then Etta will be taking care of them," Maeve said. "Sally's right. Etta is one tough cookie. She'll get through this with flying colours. If anyone can, she can." She fingered her cross. *Please, God, don't make me out to be a liar.*

Doreen patted Betty's arm. "I'll bet they're all hiding away somewhere, keeping clear of the Germans. Once the coast is clear, they'll be back before you know it."

"That's right," Sally said. "They're probably all tucked away together nice and snug." Her blue eyes gleamed. "Of course, after four days together, Lieutenant Harkness may well strangle Etta before the Germans get the chance."

"Sally!" Betty exclaimed.

"I'm just teasing, silly. We all know the lieutenant has that silly superstition about having women on his planes."

"Maybe not so silly," Thelma said primly. "After all, they *did* crash."

Maeve fixed a cold stare on the older Nightingale.

The door of the hut burst open, and Clemmie rushed in. "They're alive! They're on their way back."

Three hours later, the plane carrying the missing aircrew touched down at Down Ampney. The camp erupted in cheers when the Dakota's doors opened.

The crew deplaned carrying a stretcher, holding the injured pilot. Lewis and Dickie loaded the stretcher into a waiting ambulance, and Etta started to clamber in beside her patient. The medics stopped her. "We'll take it from here, Nurse. Get some kip—looks like you need it."

Lieutenant Harkness met Etta's eyes as the ambulance doors began to close. "Well done, Blackwood," he said.

"Sir." She saluted her commanding officer, and the ambulance drove off. When Etta turned round, she found a group of Nightingales surrounding her.

Betty squealed and launched herself at Etta, hugging her tight. "I'm so glad you're back safe and sound."

"We all are." Maeve squeezed her bunkmate's hand and gazed at her through wet eyes.

So, this is what family feels like, Etta thought.

Sally kissed her on the cheek. "Welcome home, Red. It hasn't been the same around here without you." She wiped the lipstick from Etta's face. "I'll bet you have quite the story to tell." Gently, she patted her arm. "Whenever you're up to it."

Spotting Dickie, Sally planted a kiss on his lips. "Dickie, love! Glad to see you back in one piece." She bestowed a radiant smile on the wireless operator. "We need to celebrate. Drinks are on me."

Harry rushed up with a grin that couldn't be contained. He pumped Dickie's hand up and down, slapping his pal on the back. "Welcome back, old man."

Etta glimpsed Dawkins and Lewis, leaving the runway with a cluster of officers. Seeing her, Dawkins tipped his hat above his stitched forehead and waved. When they'd finally made it to the field hospital, one of the nurses cleaned the copilot's wound and stitched him up, commending Etta for keeping his wound clean and packed in sulfa. Nodding at Dawkins, Etta turned back to her friends.

Sally was saying to Dickie, "I'll bet you can't wait to get out of that filthy uniform and get some sleep. You too, Red." She wrinkled her nose. "You're probably dying for a shower and some clean clothes. I know I would be."

Etta and Dickie locked eyes. "What we're dying for is some food and proper tea." Etta hooked her greasy hair behind her ears. "We haven't had a decent cup of tea since we left."

"Too right," Dickie said. "I'd murder for a cuppa."

After Etta and Dickie wolfed down sausages, eggs, and myriad cups of tea, Etta took a shower, scrubbing away all the dirt and grime beneath the thin trickle of cold water. Returning to the billeting hut, she collapsed on her bunk and pulled up the blanket. Etta puffed out a sigh. "This is heaven. No sleeping on the ground or a cold cellar floor."

Maeve leaned in close, speaking quietly so the chattering girls at the other end of the hut couldn't hear. "If you'd rather not talk about it, I'll understand." She patted Etta's hand on top of the blanket. "Was it terrible?"

"It wasn't too bad. The hardest part was staying on the run from the Germans. Lieutenant Harkness's injuries slowed us down."

"I'm surprised he didn't order you to abandon him to save yourselves."

"He did, actually. But I overruled him."

Maeve grinned. "I'll bet you did."

Etta shifted in her bunk, shivering. "The worst bit was being so hungry. After the first couple days, I was afraid we were going to starve to death. Luckily, a young girl, part of the Dutch Resistance, found us and hid us in her family's cellar. Audrey had gone to school in Britain, so spoke English." Etta shook her head, a faraway look in her eyes. "I didn't know the meaning of starving until we met her and her family. They were surviving on the odd turnip, endives, grass, and tulips."

Maeve's eyes widened.

"Yes, tulips. Can you believe it? Since the war put an end to tulip farming, there were all these unplanted bulbs everywhere. With food so scarce, the Dutch would grate the bulbs and use that to make some flour for bread, which they generously shared with us. They also made tulip soup." Etta grimaced. "It tasted horrible, but it kept us—and them—from starving." Her eyes drooped. "Sorry, Irish, I need to get some kip."

Maeve pulled another blanket over her friend and tucked her in.

As Etta slept, Maeve wrote to Briony. A letter she would never send. The censors wouldn't allow it. But she needed to write down what she'd learned to have a record of what happened.

Dear Briony,

My friend Etta has just returned to camp after four days missing in action. The tyre on her aeroplane burst on landing, and her Dakota crashed. She and the crew were delivering urgent supplies to British troops in the Netherlands, which the Germans have occupied since early in the war. Both the pilot and copilot on her plane were injured in the crash—their plane exploded soon after they crash-landed, but everyone had got out safely. Etta nursed the officers while they were on the run from the enemy.

The crew couldn't make it to the nearest field hospital because of heavy German sniper fire and had to flee to the forest and hide with nothing to eat. Thankfully, a young Dutch girl found them and hid them in her family's cellar. The family was starving, subsisting mainly on grass and tulips. Can you imagine? The German Army was billeted in town, but most of the soldiers were off fighting, so after hiding in the cellar for two days, Dutch Resistance members spirited Etta and the crew away at night and took them to a British field hospital. Their injuries were treated, and they finally got a flight back to camp.

I'm in awe of Etta's skill and courage under such conditions. I don't know if I could have done the same. She's an amazing, dedicated nurse, and I'm proud to call her friend. I can't stop thinking of that starving family, though, and all the starving Dutch people....

I hate this war and especially what it does to children. It breaks my heart. I pray that young girl survives. I know it's selfish of me to say this, Briony, but I'm so happy you're safe in Ireland, where the war can't touch you.

Maeve rocked the weeping soldier in her arms. "There, there, it's all right," she soothed. "Mummy's here." Across from her, Titch rubbed a young private's back, offering calming words to the lad crying out for his sweetheart.

That day, another group of bomb-happy lads had arrived, and Maeve and Titch—not Etta this time—volunteered to keep watch on them overnight. The girls moved from bed to bed, tucking the men in, laying cool hands upon fevered brows, and providing shoulders to cry on.

What horrors they must have seen, Maeve thought to herself, as another lad sobbed in her arms. *I can't even imagine.* What she could do, though, was provide comfort and a pair of arms. She stroked the soldier's back and murmured. "It's all right. You're safe now."

Another lad bolted upright in bed, crying out, "Mummy! Mummy!"

Titch hurried to his side and enfolded him in her arms. "You're all right, love. I'm here. I've got you."

Etta headed to the hospital tent to return the nursing textbook to Sister Louise. When the senior nurse saw Etta, she hurried over.

"You're back!" Louise touched Etta's hand, beaming. "So good to see you. We were all so worried."

Not knowing how to respond, Etta awkwardly extended the blue book to her. "I wanted to return this to you. Thanks for letting me borrow it. It's been very helpful."

Sister Louise held up her hand in a stop motion. "Please. I'd like you to keep it. I understand from Lieutenants Harkness and Dawkins that *you* were quite the help in the field. They said you were a fine nurse—calm and collected under pressure."

Etta's heart expanded, her cheeks pinking at the praise. "Just doing my job, Ma'am."

"And a fine job it was," a familiar voice said behind her.

Whirling around, Etta saw Matron smiling at her.

The nursing supervisor she had been trying to impress for months shook Etta's hand. "Well done, you."

Chapter Thirteen

October 1944

O n a brisk October day, a group of nursing orderlies were chatting and relaxing between flights in the communal hut when Thelma rushed in.

"Did you hear?" she asked breathlessly.

"Hear what, oh fount of all information?" Sally didn't bother lifting her eyes from her magazine.

Betty looked up over her tea to see an ashen-faced Thelma standing in the doorway, rooted to the spot. "What is it?"

The camp gossip moved unsteadily to a chair and sat down. "One of the Nightingales from Blakehill Farm was killed."

"What?!" Sally snapped her magazine shut. "Another one? Was she strangled too, like that other poor girl?"

The entire hut gazed as one at Thelma.

"No."

"What happened then?" Etta asked.

Thelma stared at them with haunted eyes. "The Germans shot them down."

Clemmie and a couple of the other girls gasped. Etta closed her eyes.

Feeling lightheaded, Betty grabbed Maeve's hand. That could have been me, she thought. Did the poor girl know what was happening? Did she know she was going to die? Over time, Betty's fear of flying had receded.

Months of flying day in and day out without incident made her think she'd overcome her anxiety. When she was focused on tending to the patients in her care, she no longer thought about being afraid. She was far too busy. Squeezing Maeve's hand, Betty took deep breaths in and out.

The door of the hut opened to admit a grim-faced Harry.

"How many patients were killed?" Sally asked.

"There were no medical casualties on board. Only the crew. All dead." Pulling a flask from his pocket, Harry raised it to his mouth and took a long drink. "It was a cargo flight from Antwerp. Apparently, they strayed too close to a German garrison at Dunkirk. Their plane was brought down by flak near St. Pol-sur-Mer."

Maeve crossed herself, and Betty bowed her head. The hut filled with the sound of murmuring and whispered prayers.

"At least it wasn't a flight full of patients," Sally said. "That's good."

"Good?" Thelma whirled on her, eyes blazing. "How can you be so heartless? A nursing orderly has died! One of us, and three crewmembers as well."

"And they were all killed doing their job," Sally said evenly, "their *duty.* They knew the risks. We all do." She looked around the room. "Anyone of us in this hut, this camp, could die at any moment. If you don't know that, you're living in a fairy tale. This is war. That's why we have to grab life with both hands and make every moment count."

Sally strode over to stand beside Harry. "Now I'm going over to the canteen to raise a glass to the departed crew. And I hope when and if *I* buy it, you'll do the same for me." Her eyes slid to Betty. She winked. "If you don't, I'll come back and haunt you." Sally linked her arm with Harry's. "Who's going to join us?"

Etta, Maeve, and Betty all stood up. Clemmie and a couple of the other girls did too. As one, the group departed for the canteen, all except for teetotalers Thelma and Doreen.

The two Nightingales who stayed behind raised a cup of tea in the fallen crew's honour. After paying their respects, Thelma leaned toward Doreen.

"That Sally is something else. She has no shame. Did you know her latest conquest is a pilot who's engaged to one of the hospital nurses?"

"No, really? Who?"

"Rumor has it Sally's been playing footsie with Flight Lieutenant Blake, the tall ginger-haired pilot engaged to that posh Sister Agatha." Thelma sipped her tea. "Evidently, Sister Agatha has heard the rumors and is none too pleased."

A pall settled over the camp as everyone thought about the lost aircrew, but, as Sally had said, this was war, and casualties were part and parcel of war. Many had lost friends during D-Day and, more recently, Arnhem. You couldn't dwell on it and let it get to you. You just had to carry on.

Betty decided to carry on and not let fear have its hold on her. She wouldn't think about the danger when flying; she would do her job and pour all her energies into the wounded men in her care. That's what she was there for, after all, and as Sally had said, that's what she'd signed up for.

She smiled when she thought about Sally. Such a jolly, happy girl, always full of fun and mischief. Some of the others in camp were unkind and whispered about Sally behind her back, but Betty reckoned that's just because they were jealous of her.

Yes, she might be rather free with her charms—freer than Betty could ever imagine being—but that was just her way of letting off steam and feeling alive. Sally had a good heart and treated her wounded boys kindly, always cheering them up with her sunny smile and flirting ways. Many's the time Betty had seen her jolly a wounded man down in the dumps, afraid he might lose his girl now that he no longer had an arm or a leg. Sally would reassure the injured lad that to the right girl, it wouldn't matter. What mattered, she said, placing her hand on his heart, was who a person was on the inside, not the outside.

Betty opened her letter from Albert.

Dear Betty,
I hope this letter finds you well.

It's a lovely October day, and I've just had a walk round the hospital grounds. There's quite a few injured lads here—I'm not the only one missing a limb. I have to say I'm glad I lost an arm rather than a leg. I think it would be a lot harder to hobble about with only one leg.

My physiotherapy is going well, and I'm determined to be home by Christmas. Mum wrote and said we lost one of our dairy cows to mastitis. The vet came round and said it was a bad case and the poor cow was suffering so much, it was best to put her out of her misery. Our land girl was apparently a right wreck about it—she'd never seen an animal put down. But that's farm life. Folks that haven't been raised on a farm like us don't understand.

That's one of the reasons I like writing to you, Betty. You're a proper farm girl and know what's what. You wouldn't lose your head over something like that. I reckon that's why you make such a good nurse, too. You're used to hard work and not squeamish about blood and such.

I know you didn't have to join up—you could have stayed home on your own farm showing the Land Girls what to do, but instead, you volunteered to help me and the other lads. Thank you. Where would we be without you?

I reckon Florence Nightingale's looking down on all you nurses and beaming with pride.

Sincerely yours,

Albert

Betty pinked with pleasure at the farm boy's words. *What a lovely lad he is.*

To stop thinking of the downed plane, Etta devoured the book Sister Louise had given her, marveling at all she learned. The blue book now competed with *Gray's Anatomy* as her book of choice. She had recently been reading about how to treat burns, which had Etta flashing back to her training days.

To prepare the nursing orderlies for what they might encounter in the field, the instructor showed the trainees a charred corpse and told them they would have to wash down the corpse before the soldier could be returned to his family. One of the girls had vomited at the grisly sight, but Etta steeled herself to look at the burnt body as an object, not a person.

The instructor also told them if a man was burnt in the cockpit, he would usually be placed on a stretcher still in the sitting position. The girl who had vomited gagged at the thought. The following day, the training instructor informed them that their queasy classmate had dropped out of the program, saying she didn't have the stomach for the job.

Etta was glad *she* had the stomach for the job.

Today, she read about syphilis and gonorrhea in the nursing textbook. Etta was already familiar with venereal disease—you couldn't grow up in the East End of London and not hear about VD. Even her brother once came home with a case of the clap, which served him right. Recently, though, at one of the field hospitals, she'd overheard a couple of doctors talking about the increase of VD among soldiers since the war began.

"Gonorrhea cases have risen fifty percent, and syphilis has skyrocketed a hundred-fold," one doctor said.

"It's the women's fault," Etta heard another doctor say. "Used to be fellows caught the clap from slags and prostitutes. These days, though, with girls in the services, munitions factories, and what have you, after putting in long workdays, these new modern women want to have a good time." She heard him snigger. "And that good time is sleeping with every Tom, Dick, and Harry that comes along. No wonder VD is out of control."

Etta saw red.

On behalf of her fellow WAAFs and munitions workers, she wanted to tell the doctors off or, better yet, punch them in their smug, priggish faces. Clenching her fists, she counted to ten, a trick she'd learned to keep her temper in check. The two were doctors, after all. Officers and *gentlemen* and she was but a lowly enlisted nursing orderly. Losing her temper and confronting them would cost Etta her job and her dream of becoming an RAF nurse.

There was one thing she could do, though.

When she returned to Down Ampney that afternoon, Etta sought out Sally. As they strolled around the camp's perimeter, she cautioned the freespirited

Nightingale to be careful, citing the rising incidence of venereal disease amongst the military.

"You don't have to worry about me, sweetie," Sally said. "I know how to stay protected." She winked. "It's called French letters."

Arms linked, Betty and Sally strolled the perimeter of the camp after dinner, knowing that soon it would be too cold to do so. Sally whistled "Swinging on a Star" as Betty looked up at the stars.

"I wonder what Wilf thinks looking down on me from heaven now, seeing me in uniform and tending to the lads on our casevac flights," Betty mused.

"I'm sure he's right proud of you," Sally said.

"I hope so. He's the reason I joined up. To bring our wounded boys back home. Back to their families." Tears pricked her eyes. "Wilf never came home."

Sally lit a cigarette with a trembling hand. "Neither did our Jimmy." She placed her hand on her heart. "But he's here with me. Always."

The door of the billeting hut opened to reveal Betty and Sally laughing helplessly and clutching their sides.

Maeve looked up from her Agatha Christie. "What's got the pair of you laughing like a drain?"

Sally's blue eyes sparkled with merriment. "You'll never believe what Titch's crazy Paddy's gone and done now." Glancing at Betty, still giggling uncontrollably, she bent over again, grabbing at her stomach.

Etta lifted her eyes from her nursing textbook. "It must be pretty funny to have reduced the pair of you to hysteria."

Sally's uniform hat bobbed up and down. "Wait'll you hear."

Maeve tilted her head. "We're all ears."

"Ears," Sally echoed, and she and Betty were off again.

"Bloody hell!" Etta threw up her hands. "Just tell us already."

Betty got hold of herself. "You know how when patients arrive, we have to let Matron or the medical officer know if there's a VIP or high-ranking officer on board?"

Maeve nodded. "Standard operating procedure."

"Well, Paddy sent word over the radio that a VIP with limb injuries was arriving on the next flight."

Cheeks flushed; a snickering Sally continued the tale. "When the plane landed, a group of officers and assorted officials were waiting for the VIP."

"Naturally."

"Only what happened next wasn't so natural, was it Betty?" Sally's eyes danced.

Betty shook her head, a smile spreading over her face. "When the medics arrived and unloaded the stretcher of this injured VIP, they found," she paused, "a crucifixion statue of Jesus."

"Jaysus." Maeve's eyes went out on stalks.

"Exactly." Sally chortled.

"Where in God's name did they find a crucifix?" Etta asked.

"One of the WAAF medics—a good Catholic girl—rescued it from a bombed-out French church and put it on board," Betty said. "You should have seen their faces when they saw the VIP."

Sally giggled. "Funniest thing I've seen in ages."

"Sorry we missed all the fun." Maeve returned to her mystery novel.

"That Paddy's a funny guy." Etta tapped her finger to her lip. "But what did the powers-that-be do as a result of this prank?"

"They gave him the biggest telling off and threatened him with disciplinary action for his 'misuse of equipment and resources,'" said Betty.

"Poor Paddy."

"I wouldn't worry too much about Paddy," Sally smirked. "Matron's always had a soft spot for him."

"And Doctor Moore has a good sense of humor," Betty added. "The whole time he was telling Paddy off, he was trying not to laugh. I think they know his hijinks are good for morale."

Sally chuckled. "I'll attest to that."

After Betty and Sally departed for the canteen, Maeve found it hard to focus on her novel, her head now full of thoughts of Doctor Moore. Thoughts that made her stomach go all wibbly-wobbly again. *Not only is he*

91

the best doctor in camp, she ruminated, *he's also handsome and has a good sense of humor to boot.* No wonder so many of the girls have a crush on him. The question is, does he have a crush on any of *them?*

The hut door banged open startling Maeve from her romantic musings and causing Etta to look up from the nursing textbook. Doreen entered, her arm around a sobbing Thelma.

Springing up, Maeve hurried over to the two girls. "What's happened? Please don't say another one of ours has gone into the drink."

Etta held her breath.

Doreen shook her head. "No, it's one of Thelma's patients."

"Little Tommy," Thelma wailed, sinking to her bunk. She rubbed her arm across her nose, leaving a trail of snot on her uniform sleeve. "My neighbor. I minded him when he was a lad."

Maeve's heart went out to the older nursing orderly. "I'm so sorry he didn't make it."

Thelma wept anew. "Tommy *did* make it. That's the problem. It would have been better had he died." She sent Maeve a tortured look. "He's lost an eye and both legs—I hardly recognized him." Closing her eyes, she sniffled. "Tommy was such a beautiful boy, the apple of his mother's eye. Tall and fit. Captain of the rugby team and the best athlete in town. Now he'll never play again." She sobbed against Doreen's chest.

Doreen's eyes filled. "I hate this bloody war."

Maeve blinked back tears. "So do I."

Swallowing hard, Etta flipped to the index of the nursing book, seeking information on prosthetic limbs.

Chapter Fourteen

December 1944

Christmas was fast approaching, but the constant stream of casualties meant no one got leave. Many felt the wrench of not going home for the holiday.

Dear Albert,

Happy Christmas! I'm so pleased by your news. By the time you receive this, you'll be home in Ludlow celebrating Christmas with your family. I wish I could say the same. Sorry, I'm feeling a bit homesick. This is my first time away from home at the holidays.

I love this time of year, don't you? Mum always bakes up a storm. The Christmas pudding will have been aging in the tin for several weeks now. Mum uses plenty of sultanas and dried apricots. Soon, she'll start making the mince pies. With rationing, though, no turkey for Christmas dinner. Last year, we had mutton with mash and sprouts. At least there was meat.

Some of the girls told me about their mum's "mock goose" (a casserole of potatoes, apples, and cheese) and nothing like goose at all. I wonder what they'll serve us for Christmas dinner in the Mess. Probably Spam. We eat a fair bit of that. And now I must stop talking about food as I'm getting quite hungry and it's still hours until tea.

Soon, Dad will be cutting down the tree. Wilf and I always went with him to make sure he got the biggest one. Evergreens have such a lovely scent, don't they? Christmas Eve, before going to church, we would make paper chains and help Mum decorate the tree. My favourite bit was putting the star on top. Dad surprised Mum one year by getting her a gorgeous gold glass star for her birthday. It's her pride and joy.

You must be thrilled to bits to be back with your cows again. I agree you should have no problem milking one-handed. You'll get that sorted in no time. Please pass on my best wishes to your family for a Merry Christmas and a Happy New Year. We're all praying 1945 brings an end to the war.

Sincerely yours,

Betty

Betty wasn't the only one missing Christmas at home.

Maeve gave a wistful sigh as she thought of Briony and their holiday traditions as a family. Each year, her mother would place the wooden nativity on the mantel, leaving the crib empty until Christmas morning when Briony—and Maeve before her—laid the baby Jesus in the manger.

Another tradition was to leave a pint of Guinness out for Santy on Christmas Eve. But the biggest treat of the season was when Dad took them to Dublin to see Jimmy O'Dea and Maureen Potter in the Christmas panto at the Gaiety Theatre. Maeve smiled, remembering how they would all loudly boo the villain whenever he came onstage.

We should've arranged to have a Christmas panto in camp, she thought. One of the men could have put on a funny little moustache and pretended to be Hitler. He'd have got the most boos of any panto villain.

For Etta, December 25th was a day like any other. Growing up, there was never a tree or presents in their flat. One year, she'd hung up her sock over the fireplace like her friends at school did. When her mother saw the holey sock, she yanked it off the nail and flung it at Etta. "What d'ya think you're playin' at?" she'd yelled. "There's no money to be fillin' that sock with anything but yer foot. And don't expect Father Christmas to be comin' down no chimney either."

Sally loved Christmas. "It meant fun and games at our house," she told Betty. "We'd do charades, which was always good for a laugh since my dad's so rubbish at it. Jimmy always had the radio playing and would dance me through the house," she revealed, lost in her reminiscences. She twirled to demonstrate. "My brother loved to dance. He would come up behind Mum when she was cooking, pull her away from the stove and spin her round the kitchen. Mum would say, 'Jimmy, you daft boy, let me go! The dinner will burn.'"

A shadow passed over Sally's face. "But she didn't want him to let her go. None of us did."

Everyone in camp, save for resident Scrooge Etta, did their best to make things festive for the holiday. Holly was collected and made into wreaths hung on doors, bits of mistletoe began showing up in the Mess, and the medics cut down a towering spruce for the main hospital hut.

For their contribution, the Flying Nightingales set about making paper chains from newspaper to decorate the tree.

"Come on, Scrooge," Sally teased Etta, whose head was buried in the ever-present nursing textbook. "Lend a hand. Have some fun for a change."

Grumbling, Etta closed her blue book.

Betty burst out singing "Joy to the World," and the others joined in. Then Sally led them in a rousing rendition of "Jingle Bells" that left them all giggling.

Finishing their paper chains, the nursing orderlies carried them over to the hospital to decorate the tree. Under Maeve's watchful eye, they were hanging the last chain when the faint sound of music reached their ears. The girls exchanged looks. Matron was quite stern about no radios in the wards, not wanting the latest war news to excite or agitate the patients. The Nightingales set off in search of the source of the music.

"Matron probably made an exception for Christmas," Etta said.

Maeve smiled. "Music does soothe the savage breast."

As they approached the main ward, the music grew louder. Sally swayed her hips. "Sounds like Bing Crosby."

All at once, Etta stopped dead in her tracks, causing Maeve to collide with her. Four mouths dropped open as one at the sight of Matron dancing with one of the patients to "Stardust."

Not only Matron.

Sisters Agatha and Louise were taking turns around the room with some patients as well. Seeing the nursing orderlies in the doorway, Matron beckoned them over. "Come in, girls. We need reinforcements." The head of nursing then explained that dancing was good exercise for the men and helped in their healing.

"You don't have to tell me twice." Smiling, Sally strolled to the nearest bed as Bing's dulcet tones crooning "I'll Be Home for Christmas" filled the room. She executed a slight bow. "May I have this dance, soldier?"

The other girls followed her lead, but Betty hung back. "I don't know how to dance," she said shyly.

"That's okay, duck." An older patient with a bandage on his neck smiled and slung his legs off the bed. "All you have to do is follow me." He held out his hand.

Matron gave her an encouraging nod. Taking the soldier's hand, a blushing Betty focused on not stepping on the man's toes.

Chapter Fifteen

December 25, 1944

The girls danced again at the camp party the next evening after first enjoying a Christmas dinner, the likes of which some had never seen. Etta couldn't get over the bounty in the Mess: Roast pork *and* roast turkey, apple sauce, boiled potatoes, sausage stuffing, carrots, and Brussels sprouts.

"Can you believe this, Irish?" she said to her bunkmate sitting beside her.

Forking up some stuffing, Maeve shook her head. "No, but I'm not going to look a gift horse in the mouth."

"Me either." Betty finished her meal with a contented groan. "Wait until I tell Mum we had turkey."

Thelma greedily tucked into her pudding. "The RAF looks after their own."

They certainly do. Etta surveyed the menu board the cook had proudly scrawled for all to see. Christmas pudding with brandy sauce, mince pies, and cheese and biscuits were still to come. *I could get used to this,* she thought.

A male voice cut through the din. "Leading Aircraftwoman Fitzgerald, would you care to dance?"

Maeve turned from where she'd been standing, chatting to Betty and Etta to see Doctor Moore behind her. Her insides did their usual wibbly-wobbly waltz at seeing him, but she maintained an outward composure as he led her to the crowded dance floor. As they passed by Sally, dressed in scarlet and entwined with one of the pilots, the blonde Nightingale beamed at her Irish pal and gave her a red-nail-varnished thumbs-up.

Taking Maeve's hand in his, Doctor Moore slipped his other hand around her waist. "That's a lovely dress. It really brings out your eyes."

"Thank you. It's Sally's, actually."

Sally, who was always perfectly kitted out and had more clothes than all the girls combined, loaned Maeve the emerald-green crepe de chine for the festivities. When they were in the hut getting ready for the party, she lifted a dubious eyebrow upon seeing Maeve's old navy wool shirtwaist. "You can't wear that."

"It's the only dress I've got. Otherwise, it's down to my skirt and jumper."

Sally made a face. "A jumper's not party clothes." Rummaging through the clothes crammed into her footlocker, she pulled out a pretty green frock, shook out the wrinkles, and handed it to Maeve. "This will go great with your eyes and that dark Irish hair."

Maeve caressed the silky fabric. "It's lovely." Not possessed of Sally's voluptuousness, the dress was a bit too big on her slender frame, but she cinched in the waist with her black belt, and that did the trick.

Betty, whose own dress had seen better days, stared at Maeve. "You look like Merle Oberon in *Wuthering Heights*," she breathed.

Sally glanced at the shapeless rayon floral print the farm girl was wearing. "I may have something for you too, sweetie."

"Oh, I'd never fit into anything of yours," Betty said. "I'm so much bigger than you."

"Where there's a will, there's a way. Now let me think..." Sally tapped a finger to her lips. Delving through her footlocker again, she retrieved a sky-blue velvet capelet. She settled the short cape over Betty's broad shoulders and stood back to admire the effect. "Perfect. Well, almost perfect."

She scrabbled through a small box of trinkets and produced a hair clip. Pulling Betty's straight locks to one side, Sally fastened the rhinestone clip in her friend's hair. For a final touch, she added a touch of lipstick. "There you go, Cinderella. You're all set for the ball." She wagged her finger. "Just make sure you're home by midnight, and don't lose your glass slippers."

Betty giggled. "I do feel like a right princess and all." Her hand moved up to touch the sparkling clip. "You have such pretty things."

"Too many. Consider that my Christmas pressie. It looks better on you anyway."

Betty flushed with pleasure. "Really? Thank you, Sally. I wish I had more than my mum's jam to give you."

"Don't be a silly goose. I *love* your mum's jam." Sally licked her lips. "The nectar of the gods." She turned to Etta, lounging on her bunk. "Now, as for you—

Etta held up her hand. "Thanks, Fairy Godmother, but I'm not one for frippery. My dress blues suit me just fine."

Maeve and Doctor Moore—Graham, he'd said to call him—danced to the strains of "Moonlight Serenade." Dancing with the handsome doctor was different than dancing with the patients. None of the men from hospital made Maeve's heart quicken or her cheeks flush with a lovely warmth. A warmth she hadn't felt since Seamus.

"I love Glenn Miller," Maeve said. "I do hope they find him."

The day before, the BBC had reported that the American band leader who'd been performing for the English troops along with his orchestra, was missing in action.

"I do, too, but it's been ten days since his plane set off for France, so it doesn't look good." Graham's voice was tinged with sadness.

Maeve closed her eyes and gave a shake of her head. "So many lost." They danced in silence. When she opened her eyes again, the doctor was regarding her with a melancholy look.

"Who did you lose?" he asked gently.

"My fiancé. Seamus was killed in North Africa at El-Alamein."

"I'm sorry. I know what it's like to lose someone you love. My wife and son were killed in the Blitz."

Maeve saw the deep sorrow in his eyes. "I'm so sorry." No need for him to know Thelma had already broadcast the news to all and sundry. "What was your son's name?"

"Theodore. Teddy. He would have been five on Valentine's Day." Graham's mouth crooked in a sad smile. "Susan and I always told Teddy he was our best Valentine."

Maeve's heart clenched. A tear slid down her face.

"I'm sorry. I didn't mean to make you cry. This is supposed to be a festive occasion, and here I've gone and spoiled our dance."

"You didn't spoil anything." She squeezed his hand.

"In the Mood" blared from the wireless, and the mood lifted. Graham spun Maeve round the floor, their feet moving in unison to the jazzy swing dance.

Betty, who'd been dancing with Dickie, made her excuses when the tempo changed and returned to the table where Etta was smoking a cigarette.

Etta blew a smoke ring at the ceiling. "Had enough?"

Betty stared wistfully at the dance floor, pulsing with people doing the Lindy Hop. "I wouldn't even know how to *begin* to do that, but it sure looks fun." Her hand tapped to the beat.

A soldier approached. "May I have this dance?"

Betty looked up, delighted to see her older, neck-bandaged partner from yesterday.

"My transport's sorted for tomorrow, but I didn't want to leave without another dance." He held out his hand.

Betty shook her head, regretfully. "I have no idea how to do that kind of dance."

"I do, and I'm a good teacher, remember? Come on, let's give it a go."

"All right then." Squaring her shoulders and adjusting her velvet cape, Betty glanced at her hutmate. "Wish me luck."

Etta gave her a thumbs-up and leaned back in her chair, puffing on her cigarette.

Harry materialized, his eyes flicking to Etta's blue uniform. "Where's your glad rags then, Red?

"You're looking at them."

"Only you." He delivered his trademark grin. "I'm here to collect on that dance you owe me."

"Sorry, Harry, I'm going to sit this one out. I'm really not much for dancing. Nothing personal."

"Message received." He gave her a mock salute. "Right. Since that's all done and dusted, I shall cast my fishing line elsewhere." His eyes surveyed the room, landing on Sally in her figure-hugging red dress.

Sipping her punch, Etta watched as Harry cut in on the ginger-haired lieutenant. As the officer released Sally, she noticed snooty Sister Agatha standing off to the side. The tall nurse with the plummy vowels cast an evil eye on the voluptuous nursing orderly. *Someone's being devoured by the green-eyed monster.* Etta released a satisfied smile. *Good for you, Sally.*

Sister Louise stopped in front of the table, fanning her face. "Mind if I join you?"

"Please." Etta pushed out a chair.

The senior nurse, who was wearing a simple, well-tailored brown dress, sank down gratefully. "Some of these lads have far too much energy for me." She blew out a puff of air, lifting the frizzy blonde fringe off her forehead. A forehead dotted with perspiration. "I'm dying for some punch."

Etta jumped up. "I'll get you some."

"You don't have to do that. I'll get up in a moment."

"It's no bother." Etta held up her empty glass. "I need a topper myself. You stay and catch your breath." There was a queue at the punch bowl, so she chatted with Doreen and some of the girls while she waited. "Are you having a nice time?"

Doreen fanned her flushed face. "I don't think I've ever danced so much in my life."

"Nor I." Thelma patted her wavy hair she'd set in pin-curls the night before. "It just goes to show one doesn't need alcohol to have fun," she said primly.

Doreen nodded her agreement. "It's a good thing beer is in such short supply and they're restricting it to one pint apiece." She and Thelma bent their heads together and proceeded to dissect what all the girls were wearing.

Reaching the front of the queue, Etta noticed Sally off to one side, whispering and giggling with Harry. The wireless operator slipped something to the Nightingale with the blonde Victory roll, which Sally hid in the folds of her skirt. Then Harry materialized in front of Thelma and Doreen as they stepped up for their drinks.

"Hello, ladies. You're both looking lovely tonight," Harry said. As she got punch for her and Louise, Etta watched as the wireless operator directed the full force of his charm on the two teetotalers. "I'm hoping you'll favor me with a dance, but since I can't dance with two at once, who'd like to go first?" He gave them a flirtatious smile.

They blushed and giggled.

While Doreen and Thelma were otherwise occupied with Harry, Etta noticed Sally pull a flask from the folds of her dress. Sally unscrewed the cap and poured some of the contents into an empty glass, topping it off with a ladleful of punch. Seeing Etta's gaze, she winked and put a finger to her lips, quickly screwing the top back on and returning the flask to her side. Sally then ladled out glasses of punch, extending one of the alcohol-free glasses to Doreen.

"Ta. I am rather parched." Doreen drank it greedily.

Sally held out the doctored glass to Thelma. "Some punch?" she said innocently.

Thelma gave Sally a suspicious glance, but Harry grabbed the other virgin glass of punch and drained it. "Drink up, Thelma. Let's you and I get out on that dance floor and show these folks how it's done." He sent her a winning smile.

Giggling, Thelma downed her punch.

Etta recounted Sally and Harry's hijinks to Louise when she returned to the table. "Those two are quite the pair." She shook her head.

"They are indeed." The nursing sister took a long drink. "Ah, that's better." Louise fastened her eyes on Etta. "It doesn't bother you that Sally's caught Harry's eye?"

"Why should it?"

"I thought you were interested in him."

Etta snorted. "Harry's the last person I'd be interested in. He's not my type."

"What *is* your type?"

Etta lifted her shoulders in a shrug. "Absolutely no idea, but definitely not Harry. Too much of a Romeo. To be honest, romance is the last thing on my mind. I'm much more interested in work."

"I hope you're finding *The Principles and Practice of Nursing* helpful."

Etta's face lit up. "Oh yes. Thanks again for giving it to me. If you ever need it back, just let me know."

Louise took another sip of her punch and studied the nursing orderly across from her. "Do you still want to become an RAF nurse when the war is over?"

"More than anything."

"How does your family feel about that?"

Etta's eyes shuttered. "I have no family." She drained her glass. "And you? Was your family happy when you became a nurse?"

"I'm actually quite a disappointment to my parents," Louise offered up a wry smile. "They sent me to all the right schools, expecting me to marry well and give them grandchildren. My brother—who scolds me for being *married to my work*—is fulfilling that family expectation instead, which is just as well." Louise gazed at Etta over her glass. "To be frank, I've never found a man half as fascinating as the work I do and I'm certainly not going to give up my vocation to become a housewife." She set down her glass with a decided thump.

Maeve danced by with Will Nichols, the nursing orderly who had a crush on her. She smiled and offered Etta a slight wave.

Louise inclined her head in Maeve's direction. "Does she also want to become a nurse? She seems a natural. She's quite good with the men, especially the bomb-happy ones. That takes a special talent."

"A talent I don't possess." Etta grimaced. "Actually," she considered, "I don't know *what* Maeve wants to do when the war is over. She's never said. I do know she misses her sister up in Ireland, so I assume she'll go back

103

home when this is all over." She added under her breath. "Although what she'll find to do in a little village is beyond me."

Thelma and Doreen dropped down at the table beside them. Thelma a bit unsteadily, Etta noticed.

"That Harry is quite a looker, isn't he?" Etta heard Thelma say loudly over the din.

"He certainly is," Doreen said, a dreamy expression on her face.

Unaccustomed to alcohol or being the object of a man's attention, Thelma glared at Doreen. "Keep your hands off. He's mine."

"Since when?"

"Since he held me close, gazed into my eyes, and murmured sweet nothings in my ear." Thelma expelled a rapturous breath.

"Harry murmurs sweet nothings into every girl's ear." Etta saw Doreen shoot her friend a sly glance. "Especially Sally's."

Thelma waved dismissively. "Sally has her eyes set on someone higher." She angled her head to the dance floor where Sally was once again plastered up against Lieutenant Blake. "Not that it's going to do her any good. She's just his bit of fun on the side." Her eyes cut to the tall nurse standing on the sidelines whose arms were crossed rigidly in front of her chest, a venomous stare fixed on the dancing duo. "Sally best be careful though if she knows what's good for her." Thelma hiccupped. "Sister Agatha doesn't take kindly to interlopers."

Thelma and Doreen weren't the only ones who'd noticed the angry nurse.

Louise shook her head. "This will not end well. Agatha knows her fiancé has a roving eye and overlooks his transgressions, but even she has her limits."

"Why does she put up with him?"

"Because Julian Blake is one of the landed gentry," Louise wrinkled her nose. "A viscount—one who's house poor and needs Agatha's money to keep his stately mansion."

Etta's eyes widened. "Sister Agatha's rich? What is she doing here then?"

"Conscription, my dear. She realized early on that single women would eventually be called up for wartime work, and Agatha wasn't about to work in a field or a factory. She told me she decided to become a nurse since it was the most *noble* of the professions on offer. But you can bet the second the war is over; Agatha won't be able to get rid of her nursing veil fast enough." Louise's eyes slid to her fellow nurse, who was still fixated on Sally. "She has her sights set on becoming Lady Muck, and she's not about to let anyone take that from her."

Chapter Sixteen

January 1945

Dear Albert,

Is it cold there? We're all freezing here. I don't think I've ever been this cold. I wish I had my dog to keep me warm. Shep's a lovely border collie who started sleeping with me after we lost our Wilf. He was Wilf's dog and always slept in his room. (He actually slept in my brother's bed, but Wilf kept that a secret from Mum, who had a rule against dogs in bed.)

After Wilf died, I curled up in his bed with Shep beside me, which was a great comfort to both of us. Shep knew Wilf wasn't coming back, and we whimpered together. The next night, my brother's dog padded into my room and started sleeping with me. What I wouldn't give to have Shep's warm blanket of fur next to me now!

I love dogs, don't you? They're such smart creatures. We have a couple cats too—two mousers named Jo and Beth after my favourite sisters in Little Women. I saw that film at the cinema when I was young—Katharine Hepburn was brilliant as Jo. Have you seen any films lately? I saw A Guy Named Joe with Spencer Tracy and Irene Dunne with my friend Sally a while ago. We've been far too busy lately to go to the cinema.

I look forward to your next letter. It's lovely having a pen pal.

Sincerely yours,

Betty

Etta searched for Louise, her mind full of questions about the latest chapter she'd read in the nursing textbook. She poked her head in a couple of the hospital huts, but to no avail. *Maybe she's stocking the medicine cupboards.* All medicine was stored under lock and key in large cupboards inside the medical supplies hut. Only Matron and a handful of doctors and nurses had access to the keys.

Etta pushed open the door of the hut, the roar of a Dakota overhead masking the sound of her entry. Seeing the cupboard in the corner with the open cabinet door partially shielding the bent-over nurse from view, she smiled in anticipation and moved forward, eager to ask Louise her questions. The nurse, whose veil obscured her face, straightened up, and Etta saw that it was Sister Agatha, not Sister Louise.

Agatha, who at that very moment was intent on plunging a morphine needle into her arm.

Well, well. Even the high and mighty have their weaknesses.

Although beer was the most popular and affordable choice of escape among East Enders wanting to forget about the squalor of their lives, Etta was well aware some sought other avenues of release. Usually illicit. Gangs of heavies peddled cocaine and heroin to addicts, and she had heard stories of her own granddad frequenting opium dens after the Great War.

As Sister Agatha pocketed the spent syrette, Etta silently backed away. *Not my business.* In her haste to leave unseen, however, she bumped into an IV pole.

Agatha snatched down her sleeve and whirled around, a guilty look on her face. Seeing Etta, her eyes glittered. "You're not supposed to be in here. What are you doing skulking about?"

"I'm not skulking. I'm looking for Sister Louise."

"Oh, that's right, you're her latest pet, aren't you?" The nurse's lip curled. "Well, you'd better not go telling tales out of school."

"I'm no one's pet, and I've been out of school for years." Etta turned to leave.

"Just keep your mouth shut if you know what's good for you. If you tell anyone, I'll make your life a living hell."

Etta was good at keeping secrets. Her brother's long-ago warning to keep her mouth shut echoed in her ears. She was thirteen the first time Donnie forced himself on her. Her parents were at the pub, and her brother was out with his mates, chasing after a blonde bird he'd had his eye on. Etta took the cherished time alone to curl up with *The Good Earth* on her cot in the corner, behind the torn curtain she'd rigged up for privacy.

Her teacher loaned her the book when Etta confessed to one day wanting to see more of the world. "China couldn't be farther away from England in many ways—not just geographic," Miss Lane told her. Handing her student the novel by Pearl S. Buck, she said, "This will broaden your horizons beyond this sceptered isle."

Etta was engrossed in the story of Wang Lung and peasant life in rural China when Donnie returned stumbling and cursing to the flat. She startled when he banged open the door. Having been on the receiving end of her brother's fist more times than she could count, she stayed still, nose in her book, as Donnie raged against the woman who'd spurned him.

If she kept quiet, maybe he wouldn't realize she was home.

Donnie glimpsed her through the torn curtain, though. Ripping aside the flimsy fabric, he stared at his younger sister. Etta saw something in his eyes she'd never seen before, something she couldn't name.

"I'll teach ya somethin' you'll never learn in yer books," Donnie said.

And he did. Again and again.

When Etta finally plucked up the courage to tell her mother what was happening, her mum slapped her across the face and called her a slut. When she got pregnant from her brother's repeated rapes, her mother took her to a back-alley abortionist.

Etta fled home as soon as she could.

The Nightingales were freezing in the metal Nissen huts. After their flights, they'd gather round the heater in the communal hut, drinking cup after cup of tea, trying to take the chill off.

Nights were the worst. Before bed, they'd all cluster round the stove in the center of the barracks to warm up. Then they'd make a mad dash to their chilly bunks, kitted out in as many layers of clothing as possible, and pull the covers up. Most of the girls slept in their uniform trousers, two pairs of wool socks, and a jumper over their pyjamas. Some tied scarves around their heads, while others placed mittens over their ears. A lucky few, including Maeve, had received quilts from home that helped to take the chill off.

Some of the girls tried to bribe those closest to the heater to change places.

"I'll give you two oranges and a jar of my mum's blackberry jam to swap bunks tonight," a shivering Betty proposed to Thelma one evening when the air was particularly glacial.

Thelma turned up her nose. "I don't like blackberries, and besides, we get an orange each time we fly."

Sally offered up chocolate and her last pair of stockings, but the older nursing orderly wouldn't be budged. Thelma had found out about the prank Sally and Harry played on her at the Christmas party and hadn't forgiven the popular nursing orderly, even after she'd apologized. Nothing would induce Thelma to give up her toasty spot.

It was so cold that if any of the women woke up in the middle of the night needing to wee, they wouldn't venture to the latrines. Instead, they would relieve themselves outside the front door or round the side of their billeting hut. Evidence of their toilet transgression would be a dark brown, snowy block of ice in the morning. Sometimes, it was so cold their urine would freeze before hitting the ground, as Etta discovered firsthand.

Flicking drops of frozen wee off her trousers, Etta slipped back into the hut, shaking uncontrollably. Unable to bear the thought of returning to her arctic bunk, she tapped Maeve on the shoulder and whispered through chattering teeth, "Move over."

Accustomed to sharing a bed with her sister, Maeve moved over. As Etta scrunched up beside her in the narrow bunk, she whispered, "Don't worry. I'll be back in my own bed by morning."

"You'd better be," Maeve murmured groggily. "I don't want my reputation ruined."

That's all we need, Etta thought as she nodded off. *More grist for Thelma's rumor mill.*

Sally found other ways to stay warm. Once or twice a week after the other girls had fallen asleep, she would slip out in the dead of night, returning before dawn the next morning, flushed and smelling of brandy. Betty knew this since her bed was next to Sally's, and her bunkmate's nocturnal wanderings had awakened her more than once.

Seeing Betty awake one morning upon her return in the wee hours, Sally placed a finger to her lips and whispered, "Sorry." That's when Betty saw the flushed cheeks and caught the whiff of brandy.

After returning from a late flight, Maeve went to the Mess in search of food. "I know I missed dinner," she said to the cook in process of shutting down the kitchen, "but I've only just got back and am starving. Do you have anything you can spare a hungry girl? Bread? Biscuits? Anything?"

The cook, a stout girl from Glasgow, jerked her head to a container on the counter. "There's some leftover minced beef I was saving for the cat that comes begging. Ye can have that." She handed Maeve a crust of bread. "Use this to sop up the grease but be quick about it. I'm after closing up for the night."

"Ta very much." Maeve inhaled the leftovers, leaving behind a bit of beef for the cat, seeing Briony's tabby in her mind's eye.

Four hours later, she awoke with stomach cramps.

Shoving her feet into her boots, Maeve wrapped her quilt around her as a buffer against the cold and headed outside, desperate for the loo. Weeing on the side of the hut was one thing, but she drew the line at defecation.

Passing Sally's bed, Maeve noticed the empty bunk. Sally was secretive about her nocturnal wanderings, so none of the girls pressed her about it. Etta and Maeve suspected she made her way to one of the men's huts and found a warm bed there, likely in the officers' quarters.

Grabbing one of the hooded torches from a hook on the wall, Maeve pointed it at the ground as she hurried to the latrine. The torch cast a dim circle of light on the snow. She hoped the light would last until she got to her destination, as she didn't fancy tripping and falling over something in the dark. She hoped *she* would last until she got there.

As the latrine came into view, Maeve sprinted the last few yards. Once inside, she turned off the torch to save the battery. She rested her forehead on the back of her hand for a moment, thinking about the Christmas party and dancing with Doctor Moore. *Graham Moore.* It had been a long time since she had danced so close with anyone. The last time was in Ballydavid, the night before Seamus shipped out.

Seamus. Maeve felt a pang, but the memory no longer cut like a knife. She remembered how she and Seamus had glided smoothly around the dance floor, their bodies in unison, melding together as one. She'd fit perfectly in Seamus's arms, her head snug against his neck. Maeve had wanted the night to never end.

But end it had.

Graham proved to be a good dancer as well, leading her effortlessly around the room. Maeve's lips curved in a smile, remembering. She wouldn't mind dancing with the good doctor again. *Doctor Moore's a fine figure of a man,* she thought. *So handsome. The girls are right; he does resemble Clark Gable...*

Wind whistled through the draughty building.

What in God's name are you doing, my girl, sitting in a cold, dark latrine? Get moving before you freeze to death.

Maeve headed to the door, steeling herself for the trek back. Outside in the pitch black, she turned on the torch. Nothing. Not even a dim circle. She would have to make her way back to her hut carefully in the dark so she didn't fall and injure herself on the uneven ground. Pulling the quilt tightly around her and holding it in place with her left hand, Maeve stretched out her right hand in front of her to avoid bumping into anything.

Then, putting one foot in front of the other, she headed back the way she'd come.

Snow began to fall. Although she couldn't see it, Maeve felt the wet flakes on her face and increased her pace. The moon came out briefly from behind a cloud, illuminating the landscape. Seeing the officers' quarters straight ahead, Maeve realized she'd got off course in the dark. Regaining her bearings, she turned, corrected course, and set off again.

The snow was now falling in earnest. Maeve hurried in the direction of her hut just as the moon retreated behind another cloud. Stumbling over something, she fell, dropping her quilt and torch in the process. "Jaysus, Mary, and Joseph!" Tears of frustration pricked her eyes.

Now's not the time to cry, my girl. Keep going.

Feeling around in the dark, her frozen fingers finally closed round the torch. Maeve gripped it and pushed herself up. As she did, the torch flickered back to life. Shining the fading circle of light on the ground, she spotted a patch of blue. *My quilt.*

Reaching down to pick up the cherished heirloom, Maeve saw it wasn't the patchwork quilt her mum made her when she was a wee lass, but rather, a blue uniform peeking out from beneath a snow-covered mound.

"Oh my God!" Maeve dropped to her knees and began digging in a frenzy. As she shoved the snow off the mound, the back of an RAF jacket came into view. Maeve's eyes darted about frantically. Finding the quilt, she grabbed it and wrapped it round the fallen figure.

Please be okay, please be okay.

And still, the snow kept falling.

Gently, she turned the fallen soldier onto his back. As she did, the torch died, plunging everything into blackness once again. Maeve flicked the torch on and off. *Come on!* The moon came out from behind the clouds, and she glimpsed gleaming blonde hair and a crumpled Victory roll.

Chapter Seventeen

"Sally!"

The moon receded, plunging everything into darkness once more. Maeve dropped her head to her friend's chest. *Was that a heartbeat? Or her own pounding heart?*

"Stay with me Sally," she yelled. "Stay with me." Remembering her training, Maeve lifted Sally's arms above her head and brought them back down to her sides again quickly. Then she did it again. Up and down, up and down. She placed her ear on Sally's chest but couldn't hear anything. Desperate, Maeve placed both hands over the Nightingale's heart and pushed up and down.

Through it all, the snow kept coming down.

A torch flared, and a yell punctured the air, but she didn't stop. Numbly, Maeve heard boots crunching in the snow and sensed someone approaching as she continued massaging Sally's heart.

"Good God!" The voice was male, low-pitched, and authoritative. "Bring those torches and blankets over here. Quickly."

Maeve felt something heavy and warm descend upon her. A hand touched her shoulder. "You can stop now, nurse," an unfamiliar voice said. "We'll take over from here." Gentle hands prised her away from Sally.

Torches illuminated the scene, and for the first time, Maeve saw the staring eyes.

"I'm sorry," the medic said. "She's gone."

"*No!*" Shoving him away, Maeve crawled over to the fallen Nightingale and lifted Sally to her chest, holding her friend tightly as she sobbed.

Swathed in blankets, her hands immersed in a basin of warm water, Maeve sat upright in the hospital bed, staring dully at the wall.

"Drink this." Sister Louise guided a cup of tea gently to her lips. "We need to get you warmed up."

Maeve drank the hot tea, not tasting it.

"I'm so sorry about your friend."

Maeve acknowledged this with a brief nod. "I have to tell Betty and Etta," she said flatly.

"Etta Blackwood?"

"Yes, and Betty Hall. We're all in the same hut," Maeve said. "Sally is," she began, then stopped. "*Was*, our friend." Fresh tears snaked down her face.

"We can send one of the medics to tell them."

"No, it needs to be me."

Graham entered the hut where Maeve had been placed apart from the men. He approached her bed. "I'm so sorry. I know Sally was your friend." He gave her a searching gaze. "Are you all right?"

Maeve looked at him through swollen, listless eyes. "I'm fine." She knew he didn't believe her.

Lifting one of her hands from the basin, Graham inspected it. Turning her hand over, he examined the palm as well. Then he repeated the process with her other hand. Next, he closely examined Maeve's chin, nose, ears, and toes. "You don't have frostbite," he said, "but you may have a mild case of hypothermia. I want you to stay in hospital overnight where we can keep an eye on you and continue warming you up."

"I'm fine, Doctor." She pushed the basin of water to one side and tried to get up, but Graham held her in place. "I need to get back to my hut," Maeve said in desperation.

Sister Louise spoke up. "Doctor, Leading Aircraftwoman Fitzgerald wants to inform Nurse Roberts' friends of her death."

Maeve delivered a pleading look to Graham. "Please. I must let Betty and Etta know. Word spreads like wildfire in camp, and I don't want them to hear it through the grapevine."

He regarded her thoughtfully. "I see. You need to stay put, though. I'll have one of the medics get the girls and bring them here." Graham focused his eyes on hers. Eyes full of understanding and compassion. "Rest assured, I will have him exercise the utmost discretion."

Maeve didn't trust herself to speak.

The doctor strode from the hut, calling for a medic. Sister Louise squeezed her hand, and Maeve steeled herself for the task ahead.

Etta and Betty rushed into the hospital hut; uniform caps jammed over mussed hair. Seeing Louise standing discreetly off to the side and Maeve pale and listless on the narrow cot, Etta's breath caught.

"What happened?" Her eyes roamed swiftly over her friend, searching for wounds and assessing Maeve's condition. Etta catalogued the absence of any cuts or bruises, the lack of bandages, and the pile of blankets covering the Irish Nightingale. She stretched out her hand to Maeve, her eyes lingering on her bunkmate's red, swollen eyes.

"I got caught in the snow on my way back from the latrine and lost my way in the dark," Maeve said. "They're keeping me in hospital overnight, but I'll be back to ours tomorrow." The image of Sally's empty bunk flashed before her. Maeve's eyes filled. Taking a deep breath, she willed the tears not to fall. "I don't know how to tell you this." Swallowing past the lump in her throat, she squeezed Etta and Betty's hands, sending them a look full of sorrow. "I'm so sorry, but Sally is dead."

"What?" Betty jerked her hand away and staggered back, her mouth a round O. "Did her plane go down? Maybe she's just missing," her brown eyes begged.

"She's not missing, love. She wasn't flying tonight. I'm so sorry, sweetheart, but Sally's gone."

Clutching the edge of the bed, Betty sobbed. "No." She shook her head wildly back and forth. "No."

Etta stared at Maeve in disbelief. "How? What happened?"

"I'm not sure. I think she may have fallen in the dark and hit her head. I found her on my way back from the latrine."

Sister Louise joined them. "We think Nurse Roberts died from exposure," she said gently. "There's no telling how long she was outside."

Betty recoiled, her eyes wide and staring. "Sally *froze* to death? Out there in the dark all alone?"

"I'm afraid so. I'm so sorry."

The young Nightingale's knees buckled, and Louise caught her as she started to fall. Betty sobbed in the nurse's arms. Great racking sobs.

Etta and Maeve exchanged a look. They knew Sally wouldn't have been alone, at least to start. Maeve remembered the night months ago when she'd happened upon Sally and some pilot—Lieutenant Blake, perhaps?—in a lover's tryst behind the women's shower hut. But that had been summer when the nights were warm. *Surely Sally wouldn't be engaging in outdoor hanky-panky now?*

Etta's hands clenched at her sides.

Betty got hold of herself. "Where is she? I want to see her. I *need* to see her."

Etta's eyes flicked to Louise, telegraphing a mute appeal.

"I'll take you to her," the nursing sister said.

"We'll all go." Pushing back the covers, Maeve slung her legs over the side of the bed. Etta and Louise worked in concert; Louise put warm socks and a pair of fur-lined boots on Maeve's feet, and Etta wrapped blankets round her friend. When Maeve stood, Betty slipped her shaking hand in hers.

The three nursing orderlies followed Louise as she passed by the men's wards and led them down the walkway to the last hospital hut. Betty tightened her grip on Maeve's hand as the nurse opened the door. Sister Louise turned on the light, passing by the blackout-curtained windows, and led them over to the bed where a still form lay covered by a sheet. Gently, she pulled down the sheet, stopping just above Sally's chest.

For the girls' sake, Maeve was relieved to see someone had closed Sally's eyes. She knew the image of those open, staring eyes would be imprinted on her own eyes forever.

Betty wiped her wet face on her sleeve and touched the golden head with a hand that trembled. "Your hair's got mussed, dear," she murmured, "but don't worry, we'll fix it for you just the way you like." She bent her head and kissed the cold cheek. "Sleep with the angels now, sweetheart, and give my brother a hug. Wilf will love you just as all your boys loved you."

Etta and Maeve said their goodbyes and Maeve returned to her hospital bed, while Betty and Etta walked slowly back to their sleeping quarters in silence. Betty's head was full of images of Sally. Laughing, teasing, flirting with her patients, jollying the men along, putting on her red lipstick, playing fairy godmother...giving her the beautiful rhinestone hair clip at Christmas. Her eyes blinded with fresh tears.

When Etta opened the door to their hut, a sea of stunned faces greeted them.

"Is it true," Clemmie asked. "Sally's dead?"

Etta's bleak gaze confirmed it.

The girls gasped, and several began to cry.

Thelma sniffed. "Can't say as I'm surprised. The way Sally drank and carried on, spreading her legs for every man in sight. Harlots never come to a good end."

Eyes blazing, Betty flew at Thelma and slapped her hard across the face. "You shut yer gob, or I'll shut it for you."

Chapter Eighteen

Etta couldn't sleep. She couldn't stop thinking about Sally. *How could this have happened? How could she have* died? She knew Sally had her paramours and sneaked out in the middle of the night to meet up with her lover of the moment. But where did they meet? The men's barracks? The officers' quarters? Could it be she had got into a fight with her latest romantic liaison?

Etta balled her hand into a fist. *Some rotter just left her out there.* Like Agnes, the dead Nightingale from Blakehill Farm.

Eyes fixed on the curved metal ceiling of the Nissen hut, Etta recalled her conversation with Sally about VD last fall. Sally had assured her she always used French letters for protection during her assignations. *Could it be one of those "letters" hadn't worked and she, like the dead Agnes before her, had also found herself in the family way?*

Etta flashed back to Christmas when Lieutenant Blake and Sally had been plastered all over one another on the dance floor. She recalled how the pilot's fiancée Sister Agatha had glared at her voluptuous friend in her snug-fitting red dress. Lieutenant Blake, counting on Agatha's family money upon their marriage, would not have welcomed an unintended pregnancy from his secret lover. Could the ginger-haired pilot have killed Sally, the same way the mystery boyfriend had killed preggers Agnes?

Etta shook her head. Sally wouldn't have allowed herself to get in that situation. She remembered her saying Agnes could have made her "little problem" go away when the girls had been talking about the dead Nightingale from RAF Blakehill and her pregnancy. Etta didn't doubt for a moment that had Sally found herself in the same predicament, she would have known what to do and where to go to take care of that kind of problem.

There's no indication Sally was strangled, she reminded herself, *or even pregnant for that matter.* A tear slid down her face and Etta dashed it away, thinking of the vibrant, laughing blonde Nightingale, so full of life. *What a terrible waste.*

Curled into a foetal position, Betty wept into her pillow so as not to awaken the other girls. *Oh, Sally.* Betty had never lost a friend before apart from her brother Wilf.

Memories flashed through her mind.

The two of them doubled over with laughter recounting Paddy's hijinks with the VIP "patient" to Maeve and Etta. Sally comforting her when Etta was missing in action. Going to the cinema together and seeing *A Guy Named Joe*. Decorating the Christmas tree with paper chains. Sally giving Betty the beautiful blue velvet capelet to wear to the dance….

The Herefordshire farm girl cried herself to sleep.

Released from hospital the next day, Maeve went straight back to work. All the Nightingales did. Matron had offered to give Maeve the day off but losing one of their own didn't stop the casualties from coming. Several flights a day continued to take off from the camp bound for France, Belgium, and Holland, returning hours later with scores of wounded. Besides, the Irish Nightingale knew she needed to keep busy.

Maeve and the crew of her Dakota had just finished loading their patients and were about to close the doors when an ambulance screeched to a stop beside the plane. Jumping out of the emergency vehicle, a medic yelled, "This soldier is severely wounded and needs to get to hospital fast. Help me get him on the plane."

Harry leapt from the Dakota, and Maeve quickly moved one of the lesser injured men from a stretcher to one of the seats. When they brought the wounded soldier on board, she saw he was missing an arm and a leg and suffering badly from internal injuries. As she tried to fit him with an oxygen mask, he moved his head wildly to and fro, letting loose a string of Gaelic. *He's Irish.*

The first Irish patient she had encountered.

Maeve responded soothingly to the wounded man in Gaelic, holding his hand, and telling him not to worry, they would take good care of him. She explained that the oxygen mask was to help him breathe and that he would be home soon. The soldier visibly relaxed, and Maeve fitted the mask on him, continuing to speak in Gaelic all the while. She asked where he was from and told him about her home and family in Ballydavid. Then she stroked his hand until he fell asleep.

"Could I have some char love?" one of the lads with bulky bandages covering his hands asked.

"Your wish is my command." Fetching the tea urn, Maeve poured him a cuppa, holding the enamel cup to his mouth as he drank greedily.

"Ta, love."

When she finished making her tea rounds, Maeve checked on the Irish soldier, making sure the tag with the time the medic had given him morphine was still attached to his collar. That way, the camp doctors would have the necessary medication dosage information when they landed.

Remembering Sally's example, Etta joked with the lads as she adjusted tourniquets, checked bandages, and went down the aisle with the ever-present urn of tea. "I think you've had enough to drink," she teased one private. "I won't have enough urine bottles to go round the rate you're going."

His face split in a wide grin. "Me mum always said I peed like a racehorse."

The corporal beside him cast the young soldier a disapproving look. "That's no way to talk to a lady."

"Sorry, Nurse," the red-faced private mumbled.

"That's okay, soldier. I've heard worse." Much worse.

Etta didn't flirt with the men the way Sally had; flirting had never been her forte. Sometimes, though, she would tell her patients bits and pieces from her days in the munitions factory—including how she and her pal Mavis used to offer up "bomb benedictions" over the bombs they were working on.

"We used to say, 'May you fall straight and true and bomb the hell out of Hitler and his crew,'" she told them.

They clapped and whistled.

"Good on ya, duck."

The Dakotas returned to camp in rapid succession. After getting their patients unloaded onto the concrete blocks so the medical officer could examine them, the girls headed to their hut.

Betty brushed her hair and applied a touch of lipstick. "Do I look okay?"

"Perfect." Maeve linked her arm with Betty. "Sally would approve."

Etta joined them, and the three nursing orderlies, along with Clemmie, Doreen, and the rest of the Nightingales headed to the canteen where Harry and the other wireless operators were waiting.

Maeve addressed the crowded canteen. "Some of you may recall when the Blakehill plane went down, and Sally raised a glass in the crew's honour." She saw tears glistening on several faces, including some of the men. "She said she hoped we'd do the same for her when and if the time came."

"And if we didn't," Harry interjected, displaying his signature grin, "Sally threatened to come back and haunt us."

Everyone laughed through their tears. Etta noticed Sister Louise and Doctor Moore standing in the back. Maeve gave Betty an encouraging nod.

Betty lifted her glass. "To Sally," she toasted in a quavering voice.

"To Sally," the room chorused.

The three Nightingales made their way over to Harry and the other wireless operators. Harry's eyes were wet. "Sally was a grand girl," he said. "Always up for some fun and a laugh."

"And boy, could that girl dance," Dickie said. "Sally did the jitterbug better than anyone."

"She danced rings around me," Frank Timmins admitted.

"Sally was a good dancer." Etta took a long slug of her beer. "She was also very good at her job. She made each one of her patients feel as though he was the only one she was caring for amongst the twenty-four wounded men on her plane. I always admired her rapport with the injured."

"Her boys," Maeve said fondly.

Harry swigged his beer. "I remember one flight back from Normandy. There was this lad who'd never flown before. He kept babbling that we were going to wind up in the drink, making the men near him nervous. Sally silenced him with a kiss and promised him another kiss when we landed if he kept quiet." He chuckled. "That lad never made another peep. Just stared at Sally with puppy-dog eyes the rest of the flight."

And so they went, exchanging stories about the friend they'd lost.

Clemmie came over to them. "I still can't believe this. One of our own dying from *exposure*. How could that happen? Are they sure that's how Sally died? It seems so strange."

Doreen shivered. "Poor Sally. All alone out there in the freezing snow." She hugged herself.

Harry's eyes flickered, and Betty began to cry.

Etta's lips thinned. "I prefer to focus on Sally's life rather than her death." Even though she'd had the same thoughts as Clemmie. She downed the rest of her beer.

Harry drained his glass. "That's what Sally would want."

Frank cleared his throat. "Has anything been said about a funeral? I expect her family will be taking her back home."

Betty blew her nose. "Sally once told me if anything ever happened to her, she'd like to be buried at All Saints in the village." She took a deep breath. "I informed Matron of her wishes and apparently, Sally had written her parents the same thing. They're coming to Down Ampney tomorrow for the funeral. Matron has made all the arrangements."

Maeve stared at Betty. *She* informed Matron. *Our youngest Nightingale is growing up.* Noticing Graham beckoning, she excused herself and made her way over to the doctor and Sister Louise. Maeve gave the two officers a warm smile. "Thank you so much for coming. I—we appreciate it. Sally would have as well."

"Of course," Louise uttered automatically. She didn't return the smile, though, and Maeve noticed she seemed uneasy. Her eyes flicked uncertainly between doctor and nurse. "Is something wrong?"

"Could we talk outside?" Graham asked.

"Certainly." Aware of the speculative glances being directed their way, Maeve followed Doctor Moore as he led her out the canteen door.

Etta came alongside Sister Louise, who was watching them leave. "What's going on?" Shifting uncomfortably, Louise didn't meet her eyes. "Sorry. If you'll excuse me, I must get back to work. She exited the canteen, leaving Etta staring after her, bewildered.

Outside, Graham cleared his throat. "Maeve…" he began, but the senior nursing sister's appearance interrupted him. As Sister Louise passed by, Maeve caught a glimpse of something in the nurse's eyes. Something she couldn't define. Louise gave them a brisk nod and moved on toward the hospital.

"Maeve," Graham began again, only to be interrupted by two laughing loadmasters approaching the canteen. Seeing the officer out front, the ground crew stopped and saluted. Returning their salute, Graham ushered Maeve away from the canteen. "Let's find somewhere a bit more private, shall we?"

He steered her in the direction of the closed Mess, stopping beside a barren oak. Glancing around to make sure no one was nearby, the doctor faced Maeve, a troubled expression on his face. "I have something to tell you."

Maeve's stomach lurched. "What is it? You're scaring me."

"I'm sorry." He gave her a penetrating look. "Sister Louise found empty morphine syrettes in Sally's jacket."

"Morphine? Nurses administer morphine—but we only do so in an emergency."

"I know." His gray eyes pinned on hers. "You realize what this means, don't you?"

She tilted her head at him, bewildered.

"Maeve," Graham said gently, "I'm afraid Sally took her own life."

She shook her head violently. "Sally would never do that. She loved life more than anyone I knew. Why would she kill herself?"

"I don't know. But the work we do is difficult. The injuries you girls see on a daily basis are horrific. It can get to you after a while." His lips tightened. "Six weeks of medical training isn't sufficient to prepare you." Graham's face took on a grim expression. "*Years* of medical training can't prepare you for the horrors of war—the damage that bullets and bombs can do to the human body. It's actually surprising there haven't been more suicides."

"Sally didn't commit suicide." Maeve whirled on him, eyes blazing. "Stop saying that! Sally seized life with both hands. She always said that in war, none of us knows how much time we have, so we need to live life to the fullest. And she did. Sally's the last person who would have taken her own life."

"Did you ever notice how, at times, she seemed a bit frenetic?"

"That was just her jolly nature. You didn't know Sally like we did."

But why did she have morphine? Maeve cast about desperately in her mind for an answer. "Sally was probably assisting the field hospital nurse when she gave the men their shots before they were evacuated. Things can get pretty hectic in the field when you're dodging German snipers and taking care of so many patients at once," she said pointedly. "In the chaos of trying to get all the men loaded, Sally may have inadvertently pocketed the syrettes and forgotten about them."

Graham lifted an eyebrow. "I admit I don't know what it's like in the field under fire and coping with so many casualties in those conditions. But I also know there are protocols in place for disposing of syrettes. Sister Louise said Sally was an excellent nursing orderly who wouldn't have made such a sloppy mistake."

Maeve knew that, but she also knew there was another explanation. There *had* to be. She just couldn't think straight at the moment, not with everything going on and Sally's funeral tomorrow. A knot formed in her stomach as she realized the implications of Graham's suggestion.

"Sally's being buried in the village church tomorrow. It's all arranged,"

Maeve said. "Her parents are coming from Sussex. If there's even a hint of suicide, the church won't allow her to be buried in hallowed ground."

"I know." Graham's mouth thinned. "I'm not a religious man, and I see no need to inform the church. The dead should be buried where they like, if at all possible. That's the least we can do for them."

Maeve expelled a sigh of relief.

"However, by law, I am required to report a suicide to the authorities."

"You can't! You don't even know if it *is* suicide. You assume so because Sister Louise found some empty syrettes in Sally's pocket. That's not fair." Realizing she was sounding hysterical Maeve took a breath. When she spoke again, her voice was steady.

"I promise you Sally did not kill herself, and I'll prove it." *I don't know how, but I will.* "Please, *please* don't report this to anyone," she begged. "Not yet. Give me some time to prove you wrong."

"All right. I won't say anything." Graham paused. "Yet." He held up his hand. "I can't speak for Sister Louise, though. She's a stickler for following the rules. She's not religious, so I doubt she'll say anything to the vicar, but Matron is another story altogether. If I were you, I wouldn't wait too long before pleading your case with Louise."

Head spinning, Maeve hurried to her hut. There were any number of reasons why Sally might have had the empty syrettes on her, but that wasn't her pressing concern. She had to tell Etta what Graham had said. Etta and Louise were friends of a sort, and Etta would have a better chance than her of persuading the nursing sister not to say anything to Matron. But she had to move quickly. Maeve had no idea when Louise planned to reveal her suspicions to the head nurse.

Sally didn't kill herself. She would never have ended her jolly, vibrant life with an overdose of morphine. Maeve knew that with every fiber of her being and was determined to prove it. *Somehow.* She shivered as a dark thought surfaced. Memories of Agnes, the dead Nightingale from RAF Blakehill, filled her head.

Sally did not end her life, but someone else may have.

Chapter Nineteen

Betty was pleased by the large turnout. All the Nightingales, save those who were flying, had come to All Saints to pay their respects to Sally. As had the aircrews, loadmasters, and several doctors and nurses, including Matron. *Mr. and Mrs. Roberts can take pride in knowing how much their daughter meant to everyone,* she thought. *How everyone liked and admired Sally.*

Unbidden, an unwelcome thought intruded. *Apart from Thelma and a few of the other girls, who thought she had loose morals.* She pushed the thought away. Once, Betty would have thought the same, but that was before she got to know Sally and recognized her big heart. Sally was the living embodiment of the Golden Rule: *Do unto others as you would have them do unto you.* She was always putting others' needs before her own. Sally had a heart of gold, and that's what Betty chose to remember: her friend's pure, generous heart.

She sat in the front pew between Maeve and Sally's mother, the three women flanked by Etta and Mr. Roberts. Mrs. Roberts, who looked like an older version of Sally, had insisted Betty, Maeve, and Etta join her and her husband. "You girls were like Sally's family here, so it's only fitting you sit with us."

Betty had managed to keep her composure throughout the service until they started to sing "The Lord is my Shepherd." Her throat felt thick with grief, and the words stuck and wouldn't come out.

After the service, Matron approached Sally's parents. "Mr. and Mrs. Roberts, please permit me to extend my deepest condolences. Sally was a fine nursing orderly. One of our best. She had a special way with the wounded, cheering them up and making each man feel as if he were her only patient. You should be quite proud of your daughter."

Sally's father puffed up with pride, and Mrs. Roberts dabbed at her eyes with her handkerchief.

Etta, who didn't usually pray, shot up a prayer of gratitude that Sister Louise had agreed not to say anything to Matron about her suspicions that Sally had committed suicide. Etta had told Louise she and Maeve were convinced Sally would never have done such a thing. She had begged the nursing sister not to say anything, appealing to her sense of compassion.

"Even if Sally *did* off herself—which she didn't—what good would come from telling Matron?" Etta asked. "She would have to report it to the authorities, word would spread, the vicar wouldn't allow Sally to be buried in church grounds, and that would devastate her parents and break their hearts." She drove her argument home. "Not to mention, her parents would have to live with the shame and stigma of their daughter's suicide forever. Why hurt them needlessly? What's the point? As nurses, we're meant to ease others' suffering, not cause unnecessary pain."

Louise had cocked her head. "Are you sure nursing is your chosen profession, Etta? You'd make a good solicitor."

After convincing Louise not to say anything, Etta had mulled over the fact of the empty syrettes in Sally's pocket. *What was Sally doing with morphine anyway? We always turn in our hampers with the emergency morphine when we land. It's inventoried and kept locked in the supply hut. So why did she have syrettes, and how did she get them?*

Then Etta remembered Sally and one of the doctors engaging in flirtatious banter at the canteen not long ago. Doctor Stone had invited Sally to his table for drinks and when Etta left, the two of them had looked quite cozy together. *Doctor Stone has access to the locked medicine cupboard. He may have given Sally the morphine. But why?*

The sight of Sister Agatha covertly giving herself a shot of morphine filled Etta's head. *Doctor Stone's not the only one with access.*

127

Betty lingered at the graveside with Sally's parents after everyone left, stepping back to give them privacy for their final goodbyes. Mrs. Roberts leaned into her husband, releasing a strangled sob as they gazed down at their daughter's grave. Mr. Roberts stroked his wife's back. He knelt down and placed a sprig of snowdrops on the fresh earth, resting his hand on the white flowers.

Mrs. Roberts looked old beyond her years. "The war's taken both our children now." Her eyes fluttered shut. "A mother's not meant to outlive her children. It's not right."

Betty's eyes filled. She clasped Sally's mum's hand and held it tight.

"The only thing that gives me peace is knowing Jimmy and Sally are together again." Mrs. Roberts released a sad smile. "When Jimmy died, I thought our Sally was going to die right along with him. She adored her big brother—thought he hung the moon. The two of them were thick as thieves, and Sally was lost without him." Her voice cracked. "Sally changed after Jimmy died. She decided she was going to live her life as if there was no tomorrow. That's when she became a WAAF. Our girl said the least she could do for her brother was take care of the lads still fighting; bring them some comfort."

Betty squeezed her hand. "That's why I became a nursing orderly, too. After my brother Wilf died at Dunkirk."

"No wonder you and Sally were such good friends." Mr. Roberts offered Betty his arm. Mrs. Roberts took his other arm and the three of them went to rejoin the others.

Maeve watched Harry push through the crowded canteen to pay his respects. The wireless operator shook Mr. Roberts' hand. "Sally was a grand girl. She will be sorely missed." Clearing his throat, he tilted his head at her mother. "It's easy to see where Sally got her good looks from. You could be her sister."

Mrs. Roberts' mouth quirked in a faint smile. "Sally said you were quite the charmer."

Dickie and Frank came up to offer their condolences, and Betty excused herself to get sandwiches for the older couple. Etta and Maeve joined her at the counter. Maeve touched Betty's arm. "How are you holding up?"

"I'm all right. Wasn't the service lovely? What a turnout. I think Sally would have been chuffed. I was happy to see Doctor Moore and Sister Louise there, especially as they didn't really know Sally. That was kind of them. It's nice to know her superiors held her in high regard."

Maeve and Etta exchanged a glance over Betty's head as she placed sandwiches on a plate. They'd not told her about the empty syrettes or that Graham and Louise thought Sally had killed herself. The girls knew the very idea would shatter Betty and saw no reason to upset their churchgoing pal. Betty's faith was simple and steadfast, yet that same faith taught that suicide was an unforgivable sin and those who took their own lives were condemned to hell. She would be gutted to think that Sally, the friend she so liked and admired, was in hell.

That's why they refused to even raise the specter of suicide to Betty.

It's all for the greater good, Maeve thought. Etta told her she'd said that to Louise when convincing her not to go to Matron: "Rules may be rules, but sometimes one has to bend the rules for the greater good."

"That *was* kind of Doctor Moore and Sister Louise to attend Sally's funeral." Maeve squeezed Betty's arm. She was just glad Thelma had stayed away. Far away. Off in one of the Dakotas to pick up casualties.

Etta had relayed to Maeve the hateful things Thelma had said about Sally when they'd returned to the hut after saying goodbye to Sally in hospital. She'd also told Maeve how Betty had slapped the self-righteous prig. Since then, the camp gossip had given Betty and Etta a wide berth and avoided the other girls in the hut. Thelma had tried to cozy up to Doreen but even her former partner-in-crime had been appalled by her pal's vitriol at one of their own and backed away from her.

Maeve would never understand women like Thelma. What caused them to be so hateful and malicious? She pulled up short, struck by a sudden thought. *Just how much did Thelma hate Sally? Enough to hurt her, maybe even kill her?*

"Maeve, are you all right?" Betty asked.

"I'm fine. Let's get these sandwiches over to Sally's parents. They need some sustenance." She flashed a smile. "So do I, for that matter." They returned to Mr. and Mrs. Roberts, where they munched on sandwiches and chatted about inconsequential things as people do in these situations.

Glancing at his watch, Mr. Roberts motioned to his wife. "We'll need to be leaving soon if we want to make our train."

Etta touched his arm. "We've packed up Sally's things for you. Harry and Dickie will load them in the truck they've secured for transport and take you to the station."

"There's just one thing before you go." Maeve prayed she could get through this next bit without breaking down. She squeezed Mrs. Roberts' hand. "This is for Sally." Stepping back, she closed her eyes and began to sing "I'll Be Seeing You" in her lilting soprano.

"Blimey, Maeve," Harry exclaimed the next morning as they prepared for their flight. "You gutted me with that Vera Lynn song."

"I wanted to give Sally a proper send-off."

"That you did, love." Harry's voice was thick as he checked his radio. "That you did."

"Harry?" Maeve spoke tentatively. *Just ask him.* "Were you in love with Sally?"

"In *love*?" He stopped what he was doing to gape at her. "Where did you get that idea?"

She lifted her shoulders. "You and Sally spent a lot of time together and the two of you were always flirting. I thought maybe it was more than flirting."

"Sally and I just liked to have a good time together. No strings, nothing serious. Just fun. An escape from all this." Harry waved his hand to encompass the plane and the camp.

In for a penny, in for a pound. Maeve plowed ahead. "Do you know if anyone else was in love with her? Perhaps one of the pilots?"

"What's with all the questions about Sally's love life, Irish? You writing a book or something?"

"I just thought it would have been nice knowing Sally had someone who loved her."

"A lot of us loved Sally. She knew how to make a man forget his troubles. Make him feel special." Harry's eyes glistened. "But as for being *in love* with her, or someone having some kind of grand passion for Sally, not that I know of—she never said."

The rest of the crew arrived and started going through their checklists. Maeve pulled out her flight log and entered the date, time, destination, and aircraft number. Then, her Dakota took off for Belgium to pick up casualties from the Ardennes offensive.

The Battle of the Bulge.

Chapter Twenty

Etta bent over the stretcher sling, making sure everything was secure before takeoff. The pilots' voices filtered back to her from the cockpit.

"Sorry you lost your bit of stuff on the side, Blake. You're really going to miss those curves."

Etta straightened, clenching the metal frame.

"I am indeed. Those curves warmed me up on these cold nights."

The copilot sniggered. "You may have to get that fiancée of yours to do the warming now."

"Not until the ring's on her finger." Lieutenant Blake grunted. "Agatha's one of those old-fashioned girls. Won't give it up until the wedding night."

"When's the wedding then?"

"The minute the war's over, I expect. The ancestral pile is falling apart, and the old man's champing at the bit for me to get it sorted. Until then, I'll have to find someone else to keep me warm. Preferably another lush blonde who knows how to keep a chap happy like that one did." The pilots laughed.

Etta gripped the frame tightly.

"All right there, Etta?" Dickie came up alongside her.

"Fine." She gave him a brief smile. "So where are we headed today?"

A shivering Betty skirted the lily ponds between the huts, holding her nose. Lily ponds were what the girls had nicknamed the trench holes dotted around the camp where the bedpans and urine bottles were emptied daily. When the ponds got too full or smelly, the ground staff filled them up and dug new ones.

Time for this lot to be filled up.

Entering the communal hut, Betty saw it was empty save for Doreen, engrossed in a magazine. She poured herself a cuppa and scooted close to the heater, eager to read the latest letter from Albert. She had written and told him about Sally, but it would still be weeks before he received her sad news.

Dear Betty,

I hope my Christmas card finally made its way to you. I'm sorry it didn't arrive before the holiday. It sounds like you had a lovely Christmas. What a feast you girls had! Made me almost wish I was a WAAF (although I don't think I'd look good in a skirt.)

We had murkey for our Christmas dinner—mutton stuffed with mostly breadcrumbs—and mash, sprouts, and swedes. If I never eat another swede again it'll be too soon. Mum also pulled out a jar of piccalilli she'd been saving which was a real treat. Our Christmas pudding didn't have much fruit this year, or even eggs, but Mum made up the difference with carrots and potatoes.

That was some sad news about Glenn Miller. At least his music will live on. It's good music to dance to. I've always liked dancing. Do you? Once you're back home, I'd like to take you to a dance. I may only have one arm, but I can still cut a rug.

How is your land-girl getting on? My brother Ronald has fallen for our land girl, Lydia, and told me he's planning to pop the question on Valentine's Day. Lydia's a nice girl, just not much use on a farm. She's trying, though; I'll give her that.

What a cold winter we're having! It's so freezing when I do the milking, I have to wear two pairs of socks. Mum knit me a fingerless glove for my hand as well. It took a bit to get the hang of milking the cows one-handed, but I've got it down now.

Everyone's saying the war will soon be over. I hope so for all our sakes, especially yours. It's a fine thing you're doing taking care of the wounded lads—like you did me—but all that flying across the Channel with the Luftwaffe still up there makes me nervous. I don't want anything to happen to you.

I pray every day for your safety.

Yours sincerely,

Albert

p.s. Since you like films so much, have you seen National Velvet? *That Violet was a real corker! Pretending to be a boy and racing her horse in the Grand National. I wonder did that really happen, or is it just a made-up story?*

Betty read the letter again, giggling as she pictured Albert in a WAAF uniform. When she came to the part where he wrote "I don't want anything to happen to you," she pressed her hand over her heart. Slipping the letter back in the envelope, she went to get another cuppa.

Two loadmasters came in, having a chinwag. "They say she froze to death on the way to her hut. Seems a bit odd that. If she'd got lost in the dark like they say, why didn't she yell for help? With all the people in camp, someone would have heard her."

"Devil if I know. She may have passed out. That one liked her liquor."

"She liked her men too, especially the officers. She was plenty free with her charms."

His pal snorted. "Why not just call a spade a spade? Or, in this case, a slag."

Betty sucked in her breath. Her stomach roiled, and the teacup in her hand began to shake. She steeled herself to say something, but Doreen beat her to it.

"I believe you're talking about Sally Roberts," Doreen said in a deathly calm voice as she stood and glared at the two loadmasters. "Or should I say *gossiping* like a pair of old women?"

The men's faces flushed.

Doreen fixed them with a penetrating stare. "Sally was a friend. A nursing orderly just like me and Betty here—a Flying Nightingale. Sally gave all she had to the wounded men in her care, and I'll thank you not to sully her memory with your thoughtless, hurtful speculation. Let the dead rest in peace." Shaking with anger, she pointed to the door. "Now get the hell out of here."

Shamefaced, the men beat a hasty retreat.

Betty covered her mouth with her hand, her eyes blinking rapidly. "How can people be so hateful?"

"They're eejits. Don't pay them any mind." Doreen laid a hand on her arm. "Now, how about we sit down with a nice cup of tea?"

When Etta and Maeve returned from their flights, Betty told them what the loadmasters had said, whispering so the other girls couldn't hear. "I hadn't thought of it before, but why do you think Sally didn't call for help? Do you think she might have been drunk and passed out?"

She told them about the night she woke up when Sally was returning from one of her nocturnal escapades and how she'd smelled brandy on her breath. "I know she was seeing someone," Betty said. "I thought maybe it was Harry, but where would he get the money for brandy? I think it must have been an officer."

An officer but not a gentleman, Etta thought. Then she, too, wondered why Sally hadn't called out for help. *Maybe because she didn't want help?* She shook her head, banishing the traitorous thought.

Maeve took Betty's hands in hers. "I don't know why Sally didn't yell for help, love. Perhaps she'd had a bit too much to drink and stumbled in the dark, hit her head, and lost consciousness. Or maybe, like me, she simply lost her way and got disoriented—something that's very easy to do, especially with the snow coming down hard like it was. When I was out there, I got all discombobulated and confused, and I hadn't had a drop to drink."

She gave Betty a small, sad smile. "I don't think we'll ever know what really happened, sweetheart, but *how* Sally died doesn't matter. It's how she *lived* that counts and what we must remember. We need to focus on her life and think about all the good times we had."

"Yeah, like the two of you laughing like a drain over Paddy's antics," Etta reminded Betty.

"And Sally playing fairy godmother to your Cinderella the night of the Christmas dance," Maeve said.

A smile broke through Betty's tears. "And how she tried to teach me to jitterbug, and I kept stepping on her toes, and she said next time she'd have to borrow a pair of some lads' combat boots." Her mouth turned down. "I just wish those chaps hadn't said what they did."

Maeve flapped her hand in a dismissive wave. "Don't give those nosy Parkers a second thought. They're small-minded men with nothing better to do with their time." She sent the girls a sly smile. "And I'll wager that's not the only thing small about them."

Betty tilted her head, confused. When she realized what Maeve meant, a blush stained her cheeks.

Etta snickered. "I'd wager the same."

"Girls!" Betty scolded.

Etta smirked. "The next time some idiot says anything stupid like that, you just slap them like you did old Thelma. I'd pay good money to see that again."

Betty giggled. "I still can't believe I did that. My mum would be shocked."

Maeve and Etta left Betty to write her latest letter to Albert and headed to the canteen for a drink. On the way, Etta shot Maeve a sideways glance. "I know those loadmasters were tossers but they raised a good point." She stopped, arms slack at her sides. "Why do you suppose Sally didn't call out for help the night she died? Could it be she didn't *want* any help? That she just wanted to end it all, as Louise and Doctor Moore suspect? I'm beginning to think they're right. Maybe Sally did kill herself." Etta stared down at her hands.

"I thought the same thing for one terrible moment when Betty told us what those idiots said. It's a good point, but I refuse to believe it. Like I told Betty, Sally may have had too much to drink, fallen and hit her head and got knocked out."

Or...someone had knocked her out then finished the job by giving her an overdose of morphine. But who? And why?

136

"Irish?" Etta waved her hand in front of Maeve's face. "You still with me?"

"Sorry. I was thinking."

"And do you think Sally took her own life?"

"Absolutely not. I think someone killed her. I just don't know who."

"*What*? You're kidding, right?"

Maeve shook her head stubbornly.

"You really think someone *killed* Sally? *Murdered* her? Why, for God's sake?" Etta remembered how she'd toyed with the same idea the night Sally died, wondering if perhaps she'd also found herself in the family way and met the same fate as Agnes, the dead Nightingale from RAF Blakehill.

"Jealousy," Maeve said. "Take Thelma, for instance." The words tumbled out as she warmed to the topic. "Thelma hated Sally and has always been jealous of her. Sally offended her repressed religious sensibilities with her free-spirited, modern attitude towards sex." She fastened her eyes on Etta. "Didn't you say Thelma called Sally a harlot? *And* she never forgave Sally for spiking her punch at the party and getting her tipsy."

"But none of those are reasons to *kill* someone," Etta said. "You don't kill someone just because they pulled a prank on you. That's ridiculous. If that was the case, I'd have killed several people by now." She flashed back to the girls in school who made fun of her for wearing the same dirty dress day in and day out. Etta had scrubbed the single dress she owned as best she could, but soap had been in short supply in the Blackwood household.

Maeve's cheeks pinked. "I guess when you put it like that it does sound rather melodramatic." She gave her bunkmate a rueful smile. "Blame it on my heritage. We Irish are well known for our love of the theatrical." Her brows knit together. "I'm just trying to find another explanation for the empty syrettes in Sally's pocket. I can't believe she killed herself. That's something depressed people do. Did you ever see Sally depressed?"

"No..."

"Exactly. Sally was the jolliest person around, always laughing, teasing, and cutting up. She *loved* life. Why would she kill herself? I'm simply trying to make sense of it all. That's why I landed on the jealousy and murder angle." Maeve pulled a face. "Maybe I read too many murder mysteries."

"Maybe. Although if you're talking jealousy, I know someone even more jealous of Sally than Thelma."

"Who?"

"Sister Agatha. Did you see her the night of the Christmas party? That nurse was pea green."

Maeve shook her head.

"Oh, that's right. You were too busy being swept off your feet by the dashing Doctor Moore," Etta teased.

"Never mind that. Tell me about Sister Agatha. What did she do?"

"Only stared daggers at Sally for dancing way too close to her fiancé. Sally and Lieutenant Blake weren't being the least bit discreet, which I'm sure was rather humiliating for the posh Agatha. If looks could kill..." Etta stopped. "Now you've got *me* doing it."

"Tell me more about Lieutenant Blake."

"He's an arse." She relayed to Maeve what she'd overheard the pilot say about Sally.

"And Sister Agatha is engaged to him? Why would she put up with that moron?"

"Because Blake is one of the landed gentry, and by marrying him, she becomes a Lady or viscountess or something. I don't know the nobility rankings and how they work, but Louise said Agatha has her heart set on becoming Lady Muck and won't let anyone stop that from happening." Etta's eyes widened.

"Anyone she might perceive as a romantic threat?" Maeve asked. "Like perhaps a certain nursing orderly?"

Chapter Twenty-One

That night, while the others slept, Etta lay awake in her bunk, unable to get Maeve's questions about Agatha out of her mind. The rain against the metal roof beat in concert with the thoughts pounding in her head.

Sister Agatha has access to morphine. Could she have taken revenge on Sally over her dalliance with her fiancé by shooting Sally full of morphine and then planting the spent syrettes in her pocket to make it look like suicide?

In her mind's eye, Etta saw the toffee-nosed nurse plunging the morphine needle into her arm. Briefly, she had considered telling Maeve or Louise of the nursing sister's morphine usage, but Etta was no snitch. Grassing on someone was not her style and hadn't served her well in the past. Her hand crept to her cheek, remembering her mum's slap, blaming her after she'd revealed what Donnie had done.

Best to keep my own counsel and just keep an eye on Sister Agatha. Etta drifted off to sleep.

The next morning, Etta and Clemmie trod over the camp's wooden planks at dawn, the mud squishing beneath their feet as rain bucketed down on their way to the Dakotas. Clemmie had forgotten her brolly, so both girls huddled under Etta's.

Clemmie shivered. "I hope the rain lets up soon. I hate flying in bad weather."

"Not my favourite, but needs must. Who's your pilot today?"

"Harkness." Clemmie grimaced. "I hate flying with him. He's convinced one of us girls will land him in the drink."

Since their crash in Holland and their subsequent hiding out from the Germans, where Etta had proven herself to the pilot by the care she'd given the injured officer, Lieutenant Harkness had welcomed her on his flights. That welcome didn't extend to her fellow nursing orderlies, though. Etta held tightly to the brolly as the wind threatened to snatch it from her hand. "Old superstitions die hard."

"I know, but believing that a woman on board is bad luck is archaic. This is the twentieth century. I'm just glad I don't see him during the flight and can focus on my job."

"Ditto."

"Who's your pilot then?"

"Blake."

Clemmie wrinkled her nose. "He's even worse. The way he looks at women makes my skin crawl. Sister Agatha's going to have her hands full being married to that one, *if* they even get married."

"What makes you think they won't?"

"The way he's always catting about and making no secret of it. Would *you* stand for that in a husband?"

"No, but then I couldn't stand having a husband. Some man always telling me what to do. I have no desire to get married."

"Ever?"

Etta set her jaw. "Never."

Arriving at the runway Clemmie gave Etta a departing wave and dashed to the shelter of her Dakota.

Etta hopped on board her plane, shaking rain from her brolly. Inside the Dakota, Lieutenant Blake gave her a slow once-over, starting at her chest and moving down to linger on Etta's thighs, where her damp uniform clung to her legs. He ran his tongue slowly over his top lip. "I prefer wet WAAF uniforms to dry ones—they show off what you have on offer so much better."

Crossing her arms, Etta gave Sister Agatha's fiancé a cool look. "I'm not offering anything."

The pilot's neck turned a dull red, and his eyes narrowed to slits.

"Don't waste your time, Sir." Harry shot a playful grin to his superior officer. "Red here has shot me down countless times. She's just not interested. Isn't that right, Red?"

"Harry, you know me so well." Etta flashed him a brief smile as she pulled out her flight log. Turning her back on the randy lieutenant, she entered the date, time, destination, and aircraft number in her log and prepared for the flight to France.

Wandering away from the airstrip cut from the French cornfield Etta searched for a bit of privacy as the crew unloaded the supplies. There were never any facilities for women, so the nursing orderlies had learned to make do with the nearest bush or tree. Spotting a small copse of trees ahead, Etta hurried toward it.

Finished answering the call of nature, she was buttoning up her trousers when she heard a faint rustle behind her. Etta bent over, pretending to tuck in her trouser leg, and removed the pocketknife from her boot. After the crash in Holland and finding herself the only one of the aircrew without a weapon to defend herself when they were on the run, Etta refused to be in that vulnerable position again.

As she started to straighten up, someone grabbed her from behind in a headlock. "Hallo, Fraulein," a man whispered.

Turning her head to the side, Etta grabbed onto her attacker's arm. Raising her shoulders, she tucked her chin into the crook of his elbow and bent her knees. She took a step back and locked her foot around the German's leg. Keeping her hands on his arm, Etta turned towards her foot, pulled across her body, and threw the soldier to the ground.

Before he had time to react, she kicked him hard between the legs. He grunted in pain, his hands flying to his crotch. Etta knelt down and pressed her knife against his neck. "One more sound, Jerry, and I'll slit your throat." Keeping the knife pressed against his throat, she reached down with her other hand and relieved him of his pistol.

Etta marched the German prisoner back to the airstrip, his hands on his head and his pistol in her hands. Trained on his back.

Betty couldn't find her lucky charm anywhere. Sally had given her the rabbit's foot after her first Down Ampney flight when she'd found the farm girl alone in their hut, shaking uncontrollably.

"What is it love?" Sally had hurried over, her big blue eyes full of concern. She sat on the edge of the bunk and patted Betty's arm. "Tell Sally."

She had blurted out her fears of flying, begging the glamorous nursing orderly who looked like a film star not to tell anyone, especially the other girls.

Sally held up her hand. "Scout's honour. It will be our secret." Reaching into her pocket, she pulled out a rabbit's foot. Pressing the lucky charm to her lips, she kissed it before handing it to Betty. "This little guy was given to me by one of the wireless operators when I first arrived. Peter Rabbit has kept me safe and sound on oodles of flights, and I know he'll do the same for you."

"But don't you need him?"

"I make my own luck now."

Betty couldn't believe she'd lost the charm. She had searched her uniform pockets for the lucky talisman and come up empty. She'd also searched her plane, her hamper of medical supplies, footlocker and hut, to no avail. *Where are you, Peter?*

Peter was precious to Betty. Not only because he was a good luck charm, but because Sally had given him to her—the first gift from her lovely, big-hearted friend. A gift that bore a trace of Sally's red lipstick on its fur.

Rocking back on her heels, Betty had a think. *You need to retrace your steps, you silly moo. Think of everywhere you went after putting Peter in your pocket.* Closing her eyes, she relived the day, seeing all the places she'd gone unspool in her mind's eye like watching a film. Betty made a mental list: women's shower hut, Mess, medical supply hut. Then she set out, a woman on a mission.

The only thing she found in the shower hut was a sliver of soap and Doreen singing off-key. Next, Betty scoured the Mess, making a beeline to the table where she'd sat earlier that day eating her porridge. She looked beneath the table and under the bench. Nothing. She searched the surrounding tables as well without any luck.

Hesitantly, she approached the stout Glasgow cook, who was stirring something on the stove. "I don't suppose you've found a rabbit's foot round here by chance. Did anyone turn one in?"

"Do I look like the bloody Lost and Found? Now get away with ye. I'm busy."

Shoulders hunched Betty trudged over the muddy planks toward the supply hut. She'd had her medical hamper replenished earlier that day with the supplies she'd needed for the men on her flight. *If I don't find Peter there, he's gone. Lost forever.*

Nearing the metal building, her eyes scanned the area to see if anyone was about. Orderlies weren't supposed to enter the medical supply hut without being accompanied by one of the nurses. All medications were kept under lock and key inside. The nursing sister would give the girls the medical provisions needed for their flights, including emergency morphine.

Seeing no one around, Betty slipped inside. She'd just have a quick look round for the missing rabbit's foot and be in and out in a jiffy. Hurrying over to the bank of tall cupboards where all the bandages were stored and where she'd had her kit restocked earlier, she squatted beside the cupboards, peering at the ground in the murky hut.

A small, furry object caught her eye. *Is it Peter or a mouse?*

Betty stretched out her hand to the unmoving object. Mice didn't bother her—she was used to them on the farm. She smiled, remembering her mum's recounting of their land girl's hysteria at her first sight of a field mouse. Betty's fingers closed around the furry article. There *you are, Peter. At last.* Tucking the lucky charm in her pocket, she started to stand.

A shaft of sunlight pierced the dimness as the door slowly began to open. *Oh no, I'm in for it now.* Silently, Betty ducked behind the end of the cupboard, shrinking into the shadows and praying she wouldn't be caught out. *I'm sorry, God. I promise never to do something like this again.*

The door shut, and a torch clicked on, casting a dim circle of light on the floor. Soft footsteps sounded, and she heard the jangle of keys. Betty scarce dared breathe. The faint circle of light moved forward, getting closer. Then it bounced to the left, away from the bank of cupboards where she crouched. The torch flickered upward, spotlighting the medicine cupboard opposite her hiding place.

A tall figure moved towards the cabinet, and Betty saw a flicker of white—a nursing veil. The nurse directed the beam of her torch to the locked cupboard, fitted a key into the lock, and opened the cabinet door in one swift motion. As the torch splayed over the shelf of medicines, the hidden Betty glimpsed a pale hand dart out and grab two morphine syrettes. That same hand quickly closed and locked the door, placing the torch atop a nearby cabinet, positioning it at an angle so she could see what she was doing.

The white-veiled figure bent slightly, revealing a glimpse of her face as she pushed up her sleeve. Betty watched in horror as Sister Agatha plunged a syringe into her arm, expelling a sigh of bliss.

Back in their hut, Maeve pulled out pen and paper to write to her sister.

Dear Briony,

Sorry I haven't written in a while, love. Things have been pretty busy. How's everything there? Does Patrick still have the same girlfriend, or has he got a new one now? I can't keep track of all his girls. I wonder if our brother will ever settle down. I have a feeling Andrew will get married and settle down long before our Patrick.

What about you? Have any lads caught your eye? You know you can always tell your big sister, and I won't say anything to Mam and Da. It will be our secret. I hope you know you can always tell me anything, Briony—unless it has to do with maths. That will go right over my head. You're the brain in the family. I expect great things from you. I wouldn't be at all surprised to see you teaching at Trinity College one day. Professor Fitzgerald has a nice ring to it, don't you think?

Thank you for letting me know Seamus's mother has passed. May she rest in peace. Now, she's reunited with her son and her husband.

Is old Dr. Byrne still going strong? That man is a marvel. I hope I'm still as spry as him when I'm in my seventies. (Perhaps I'd best stop eating so much cake.) Did I tell you the cake at the canteen is dry as a bone? Nothing like Mam's. Ah, what I wouldn't give for a slice of her Dundee cake about now. I'm actually missing a lot of Mam's cooking—especially her Guinness stew and soda bread. That's the first thing I'll ask her to make when I get home. Whenever that may be.

Is Fiona still working in the shop? Tell her hello from me.

Give Mam and Da a hug from me and tell them they can expect a letter soon.

Love,

Maeve

p.s. Tell Mam to feel free to send me some Dundee cake if she has any.

As she sealed the letter, Maeve's thoughts turned to Graham. She had been thinking about the widowed doctor a lot lately, daydreaming about him and his lovely eyes and kind manner. She had glimpsed him a couple of times, but it was usually when one of them was coming or going, and busy with patients. She hadn't actually talked to him since Sally's funeral.

After the funeral service, Maeve went up to Graham and thanked him for coming. She had also wanted to thank him again for remaining quiet about his suspicions that Sally may have killed herself, but one of the girls interrupted her.

Sally.

Reflecting on her conversation with Etta from the night before, Maeve wondered if Sister Agatha might be the answer to Sally's death. Had the posh nurse with the plummy vowels killed the blonde Nightingale in a fit of jealous rage to prevent Sally from ruining Agatha's plans to become the lady of the manor?

Or... was Sister Agatha not in a jealous pique at all? It's not like nurses go walking around with morphine syringes in their pockets—especially in the dead of night. Why would they? A shiver snaked down Maeve's spine as she realized what that meant. Killing Sally with an overdose of morphine had to be methodically planned and executed.

If that is indeed what happened, it meant Sally's death was cold-blooded murder.

Etta moved amongst her patients, dispensing tea. As she passed by a wounded sergeant, he reached out and pinched her bum.

"None of that now," she said.

Harry piped up. "Best be careful if you know what's good for you, chaps." He winked at Etta. "You don't want to get on the wrong side of Red here. She just overpowered a Jerry without batting an eyelash and marched him back to camp, bold as brass."

The casualties stared in disbelief at the petite nursing orderly. Then, the entire plane erupted in cheers and applause.

"Good on ya, duck."

Etta grinned. "I knew my East End upbringing would come in handy one day."

Beneath her bravado, though, lurked the memory of her brother's repeated attacks. No man will ever assault me again, she vowed.

To distract the men on her flight from their injuries, Betty regaled her patients with funny stories from Cherry Tree Farm as they left France. Recounting Tillie the land girl's escapades never failed to garner a laugh. So did the comic anti-Hitler ditties that Betty sang to them. The lads always asked her when they were over the coast. When that sceptered isle came into view, she told them it wouldn't be long now before they were home, and they all cheered.

After landing, Betty got her patients settled onto the waiting concrete blocks for the doctors to examine. As she worked, news of her friend's derring-do escapade filtered to her ears.

Betty rushed into the hut, startling Maeve. "You'll never believe it! Etta captured a German singlehandedly!"

Chapter Twenty-Two

February 1945

Everyone knew the war couldn't last much longer. Hitler was in retreat, and his Nazi regime was fast unraveling. The Allies were now pushing into Germany from the west, and Soviet troops had reached Poland in the east. Only last week Churchill, Roosevelt, and Stalin had met at Yalta and agreed to demand Germany's unconditional surrender.

The Germans, however, weren't ready to surrender.

And so, the fighting continued. As did the casualties.

The Nightingales continued to bring wounded men from Europe to Down Ampney, where they were evaluated by a medical officer and evacuated to the appropriate hospital for treatment. As Doctor Moore stopped at the cement blocks holding the stretchers from the most recent evacuation, he examined each patient and announced which hospital he would be transferred to.

Maeve filled out the destination tags and attached them to the wounded men. Her latest flight had several burn victims who were being moved on to Odstock. The smell from the butter-treated burns was horrendous, but she had discovered that placing a bit of Pond's cold cream inside her nostrils helped to mask the overpowering odor. Maeve soothed a frightened young lad swathed in bandages. Placing her hand gently on his cheek, she gave him a reassuring smile. "You'll be in hospital soon, love. They'll take good care of you."

Another lad whimpered in pain. His head and face had been badly burned, and only one eye was visible through a slit in his bandages. Doctor Moore gave him a shot of morphine, marked the dosage on his tag, and pinned the syrette to the wounded soldier's collar.

Bending close over the burned man, Maeve captured his lone visible brown eye with her two green ones. "There now," she murmured. "Don't you fret. You'll be home soon." At those magic words, the wounded man drifted off to sleep, and the stretcher-bearers carefully loaded him onto the truck bound for the railway station.

Maeve looked up to see Graham watching her. Their eyes met, and something passed between them.

Another flight of casualties arrived, and Doreen accompanied her patients to the waiting cement blocks, delivering a quick smile to Maeve.

"Hey, Moore, take a break," one of the medical officers called. "I'll handle this one."

Maeve watched as Graham stretched and rubbed the back of his neck. Her stomach fluttered as he approached. *Don't get excited. He's just going to ask you something about a patient.*

Graham smiled at her. "Would you like to get a bite at the canteen?"

She stammered out a yes. Although fraternization between officers and enlisted ranks was forbidden—each having their own separate quarters, communal huts, and Mess—the commercial canteen, run by NAAFI, was where the powers-that-be turned a blind eye to mixing between the ranks.

When Graham and Maeve arrived at the canteen, they found it nearly deserted. Two corporals were having a beer, and Clemmie Brown was in a corner, engrossed in a novel.

"Would you like a beer and sandwich," the doctor asked Maeve, "or tea and cake?"

"Tea and cake, please." The sides of her mouth lifted up. "I've quite the sweet tooth."

The cake was dry, but the tea was hot, and Maeve sipped it gratefully. "It's nice things have quieted down to only one flight a day."

"We're all enjoying the respite." Graham took a bite of his fish paste sandwich and tilted his head at her. "What will you do after the war?"

"Go home, I suppose."

"Back to Ballydavid?"

"You remember the name of my village?"

"I remember a lot of things." His gray eyes locked on hers. "Like the Christmas dance and how lovely you looked and how right you felt in my arms."

A wave of yearning rippled through her. Maeve lowered her eyes.

"Am I being too forward? I'm afraid I'm out of the habit. I haven't done this in a long time." Graham looked at her intently. "I know we haven't spent much time together, Maeve, but I'd like to change that. Now things are starting to wind down. I hope we'll have time to get to know one another better."

"I'd like that."

"Fire away," he said.

"What?"

"We've some time now. What would you like to know about me?"

"I don't know…where are you from?"

"Devon. A small coastal town called Beer." Graham's eyes crinkled at the corners as he drank his draught.

"Sure, and I'm from Guinness."

"I can show you on a map. Where do you think my love of beer comes from?"

"I suppose it could be worse. You could be from Looe."

He laughed.

Maeve sipped her tea. "Do you have any brothers and sisters?

"Unfortunately, no. I'm an only child. How about you?"

"I have two older brothers, Patrick and Andrew. They work at the Guinness factory in Dublin. There's not much work to be had in Ballydavid. I also have a younger sister Briony, who I miss something fierce. Briony's a bright lass, very clever with sums and such. Unlike her sister." Maeve made a face.

"You have other talents. You're very good with the wounded, Maeve. You have a kind heart and a calming way with the men. That's a gift. I don't know if you realize that."

"I just wish there was more I could do to ease their pain."

"So do I." Graham's lips tightened. "The kinds of injuries these boys suffer are like nothing I've seen. And hope to never see again once this bloody war is over." He murmured, "'*It is only those who have neither fired a shot nor heard the shrieks and groans of the wounded who cry aloud for blood, more vengeance, more desolation. War is hell.*' General Sherman said that about the American Civil War. It appears we've learned nothing since then."

"War *is* hell. And not just on the soldiers." Maeve saw in her mind's eye the face of the Dutch refugee mother who'd lost all four of her children, including her wee babe, in the bomb blast. "So many mothers have lost their children. It doesn't bear thinking about." Thinking of her own child who never got to take a breath, Maeve mourned the loss anew.

"Do you want children someday?"

Her face shuttered. Still in the grip of her grief, she blurted, "I had a miscarriage. I lost my baby. Seamus's baby."

"I'm sorry." Graham placed his hand on hers, his grey eyes full of sympathy.

Maeve gave a brisk nod, willing away the tears and changing the subject. "What's your favourite food then?"

"Fish and chips." He grinned. "I'm a Devon lad born and bred. We love our fish. And our cream teas, of course." He puffed out a sigh. "What I wouldn't give for some proper Devonshire cream and jam on a scone right now."

"Stop. I told you I have a sweet tooth." She polished off the crumbs on her plate.

They exited the canteen as a small group of medics and nursing orderlies arrived. Thelma's eyes bulged, seeing the doctor and Maeve together. She whispered to the girl beside her.

The camp will certainly be buzzing tonight, Maeve thought, but she didn't care.

As she walked to her hut, the moon lighting her way, Maeve savored Graham's words of praise. His complimenting her kind heart and calming way swelled her heart. That heart—and stomach—fluttered at thoughts of the doctor's more than professional interest. Looking up at the moon, she said her daily goodnight to Briony. Then she added softly, "Goodnight, Graham."

Continuing on her way, Maeve reflected on her work. At times, she wondered if the tea and sympathy she and the girls provided made any kind of difference to the men in their care. She knew being a nursing orderly wasn't enough for Etta, who wanted to become a "proper nurse." But Maeve also knew that a kind word and a gentle touch helped settle those who were fearful and anxious.

"*There* you are," Betty exclaimed as she pushed open the door of her billeting hut. "Where have you been? We've been waiting for you for *ages*."

"Sorry. I was um…talking to one of the doctors about the patients."

Etta, leaning casually against Betty's bunk, gave Maeve a sideways glance, her mouth crooking upward. "Hmm, I wonder what doctor that might be."

Ignoring her, Maeve focused on Betty. "What's got you all in a dither?"

"We got a package!" Bubbling with excitement, she inclined her head to a brown-wrapped parcel on the end of her bed.

"*We?*"

"All three of us." Betty beamed. "You, me, and Etta. From Mrs. Roberts. We've been waiting for you so we can open it together."

Maeve smiled. "Well, then, let's open it."

Betty cut the string on the package and unwrapped the overlapping brown paper. She sucked in her breath. "Oh." Slowly, she removed the blue velvet cloth. "It's the cape Sally let me wear at Christmas." Clutching the capelet to her chest, Betty bent her head.

Maeve blinked back tears.

"Is there a letter?" Etta asked, but Betty was incapable of speech. Reaching into the package, Etta retrieved a piece of paper and read aloud:

> *"Dear girls,*
>   *When I was going through Sally's things, I found a letter at the bottom of her footlocker addressed to her dad and me. Sally wrote if we were reading it, that meant she hadn't made it.*

A splotch on the paper blurred the ink.

> *Sally told us not to be too sad as she and Jimmy were together again now, and her big brother would take good care of her just as he always had.*

Another splotch.

> *Our Sally told us how proud she was of the work she'd done as a nursing orderly, a "Flying Nightingale," helping all those wounded lads. She wrote that she saw Jimmy in each one of their faces. She also talked about the friends she'd made at camp. Betty, she said that if she'd had a little sister, she would have liked her to be like you. She asked us to send along these keepsakes and told us she'd tucked a little note into each one..."*

Betty's head snapped up. Springing to her feet, she shook out the velvet cape. A piece of paper fluttered to the floor. Picking it up, she unfolded it with a shaking hand:

> *Cinderella,*
> *Here's a little something from your fairy godmother. I hope you'll think of me whenever you wear it. Be sure to always accessorize, with the hair clip and red lipstick. A girl can never go wrong with red lipstick. You'll dazzle that dairy farmer!*
> *Love,*
> *Sally*

Betty dropped on the bed, shoulders heaving. Maeve hugged her as she wept.

Clearing her throat, Etta continued with the letter.

> *Sally said if anything happened to her, she wanted you all to have*

something to remember her by. I think she may have had a premonition she was going to leave us—

Etta's eyes flew to Maeve. The girls exchanged a disbelieving look over Betty's bent head.

Maeve's heart clenched. *Does this mean what I think it means? Did Sally end her life?*

Beside her, Betty sniffled. "See what else is inside."

Maeve parted the paper. A mass of silky green fabric greeted her. Slowly, she lifted out the party frock Sally had loaned her the night of the dance. She opened the note tucked within the folds of the dress.

Hey Irish,

This was meant for you and your beautiful green eyes. A perfect match. You'll have to fight the lads off with a stick. All except a certain doctor, I think. With this, I officially pass my belle of the ball crown to you.

Love,

Sally

Maeve's eyes brimmed with tears. Her hands shook as she folded the note.

"There's something for you too, Champ," Betty said. She had given Etta the nickname after she'd singlehandedly taken down the German soldier in France. Betty handed Etta a smaller brown-paper parcel with a note attached to the top in familiar handwriting.

For Etta (to offset all those dreary nursing books),

Maybe this will entice you to cuddle up with something that has two legs and is breathing. You don't want to stay tucked away on a dusty old bookshelf forever. Go on and live a little, Red.

Love,

Sally

Unwrapping the book, Etta barked out a laugh.

"What is it?" Betty asked.

Etta turned the book around so they could see the cover: *Lady Chatterley's Lover*.

Two red spots appeared on Betty's cheeks. "That sounds like a naughty book."

"Oh, it is, Betty," Maeve said, laughing. "It very much is."

"Good one, Sally." Etta chortled.

"Did Mrs. Roberts say anything else?" Betty asked.

Etta scanned the letter. Biting her bottom lip, she delivered an inscrutable look to Maeve. "Only this—

> *Sally said she wanted to make sure everything was sorted. Our Sally always liked everything neat and tidy and tied up with a bow, even as a child. I hope you'll enjoy her things and never forget her. Please stay in touch. You're our last link to our girl.*
>
>> *Sincerely yours,*
>> *Edna Roberts*

The three friends gazed at each other through wet eyes.

Maeve felt as if a heavy stone had taken up residence in her chest. *Graham and Louise were right. She did commit suicide. Oh Sally, why didn't you talk to one of us and tell us what was troubling you? We could have helped.*

Through blurry eyes, Betty reached for the brown paper. As she started to fold it, she felt something. "There's something else." Her fingers closed around a small, cylindrical object. She held it up.

A half-used tube of red lipstick.

Chapter Twenty-Three

Betty snuggled under the covers with Albert's latest missive. When she lifted the letter from the envelope, a prayer card fell out. Betty studied the picture of Saint Francis and turned the card over to read the words of the much-loved prayer, *Lord, make me an instrument of your peace. Where there is hatred, let me sow love...*

She held the prayer card to her chest as she began to read.

Dear Betty,

I'm so sorry about your friend. Please accept my deepest condolences on the loss of Sally. I'm enclosing this prayer card of Saint Francis in hopes it will bring you some comfort. Francis is my favourite saint. He had such a way with animals.

It's so hard losing our friends. The friendships we make in wartime are much deeper, aren't they? I think it's because we're all fighting side-by-side together against an enemy bent on killing us and destroying all that we hold dear. Fighting such evil binds us together in a common cause. In war, we depend upon our fellow soldiers for our very lives. That creates a bond, an unshakable bond that will never be broken, even in death. I know because I too lost one of my friends—a lad from Cornwall named John, who was killed on D-Day at Caen. I still write to John's parents, and always will.

I like writing to you, Betty. You're so easy to talk to. Letter writing is a kind of talking, isn't it? It was my lucky day when I met you on that plane.

How many times a day do you fly across the Channel picking up the wounded? I suppose you really can't say with the censors and all. Just stay safe up there, please.

As for your friend Sally, remember the prayer of Saint Francis: "And it is in dying that we are born to eternal life."

In sympathy,

Albert

Through wet eyes, Betty touched the prayer card to her lips before tucking it under her pillow.

Thelma entered the hut giggling with Joyce, the new girl whose braying laugh set Etta's teeth on edge. Joyce Gibson, a transfer from RAF Broadwell, had taken over Sally's bed, and Thelma had taken over Joyce. Befriending the newest Nightingale before any of the girls could warn her about her poisonous ways, the camp gossip had taken young Joyce under her wing.

Thelma showered the frizzy-haired orderly with compliments and food. "Joyce, you're so lucky to have naturally curly hair. I have to put mine up in pin curls just to get a wave."

"I can't eat the rest of my porridge would you like it, dear?"

"Joyce, would you like my barley sugar?"

Taken in by all the attention, Joyce had fast become Thelma's best friend, devotee, and sycophant. When she first arrived, Thelma had tried to get Doreen to switch beds with her so she and Joyce could be near each other.

Doreen, however, wasn't giving up her warm spot near the heater for anyone.

"But Joyce is young and doesn't know anyone," Thelma had pleaded. "That's why I've taken her under my wing. I guess you could say I'm sort of a mother hen."

"Well, Mother Hen, you've just laid an egg. I'm not moving. Why don't *you* move closer to Joyce's bed?" Doreen said innocently. "I'm sure one of the other girls would be happy to swap bunks with you. Ask Clemmie or Betty."

Thelma glared. "I'm not giving up my warm bed by the stove."

"Neither am I."

Now, as Joyce sat next to Thelma on her warm bunk, the two curly heads bent together,

Doreen sniffed the air. "Who's wearing scent?"

"I am," Joyce preened. "Isn't it divine? Thelma's a dear to share her lovely perfume with me."

"What are friends for?" Thelma held out a small bag to Joyce. "Would you like another pear drop?"

"Pear drops?" Betty groaned. "Where did you get pear drops?"

"Swindon."

"And how did you pay for them? And the scent?" Doreen asked suspiciously, knowing full well Thelma was as skint as the rest of them.

"Ask me no questions, and I'll tell you no lies."

"Thelma got an inheritance from her rich aunt in Scotland," Joyce said self-importantly. "They were very close."

Thelma cut a side look at her, and Joyce clapped a hand over her mouth.

Doreen narrowed her eyes at Thelma. "You never told me you had an aunt in Scotland, rich or otherwise."

"That's information I reserve for only my closest friends." Thelma offered a syrupy smile to Joyce, who flushed with relief. The two girls bent their heads together, whispering and sniggering, and Joyce let out her braying laugh.

"Bloody hell!" Etta slammed her book shut. "It sounds like a bunch of cackling hens in here." Grabbing her Hairy-Mary jacket, she stalked out of the hut.

Etta headed in the direction of the hospital, thinking she might seek out Sister Louise. *She* didn't bray like a donkey. Louise was an intelligent, interesting woman and a good conversationalist, whose company she enjoyed. As well, Etta wanted, no, *needed*, to talk to her about a couple of things.

Approaching the back of the main hospital hut, Etta noticed Sister Agatha off to one side having a heated exchange with her pilot fiancé. The nurse's face was red and contorted with rage. Agatha was so caught up in her conversation with Julian Blake, she didn't even notice the nursing orderly. Slipping past the squabbling couple unobserved, Etta heard Agatha snarl. "How many times must I pay for your indiscretions? I'm sick to death of it!"

No wonder she needs her morphine high. Betty had recently confided in Etta about seeing Sister Agatha inject herself with the pain medication. She knew then that her observance of the same thing hadn't been a one-off. Betty had been worried, wondering if she should do something about it. Perhaps report the nurse to Matron?

"Did Sister Agatha see you?" Etta had asked.

"No. I was hiding behind the cupboard."

"And why were you hiding?"

Betty's face flushed. "Because I wasn't supposed to be there."

"Right. So why open yourself up for reprimand? Besides, it would be an officer's word against yours. If I were you, I'd keep my mouth shut. Don't borrow trouble."

Betty had given her a wretched look. "But what if Sister Agatha's habit interferes with her taking proper care of her patients? Maybe harms them?"

At that, Etta had been brought up short. She frowned. "That's an entirely different story. Let me think about it. Maybe I can talk to Sister Louise, see what she thinks. Leave it with me."

She went in search of Louise, checking the various wards, but they were all empty. The patients had been moved on to the various treatment hospitals. At last, Etta located the nurse in one of the tents, standing before an open cupboard, marking something on a clipboard. "Sister Louise?"

Louise turned round, a pleased smile lighting up her face. "Etta! You're just the one. Would you assist me with this inventory? Agatha was meant to be helping, but she wasn't feeling well and went to sick quarters."

Is that what they're calling it now? "Just tell me what you need."

"We have to count all the supplies so we'll know how much to replenish before the next load of patients arrive. I've already finished the top shelf, so if you take the middle shelf and I take the bottom, we'll be finished in a jiffy." Louise handed Etta a piece of paper so she could keep track, and the two went to work rapidly and efficiently, finishing up in less than a quarter of an hour.

"My mother always said many hands make light work. Of course, she said that to the staff." Louise cast a wry glance at Etta. "I don't think mother's ever done a scrap of real work in her entire life."

"You had staff? As in servants?" Etta suddenly felt uncomfortable in the nursing sister's presence. *Just imagine what she'd think if she knew where you came from.*

Louise wrinkled her nose. "A cook, housekeeper, gardener, and all-around dogsbody who did repairs round the house and kept everything sorted."

Sensing Etta's discomfort, she explained. "My father is a barrister, and my mother's family are all bankers. Mother was raised to never do anything except look decorative, be a good wife and hostess, and give fabulous parties. I don't think she can even boil an egg. I didn't fancy following in her footsteps, so here I am. No servants for this nurse. I actually *do* know how to boil an egg, and I quite enjoy cooking." Louise's mouth crooked up.

Etta relaxed. "What do you plan to do after the war?"

"Continue nursing. I haven't worked out yet if I'll stay in the RAF or not and go wherever they send me." Her eyes gleamed. "It could be someplace exotic like Singapore or Egypt. I've always wanted to see the pyramids." Louise pulled a face. "Then again, they could send me to Croydon."

"And what will you do if you leave the RAF?"

"Return to Radcliffe. That's where I worked before the war—in the surgical theatre."

"You were a *surgical* nurse in hospital? That's what I want to do! What sort of operations did you get to be part of?"

"Appendectomies, hysterectomies, Caesarean sections—" The arrival of Will Nichols carrying a large container interrupted the nurse.

"Hello, Sister. I'm restocking the tents," Will said. "Do you need any more bandages?"

Louise nodded, stepping back to give him access.

"Hiya Etta," Will began replenishing the rolled white bandages. "How's your Irish pal?"

Etta smiled, knowing of Will's crush on Maeve. "She's well. Busy but well."

"Has she come to her senses yet and realized what a great catch I am?"

"Not yet, I'm afraid." Etta didn't want to burst Will's romantic daydreams by telling him she suspected a certain doctor was already making inroads into Maeve's heart.

"Put in a good word for me, will you?"

"I'll do that." After they exited the tent, Etta said casually to the senior nurse, "Do patients ever get addicted to morphine?"

"They can. It's quite an addictive narcotic. That's why we carefully monitor the dosage and keep a record of how much each patient has been given and when. That's also why we have you and the other nursing orderlies note the dosage from the field nurses on the patient's tag before you load them for evacuation." Louise sent her a searching look. "Why do you ask? Do you think one of your patients might be addicted?"

"I was just wondering. I want to learn all I can about different medications."

"Good for you. That's an important part of nursing."

As they walked past the row of hospital tents, Etta asked offhandedly, "Can an addiction to morphine impede a person's ability to think? To function normally and do their job properly, for instance?"

Louise stopped. Her eyes probed Etta's. "Are you speaking about Agatha?" she said quietly.

Etta tried, unsuccessfully, to mask her surprise.

"Suffice it to say, that problem has been dealt with accordingly." Louise's lips tightened. "I'm not at liberty to say anything, but rest assured, our patients were not in danger and won't be. Matron has seen to that. Now can we talk about something else?"

They resumed walking, Etta heavy-footed as she remembered why she'd originally sought out Louise. In a halting voice, she told her new friend about the parcel from Mrs. Roberts, the gifts inside, and the notes Sally had written to each of the girls.

"They were obviously goodbyes," she said in a flat monotone. Etta revealed the additional evidence: Sally's farewell letter to her parents saying at last she was reunited with her brother and her mother's thinking her daughter had had a *premonition* of her death. "It looks like you were right," she said, her throat dry. "Sally did take her own life. I know you have a responsibility to inform Matron, so I wanted you to know."

With eyes full of compassion, Louise placed her hand on Etta's arm. "I'm sorry. I take no pleasure in being right." Her voice was tinged with regret. "The poor girl. We none of us know the burdens others carry." Louise gazed pensively into the distance.

The beery face of her brother looming over her flickered in Etta's subconscious. She shoved the memory away.

"However," the nursing sister continued, "I see no reason to report this to Matron. As you said, what good would it do? Revealing Sally committed suicide would only hurt her parents and others. Sally is gone. Let us allow her to rest in peace.

"Thank you," Etta mumbled.

Louise gave her a sideways glance. "Something you might want to consider… Why do you suppose Sally killed herself outdoors in the cold?"

"I don't know, I hadn't really thought about it."

"I think it was because she didn't want her friends, the people she cared about most, to find her."

"But Maeve *did* find her."

"Yes, but she got disoriented in the dark and snow," Louise said. "She found Sally in the vicinity of the officer's quarters—a place Maeve wouldn't usually go, correct?"

Etta nodded.

"I speak from experience," Louise said. "Years ago, a friend of my brother's committed suicide. To ensure his wife and children didn't find him, James drove behind the local constabulary, parked his car, and shot himself there." She gave Etta a gentle look. "Perhaps knowing this—that Sally was thinking of her friends with the place she chose to end her life—will help you and Maeve."

That's so like Sally, Etta thought, *always thinking of others and generous to a fault.* She closed her eyes. *Thank you, Sally.* When she opened her eyes again, she noticed snowdrops poking out of the snow.

"The first signs of spring." Louise murmured, "*Chaste snowdrop, venturous harbinger of spring, And pensive monitor of fleeting years.*"

Etta tilted her head at the senior nurse.

"Sorry. Poetry is a love of mine, and I tend to quote it randomly. My brother's forever teasing me about it."

"I learned some poetry in school, but that was ages ago." Etta screwed up her face in concentration and recited, "*If you can keep your head when all about you/Are losing theirs and blaming it on you.* That's all I can remember."

"Kipling." Louise favored her with a smile. "I love *If*."

Pleased, Etta asked Louise for the name of the author of the snowdrop poem.

"Wordsworth. He's not much in favor now, but I like him. I also quite like the American poet Edna St. Vincent Millay. Have you read her?"

Etta shook her head.

"I have a book of her poetry I can lend you if you like."

"First, I have to read *Lady Chatterley's Lover*."

Louise's eyebrows shot up.

"Sally's parting gift to me. She thought it would encourage me to *live a little*."

Louise threw back her head and laughed.

Folding the velvet capelet, Betty placed it reverently in the bottom of the cupboard. Then she tucked the tube of lipstick into the small drawer where she kept the rhinestone clip and her other treasures, including Albert's letters. Pulling out a piece of stationery, she began to write.

Dear Mrs. Roberts,

Thank you so much for the lovely remembrances from Sally. I can't tell you how much it means to me. To us. We were all fair astonished when your parcel arrived.

I burst into tears when I saw the velvet cape. I've never had anything so beautiful, so glamorous. That was so like Sally. And when I read her note, I cried even more. Sally was always so kind to me. I couldn't believe someone with her movie star looks would want to be friends with the likes of me. I quickly discovered that Sally's beauty wasn't only on the outside, though. She had a heart of gold, especially towards her "boys," as she called them. They all loved her. She treated them so tender and kind. I hope knowing that will help ease your grief. In her own way, your daughter was a hero.

Maeve and Etta loved their special gifts as well.

Betty paused her pen. Should she mention the book and how much it made the girls laugh? She blushed, recalling the title and Maeve and Etta's confirming it was indeed a naughty book. Some things are better left unsaid. She didn't want to embarrass Mrs. Roberts. She continued her letter.

How is Mr. Roberts? Please give him my kind regards. I know men tend to put on a brave face when something like this happens. They may not say much—at least my dad didn't when our Wilf died—but I know Sally's dad must be fair broken-hearted over losing his little girl. I'm glad he has you to comfort him, and you have him to do the same.

I hope it will also comfort you to know that I visit Sally's grave. Last week, when I visited, I'd hoped to bring her flowers, but flowers are in scarce supply these days. Instead, I put a sprig of rosemary on her grave for remembrance.

I will always remember Sally.

Thank you again for the beautiful cape. I shall treasure it forever.

Yours sincerely,

Betty Hall

Maeve couldn't stop thinking of the patients on her second flight. Flame-throwing tanks had caused the men's horrific burns, the field nurse informed her. Burns that had been treated with butter. She felt helpless in the face of such unbearable pain, knowing the worst was still ahead. Once the patients were at the burn hospital, the nurses would have to repeatedly debride—remove—the men's skin to get rid of the burned tissue and prevent infection. Her stomach turned. She'd been told the pain was excruciating.

Shuddering, Maeve put it out of her mind, deliberately turning her thoughts to more pleasant things. Her lips curved up as she recalled her canteen chat with Graham. Remembering his gray eyes holding hers. His saying how right she had felt in his arms when they danced… She had felt the same. Maeve burrowed under the covers, replaying every detail of their conversation in her head. She still didn't know if Graham had been teasing when he said he was from a town called Beer. She'd go to Admin tomorrow and look at the map.

Then she remembered what she had said.

Her cheeks burned, recalling how she'd blurted out the news of her miscarriage—something she'd never told another soul. *What in the world came over me?* After revealing her secret, Maeve was certain she'd ruined any chance she might have had with the good doctor. But Graham hadn't looked at her with disapproval or dismay; he had shown compassion.

He was a good man. A good doctor. The best in camp.

Recalling his saying her calming way with the men was a "gift," Maeve grew pensive. Her thoughts turned to the bomb-happy boys she had sat with through those long nights and how natural it had been for her to calm and comfort them. *Perhaps I might be able to use this gift after the war to help those who are wounded in spirit,* she mused.

Unbidden, the unwelcome thought came that she had missed the signs with Sally.

What was it she had said in her note again? Something about passing on the belle of the ball crown to me. A cold certainty gripped Maeve. A crown was only passed on at the end of a ruler's reign, usually by death.

Why did Sally take her life? If she was upset or depressed about something, why didn't she talk to me or Betty? she wondered. Even as Maeve thought that she realized that if the issue had been anything sexual in nature—like Sally's assignations with Julian Blake—she wouldn't have confided in innocent

Betty.

I would have understood, though.

And how would Sally have known that? Maeve castigated herself. *It's not like the two of you had heart-to-hearts.* She thought of all the times Sally had invited her to have a drink and how she had always fobbed her off. *Now, we'll never have that drink.*

Sally's crumpled Victory roll and staring eyes filled Maeve's head, evoking memories of her desperate efforts in the snow to revive the fallen Nightingale. Her breath caught, and she began to shake. *Deep breaths,* she told herself. *Breathe in. Breathe out.*

When Maeve had got herself under control, her thoughts returned to Graham and how he'd told her early on; it appeared that Sally had given herself an overdose of morphine. She had refused to believe him, insisting that she knew better and would prove it.

Except now, there was nothing to prove.

Both Graham and Louise, her superior officers with years of medical training between them, each far more qualified than her, had been right. Maeve resolved to go to Graham tomorrow and admit she'd been wrong.

Chapter Twenty-Four

March 1945

The next day, each of the girls had only one flight—Maeve to the Netherlands and Betty and Etta to Belgian airfields.

The Dakotas carrying casualties usually flew "low and slow" since the head and chest patients needed to stay in low altitude to avoid drops in air pressure. This time, though, Etta's plane ascended rapidly, and she noticed a soldier with a stitched abdomen in distress. Hurrying over, she saw that his stomach had swelled. She pulled out her pocket knife and cut the sutures to prevent any further damage. Then she wrapped a clean bandage tightly round the open wound to hold it in place until they landed.

When she'd finished a skinny sergeant called out, "Hey Red, you got some tea for a thirsty man. Or maybe something a bit stronger?"

"If I had anything stronger, soldier, *I'd* be drinking it."

As she dispensed tea to the men, Etta thought of her conversation with Louise from the day before. She couldn't wait to talk to Louise again and hear stories from her days as a surgical nurse and all the different operations she'd assisted with in theatre.

She couldn't imagine anything better. Etta had been to the four-story Radcliffe Infirmary in Oxford when delivering a head injury patient once and been fair impressed by all she'd seen.

While clearing a blocked tracheotomy tube, Betty overheard one of the lads on her flight say he couldn't wait to get home. She was overcome by a wave of homesickness. Her mum's latest letter had been full of all the goings on at the farm. The victory garden had yielded a bumper crop of carrots. Land Girl Rose was marrying Wilf's friend John, and soon, they'd be planting peas for summer.

Betty's mouth watered at the thought of popping fresh peas from the garden into her mouth, something she and Wilf had always done. *I miss you, Wilf. I hope you've met my friend Sally in heaven.*

Maeve adjusted the bandage on a young lad's leg that had started to slip. After giving tea to several of the injured, she cast an indulgent smile at Harry, squatted between two stretchers showing off his pin-up cards and regaling a group of lads about his romantic exploits.

I wonder if Harry will ever settle down with a nice girl, she mused. He's one of the most popular lads in camp. Somehow, though, I get the feeling he won't get serious about anyone until after the war. Harry does like playing the field.

She recalled the words she'd said to Betty when she first arrived. "Men's heads may be easily turned by a pretty face, but in the end, you'll find most just want to settle down with a nice girl." Maeve's thoughts moved from Harry to Graham. She wondered whether having been married before if the good doctor wanted to settle down again and start a new family? *Or was he more like Harry, only wanting a wartime dalliance?*

Back at camp, Etta cut away the blood-soaked trousers of one of her patients. After giving him a wash, she applied clean dressings to his bullet wounds and helped him into a new uniform. "There you go, soldier. Fresh and clean as a whistle."

Continuing down the row of cots filled with the wounded from the last two flights, Etta, Doreen, and Will washed each man, applied clean dressings, and kitted them out in fresh uniforms as needed, to ready them for transport to their respective hospitals. When they'd finished for the day, Will suggested going to the canteen for beer and sandwiches.

"Sounds good to me," Doreen said. "Etta?" Having relaxed her former teetotaling stance, Doreen now enjoyed an occasional beer.

Etta, however, had noticed the covert looks her fellow Nightingale had been sending Will throughout the afternoon and realized her hutmate had a crush on the male nursing orderly. "You go on without me. I think I'm going to get some kip." Behind Will's back, she winked at Doreen.

Etta yawned as she walked to her quarters on the overcast March day. *A nap will be just the ticket,* she thought. Most of the girls are flying, so with any luck, the hut will be empty. She relished the quiet, which was in short supply on base, especially in a billeting hut full of chattering girls. Etta looked forward to the day when she would once again share a flat with just one or two girls. Ones who didn't natter on all the time.

Slipping inside the hut, Etta was gratified to find it empty. As she approached her bunk, however, she saw the hut wasn't empty after all. Thelma crouched over an open footlocker, so engrossed in what she was doing, she didn't hear Etta approach.

"What the bloody hell do you think you are doing?"

Thelma startled and dropped the book she'd been reading. She shot to her feet and whirled around, a guilty look on her face. Her hand fluttered to her chest. "You scared me."

Etta pinned Thelma with her eyes as she closed the distance between them. "Let me repeat," she said in a slow, deliberate voice. "What the bloody hell are you doing in my footlocker?"

"I, um, was just looking for some plasters. I cut my finger."

"Oh, I hope it's not a deep cut," Etta said in a voice full of mock concern. "You might need stitches. Let me see."

Thelma's hand flew behind her waist. She took a step back. "It's not that bad. I'll just get a plaster from the First Aid kit."

Etta regarded her with a steady gaze. Glancing at the open footlocker, she knelt down, removing *Lady Chatterley's Lover.* "Thelma, if you wanted to read this, all you had to do was ask."

"I would never read such filth! I can't believe you even brought it into our hut. Wasn't that book banned?"

169

"Could be." Etta grinned. "That would be just like Sally."

Thelma sneered. "I should have known Sally was the one who brought that trash in here. Even in death, the stench of that hussy lingers."

Etta punched her in the face.

Betty read the latest letter from Albert, her mouth turning up at the corners. Albert wrote her several times a week now, regaling her with daily stories from the farm and sharing his hopes for the future. Betty had never known a boy like him before—they both liked many of the same simple pleasures. Spending time with family, taking long walks in the country, tending the animals, singing in the church choir, and playing with children.

Albert loved children. He'd written that he couldn't wait for the day to have children of his own. Betty had blushed, feeling the same. Albert was a good man. A good friend. Always showing an interest in her, wanting to know her thoughts, her dreams. More and more, she found herself daydreaming about him. Longing for the day when she would see him again. Hardly daring to dream that their friendship might blossom into romance. *Could Albert be my happily ever after?* Betty wondered.

After cleaning up her patients and seeing them off on their hospital transports, Betty made her way to the communal hut, desperate for a cuppa. Inside, lovebirds Titch and Paddy sat close to each other chatting while Lilian and Rita from one of the other huts shared a newspaper and drank their tea. Betty noticed quiet Margaret off in the corner intent on her fortune-telling cards.

Acknowledging the others, she went to get herself a cup of tea.

"Pour one for me too, would you?" Maeve, who'd just arrived, asked.

Carrying two cups, Betty handed one to her friend and sat down beside her.

Maeve smiled, thinking of the incident she'd just witnessed. A chuckle escaped.

"What's so funny?"

Maeve glanced around the room, noting the presence of the others. "I'll tell you later."

"How did it go today?" Betty asked.

"No burn injuries, thank goodness. Those really get to me."

"Me too."

The girls drank their tea in silence, thinking of their patients.

"Have you heard from your mum lately?" Maeve asked.

Betty nodded. "The big news is our Land Girl Rose is getting married to the lad on the farm next to ours. Mum's fair excited. She loves weddings." She sighed. "So do I." Betty rested her chin on her hand, a dreamy expression stealing over her face. "It's so romantic. Seeing a young couple in love, starting out their lives together. Like Cary Grant and Irene Dunne in *Penny Serenade*."

Maeve gave her a quizzical look.

"You've not seen *Penny Serenade*?"

Maeve shook her head.

"Ooh, it's a lovely film. Cary Grant is wonderful. Irene Dunne, too. It shows how they first met in a record shop and fell in love and got married. There's some sad things, too." Betty blinked back a tear. "It's quite a tearjerker, but it has a happy ending. My favourite kind of film." She blushed. "Albert likes it too."

Maeve thought about teasing her young friend but decided not to. It was plain Betty harbored secret dreams of marrying Albert, the dairy farmer. Acknowledging that would just embarrass her. Instead, she filled Betty in on the latest about her family.

"Since my brothers left to work in the Guinness factory, Mam's started working in the pub with Da. Briony's older now and doesn't need her as much at home. Mam writes she's having a grand old time. She says if she'd known how much fun pouring beer and chatting with men was, she'd have done it years ago." She chuckled. "I'm not sure how much fun Da thinks it is, but he'll get used to it."

Titch gave the girls a half-wave as she and Paddy left. Lilian and Rita followed suit soon thereafter. Apart from Margaret, intent on her cards, the hut was now empty.

Maeve scooted closer to Betty, keeping her voice low. "Earlier, after I got my patients sorted for transport, I took a shortcut, needing the toilet. I was hurrying to the latrine when I went round the corner of the hospital hut and almost collided with Thelma. She was having a proper argy-bargy with one of the nurses."

"One of the *nurses*?" Betty's eyes bulged. "Who?"

"Sister Agatha. The tall, snooty one who's engaged to Lieutenant Blake." *The same Lieutenant Blake who was engaged in hanky-panky with our Sally.* But Maeve didn't say that aloud. "She and Thelma were going at it tooth and nail, although it looked like I missed the best bit."

Conscious of Margaret in the corner with her cards, Maeve leaned closer. "Thelma's face was red and swollen. She looked the way my brothers look when they've been brawling and get a punch in the nose. It won't be long before that redness turns into a black eye."

Betty's mouth formed an "o." "You think Sister Agatha punched Thelma in the nose?" she whispered.

"It certainly looks that way."

"What in the world did Thelma do, I wonder?"

"With Thelma, it could be anything. Some rumor she was spreading, I'll wager."

Margaret departed as Etta entered.

Betty motioned Etta over. "Hey, Champ, you won't believe what Maeve just told me!"

"Let me get a cuppa and then you can tell all." When she returned with her tea, Etta stretched her legs out to the heater. "Okay, spill."

"You tell her, Maeve. It's your story."

Maeve recounted the juicy goings-on.

"Sounds like quite the argy-bargy," Etta said.

"I know." Betty giggled. "Can you believe one of the nurses punched Thelma's lights out?"

"Actually, that was me."

Maeve and Betty stared at her open-mouthed.

"What did Thelma *do*?" Maeve asked.

172

"I caught her going through my footlocker and confronted her. She made a nasty crack about Sally, and I laid her out." Etta lifted an eyebrow at Maeve. "Your turn now. Betty and I have both got in our licks against the dreadful Thelma. What do the Americans say? Three strikes and you're out?"

Betty nodded. "I learned that in *Pride of the Yankees.*"

"I'm up for the challenge." Maeve grinned and punched her fist into her palm. "Thelma won't know what hit her."

Etta sipped her tea. "It should make for an interesting evening in the hut tonight."

Betty fastened worried brown eyes on her. "Do you think Thelma will report you to Matron?"

Etta waved her hand in a dismissive motion. "Thelma's not going to say anything. If she does, she'll have to explain why she was going through other people's things. She'll just make up some feeble excuse for her black eye, saying she ran into a door or something."

"That's a relief." Betty stood. "Well, I need to write my letters. Speak to you later."

"Careful how you go," Maeve warned. "It's getting dark. You'll want to skirt the lily ponds."

"Always." Betty shuddered. "Can you imagine falling in that muck?"

After she left, Etta gave Maeve a speculative look. "Sister Agatha seems to be having her fair share of dust-ups of late. I wonder if her fight with Thelma has anything to do with the argument she had with her fiancé?"

"Perhaps she caught Thelma *in flagrante delicto* with Lieutenant Blake and was giving them both what for."

"I can't imagine Thelma *in flagrante delicto* with *any*one." Etta wrinkled her nose. "I'd prefer not to, thank you very much."

"Nor I." Maeve winced. "I herewith scrub my mind of that unappealing image."

"Besides, after Sally, what man would choose Thelma?" Etta told Maeve she had talked to Louise about how everything added up to Sally having taken her own life. "Louise isn't going to tell Matron about Sally's suicide. She sees no need."

"I hope Graham feels the same. I was going to tell him today," Maeve said, "but he was too busy with patients. I'll tell him tomorrow."

But there was no time for conversation the next day or the day after that.

Chapter Twenty-Five

In early March, the Americans captured the bridge at Remagen, allowing the Allies to transport troops and tanks across the southern part of the Rhine. Now, in the largest amphibious and airborne operation since D-Day, Field Marshal "Monty" Montgomery led British troops across a twenty-mile stretch of the heavily fortified northern Rhine into the heart of Germany in "Operation Plunder."

"Aye, laddie," one of the bandaged Scottish soldiers on Maeve's plane crowed to the injured Scot on the stretcher beside him, "Monty's done it. It's the beginning of the end for Herr Hitler."

"You're right there. And it was the *Scots* Monty chose to lead the way across the Rhine." The baby-faced lad, who'd suffered machine gun wounds to both legs, broke into a rousing rendition of "Scotland the Brave."

The other Scots on board joined in, and Maeve beamed at them. "That calls for a cuppa."

"I don't suppose you have any whisky in one of those urns, do ye, lassie?"

Betty spoon-fed a sullen private missing an arm. "Here you go, love," she coaxed the one-armed soldier in the hospital bed, "a nice bit of egg for you." After they'd landed and she had got her patients cleaned up, the Mess waitresses served plates of food to the men before they were sent off to hospitals. Betty helped those who couldn't feed themselves. Forking up a bite of sausage, she guided it to the private's mouth.

He gave a snort of disgust. "So, this is what the rest of my life will be like. Being fed like a baby, not able to do anything ever again. A useless cripple."

"Don't say that." Betty's eyes flashed. "My friend Albert lost his arm, just like you. He went on to hospital in Stoke Mandeville, just like you'll be doing. The doctors and nurses there are a great lot. They'll give you physiotherapy and teach you to do things one-handed, just like they did for Albert. And my Albert is now back home on the farm milking cows one-handed," she declared, her voice full of pride.

"Ta, nurse." The soldier sat up straighter. "You sound like my ma. She'd say, 'There's no point feeling sorry for yourself,' when things went wrong." He regarded her with determination. "If your man can do things one-handed, so can I."

My man? Betty blushed, realizing she'd called Albert *my* Albert.

Etta removed the bloody dressing from her patient's chest, washed the wounded area, and applied a fresh bandage. Then she helped the injured man into a clean uniform jacket, settled him into a chair, and tucked a blanket round him.

Advancing through the hospital hut, she performed similar clean-ups for the remaining patients from her flight. As she neared the last bunk, the injured man held up a copy of *The Daily Express* and read aloud, "*Mighty Blitz Hits Germans Facing Monty's Army. Anything that moves target for RAF,*" he crowed. "Take that Hitler! The RAF doesn't mess around."

"Watch out, Adolph," a young private with a bandaged leg announced. "We're comin' for you."

"We are, indeed," Etta said, a determined glint in her eye. "You can run, Herr Hitler, but you cannot hide."

Gazing up at the pink-ribboned sky, Betty recalled the sunsets at Cherry Tree Farm and wished she was back home. Her mum's oft-repeated saying filled her head. *If wishes were horses, beggars would ride.* Smiling, she entered her hut, intending to answer Albert's latest letter.

Doreen waylaid her, waving a piece of paper in the air. "Look at this, Betty."

"What is it?"

"A letter to Sally from one of her boys."

"To Sally? After all this time?" She hurried over to Doreen's bunk. "How did you get it?"

Doreen blushed. "It was addressed to the 'pretty blonde nurse.' Admin handed it to me after I missed mail call today."

"But how do you know it was for Sally?"

"Just read it, and you'll see." Doreen thrust the letter at her.

Betty read aloud.

Dear Nurse (or as I think of you, my flying angel)

If you don't mind my saying, you're the prettiest thing I ever saw. You look like Lana Turner or one of those film stars. It was my lucky day to land on your flight. Who knew someone so pretty could also be nice and kind? I wanted to thank you for taking such good care of me on the way home. It was my first time in a plane and I don't mind telling you I was right scared to be flying so high in the sky in that giant metal bird.

I was sure we were going to crash, but you made me forget being afraid when you said you bet I had a boatload of girls waiting for me at home.

I don't have any girls at home. I'm usually shy around girls. I didn't feel shy around you, though. You got me laughing and made me feel comfortable. And it didn't seem to bother you one bit I've only got one leg. I figured no girl would ever pay attention to me now, but you did. You were so nice and even gave me a kiss on the cheek. Do you remember? I'll never forget it. I didn't wash my cheek for days—not wanting to remove your red lipstick, which proved that the prettiest girl I ever saw kissed me.

You probably have a fella, maybe even more than one. I'd like to write to you if that's all right. You'll need to tell me your Christian name, though, please.

Until then, I'll call you Angel because that's what you were to me.

Sincerely yours,

Virgil Ross
p.s. All my friends call me Virge.

Betty regarded Doreen through blurred eyes. "Someone needs to write to this lad and tell him Sally really is an angel now, and she's looking down on him from heaven."

"Would *you* do it? You're good at writing letters, Betty. I wouldn't even know what to say."

"It's *your* letter. It came to you."

"Only because I have blonde hair. This is Sally's letter," Doreen said, "and you were Sally's good friend. I'll bet she'd want you to write back to one of her boys. Please?"

Betty considered, a thoughtful expression on her face. "She would, wouldn't she? Sally always answered letters from her boys." She straightened. "I'll do so on her behalf. Right now." She pulled pen and paper from her drawer and set to work.

> *Dear Virge,*
>
> *My name is Betty. I'm a friend of Sally Roberts, the pretty blonde nursing orderly you wrote to. The one who looked like a film star. I'm afraid we've only just received your lovely letter—sometimes the post can take several weeks to arrive. I'm sorry to have to tell you this, but we lost our sweet Sally in January.*
>
> *She would have loved your letter. Sally always enjoyed receiving letters from her "boys," as she called you, and would have written you back straightaway.*

Betty paused, trying to decide what to say next. *What would Sally have said?*

> *Virge, it wouldn't have bothered her one bit that you only have one leg. She always looked at the inside of people, not just the outside. She knew that's where our true value lies. In our souls. Our hearts. Sally had the biggest heart of any girl I've ever known. She was my dear friend, and*

I miss her terribly.

A tear plopped onto the paper.

> *Thank you for taking the time to write. I know Sally would have been right touched by what you said. I'm going to send your letter on to her parents. It will bring them comfort knowing how much their daughter meant to her patients. She had a special way about her—she could always lift the spirits of the lads on her plane. I'm so glad she lifted yours.*
> *Thank you for writing her, and God bless.*
> *Sincerely,*
> *Betty Hall*
> *p.s. You said you'd call her Angel until you learned her name. Sally's an angel to all of us now.*

Maeve caught herself daydreaming about Graham again. *You silly goose, you're as bad as Betty. Pull yourself together. Just because you danced together and shared a few conversations doesn't mean he's interested in you. Certainly, there's an attraction there, but don't be reading anything more into it than that.*

Unbidden, the thought entered her head. *And would it be so bad if we acted upon that attraction? Neither of us has anyone waiting for us back home. We've both lost the loves of our lives. What could it hurt if we had a wartime romance?* She closed her eyes, imagining herself in Graham's arms, a welcome respite from the daily horrors they encountered. *Before anything like that could happen, though, you've got something important to tell him.*

Maeve went searching for Graham after finishing with her patients. She found him in one of the hospital tents, washing his hands. "Doctor Moore?" Conscious of the medic and nursing sister conferring in a corner, she asked, "Do you have a moment?"

Graham turned, his gray eyes lighting up at the sight of her. "Certainly. I've just finished up here."

As he led her from the tent, the nurse and medic gave them a speculative glance.

"It's lovely to see you again," Graham said, looking at Maeve in a way that made her heart thump. *Could he hear it?*

He smiled. A smile that took years off his careworn face and turned her insides to mush. "How are you? I haven't seen you since we talked at the canteen."

"Things have been so busy."

"Are you off duty now? Would you like to go to the canteen and have a cup of tea? And cake, of course." Graham gave her a sly look. "I haven't forgotten your sweet tooth."

"I'll never say no to cake." As they walked through the camp, Maeve said, "You were right."

"About what? I'm right about so many things it's hard to keep track."

"You are quite a fount of wisdom and knowledge." A smile tugged at the corners of Maeve's mouth. "There *is* a town in Devon called Beer. Near Lyme Regis, which I recognized from *Persuasion*."

"You like Jane Austen?" Graham regarded her with obvious delight. "She was my wife's favourite author. Susan made me read all her books when we were courting—told me she could never marry a man who didn't appreciate Austen."

"Smart woman." Maeve stopped beside a large oak in front of the canteen. Turning, she faced the doctor, a somber expression on her face. "You were also right about Sally. It appears she did kill herself." She explained how she'd arrived at that conclusion.

"I'm sorry." Graham's voice was tinged with regret. "For your sake, I was hoping there was another reason for her death, although I couldn't imagine what that might be."

Do NOT tell him about your dramatic murder musings. "I'd hoped the same. Etta's told Sister Louise so she could inform Matron, but Louise said she saw no reason to say anything, that we should let the dead rest in peace."

"It's the least we can do for them. May they all rest in peace." There was a note of finality in Graham's voice. He brushed a stray hair off Maeve's face, his hand lingering on her cheek.

Shivering at his touch, Maeve closed her eyes, her breath quickening. When she opened her eyes again, it was to find the doctor gazing at her with a look of yearning. *This is it. It's going to happen.* She closed the distance between them.

Graham bent his head and kissed her. A light whisper of a kiss. "I've been wanting to do that for some time," he said.

"Me, too." Taking his hand in hers, Maeve led Graham behind the tree. She slipped her arms around his neck and kissed him back.

Enfolding her in his arms, Graham returned her kiss, murmuring in a husky voice. "It's been so long."

So long. All her senses reawakening, Maeve kissed him with renewed vigor.

The canteen door slammed, breaking them apart. The next sound they heard was a soldier relieving himself.

Maeve stifled a giggle as the soldier stumbled away.

"Well, that killed the mood," Graham said. "Shall we go inside and have that drink now?"

"And cake. Don't forget the cake."

Everyone in the crowded canteen was celebrating Monty's success. Loadmasters and wireless operators mingled with ground support staff, and typists and supply clerks chatted to cooks. A cluster of pilots and navigators chatted up the nurses. Maeve spotted a few Nightingales scattered around the room, including Doreen and Etta. Doreen was smiling and talking to Will while Etta was squeezed into a corner with Louise, their heads bent over a familiar blue nursing textbook.

Maeve smiled to herself. Looks like Etta has found someone who shares her passion.

A beaming Dickie strode over, beer in one hand, *The Evening Standard* in the other. "Have you seen this?" He flapped the newspaper and read aloud with glee. "Berlin Reports Huge Military Barrage." "Monty: We'll Chase Them from Pillar to Post.... "This Brings Victory Near—Mr. Churchill."

Dickie's eyes shone. "If *Churchill's* saying victory is near, you can count on it! Not much longer now, and the Nazis will be done and dusted."

"From your lips," Maeve murmured.

Dickie rejoined Frank and Harry, who were standing off to the side laughing with some pilots. Seeing Maeve, Harry smiled and waved. She watched as he scanned the room, his eyes gleaming when they landed on a trio of typists. Harry sauntered over to the girls and said something that made them giggle.

Graham steered Maeve through the crowd to a table where two medics had just stood up. "Mind if we sit here?"

"It's all yours, Doc."

"I'll get the drinks." Graham's mouth quirked. "And your cake, of course. Tea?"

"I'll have a beer. I feel like celebrating as well." Her eyes locked on his.

Graham's fingertips brushed her hand, sending a tingling down Maeve's spine. She tried to steady her breathing as he left to get their drinks. It had been a long time since she'd responded this way to a man. *Since Seamus.* She touched her lips, thinking of Graham's lips on hers, his gentle kiss. Maeve turned pink, recalling how she'd pulled the doctor behind the tree and kissed him with such fervor.

A braying laugh from across the room punctured her daydreaming. *Joyce.* She pulled a face. If Joyce was here, that meant Thelma was close by as well. *I wonder how she explained her black eye to her new pal.*

"Why, hello. I don't believe I've had the pleasure," a male voice said in a seductive tone.

Maeve looked up to see Sister Agatha's ginger-haired pilot fiancé standing before her.

"Julian Blake." The flight lieutenant extended his hand with a cocky air.

Maeve placed her hands in her lap. "I know who you are." She recalled the cockpit conversation Etta had relayed to her after Sally died and remembered Clemmie's interaction with the randy pilot. "Sally Roberts was a friend of mine."

His hand dropped to his side. "Such a shame. Lovely girl. She was a lot of fun."

Maeve fixed him with an impenetrable stare. "Was that all Sally was to you?"

The lieutenant shifted his eyes. "We had some jolly times together, but it was just a lark. Sally knew that."

Did she? Maeve thought. *How do you know? If it was just a lark, then why did Sally kill herself?* She blinked back sudden tears.

Graham reappeared and set two glasses on the table. "Never fear. Your cake is on its way." Noticing the wetness in her eyes, his smile was replaced with a look of concern. "Everything all right?"

Maeve nodded, not trusting herself to speak.

Graham narrowed his eyes at the pilot. "Were you bothering this lady?"

The pilot held up his hands. "Sorry, old man. Didn't know you'd already staked your claim." His eyes flicked to Maeve, dismissing her before departing the canteen.

"Goodbye and good riddance," she muttered.

"Do I need to punch the lieutenant's lights out?"

"No." Maeve's lips tightened. "Lieutenant Blake and Sally were involved. Merely a fling, according to him." She gave a brisk shake of her head. "But let's not talk about that. I'd rather forget all about the odious lieutenant."

"Here you go, love." The waitress appeared with her cake.

Smiling, Maeve picked up her fork. "This helps." She took a bite and washed down the dry morsel with a drink of beer. "This helps even more."

"Shall we pick up where we left off?"

"Here? In front of everyone? People will talk, Doctor Moore."

Graham chuckled. "We will pick that up again and soon." His eyes lingered on her lips, and a delicious warmth spread through Maeve. "I meant picking up where we left off getting to know each other. You know *my* favourite food is fish and chips, but I never found out yours."

"My mam's Guinness stew," she answered promptly. "Beef, onions, potatoes, and carrots in a Guinness broth. What more could you ask for?"

"I don't suppose you know how to make this delectable stew." He gave her a hopeful look.

"What self-respecting Irish lass doesn't? Especially one raised in the family pub. Mam's stew was the favourite dish on the menu."

"Perhaps you might make it for me sometime."

"I think that could be arranged. After the war, of course. I doubt the cook would let me into the Mess kitchen."

"I'll hold you to that. You, me, and Guinness stew. It's a date. Now then, what food can you not abide?"

"Tongue." Maeve shuddered. "Nasty stuff."

"Shame. After fish and chips, that's my favourite meal. In fact," Graham said with all innocence, "I was hoping you might cook me braised tongue sometime."

"Keep hoping." She grinned. "Right then, my turn. What's your favourite song?"

"That's a tough one. There are so many." His eyes crinkled at the corners. "I quite like 'Boogie Woogie Bugle Boy.'" Graham drummed his hands on the table. "I'd have to say my current favourite is 'Moonlight Serenade,' though." He touched her hand. "That song holds a special place in my heart."

Maeve recalled the Christmas dance and the first time Graham had held her in his arms. "Mine too." She gave him a shy smile before tilting her head at him. "I never got to ask. What do *you* want to do after the war?"

"Open a doctor's practice again, but not in London." A shadow crossed Graham's face. "Some place small and quiet."

"Like Beer? Are your parents still there?"

He shook his head. "They died years ago. There's nothing for me in Beer anymore. Or London, for that matter." Graham gave her a forlorn smile. "I'm a man without a home."

Pushing down her romantic daydreams, Maeve squeezed his hand. "You'll find the right place."

"All right then, Irish?" a familiar voice asked.

Maeve looked up to see Etta and Louise standing before them. Her bunkmate's eyes zeroed in on Maeve's hand atop Graham's. Etta smirked.

Removing her hand, Maeve nodded at the blue textbook Etta was holding. "Did you two solve the nursing problems of the world?"

"Not all of them," Sister Louise said, "but we made a good start. Etta's going to make a fine nurse."

Etta basked in her mentor's praise.

"What type of nursing do you want to do after the war?" Graham asked Etta.

"Surgical," she answered without hesitation.

"That's quite a challenging job."

"Etta's up for the challenge," Louise said. "I have every confidence in her." Etta's face shone.

"So do I." Maeve smiled at her bunkmate.

"Sounds like a quorum," Graham said. "Good luck, Etta. I wish you all the best."

"Thank you, Sir."

"Are you two leaving?" Maeve asked.

Louise nodded. "I have an early shift tomorrow."

"So do we. Etta and I are flying first thing." Maeve gave Graham an apologetic shrug. "I guess we should go."

The foursome departed the canteen, followed closely by Will and Doreen.

"Looks like everyone's got an early start tomorrow," Doreen said.

"*Time and tide wait for no man*," Louise quoted. "Sorry." She shrugged. "I have a tendency to utter random lines of poetry."

Maeve saw Etta furrow her brow in the moonlight. "I know that quote," she said, "but I have no idea who said it."

Doctor and nurse replied in unison. "Chaucer."

They all laughed.

Up ahead, torches bobbed over the uneven ground. "Oops," a beery male voice cut the night air. "Looks like some WAAF celebrated too much and fell in the lily pond." A loud belch erupted.

"That's going to be a right stink," a second male voice declared. "Let's rescue the damsel in distress, but be careful you don't wind up in the drink, too." The torches bobbed off to the right.

One of the men cursed. "Watch it. You just stepped on me bleedin' foot."

Graham strode forward to help, the others following. Will, the only one with a torch, clicked it on and pointed it at the ground in front of them.

The beery-voiced man belched again. "Jaysus, that reeks!" The sound of vomiting followed.

As they approached the trench, Will's torch spotlighted the trouser-clad legs of a WAAF on the ground. But only her legs. Her torso and head were sunk in the lily pond.

Graham and Etta sprinted forward, Louise and Will fast on their heels while Maeve and Doreen stood rooted to the spot in horror.

As if in slow motion, Maeve watched as the others pulled the submerged WAAF from the trench. She heard Graham's voice issuing urgent commands and other voices overlapping, but it was as if it was all from a great distance. Frozen in place, she watched as Graham and Will turned the WAAF on her back. Louise yanked off her nursing veil and began wiping the muck from the woman's face. Yanking off her jacket, Etta assisted Louise.

"Oh my God," Doreen cried as Will's torch illuminated the bruised face. "It's Thelma."

And for the second time in a matter of weeks, Maeve looked into the staring eyes of a dead Flying Nightingale.

Chapter Twenty-Six

What happened to Thelma? The camp buzzed with conjecture. Many, like the tipsy soldiers who'd first spotted the nursing orderly in the lily pond, assumed she was drunk and had passed out and fell in the trench, suffocating in all the waste.

Others speculated she'd been in a fight and got the worst of it. "They say she had bruises on her face," one of the typists in Admin whispered to the girls in the typing pool.

"I heard she had an awful black eye. Do you suppose her boyfriend did that?"

"I don't think she had a boyfriend."

The gossip flew, fast and furious.

"I heard she got mixed up in the Black Market. My friend said she was wearing posh perfume."

"How could they tell?"

Thelma's hutmates recalled the scent she'd begun wearing and sharing with Joyce. They also remembered her coy reply when asked where she'd got the money to buy the expensive scent: "Ask me no questions, and I'll tell you no lies."

The nursing orderlies who billeted with the fallen Nightingale also knew Thelma didn't drink. "Just that one time when Sally and Harry spiked her punch at the dance," Doreen said as they huddled together discussing their fellow nursing orderly's shocking demise.

"Sally." Betty's eyes filled with tears. "First Sally and now Thelma. What is *happening*?"

DEATH OF A FLYING NIGHTINGALE

Clemmie's mouth thinned. "That's what I was wondering. They both died outside, too. At night, alone in the dark. Like that Nightingale Agnes from RAF Blakehill who was strangled. Seems suspicious if you ask me."

Doreen agreed.

Betty stared at them. "Sally got disoriented in the snowstorm and lost her way. Sister Louise said she died of exposure. There's nothing suspicious about that." She didn't tell the other girls Sally may have been drinking and passed out in the snow. Betty refused to besmirch her friend's memory.

Clemmie looked thoughtful. "But that was in January when it was arctic. Now it's almost spring, nowhere near as cold."

"Thelma would never be caught dead by the lily ponds," Doreen declared. "She hated them." Realizing what she'd said, she burst into tears.

After pulling Thelma from the lily pond, Graham did a cursory examination. It was obvious to all of them, though, the moment they saw Thelma that she was gone. Etta covered the dead Nightingale's face with her jacket, and Will left to get a stretcher.

Doreen wept for her former friend, burying her face in Maeve's chest and bringing her out of her trance. Maeve patted Doreen's back and murmured comforting words.

Graham conferred with Louise while Etta stood apart, recalling her last encounter with Thelma. Since she had punched her in the nose, Thelma had taken care to maintain her distance from Etta, a distance that suited them both. Now, as she stared down at the body of her former hutmate, Etta thought, *what the hell happened?*

Louise approached. "Are you all right?"

"I'm fine." In the moonlight, Louise looked different—younger and more vulnerable somehow, Etta thought. Then she realized the nursing sister was without her usual veil. The veil she'd used to remove the waste and muck from Thelma's face.

"When Will returns with the stretcher, we'll take Thelma to hospital, and Doctor Moore will inform Matron," Louise said. "Would you be able to help me wash and prepare her?"

"Of course."

"If you'd rather not, I can get one of the other nurses to help me. I know you and Thelma lived in the same hut."

Etta donned her professional mantle. "It's fine."

Graham walked over to Maeve and the sniffling Doreen beside her. "How are you?"

"Fine, but I think I should take Doreen back to our hut."

Will appeared with the stretcher. Graham squeezed Maeve's hand and returned to Will and the waiting Louise and Etta.

In the hospital hut, Louise and Etta worked side by side, removing the dead woman's uniform. They stuffed the filthy clothes in the rubbish and bathed Thelma, washing the waste from her hair and taking great care to remove every trace of sludge and sewage from her body. Etta's jaw worked as she viewed the pale, nude form on the hospital bed, so defenseless and vulnerable in death. She swallowed hard.

I'm sorry, Thelma. We had our differences, but you didn't deserve this.

Pushing aside thoughts of Thelma's venomous tongue, rumormongering, and all-around spitefulness, Etta closed her eyes, trying to find something good to remember about the older nursing orderly. A wisp of memory fluttered at the edges of her mind. An image of Thelma weeping over her young neighbor who'd lost an eye and both of his legs. Followed by another image of Thelma in her crisp blue uniform dispensing tea to her patients on the ground while they awaited transport.

Like Etta, Thelma had been a Flying Nightingale. For all her faults, she had done her job. Raising the arm of her fallen comrade, Etta slipped Thelma's hand through the sleeve of a clean hospital gown.

Louise did the same on the other side of the cot. Returning the dead Nightingale's arm to her side, Louise, who had donned a fresh nursing veil, murmured, "*With brooks too broad for leaping/the lightfoot boys are laid; The rose-lipt girls are sleeping/In fields where roses fade.*"

Staring down at Thelma's bruised face, Etta said, "I hit her."

"What?"

"I hit Thelma. I'm the one who gave her that black eye."

"When?" Louise asked in an odd voice.

"A couple days ago. I found her going through my things and confronted her. She got defensive and made a vicious crack about Sally, so I punched her in the nose."

"Sounds like she deserved it."

"She did." Etta looked down again at the still form. "But she didn't deserve this. What do you suppose happened?"

"I have no idea, but she has a huge goose egg on the back of her head. I felt it when we were washing her hair."

"Where?"

Turning Thelma's head to one side, Louise parted the hair at the base of her skull. "There."

Etta felt the lump and frowned. "Do you think she got it when she fell?"

"I'm not sure she *did* fall. If she had, this goose egg would be on the front of her head, not the back. Remember, she was face-down when we found her."

"What are you saying?"

"I'm saying I don't know what happened, but I think there's a possibility someone may have hit her."

Etta recalled the heated argument Maeve had witnessed between Thelma and Agatha. Had the two of them had another confrontation, except this time the nursing sister lashed out and struck Thelma in her anger?

Logic intervened. *In the back of the head? You punched Thelma in the nose, and Betty slapped her in the face.* "Maybe she tripped over something in the dark and got a bump on her head that way," Etta mused.

"Maybe…" Louise said, doubt in her voice. "But in that case, why didn't we find her lying on her back on the ground instead of submerged in the sludge?"

"I don't know." What Etta did know is that everyone in camp knew where the lily ponds were. The girls were all careful to give them a wide berth, Thelma in particular. She couldn't stomach certain smells. Etta had stepped in more than once to take over the care of a colostomy patient from the squeamish nursing orderly, who gagged at the stench. Thelma always held her handkerchief to her nose and stayed as far away as possible from the trenches full of waste.

So, what was she doing at the lily pond?

"Etta," Louise interrupted her musings, "I think we have to face the very real possibility someone may have struck Thelma from behind and left her in the lily pond to die." The nurse looked as if she was going to be sick.

Etta felt as sick as Louise looked. Pushing down the bile, she said, "I'm going to Matron. I need to tell her I punched Thelma in the nose."

Maeve lay on her bunk, the events of the night unspooling before her.

When they'd returned to the hut, Doreen had taken Joyce outside to tell her about Thelma while Maeve informed Betty, Clemmie, and the other girls. While Maeve was explaining to her disbelieving hutmates what had happened, they heard a shriek followed by hysterical sobbing.

Betty hurried outside to comfort the distraught nursing orderly, but Joyce wouldn't be comforted. She flew into the hut, her face contorted with grief, tears coursing down her cheeks.

"You all hated her!" Joyce yelled. "I was her only friend, and now she's gone. I hope you're happy!" She flung herself across Thelma's bunk, sobbing.

It had taken over an hour to get the grief-stricken Nightingale under control. At last, Joyce cried herself to sleep. Everyone now slept.

Everyone but Maeve. She couldn't get the image of Thelma's staring eyes out of her head or the smell of the lily pond out of her nose.

The next day, the lily pond was filled in, and a fresh trench hole dug beside it. A hysterical Joyce decided her billeting hut was cursed and moved to another hut.

Passing by the two empty bunks when she returned after speaking to Matron, Etta took Maeve aside and told her there was a possibility Thelma may have been murdered. She warned her Irish friend not to say anything, though, since it was all conjecture at this point.

Maeve acquiesced, seeing Thelma's open-staring eyes again in her head.

Then Thelma's staring eyes were replaced by Sally's.

Someone's killing Nightingales.

Chapter Twenty-Seven

April 1945

Etta removed her gear from the plane. She'd got her patients sorted and off on transport to the different hospitals. Now, she just needed to stash her gear and get something to eat. Before heading to the Mess, though, she made a detour.

Ever since the night she and Louise had cleaned and prepared Thelma's body, Etta hadn't been able to get Louise's suspicions about the goose egg on the back of the dead nursing orderly's head out of her mind. Etta knew full well her squeamish hutmate would have never gone near the lily ponds willingly. Prissy Thelma had always made a point of steering clear of the waste-filled trenches.

So, then, what was she doing there? Every time she thought of the grotesque way Thelma had died, Etta felt sick. Especially since her last interaction with the dead Nightingale had been to give her a black eye.

Matron had commended Etta for her honesty in coming forward. "You'll have to make a statement to the military police investigating Thelma's death, however," the nursing supervisor had said. The following day, Matron called the MPs into her office, shut the door, and stood beside Etta as she admitted to striking Thelma.

"You confess to having an altercation with the deceased and punching her in the face?" the older of the two MPs asked Etta.

"Yes, two days before her death."

"Why did you hit your colleague?" the younger MP, taking notes, asked.

"I caught her going through my footlocker, and when I confronted her, she lied and said something nasty about a friend of mine." Etta's hands clenched at her sides, recalling Thelma's ugly words about Sally.

"Are you in the habit of hitting people whenever they say something you don't like?"

"No."

"So, the black eye came from you. Did the goose egg on the back of the head also come from you?"

"No!"

The MPs exchanged a look.

"Sounds like someone's got a hair-trigger temper," the older MP said. "Could it be that Leading Aircraftwoman Jenkins said something you didn't like again, and you hauled off and hit her a second time?"

"Except this time, you hit her so hard, she died?" the note-taking MP added.

"No," Etta answered in an even voice.

"And then, to cover up your crime, you dragged the dead woman over to the trench and left her there with the rest of the waste?"

"I would never do something like that."

"That's enough, Corporal." Matron gave him a stern look. "Nurse Blackwood is not a killer. She's the best nursing orderly I know. She *saves* lives; she doesn't take them. She is also a woman of honour and integrity. Leading Aircraftwoman Blackwood came to me of her own volition to tell me she struck Thelma and gave her a black eye."

Etta flushed at Matron's praise.

"Not until *after* Jenkins was dead," the MP said. "She could have been trying to cover her tracks. She could have hit her fellow nursing orderly in anger again, except this time she wound up killing her and tried to make it look like an accident."

"No, I couldn't have," Etta said.

"Why is that?"

"Because I was at the canteen all evening. A crowd of people saw me there, including Sister Louise. We were discussing diseases, and she was explaining what it's like to be a surgical nurse."

Matron called in the senior nurse, who confirmed that Etta had indeed been with her all evening.

"Etta never once left the canteen until a group of us did together at the end of the night," Louise said. She gave the MPs a measured look. "It may interest you to know that Etta helped Doctor Moore pull Thelma Jenkins from the trench when we discovered her to render aid. She then helped me remove the sludge from the poor woman's face in an effort to help her breathe. Unfortunately, we soon realized our efforts were in vain."

Louise pinned her eyes on the older MP. "After we took Thelma to the hospital, Leading Aircraftwoman Blackwood spent hours assisting me in cleaning her colleague's body to afford her the proper dignity everyone deserves in death." She spoke in a cool, measured voice. "Not only was it impossible for her to have killed Thelma, but Etta did not hesitate to assist me in one of the most difficult tasks a nurse must undertake, doing so with the utmost compassion and respect."

Matron stood. "And that, gentlemen, is that." She dismissed the two MPs. "I suggest you look elsewhere for someone who may have wanted to harm Nursing Orderly Jenkins. It might behoove you to start with somebody who wasn't in the canteen all night long."

Recalling Matron's admonition to the MPs, Etta poked her head into the first hospital tent in search of the nursing sister. Empty. The second tent was also empty. When she stuck her head in the third tent, at last, she found who she sought. And better yet, she was alone.

"Sister Agatha?" Etta approached the kneeling figure who was pulling rolled bandages from the cupboard.

"What is it?" The nurse flicked her an impatient look. "In case you can't see, I'm busy."

"This will only take a minute of your time."

"What do you want?"

"I wanted to know if it was *you* who bashed Thelma in the head and left her to die in the lily pond," Etta said with an innocent air.

Agatha's face paled. She rocked back on her heels. "Are you quite mad? What in God's name are you talking about?"

"Thelma Jenkins, the nursing orderly from my hut. Now dead. The one you were having a violent argument with the day before she died."

"You have an overactive imagination. Now get out of here and leave me alone."

Etta shrugged. "Sure. I'll just go to the MPs investigating the death and tell them what I saw. I'm sure they'll be quite interested."

"Wait." Agatha sank down on a nearby cot, rubbing her forehead. "How much?"

"Pardon?"

"How much do you want to keep quiet?"

Etta closed her eyes and shook her head. "You *did* kill Thelma."

"No!"

Etta's eyes flew open in time to see the nursing sister shoot to her feet, a horrified look on her face. "I could never kill anyone," Agatha said. "I'm a *nurse*, for God's sake."

"Then why did you offer me money to keep my mouth shut?"

"To keep you quiet about my argument with Thelma. When I heard she had died, I thought this was finally all over."

"*What* was all over?"

"The blackmail. Thelma's been bleeding me dry for months."

"Over what?"

Agatha's mouth curled. "My fiancé's indiscretions. That's what we were arguing about. I told Thelma I wasn't going to pay her anymore. I didn't have the money."

"Was this about Lieutenant Blake's dalliance with Sally?"

"Among others." The nurse gave a bitter laugh.

A medic hurried into the tent. "Sister Agatha? Doctor needs you straightaway."

"Coming." Agatha sent a pleading glance over her shoulder to the Flying

Nightingale as she exited the tent.

Etta recognized the truth in the nurse's statements. *This explains Thelma's recent sweets and perfume indulgences.* She wondered if everything else Agatha had said was also true. The nursing sister had seemed genuinely horror-struck at the prospect of anyone thinking she could kill another person.

Etta decided to ask Louise her thoughts. She had worked alongside Agatha for a while now and knew the nurse much better than she did. Louise had even known about Agatha's morphine addiction. Leaving the tent, she spotted the nurse she sought heading in the direction of the Officer's Mess. "Sister Louise," Etta called, hurrying to catch up with her.

Louise turned, a smile brightening her face at the sight of the nursing orderly.

"May I speak to you for a moment?"

"Walk with me to the Mess. I'd invite you to join me for lunch, but..." Louise rolled her eyes. "I understand the reasoning for separation between the ranks," she said, "but having separate latrines and eating facilities for officers and enlisted seems silly. It offends my egalitarian nature. You're my friend, and we can't share a meal together because you're enlisted, and I'm an officer." She made a face.

"It's not a problem." The strict rules of separation between the com-missioned and non-commissioned ranks didn't bother Etta. She was just pleased Louise viewed her as a friend, coming from such different worlds as they did.

"Right. I'll get off my soapbox now." The nurse's eyes crinkled at the corners. "What did you want to speak to me about?"

Etta recounted her conversation with Agatha.

Louise stopped in her tracks to stare at Etta. "Let me get this straight." She lowered her voice. "You asked Agatha outright if she *killed* Thelma?"

"I've always found being direct is better than beating around the bush."

Louise doubled over with laughter. "Etta, you are one of a kind."

"I'll take that as a compliment." As they resumed their walk, Etta gave her mentor a probing look. "You know Agatha much better than me. Do you think she's capable of killing someone?"

"With her *eyes*, yes, but not more than that." Louise shook her head. "She doesn't have it in her. Agatha is many things, but a murderer is not one of them. Killing Thelma, killing *anyone*, would destroy her well-laid plans for the future, and she won't do that."

"Well, that's sorted then."

Louise laid her hand on Etta's arm. "We don't even know *if* Thelma was murdered. The MPs are looking into it, and I think we should let them do their job." She fastened a steady gaze on Etta. "And if someone *did* kill Thelma, what's to say they might not kill again? Especially if they discover someone's poking around. Don't play detective, Etta. Please. It's not safe, and I would hate for anything to happen to you."

A sudden wave of emotion flooded Etta. She wasn't used to having people care what happened to her. She pushed down the feelings that threatened to overwhelm her. "Right. I'll hang up my deerstalker hat."

"This is me," Louise said, nodding to the Officer's Mess in front of them. "I wonder what epicurean delights the cook has in store for us today. Rack of lamb with mint jelly, I hope." She crossed her fingers.

"I'd settle for some fried Spam."

"Would you like to go to the canteen later for a cup of tea and their signature dry cake?"

"My mouth is watering in anticipation," Etta said.

Walking to her hut, Etta thought about Louise. She'd never known anyone like her. So kind and smart, and accomplished. She loved spending time with the nursing sister. Although their backgrounds couldn't have been more different, Etta was beginning to feel more and more that she and Louise were birds of a feather.

Kindred spirits.

Chapter Twenty-Eight

Betty sat beside the heater in the communal hut with a cup of tea. She opened the letter from Albert first.

Dear Betty,

The papers are all saying the war will be over soon. It can't come soon enough for me. We lost Ronnie Trask last week from the farm next to ours. Ronnie was a pal of mine. We were in the same class at school together. He was a great lad—quite the cut-up. Ronnie always kept everyone laughing. His mum and dad are that devastated. I don't know if they'll ever laugh again.

Losing Ronnie made me realize all over again that life is short. I first realized it in France when my arm was shot off and hanging by a thread. I begged God to let me live so I could come home to my family, the people I love. That's what's most important. None of us knows when our time will be up, so we'd best not be wasting what time we have.

I know we only met that one time, Betty, but I've got to know you so well these past months through all the letters we've exchanged. Well enough to know how much I like you. In fact, I like you so much I've started thinking of you as my girl. Pretty cheeky of me since I never even asked how you felt.

I'm asking now: Betty Hall, would you be my girl?

Betty gasped. Her heart began racing so fast she thought it might burst out of her chest.

"You okay?" Dickie asked.

"I'm fine." Warmth spread through her all the way down to her toes. *Of course, I'll be your girl, Albert. I can't think of anything I'd like better.* Flushed with happiness, Betty returned to her letter.

> *Please write straightaway and let me know. I can't wait for the war to be over and for you to be safely home again. I've told Mum all about you, and she's fair itching to meet you. I look forward to meeting your mum and dad as well. Maybe you could send me a telegram once you're demobbed and let me know when you're coming home. I'd like to meet you at the train station if you don't mind.*
>
> *I can't wait to look into your lovely brown eyes again. You have the kindest eyes of any girl I've ever known.*
>
> *I'll be counting the days.*
>
> *Hopefully yours,*
>
> *Albert*

Betty read the letter again, scarce able to believe her eyes. Her *lovely brown eyes,* Albert had called them. No one had ever said that to her before. She wished Sally was here so she could show her Albert's letter and talk to her about it. Betty decided to pay a visit to Sally's grave the next day. It had been a few weeks since she had been to the graveyard, and she wanted to catch Sally up on everything, including Thelma's shocking death. Although, of course, Sally would already know about that.

The girls in her hut knew Betty visited Sally's grave, but none of them knew about her one-way conversations with the dead Nightingale. They wouldn't understand, except maybe Maeve, and she didn't want the girls to tease her. Talking to Sally made Betty feel closer to her, and she always felt better afterwards.

"What's got you beaming like the sun, and could I have some of that?" Maeve gave Betty a tired smile as she sat down beside her.

Maeve's smile didn't reach her eyes, though. Betty noticed the dark circles under her friend's eyes. The Irish girl hadn't been herself since the night Thelma died, which surprised Betty since Maeve and Thelma hadn't been close.

Maybe it has nothing to do with Thelma, Betty thought, *but with a certain Doctor Moore.* Maybe things aren't going well between them. In that case, it wouldn't be right for her to rub Maeve's nose in her happiness with Albert. She answered Maeve's question. "Just some nice letters from home." Betty focused on her friend to deflect the conversation away from herself. "How is your sister? Have you heard from Briony lately?"

"Aye." Maeve's eyes brightened. "Briony's grand. She's doing well in school, making us all proud. Top marks in her class. She's running rings round the rest of us."

"And how are *you*?" Betty's brown eyes were full of concern. "You look done in, Maeve. You should get some kip."

"I might do." *Without Joyce's braying laugh in the hut anymore, I might actually be able to get some sleep.* Although Maeve doubted it. She hadn't slept well since the night of Thelma's death and Etta telling her their fellow Nightingale might have been murdered. She had kept her word, though, and not said anything to anyone. Except Graham.

Graham had sought Maeve out the morning after they'd found Thelma, telling her in private he had concerns that the nursing orderly's death may not have been accidental. As such, the MPs would conduct a discreet investigation into Thelma's death. Very discreet, so as not to alarm the other nursing orderlies

Maeve shivered when Graham told her about the investigation. "These suspicions over Thelma's death have me wondering all over again if Sally's death was suicide after all." Her eyes darted about. "Could there be a modern-day Jack the Ripper targeting Nightingales?"

Graham squeezed her shoulder. "I doubt that's the case. These deaths are different—Sally had spent morphine syringes in her pocket. And don't forget the letter from her mum and the gifts she bequeathed to you and the other girls."

"You're right." Maeve ran a shaking hand through her hair. "I'm just letting my Irish imagination run wild again. That happens when I haven't had enough sleep."

Graham took her in his arms. "You've had quite a shock. Seeing Thelma like that brought back the trauma of your finding Sally and reawakened that painful memory, making it fresh again."

Maeve wept against his chest. "You're right. I haven't been able to get those images out of my mind. Every time I close my eyes, all I see is their staring eyes. First Thelma, then Sally, then Thelma again. Staring up at me. Dead." She trembled. "It goes round and round in my head as if I'm on some terrible merry-go-round, and I can't get off. Or a house of mirrors at a carnival. Except everywhere I turn, it's not my face I see, but Thelma's and Sally's. Agnes's, too."

Maeve choked out a sob. "Three dead Nightingales in a matter of months."

Graham stroked her back in a gentle circular motion. "It's all right. It's good to cry," he soothed. "Let it all out."

At last, Maeve gave a shuddering sigh and extricated herself from Graham's embrace even though she'd like to have stayed in his arms forever. "I don't know what came over me. I'm not usually prone to hysterics."

"You've suffered a trauma, like the bomb-happy boys. You came upon two women dead in a short span of time—actually, three, if you count the nursing orderly from Blakehill. One of those women was a good friend, someone you lived with whose life you tried to save. You don't get over that easily," Graham said. "Your mind needs time to heal and recover, and your body needs rest. Lack of sleep exacerbates the trauma and magnifies it in your mind."

He adopted his doctor demeanor. "I'm going to give you a sedative to help you sleep. Meanwhile, you need to rest and take it easy. I'm going to prescribe a few days off."

"I can't take time off. We're down two girls already."

"You're no good to yourself or to your patients like this, Maeve. I'll speak to Matron and the duty CO and get it sorted. You need a rest. Doctor's orders." His smile faded. "Meanwhile, until the MPs figure out if Thelma was murdered, I don't want you going out alone at night. Even to the loo. Make sure Etta or one of the other girls is with you." Graham gazed deep into her eyes. "I've only just found you. I'm not going to lose you now. Promise me."

"I promise."

"And to help get those images out of your head, you need to fill your mind with better pictures—pictures of lovely things, lovely places." He studied her face. "When's the last time you went home?"

"To Ballydavid? I can't remember. It's been ages. We've been so busy and for so long we weren't allowed to take leave."

"Now that things are quieting down, leave restrictions have been lifted. I think you should go home and see your family. Have a rest. Get away from all this for a few days."

"It *would* be lovely to see everyone, especially Briony," Maeve said. "I miss her. But it's such a long journey, too long for a short visit." She gave Graham a dry look. "You've obviously not been raised in a pub. It's not the most restful environment."

He chuckled. "I suppose it wouldn't be. In that case, we need to find you a quiet, restful place not so far away." He pondered for a moment, a thoughtful expression on his face. "A friend of mine has a cottage in a village north of here he rarely uses. George has offered the use of the cottage to me in the past, but I've never taken him up on it. Sounds like now might be the time. I'll check to see if it's still available. How does that sound?"

"Lovely." *All right, my girl. It's time. Take the plunge.*

Screwing up her courage, Maeve took a deep breath. "What would be even lovelier is if you could join me there." She offered a shy smile.

Graham went still. He caressed her cheek. "I can't think of anything I'd like more."

Chapter Twenty-Nine

"I hope Maeve is having a lovely time at her friend's in Dorset," Betty said to Etta that evening in the hut. "I think the sea air will do her a world of good."

"So do I. I'm glad she was able to get some leave. She needed a change of scenery."

"Poor lamb. I hope a nice rest and some time away will help her put the memory of that awful night at the lily pond behind her." Betty shuddered. "Although," she said, considering, "I'd have thought she would have gone home to Ireland to see her family rather than Dorset. If *I* got leave, I'd go home straightaway. I miss Mum and Dad and everything so much."

"Everything or every*one*?" Etta teased. "Doesn't your Albert live close by?"

Unable to hold it in any longer, Betty had confided to Etta how Albert had asked her to be his girl and how proud she was to call herself that. She had never been anyone's girl before except her Dad's, and she liked the feeling.

Betty blushed. "Albert's in Ludlow, ten miles from us." *Just a short bus ride away.* "Ireland is so much farther," she acknowledged. "I expect it's a long journey to Ballydavid."

"Maeve said between the train and the ferry it would have taken her well over a day to get home," Etta recounted, "and then the same again on the return. With only a few days leave, that wouldn't be very restful."

"And she needs her rest." Concern creased Betty's forehead. "I've been worried about Maeve. She's usually so strong and capable. Remember how good she was with those bomb-happy lads?"

Etta remembered it well. That was when she'd realized she didn't possess her bunkmate's maternal instinct. Maeve had become an instant mum to the shell-shocked lads, soothing them and rocking them like babies, even singing them a lullaby, for God's sake.

"Maeve took me under her wing when I first got here and showed me the ropes," Betty said. "I was nervous being away from home, wondering whether I was up to the job, but she gave me confidence. I'm praying this rest at her friend's will bring her confidence back."

"I have no doubt. Maeve just needed a break, to get away from everything for a bit. She'll be right as rain when she returns." Etta smiled to herself, having sussed out that the *friend* Maeve was visiting was, in fact, the handsome Doctor Moore.

"Good for you, Maeve," Etta said when she made the connection. Louise had told her Doctor Moore had taken a couple days leave to tend to a sick uncle in Devon. Etta then informed Louise that Maeve had left camp a day earlier to stay with her Dublin *friend* Fiona, who'd married an Englishman and moved to Dorset. She smirked. "I think my Irish pal Maeve has a touch of the blarney in her."

"I think you're right. I also think this is just what Maeve needs. What they *both* need." Louise liked and respected Graham Moore. He was a good doctor and a good man—not arrogant or condescending like so many of the doctors. The nurse had seen the sadness in Graham's eyes, the haunted look he often wore. Since Maeve, though, that haunted look had disappeared, and the doctor's eyes had come alive again.

"May the road rise up to meet them, and may the wind be always at their back."

Maeve arrived before Graham in Woolton-on-the-Water. He had only been able to secure two days leave and since she had got four days off, they'd agreed she would precede him. That way, Maeve could have a day in the village on her own before Graham arrived and another day of solitude after he left. Their different departure and arrival days would also prevent rumors from flying.

Fingers crossed.

Am I going to regret this, she wondered? I've only ever been with Seamus before, and we were in love and engaged to be married. I was going to spend the rest of my days with him.

Graham and I have never even spoken of love. There's a strong attraction between us that I can't deny it. But is it love? Or is the reason I asked him to turn this into a romantic getaway a reaction to Thelma's death and all the horrors we see every day? A need to escape from all the awfulness for a bit. To forget everything and just surrender to the passion I feel whenever I look at Graham?

Would that be so wrong?

Maeve boarded the train at Cirencester, clad in her dress blues, case in hand. Being in a skirt rather than the daily battledress trousers she wore on the planes was a welcome change. She found an empty railway carriage and placed her case on the seat beside her as she settled in for the train ride. Expelling a weary breath, she banished all thoughts of Thelma, Sally, Agnes, and the camp from her head.

Following doctor's orders to fill her mind with pictures of lovely things and lovely places, Maeve gazed out the window, drinking in the pastoral scenery. Rolling green hills dotted with sheep penned in by centuries-old stone walls and golden fields of rapeseed as far as the eye could see lifted her spirits. The train passed by villages, churches, and farms with cows in the pasture and land girls plowing the fields. She waved at the land girls, and as the train moved on, her mind filled with new images.

Images of Graham.

His eyes. His smile. His lips. His arms around her. His tenderness, gentleness, and the way he looked at her... Graham had told her to rest and relax before he came, but she had decided she wanted to surprise him by making Mam's Guinness stew tomorrow—*if* she could get the necessary foodstuffs.

Maeve scribbled a list: potatoes, carrots, onions, flour, beef, and Guinness. She knew the chances of finding beef were next to none, but she had to at least try. Graham's friend George had told him he would find staples in the cottage kitchen, and she hoped those included salt and pepper.

The train arrived in the large market town of Moreton-in-Marsh, where Maeve would catch the bus into the nearby village of Woolton-on-the-Water. The bus wasn't due for another hour, though, so she decided to use the time to go shopping. Spotting a green grocer's, Maeve went inside. Using her emergency ration card, she bought spuds and carrots.

"Are there any onions?" she asked.

The grocer snorted. "Onions are as scarce as hen's teeth, love. I've got some nice leeks, though."

Maeve bought the leeks and another potato, thinking she'd make potato leek soup for their second day. Walking through town, she enjoyed looking in the shop windows. It was almost like being in Dublin again, although on a much smaller scale. She sucked in her breath as she stared at the dress shop window in front of her. A pale pink bed jacket with a delicate lace collar shimmered in the morning sun.

Maeve had never had a bed jacket before, but she had always yearned for the ones she'd seen in magazine adverts. Packing her case that morning, she'd given a rueful glance at her shabby dressing gown, wishing she had something new and nicer to wear for Graham.

The bed jacket in the window beckoned.

She reckoned the price would be too dear but had to find out. Having only used her clothing allotment for shoes and her fur-lined flying boots up to now, she still had plenty of clothes coupons left. Maeve pushed open the door of the dress shop, jangling the bell at the top.

The whir of a sewing machine stopped. Moments later, a trim, middle-aged woman in a navy dress with a pale pink collar stepped through a curtained doorway. "Good morning, Miss," she said politely. "How may I help you?"

"I'd like to see that bed jacket in the window if I may."

The shopkeeper smiled. "You're lucky. I've just put that out. I knew it would catch someone's eye." Removing it from the window, she brought over the piece of lingerie. "I haven't made any bed jackets in some time—it's impossible to find satin and silk these days." She wrinkled her nose.

"Everything is so dreary and utilitarian now—so much brown, gray, and drab green. A woman needs a bit of colour and frilliness now and then to keep her spirits up."

The shopkeeper held the bed jacket up against the woman in the RAF uniform. "That pink is lovely with your complexion, my dear. Why don't you try it on and see how it fits?"

Maeve set down her suitcase and bag of veg and removed her blue uniform jacket. When she tried on the pink dressing jacket, her hands lingered on the lightweight fabric.

"I salvaged the rayon from my mum's bedroom curtains after she died." The shopkeeper fingered the pink collar of her dress, "Kept a bit in remembrance." She led Maeve over to a cheval mirror in the corner. "It's as though it was made for you."

Looking in the mirror, Maeve imagined Graham's eyes when he saw her in the pale pink lingerie. Imagined him removing it...

Her cheeks warmed. "It's lovely," she breathed. "You're right. It *was* made for me." When she glimpsed the price, though, she gulped. Buying it would eat up most of her month's wages.

Maeve looked in the mirror again and decided. *If I'm going to do this, I might as well go for broke, as the Yanks say.* She'd still have enough money left to buy the remaining provisions she needed, and when she got back to camp, she'd be eating in the Mess. She would just have to forego tea and cake in the canteen for a bit.

Maeve got off the bus in Woolton-on-the-Water, case and parcels in hand. Checking Graham's directions, she crossed a small stone bridge over the River Windrush that ran through the center of the village. She noticed a couple old-timers sitting on a nearby bench chatting as they ate fish and chips.

The aroma of fried fish wafted to her nose, reminding her she hadn't eaten since early morning porridge. First things first, though. Passing by shops and a cluster of stone cottages opposite the village green she carried on down a narrow side street, past a row of honey-coloured cottages made of

Cotswold stone. Turning right at the end of the street, she passed a pub and a garage where a mechanic was tinkering with a Morris Saloon.

The mechanic smiled at the woman in uniform. "All right then, love?"

Maeve waved, not wanting to stop and talk. Turning left, she passed more cottages, and a large brick manor house set back from the street. The stately manor house was fronted by a gravel drive and a manicured lawn and rose garden that would be gorgeous in a couple months with the roses in bloom. Horses grazed in a paddock beside the grounds.

Continuing on, Maeve made a final turn and found herself on a quiet country lane. At the end of the lane, tucked behind a copse of blooming magnolias, she arrived at her destination: Ivy Cottage.

A riot of colour greeted her beyond the metal front gate. Lilacs and forsythia mixed with a profusion of daffodils, irises, tulips, and crocuses in the unruly cottage garden. She basked in the beauty. Maeve had always preferred the wildness of an unstructured cottage garden over more formal, manicured gardens.

She pulled out the key Graham had got from his friend and inserted it into the blue door of the ivy-covered cottage. Once inside, she made straight for the kitchen with her bag of veg. Maeve set the potatoes on the counter, and placed the leeks and carrots in the larder.

She retrieved the jar of blackberry jam from her case and placed it on the counter. Betty had pressed the last of her mum's blackberry jam on Maeve before she left, insisting she take it. "Something sweet for your getaway. You just put your feet up and enjoy a nice cup of tea with jam and bread with your friend."

Seeing the jam reminded Maeve of her hunger, but first, she needed to check the kitchen staples to see what she'd need to buy from the shops. Inside a blue cupboard, she found salt, pepper, tea, Bovril, a jar of oats, and some tinned tomatoes.

Pulling out the crumpled paper carrier the greengrocer had given her, she returned to the village center to stock up. At the corner shop, she bought bread, margarine, a pint of milk, a tiny bit of bacon and sugar, and the lone egg her ration book allowed. Next door at the butcher's, Maeve asked in a hopeful voice, "I don't suppose you have any beef?"

He snorted. "You're joking, right? We haven't had beef in months, love. I have a small chump end of lamb, though."

She bought the lamb and went in search of the chippie.

Returning to Ivy Cottage after polishing off her fish and chips, Maeve put the perishables away and took her case upstairs to unpack. When she saw the bed—a proper double bed with a lovely counterpane and two fluffy pillows, rather than the hard military bunk she was used to—she dropped her case and jumped on the mattress, letting out a shout of joy. Sinking into the pillowy comfort, she promptly fell asleep.

Three hours later, Maeve woke up, not knowing where she was. The sprigged rose wallpaper and large walnut wardrobe were unfamiliar. Then she spied her case on the floor and remembered. She was on *leave*.

Swinging her legs over the side of the bed, Maeve stood up and stretched. Divesting herself of her uniform, she hung her blues in the wardrobe and unpacked her case. Pulling on her old dressing gown she sat on the edge of the bed, unwrapping her new bed jacket. Her fingers stroked the lace collar. She hung the lingerie on the wardrobe door to admire it, a slow smile stealing over her face, imagining Graham's reaction when he saw her in it.

How much longer until he gets here? Maeve glanced at the clock on the bedside table. Eighteen more hours. She decided to explore the cottage. She'd been too busy when she arrived sorting out the food and going to the shops and then falling asleep, she hadn't paid much attention to her surroundings.

The bedroom was neat and tidy and smelled of beeswax polish. Graham's friend George had arranged for a local cleaner to tidy and air out the cottage beforehand since nobody had been there in well over a month. A gas fire hugged the opposite wall, and next to the bedside table, a cozy chair covered in faded chintz snugged beneath the window, the requisite blackout curtains pulled open in the light of day.

Moving to the window, Maeve took in the view of the surrounding countryside.

A flicker of movement below caught her eye. She watched as a calico cat in the garden gave chase to a rabbit. *Run, Rabbit, Run.* Maeve smiled, thinking of the title of Churchill's favourite song. Rumor was the prime minister sang snatches of the popular tune using the new war lyrics "Run, Adolph, Run."

Exiting the bedroom, she moved down the hall. Maeve opened a closed door and squealed with delight. "A tub!" It had been ages since she had had a bath. A situation she planned to remedy soon. A door beside the bath revealed a tiny water closet that looked to be a recent addition. Recalling the draughty camp latrine and showers with lukewarm water that came out in a trickle, Maeve felt like she'd landed in the lap of luxury.

Downstairs, she explored the snug sitting room with its velvet settee and comfy chintz chair by the fireplace. Beside the fireplace stood a wooden bookcase dotted with bits and bobs amongst the books. Perusing the titles, she found classics and a handful of Ngaio Marsh and Agatha Christie mysteries. Next to *The Body in the Library* sat a pack of playing cards and the Happy Families game Briony had always loved to play.

The modest cottage didn't have a dining room, but earlier, Maeve had noticed a small table and chairs in the kitchen. Returning to the kitchen, her eyes roamed the narrow room, taking in the cooker, cupboards, larder, and a door leading outside.

Opening the door, she stepped into another world. A world bursting with colour and birdsong. As Maeve wandered through the higgledy-piggledy garden full of lilac bushes, fruit trees, and bramble roses yet to bloom, she inhaled the scent of jasmine and forsythia. Bending down to pick some forget-me-nots, a pair of green eyes startled her.

"Hello, Puss." She reached out to stroke the calico cat she'd seen from the window, but it streaked away.

Taking the forget-me-knots inside, she put them in a glass of water on the table. Then, rummaging round for a pair of secateurs, Maeve returned to the garden and cut a bunch of daffs. She placed the sunny flowers in a vase on top of the bookcase beside the radio so she could enjoy them from the settee. Then she plucked an Agatha Christie from the bookcase and settled into the settee for a long, relaxing read.

For dinner, she had a cup of Bovril and some tea and toast. Maeve spread the jam from Betty's mum on thick to disguise the taste of the dreadful National Loaf. After dinner, she drew a scalding bath and soaked in the tub for an hour. Then she curled up in bed with *Lady Chatterley's Lover*.

Etta had slipped the scandalous book into her suitcase before she left. "Something to help you relax and keep you warm," she'd said with a sly wink.

Chapter Thirty

Maeve slept in the next morning, having stayed up late reading. Her dreams had been full of the lusty gardener Oliver Mellors. Only the gardener had been Graham. She smiled at the memory, a fluttering in her midsection. Her eyes drifted to the forget-me-nots she'd placed on the bedside table.

That's when she saw the clock.

Eight-twenty-seven. Graham's bus would be here in half an hour!

Maeve jumped out of bed and sprinted to the bathroom, where she cleaned her teeth and washed her face. Returning to the bedroom, she quickly made the bed and fluffed the pillows. Pulling on her ivory blouse and black skirt, she fastened a small cluster of forget-me-nots to her bodice for a touch of colour.

As she arranged her hair in front of the mirror, Maeve regretted not bringing along Sally's tube of red lipstick. *And what reason would you have given Betty for asking to borrow the lipstick when you're off on a restful leave to your friend "Fiona's" house,* she asked herself. Her hand moved up to pinch her cheeks, but when she looked in the mirror, she realized there was no need.

Maeve hurried from the cottage to meet Graham, humming "Moonlight Serenade" as she walked beneath a blue sky studded with candy floss clouds. She arrived at the bus stop in front of the village green just as the nine o'clock bus pulled up. Smoothing down her skirt, she scanned the departing passengers, her eyes alight with anticipation. Two women got off, followed by an elderly man. Finally, she spotted a blue RAF uniform.

Graham stepped off the bus, carrying a case and a paper bag. A young woman passing by gave him an admiring glance, but Graham only had eyes for Maeve. His face lit up like candles on a birthday cake when he saw her. "Maeve."

"Graham. You're here."

He closed the distance between them and kissed her on the cheek. "You look beautiful. I'm dying to kiss you properly," he murmured, "but we have an audience."

Maeve noticed a trio of middle-aged women peeking their way and whispering and the butcher standing in his shop doorway regarding them. "Let's get out of here." She linked her arm in Graham's as they made their way to the stone bridge over the river. "Lovely to see you," she remarked in a normal voice for the benefit of the village gawkers. "Did you have a good journey?"

They chatted as they strolled across the bridge, with Maeve nodding to the butcher as they passed. Making the circuitous route to the cottage, they ambled by the cluster of cottages and the manor house, where Graham stopped to admire the horses in the paddock.

As they carried on in the direction of the pub, something in his paper bag clinked.

"What have you got in there?"

"It's a surprise."

At last, they turned down the country lane. As the copse of trees came into view, Maeve's breath quickened. The blue cottage door had scarce shut behind them before the couple was in each other's arms.

When they came up for air, Graham asked, "What would you like to do first?"

Maeve lifted an eyebrow.

"I meant, would you like to go for a walk or a bicycle ride? Explore the area, perhaps?"

She decided to be bold. "All I want is to be with you."

"And I with you." Graham's eyes darkened with desire. "More than anything."

"I'm going upstairs," she said. "Give me a couple minutes."

"I've some things to put away in the kitchen. Then I'll be up."

In the bedroom, Maeve undressed and donned her new lingerie. Slipping beneath the covers, she propped a pillow behind her as she sat in bed waiting for Graham. Adjusting the lacy collar and arranging the bed jacket just so her heart raced when she heard footsteps on the stairs.

Good thing you've left the church, my girl, as you're about to commit a mortal sin. Again.

Graham entered the room, minus his uniform jacket and hat, his tie loosened and case in hand. He stopped in the doorway. "You're so beautiful." His voice was husky. Setting down his case, he crossed to the bed.

Maeve snuggled against Graham, her dark head on his bare chest. "I've never made love in the morning before. I feel quite scandalous."

He kissed the top of her head. "Get used to it." His arms tightened around her. "There will be many more mornings like this if I have anything to say about it." Bending his head, he captured her mouth with his again.

Later, as they nestled together, flushed and content, Maeve's stomach growled.

Glancing around the room, Graham leaned over the side of the bed and peered beneath it. "Is there a lion in here?"

"A very hungry lion. I didn't have any breakfast."

"Well, we can't have that." Swinging his legs over the side of the bed, Graham strode to his suitcase. And Maeve admired the view.

Graham plopped his case on the bed, opened it, and removed a navy dressing gown. Pulling on the dressing gown, he belted it at the waist. "Would you like egg, tea, and toast, or just tea and toast?"

"There's only one egg."

"There *was* only one egg. Now, there are two. I got groceries in Moreton-in-Marsh."

"So did I."

"Great minds think alike. Now, would Madam like an egg?"

"Let's save the eggs. I'll make us a proper breakfast tomorrow."

"As you wish." He gave a slight bow. "You stay there, and I'll bring you a tray."

"You're spoiling me." No one had ever spoiled Maeve before. Not even Seamus.

"And rightly so."

"Graham?"

He turned, giving her a quizzical look.

"There's some lovely jam in the cupboard."

Maeve snuggled under the covers, reliving the past few hours. She had thought she'd be shy since the only man she'd ever been with had been Seamus, but she and Graham had joined together so naturally, she didn't feel the least bit shy. The handsome doctor had reawakened feelings in Maeve she'd long thought dead.

Graham held Maeve in his arms, stroking her hair. "I didn't think I could ever feel this way again. After Susan and Teddy died, I wanted to die right along with them. I didn't, though. I stayed alive, going through the motions of living, anaesthetizing myself with my work. All the time, though, I was dead inside. A dried-up husk of the man I used to be." He laced his fingers with hers. "Then I met you, and you brought me back to life."

"You did the same for me."

"Aren't we the lucky ones?" Graham squeezed her hand and gazed at Maeve with such tenderness it made her weep.

They held each other tight and wept together.

The couple took a long walk, hand-in-hand, down the country lane, chatting and talking about the future, wondering what life would be like after the war.

"I don't suppose they need a doctor in Ballydavid, do they?" Graham teased.

"Not at the moment," Maeve replied in as steady a voice as she could muster. "Old Doctor Byrne has been there forever. He says the only way he'll leave Ballydavid will be in a pine box."

"Well, I wouldn't want to wish death on anyone." Graham gave her a sideways look. "I imagine you'll return to Ireland after the war?"

"I suppose. I've missed my family. Although," She made a face, "I don't much fancy working in the pub again."

"Have you thought of staying in nursing?"

"Maybe, but I don't want to go on to nursing school like Etta, and I *definitely* don't want to become a surgical nurse. I've seen enough open bleeding chests, stomachs, and the like to last a lifetime." Maeve shuddered. "Not to mention the burned flesh. I've never been squeamish, but I couldn't do what the burn nurses do, having to remove the skin and cause such agonizing pain. I prefer listening to the lads, reassuring them, comforting them, and the like."

She peered off in the distance, her eyes haunted. "I've seen things I hope to never see again."

Graham squeezed her hand. "No more talk of work now. This is meant to be a time of rest. Some much-needed R and R for you."

"Too right." Maeve's eyes gleamed. "And we're going to continue that R and R right now." She tugged at his hand. "Come with me."

"Where are we going?"

"You'll see." She steered him back toward the village. As they drew near to Maeve's intended destination, she made Graham close his eyes.

"Then I can't see where I'm going."

"Don't worry, I'll guide you. Now close your eyes, Doctor," she ordered.

"Yes, ma'am."

Maeve led him down a side street off the village green and stopped. "You can open your eyes now."

Graham inhaled the scent as he gazed at the chippie in front of him. "Fish and chips!" He salivated. "I don't remember the last time I had fish and chips." Whirling Maeve around, he planted a resounding kiss on her lips.

"If I'd known that's all it took to warrant a kiss from a dashing man, I'd have done that years ago," said a gray-permed woman standing outside the shop.

Her silver-haired pal gave her a sly wink. "You can always bring Harold to the chippie."

"I said dashing. Harold's not been dashing a day in his life. He looks nothing like this Clark Gable here; my Harold's more like Mickey Rooney."

Cackling, the women walked away.

When Graham and Maeve finished their fish and chips, which he pronounced delicious, though not *quite* as good as the fish on the coast, Graham put his arm around Maeve's waist, and they made their way back toward the cottage. Halfway there, it started to rain, and within moments, it was bucketing down.

Graham grabbed Maeve's hand, and they ran the rest of the way.

Inside Ivy Cottage, they exchanged sodden clothes for pyjamas and jumpers. Graham built a fire, and Maeve made them cups of tea. Snuggling together on the settee, she released a contented sigh. "I love a cuppa in front of a cozy fire."

"Nothing better." Threading his hand through her hair, Graham stroked the back of her head.

Maeve nestled against his chest. "Tell me about your parents. What were they like?"

"My mum was lovely. Kind and gentle. Beautiful like you—the same dark hair. Mum was loads of fun. She would get down on the floor and play with me when I was little. She always read Beatrix Potter stories to me at bedtime." His mouth curved up in remembrance.

"And your dad?"

"He was the farthest thing from fun there could be. Father was always working or in his study where I was never to disturb him."

"What kind of work did he do?"

"He was a solicitor, like his father before him. He wanted me to become a solicitor too and join the family firm, but I had no intention of following in my father's footsteps."

"I can't imagine you as a solicitor. You're such a brilliant doctor."

Graham kissed her on the cheek. "But enough about me, I want to focus on *us*. Shall we go out to dinner tonight and perhaps dancing after?"

"No, I'm cooking," Maeve said. "I've got it all planned, and we can dance here. I'd rather not be around other people. We'll be surrounded by loads of people soon enough. For now, I want you all to myself."

"You won't get any argument from me." He kissed her. "So, what's on the menu?"

"Guinness stew, but with lamb since there's no beef to be had." Maeve's hand flew to her mouth. "Oh no! I forgot the Guinness. I meant to get it from the pub down the road."

"Never fear." Graham went to the kitchen and returned with four bottles of Guinness.

All too soon, their romantic idyll was over. When it was time for Graham to leave, he asked her not to walk him to the bus stop—he'd rather say their goodbyes in private. Taking Maeve in his arms, he gave her a long, lingering kiss. "I don't want to go."

"I don't want you to go either." Maeve hugged Graham tight, her heart full in a way it hadn't been since Seamus.

Chapter Thirty-One

Clementine Brown lay on her bunk, trying and failing, to read Virginia Woolf's *To the Lighthouse*. Try as she would, though, she couldn't concentrate. The MPs had been nosing round, asking questions about the night Thelma died.

"Did you see anything out of the ordinary? Did Nursing Orderly Jenkins mention if she'd been having trouble with anyone? Do you know if she'd been seeing anyone?"

It was obvious the authorities thought someone had killed Thelma.

Clemmie had been thinking the same thing ever since her hutmate's body had been found in the lily pond. Her suspicions were confirmed when Matron recommended to the nursing staff they pair up when they went out at night, "just to be on the safe side."

What Clemmie didn't understand was why such a recommendation hadn't been made after Sally Roberts had died, or why the MPs hadn't investigated her death as well. She hadn't known the popular nursing orderly well, but the two deaths were similar, both women dying outside and alone.

Her eyes slid to the other end of the hut, where Etta was engrossed in the blue nursing textbook she read religiously. Closing her novel, Clemmie approached the redheaded Nightingale. "Sorry to disturb, Etta. Could I speak to you? It's about Thelma and Sally."

Etta snapped her book shut, giving Clemmie her full attention. "What about them?"

"It's obvious the powers that be think someone killed Thelma. What I want to know is why didn't they respond the same way when Sally Roberts died? If they had, perhaps Thelma's death might have been prevented." Clemmie's voice shook. "It appears someone is killing Nightingales. Who knows which one of us might be next?" She sank down, shaking, on Maeve's bunk.

Etta sat down beside her. "I don't think you need to worry about that. Sally's death and Thelma's death were completely different. I agree there's a possibility someone may have killed Thelma—that's why the MPs are investigating. Supposedly, discreetly." She rolled her eyes. "Although I don't think they know the meaning of discreet. If someone did kill Thelma, though, I'd imagine it was for a more personal reason, not because she was a Nightingale."

"And what about Sally?"

Etta took a deep breath. She glanced around the hut to make sure they were alone. "What I'm about to tell you is just between us. It must never leave this room. Do you understand?"

Clemmie nodded, wide-eyed.

"Sally committed suicide," Etta said in a voice tinged with regret. "Only a handful of people know that, though, and we need to keep it that way. Betty, especially, must never know. It would devastate her. She adored Sally, and it would break her heart." Etta pinned her eyes on her fellow nursing orderly. "Do I have your word you'll never repeat this to anyone?"

Clemmie shook Etta's hand. "On my honour as a Nightingale."

Later that day, Etta sought out Louise. "Have you or Matron heard anything from the MPs yet about their investigation into Thelma's death?" she asked.

"Only that they haven't found anyone who saw her or was with her that night. No one noticed anyone lurking around the lily pond. The MPs questioned Agatha, but she's in the clear because the night Thelma was killed, she was pulling a late shift. Her presence was vouched for by another nurse working the ward with her."

"We'd already worked out Agatha didn't kill Thelma." Etta scowled. "The MPs remind me of the bumbling police detectives in the Miss Marple stories."

221

"Just so long as you don't go trying to play Miss Marple. Unless you've given up your nursing aspirations in favor of becoming a detective?" Louise teased.

"Miss Marple's an amateur sleuth, not a detective, but point taken. I'll leave the detecting to the police. It's not like I don't have enough to keep me occupied."

Maeve returned to camp rested, refreshed, and ready to take on the world. Pushing open the door of her hut, she announced, "I'm back, girls. Did you miss me?"

The sound of weeping greeted her.

Maeve's eyes flew to the end of the hut where Etta was holding a blubbering Betty. The Irish Nightingale flew to her friends' side, her pulse ratcheting up. Maeve knelt beside her young friend, who was sobbing as though her heart was breaking. "What's happened, sweetheart? Are your mum and dad all right?"

Betty nodded, gulping back sobs.

"And Albert?"

She nodded again, unable to speak.

Maeve turned horrified eyes on Etta. "Don't tell me we lost another Nightingale."

"No." Etta's voice was grim. "It's Bergen Belsen."

"Bergen Belsen?" Maeve was at a loss.

"The Nazi concentration camp. Monty liberated it a few days ago, and Betty was on a flight evacuating some of the survivors to Switzerland."

Betty lifted her head and stared at Maeve through swollen eyes. Eyes stricken with horror. "Oh, Maeve, it was horrible. Those poor little lambs. I've never seen anything like it. They looked like skeletons." She sobbed anew. "How can people be so evil? Do such terrible things to other people? To *children*?"

Etta said in a bleak voice, "The BBC broadcast the liberation and what the Army found when they arrived. Thousands upon thousands of dead bodies everywhere they turned. Mass graves. Corpses stacked like firewood.

Walking skeletons suffering from typhus, dysentery, and starvation."

Maeve rocked back onto her heels. She stared at the girls, feeling sick. "I hadn't heard." She clasped Betty's hands in hers. "I'm so sorry, sweetheart. I can't even imagine how awful that must have been."

"Harry and I got sick to our stomachs," Betty said in a shaky voice. "Luckily, we were at the back of the plane away from the children." She stared at Maeve. "Although I don't think they'd have even noticed. Their eyes were so empty it was like being on a plane with ghosts."

"Skeleton ghosts." Doreen joined them. She had been on another of the flights ferrying children from Bergen to Switzerland, where the Swiss had offered to take the orphans into their homes. "I'll never forget the sight as long as I live." She swiped at her eyes. "I'd like to try though. Can we talk about something else, girls? Please. Anything to get those images out of our minds. I don't want nightmares tonight." She turned to Maeve. "Tell us about your leave. Did you have a lovely time?"

"Yes, it was just what the doctor ordered."

Etta smirked at Maeve behind Betty's back, but Doreen didn't notice.

Trust Etta to figure it out, Maeve thought. *I guess we weren't as discreet as we thought.*

"Did you go swimming?"

"It was too cold for that."

"What did you and your friend do?" Betty asked. "Her name's Fiona, right?"

Maeve felt guilty deceiving Betty. "We just took walks and talked. I read a bit and took long naps. It was very relaxing—just what I needed." Her mouth crooked. "Your mum's jam went down a storm."

"I'm glad." Betty released a wan smile.

Maeve tilted her head, a smile playing at her lips. "Do you know what was the best thing of all?"

Etta gave her a lazy smile. "Do tell."

"I had a long, lovely soak in a hot bath. *Two* baths, in fact. It was heaven."

"Lucky duck." Betty expelled a sigh of envy. "I'd kill for a hot bath."

"I'd sell my soul," Etta said.

"I wouldn't go quite that far, but I *would* give a month's wages for a nice long soak in a scalding hot tub." Doreen lifted her shoulders in a shrug. "But since there are no tubs to hand, I'll settle for a beer. Anyone want to join me at the canteen?"

"I will," Betty said. "After today, I need it. Maeve, will you come too? You can tell us more about your trip." She turned to Etta. "I'll buy you a beer for letting me cry on your shoulder."

"I'll never turn down free beer."

Maeve gave Betty a look of regret. "I need to unpack my case before my clothes are wrinkled beyond belief. I don't fancy ironing at the moment. Perhaps I'll join you later."

Betty smiled at her. "I'm so glad you're back, Maeve. I missed you. We all did."

"We did at that, Irish," Etta said. "Good to have you back."

The girls departed for the canteen.

Alone in the hut, Maeve placed her case on her bunk and opened it. She pulled out the pink bed jacket and hugged it to herself, thinking of Graham. Closing her eyes, she remembered how he'd eased the lingerie off her shoulders and…

A long, slow whistle from the doorway interrupted her romantic reverie.

Dropping the jacket as if scalded, Maeve whirled around to see Etta approaching at a languorous pace.

"Well, isn't that pretty? I don't go for pink myself, but it suits you." Etta picked up her hat and clapped it on her head. "I forgot this." She sauntered out again, whistling "Our Love Affair."

So much for keeping our romantic getaway secret. Maeve was relieved it had been Etta who'd seen her new lingerie rather than any of the other girls, though. She knew her pal would tease her in private, but Etta would also keep her mouth shut. Folding the bed jacket, she tucked it out of sight in the bottom of her footlocker. She regretted not being able to join the girls at the canteen, but after her extravagant purchase, her purse was empty until payday.

Instead, she sat and wrote a letter to her sister.

Dear Briony,

How are you love? I hope all is well. Please don't say anything to Mum and Dad, but I have a lovely secret I wanted to share with you and you alone, sweetheart. I never thought I'd say this again, but I've met someone....

Betty couldn't get the children from Bergen-Belsen out of her mind. Her heart. She knew Doreen didn't want to think about it or talk about it, but she couldn't *stop* thinking about it. She kept seeing the children's haunted, desolate eyes and skeletal bodies. She had to talk to someone about what she'd seen, or she'd go mad.

Dear Albert,

I received your last letter and enjoyed reading about the latest calving on your farm. There's nothing like watching new life being born is there? I miss that. Many's the time I helped Dad deliver a calf or watched a litter of piglets being born. Once they were old enough, I loved giving them a cuddle. Pigs love a good cuddle.

Recently I got to cuddle some children, but I had to do so very carefully as they were so thin and fragile, I was afraid their bones might break. The poor lambs were orphans from a concentration camp in Germany. You've likely seen the newsreels where Monty liberated Bergen-Belsen and the terrible things he and our lads encountered there. It doesn't bear thinking about.

We have *to think about it, though. We have to talk about it to prevent such evil from ever happening again.*

I saw the aftereffects of this evil firsthand when we loaded up flights of starving little ones who'd been orphaned at the camp to take them to new homes in Switzerland. The poor children lost their mothers and fathers to disease, starvation, and so much worse. The terrible things they've been through are beyond imagining. When I first saw them, I had to bite my lip to keep from bursting into tears.

I wanted to scoop up all the kiddies and bring them to Cherry Tree

225

Farm, where they'd have lots of room to run and play and plenty of food to eat. Mum and I would feed them proper and put some meat on their bones. They were like skeletons.

As much as we wanted to feed them, though, we were under strict instructions not to give them food because they were too weak to digest it—food could kill them. That's what happened to some of the prisoners when our soldiers first entered the camp. The lads were so desperate to relieve the starving, and suffering, they gave the prisoners their Army rations. Heartbreakingly, it proved fatal; their poor stomachs simply couldn't digest the food.

We could give the children a bit of broth and tea, but that was all. They needed to build up their strength slowly and get their stomachs used to being fed again, so the doctors said no chocolate or other solid foods.

It was the hardest thing I've ever done, especially when I had some chocolate in my pocket. All the children had had their heads shaved, even the girls, to delouse them, and they'd been given "new" clothes to replace the rags they'd been wearing, one of the nurses told me. The clothes simply hung on their frail bodies.

There was one little girl who clung to me and didn't want to let me go when we landed in Switzerland. I didn't want to let her go, either. For a brief moment, I had a mad thought to hide her on the plane and bring her back to camp with me, then adopt her and raise her as my own. Of course, that was impossible. I still have a job to do and a duty to serve my country. That duty as an air ambulance nursing orderly is taking care of casualties, not being a mum to one lost little girl, but oh, how I wanted to...

Tears plopped on the paper.

Instead, I held little Greta's hand (that was her name) as we disembarked and told her she would be getting a new mummy and daddy who would love her very much and take good care of her. Greta didn't speak

English, so I doubt she understood me, but I tried to communicate to her with my eyes. And then I turned her and the other children over to the waiting Red Cross, got back on my Dakota, and cried.

It was one of the hardest things I've ever done. Absolutely broke my heart.

Yours,

Betty

Betty set down her pen, feeling better after writing to Albert and unburdening herself to him. Lighter, somehow. After posting her letter, she returned to work, ready to face the challenges of a new day.

Chapter Thirty-Two

Late April 1945

The war was almost over. Patton's Army was advancing in the west and the Russians were approaching Germany from the east. After the liberation of Bergen Belsen and the Germans' surrender of the concentration camp, the advancing Allies then liberated prison camps—stalags, as the Germans called them.

The prison camps that stretched across Germany, Austria, Poland, and Italy held British, French, Russian, Polish, and American prisoners. Allied troops began liberating camps and repatriating hundreds of prisoners, bringing British soldiers back home to English soil at last.

Maeve moved among the POWs on her plane, dispensing tea, kind words, and a gentle touch. "Would you like some tea, soldier?" she asked a haunted-looking lad with sunken cheeks.

"Ta. It's nice to have proper English tea again after four years."

Four *years*? Maeve squeezed his shoulder and moved on to the next man. She'd fast learned that most of the prisoners didn't want to talk about their time in the stalags, especially to a woman, so she didn't press them. She recognized that although these men didn't bear the external injuries she was accustomed to seeing on her evacuation flights, it was clear they had internal wounds.

After returning to camp, she headed to the communal hut for a cuppa. Inside, Maeve found Harry and Dickie comparing notes about the POWs they'd chatted to on their respective flights.

Harry slammed his beer down on the table. "What about the bloody Geneva Convention? That's supposed to make sure prisoners are taken care of properly, given enough food and decent living conditions. Not starved, having the Jerries steal their Red Cross parcels, and living in filthy, overcrowded barracks teeming with lice and rats. Those camp commandants need to be strung up for how they treated our lads."

"Not all the camps were like that," Dickie said. "The lads on my flight said they respected their camp commander and how he treated them. He followed the Geneva rules. They said the worst thing about being prisoners— besides being incarcerated—was the boredom." He shook his head. "I can't imagine being stuck in the same place, penned in for years with nothing to do. Every day, the same, day in and day out. Never able to leave. I'd go bloomin' crazy."

"Some of them did," Harry said grimly.

And if not crazy, then depressed, Maeve thought. She saw again the empty eyes and dispirited demeanor of some of the POWs on her flight and hoped they would get the help they needed. Pouring herself a cuppa, she joined Betty and Doreen, feeling the need for some friendly conversation. "Hello girls, what are you talking about?"

"The new Sherlock Holmes film." Betty turned animated eyes on her. "Will took Doreen to see it."

"Will's a big Sherlock Holmes fan," Doreen said. "I'll bet he's read every one of the Arthur Conan Doyle stories."

"I've not read the stories, but I like the films with Basil Rathbone," Betty said. "*The Hound of the Baskervilles* gave me a real fright." Her eyes sparkled with cinematic fervor. "Did you see it, Maeve?"

"I missed that one." She delivered a grin to her young friend. "I hope your Albert likes films as much as you do. Otherwise, he'll find himself left out in the cold."

Betty stared at Maeve wide-eyed. "I would never leave Albert in the cold."

"I know you wouldn't, sweetie. I'm just teasing you. How is Albert these days?"

"I just got a letter from him, but I haven't had a chance to read it yet."
Doreen had waylaid her, wanting to chat about Will. Betty stood up. "Would
you excuse me, girls? I'm fair itching to read my letter."

"Go on then." Doreen smiled. "But I want to hear all about it later."

"Me too." Maeve gave Betty an affectionate push toward the door. "Now
get out of here."

"Someone is smitten," Doreen said, watching the young Nightingale
depart.

"I wonder how long before we hear wedding bells."

"I was wondering the same about you." Doreen smirked. "Anyone with
eyes can see that Doctor Moore is besotted and vice-versa. Will saw it
straightaway and knew he didn't stand a chance with you. That's when he
finally looked *my* way."

Maeve felt a flush creep up her neck. "I-uh," she stammered.

Doreen flapped her hand. "No need to say anything. I know you have
that no-fraternization rule hanging over you and have to be discreet. You
won't have to put up with that much longer, though. Meanwhile, I'm happily
enjoying your cast-off." She grinned and took her leave.

As Maeve started to follow Doreen, she noticed Margaret Walsh in
the corner; head bent over her beloved Romany fortune-telling cards.
Knowing how it pleased the quiet nursing orderly to read the girls' cards,
she approached with a smile.

"Hello Margaret, would you be up for telling me my fortune?"

Strolling back to her hut, Maeve wondered what Graham was doing. She
hadn't seen him in a few days and missed him. She thought about himm all
the time now, reliving their romantic idyll, remembering his lips on hers,
the feel of his skin against hers, and wondering when they could get away
to be alone again.

Not anytime soon, my girl. You were lucky to get leave when you did.

She wondered where Sally and Lieutenant Blake had conducted their
clandestine affair. There had to be somewhere in camp a couple could
steal away to be together. But where? Then Maeve remembered how she'd

stumbled upon Sally and the pilot behind the women's shower hut ages ago. She shook her head. *That's not for me. I'll not be making love to the man I love where anyone could happen upon us.*

Maeve stopped walking. Did I really just say that Graham is the man I love?

Aye, ye did. There's no denying it, my girl. You're in love.

Stop right there, Maeve Fitzgerald, her rational side told her. *Wartime is no time to fall in love.*

Still…the warmth unfurled in her stomach, blossomed to her chest and up her neck, exploding in a smile as bright as the Dublin fireworks on New Year's Eve. She decided it was time to stroll over to the hospital huts to pay a visit to the good doctor. When Maeve arrived, though, Graham was deep in conversation with another doctor and nurse. She turned and began making her way back to her hut.

"Maeve!" Graham hurried over to her. "You are a sight for sore eyes." He kept his voice low, giving her a hungry gaze. "The most beautiful sight these eyes have seen. We're discussing a difficult case, though, so I can't stay." Removing a folded piece of paper from his pocket, he pressed it into her hand. "For now, this will have to suffice."

Betty knelt and brushed a bit of dirt from Sally's headstone, placing the daffodils she'd picked beside her friend's name. Her fingers traced the letters S-A-L-L-Y. Then she bowed her head and prayed.

"How's everything in heaven, Sally? You've got a birds-eye view of all that's happening down here so you can see the war's in the final stages now, thanks be to God. I don't mind telling you, I'm fair ready to go home. I wouldn't say this to the other girls, but between you and me, I've had enough. Enough of the fighting, the death and destruction, the horrible injuries to our lads, and the pure evil that's been unleashed on our world."

"Such evil as I've never known before."

Tears fell from Betty's eyes. "I can't bear it. I shall never forget the sight of those poor lambs from Bergen-Belsen and learning of the horrors they endured. The unspeakable things the Germans did to all those people

231

in the concentration camp and to the thousands upon thousands who didn't survive those horrors." She wept. "Every one of those thousands was someone's child. Someone's mother, father, sister, brother, friend...." Her voice trailed off.

She pulled her hankie from her pocket, wiped her face, and blew her nose, trying to get hold of herself. "I love the friends I've made here, Sally, especially Maeve and Etta. I'll miss them terribly when we leave, but I know we'll keep in touch, and I'll never lose their friendship. We've been through so much together."

A wave of homesickness washed over Betty. "I miss my family something fierce, though, and I'm ready to go home." She opened the letter from her mother first, wanting to save Albert's letter for last.

Dear Betty,

Every day, your dad and I wonder, is this the day our girl's coming home? Your room's just as you left it with your flowered counterpane on the bed and the yellow curtains at the window. Your bottom drawer's still full of your linens and embroidered tea towels and such for when you get married. (Which I have a feeling is going to be sooner rather than later.)

We met your young man. He came to see us.

Betty's hand flew to her chest as she gasped. "Sally, you won't believe it! Albert went to our farm and met my parents."

Good on him. She could hear Sally's approving voice in her head. Swallowing past the lump in her throat, Betty continued reading her mum's letter.

Albert said he'd heard so much about us, he felt he knew us and wanted to meet us in person. Said he wanted to see the farm where you grew up. Your Albert is a lovely lad, love. Having only one arm doesn't seem to have slowed him down at all. Why when he was here, he helped your dad feed the cows, bring in a bucket of milk, and all sorts of things. He's a big strong lad that one.

He brought us a bit of cheese and some milk from their dairy which went down a real treat. I gave him tea and some bread and jam. You should have seen the smile that came over his face when he tasted my blackberry jam. Albert said, "Betty was right. I can see now why your jam wins all the prizes." He whispered that it was better than his mum's, but said he'd never want her to know that. He'd never hurt his mother's feelings.

That's a good lad you've got there, Betty.

Tillie was making goo-goo eyes at Albert, but he didn't pay her any mind. It's clear his heart lies elsewhere. When he left, I told Tillie to stay clear if she knows what's good for her. Albert is our Betty's, I told her, so she'd best watch her step.

Love,

Mum

p.s. Your dad liked him, too. Said he couldn't have picked a better lad for his daughter.

The words blurred in front of Betty. Closing her eyes, she let the happy tears run down her face unchecked. "Oh my gosh, Sally. Oh my gosh. Can you believe this?"

Of course, I can. And now you need to read Albert's letter.

Swiping at her eyes, Betty opened the second letter with shaking hands.

Dear Betty,

I hope you don't mind, but I went to see your parents yesterday. I know that's a bit presumptuous on my part, but I really wanted to meet them. I needed to meet them. I hope you know by now how much you mean to me, Betty. You've stolen this dairy farmer's heart. I can't stop thinking about you, worrying about you, and praying for your continued health and safety.

Every day when the postman comes, I rush out, hoping for a letter from you. I'm sore disappointed when there isn't one, but I'm over the moon when there is. I've never felt this way about any girl before.

And I hope, I pray, you feel the same for me.

I won't say what I really want to say, though. Those words aren't for a letter. They need to be said in person. Once you're standing before me again and I can look into your beautiful brown eyes, I'll finally say them face-to-face.

I like your mum and dad. We got on well. They're salt of the earth, like my parents. Your mum gave me some of her jam; that was a real treat. The sweetness with just the right amount of tart fair to burst in my mouth.

I saw the picture of your brother Wilf on the mantel, and I could see he was a good lad. When I saw the picture of you in your WAAF uniform, it felt like there was a hive of bees buzzing inside my chest. After all this time, it was so good to look into your lovely brown eyes again.

Your mum also showed me a photo from when you were young. I like your hair in pigtails! Even then, you had kind brown eyes. They looked at me as if to say, "I knew you'd come someday."

The papers and the wireless say it won't be long now until our boys are back home again. I long for the day when my girl will be back home again.

Love,

Your Albert

P.S. One of the first things we'll do when you get home is go to the cinema. I know how much you love films.

Betty held Albert's letter to her chest, her heart full to bursting. "Can you believe it, Sally?"

Hang on to that red lipstick, my friend. You'll be needing it soon.

Maeve pushed open the door of her hut, hoping to find it empty. She wanted to read Graham's note in private without being interrupted. Relieved to find only Clemmie inside, her nose buried in a book, she continued on to her bunk.

Clemmie, like Etta, was always reading. Unlike Etta, though, Clemmie preferred novels to "boring medical tomes," she'd told the girls. Clemmie's aunt, an English professor at a women's college in Oxford, sent her niece a novel every month. This month's offering was *The Grapes of Wrath*.

Maeve didn't worry about her hutmate disturbing her as she read Graham's message. When Clemmie read, she disappeared into a book. Shucking off her boots and jacket, she settled into her bunk and unfolded the piece of paper from Graham.

My beautiful Irish lass,

Thank you for the most wonderful two days. You have bewitched me, Maeve Catherine Brigid Fitzgerald. I can't stop thinking about you. You consume my every waking thought. My sleeping ones, as well. You have invaded my dreams. My darling, you fill my senses in a way I never imagined they could be filled again. I don't know if you realize the effect you have on me, my green-eyed girl. I wish we were back in Ivy Cottage so I could show you how much you mean to me. You take my breath away. But more than that, you are an oasis of life-giving water in the desert that was once my heart.

Thank you, Maeve, for opening my heart back up again.

Chapter Thirty-Three

Betty closed her eyes and took a calming breath. *You can do this*, she told herself. *Scripture says we are to love our enemies. Remember, we are all children of God.* Rubbing her hands down her trouser legs, she pasted on a smile and made her way through the group of wounded German soldiers on her Dakota.

"*Willkommen.*" Delivering an apologetic smile, she added the only other German she knew. "*Nein sprechen sie Deutsch.*"

A fair-haired lad with a broken leg returned Betty's smile. "*Nein Sprechen sie English.*"

Two bandaged officers on the floor stretchers opposite stared at her with contempt. "*Dummkopf,*" muttered one. His companion, a florid-faced man whose uniform strained against his midsection, looked Betty up and down, his eyes lingering on her chest.

She flushed and lifted her urn, miming drinking. "Would you like some tea?"

The officer's fleshy lip curled, and he said something to his injured pal. They sniggered and sent Betty scornful looks.

Right, then. No tea for you. She carried on, intent on her other patients. As Betty passed the officers, the florid-faced German thrust out his leg, tripping her. She fell and dropped her urn, splashing tea on her uniform.

The two officers laughed.

Frank, the wireless operator, rushed to Betty's side, helping her up. "Are you all right?"

"I'm fine. Wet, but fine." She gave Frank a shaky smile. *Turn the other cheek.*

Turn the other cheek, Betty told herself as her knees throbbed.

Frank cursed the beefy officer and strapped his legs down on the stretcher.

Another German officer with a bandaged head directed a torrent of angry words to the offender, who thinned his lips and regarded him with cold eyes. The officer turned, shamefaced, to Betty. "Fraulein, on behalf of my countrymen, please accept my apologies. Not all Germans are barbarians."

Frank snorted.

Betty acknowledged the apologizing officer with a brief nod. *I won't be writing home about this,* she thought, *especially not to Albert.*

Louise and Etta sat together in the canteen, chatting in a corner, away from a noisy group of loadmasters and ground crew. Etta nibbled her fish-paste sandwich. "I'm trying and failing to pretend this is roast beef," she said.

"I'm pretending mine is ham, cheese, and pickle." Louise followed a bite of her sandwich with a chaser of beer. "What I wouldn't give for some of my gran's chutney."

"Is your gran still alive?"

"No. More's the pity. She died several years ago. Gran was a real corker." Louise released a fond smile. "Ahead of her time—a suffragette. She marched on Parliament with Emmeline Parkhurst." Her voice rang with pride. "Gran fought for more than twenty years for women to get the right to vote. When I was ten, she took me along on one of her marches. My father nearly had apoplexy when he found out."

"Did your mother march as well?"

Louise snorted. "Not likely. Mum is worlds apart from Gran. She hated her mother-in-law's *stridency,* as she put it. Mother was even more furious than Dad when she found out about the march. She forbade Gran from ever seeing me again. Mum told her," Louise pursed her lips, "'No daughter of mine is going to become one of your angry activists. Louise is going to grow up to be a proper wife and mother.'"

She smirked at Etta over her glass. "That didn't quite work out the way Mother intended, to her everlasting dismay. *I, being born a woman and distressed.*"

"Who said that?" Etta asked.

"My favourite poet, Edna St. Vincent Millay."

"I'll need to read her one of these days." Etta finished her sandwich. "Did your mum relent and let you see your gran again?"

"Not until the year women got the vote. Once that happened, Mother figured Gran's marching days were behind her and she couldn't unduly influence me anymore." Louise got a far-off look in her eyes. "Gran and I had missed each other terribly and didn't want to be parted again. We decided until I was of age that we would play by the roles Mother expected—at least in her presence. When we were alone, though, we would be our true selves."

She smiled, remembering. "You'd have liked Gran. She was curious about everything. Interested in everything: politics, religion, literature, travel...." Louise's voice trailed off. "For my eighteenth birthday, she was going to take me to Egypt. We were excited to see the Sphinx and the pyramids, but sadly, Gran died the week before we were meant to leave."

"I'm sorry."

"I never did make it to the pyramids, but I'm determined to go one day in Gran's honour." Louise released a fond smile. "Gran left me a lovely surprise in her will, though—her cottage."

"A cottage?" Etta stared at her friend in wonder. "Where?"

"Tackley, a small village north of Oxford." Louise quaffed her beer. "Like Virginia Woolf, Gran believed every woman needs a room of her own. Or, in the case of her spinster granddaughter, a *house* of her own." She paused. "Gran knew long before I did that I would never marry. She didn't want me to have to be dependent on a man to have a home, like she had been. Gran wanted to be sure I would always have a home of my own."

Etta couldn't even imagine the prospect. She'd never lived on her own. The closest she'd come had been the postage-sized flat she'd shared with Helen and Mavis in London. But to actually *own* your own home? "It sounds like heaven," she said. "Is someone living in the cottage now?"

"I have some tenants renting it—a family who was displaced early in the war."

"So, you're a landlord as well as a nurse." Etta's eyes flickered. "I'm sure you're a better landlord than the ones I've known. Or should I say slumlord?" A sour expression crossed her face.

"Where are you from, Etta?"

Now you've done it.

"Somewhere I daresay you've never been." She gave a careless shrug. "The wrong side of the tracks. Otherwise known as the East End."

"I *have* been there, actually. My first nursing job was at London Hospital in Whitechapel. I worked there for two years." Louise tilted her head at Etta, sitting across the table from her. "You don't have an East End accent."

"I should bloody well hope not."

A trio of nurses nearby shot her a disapproving glance.

Etta tucked her arms in at the sides. "Evidently, you can take the girl out of the East End but not the East End out of the girl." Leaning toward Louise, she lowered her voice. "When I decided to become a WAAF, I determined to become a whole new person, leaving behind the slum girl who left school at fourteen and couldn't speak properly." Etta looked at Louise. "When you have an East End accent, people assume you're stupid and treat you as such."

She paused, remembering all the slights and indignities she'd encountered, first working in the dress factory and then the munitions factory. "I wanted to be judged on my own merits," Etta said, "not my background. In basic training, I listened to the other girls, studied the way they spoke, and learned to talk like them." She drained her beer. "It wasn't hard. I've always been a quick study."

"Which is why you'll make a good nurse," Louise said. "As a nurse, you need to be able to think fast on your feet and respond quickly." She regarded Etta with an intent expression. "Do you have your heart set on becoming a member of Princess Mary's Royal Air Force Nursing Service?"

"I have my heart set on becoming a *nurse*." Etta lifted her shoulders. "Since I'm already a WAAF, the RAF seemed the easiest, most affordable way to do so."

"There are other options," Louise said. "For instance—"

The canteen door banged open, revealing a white-faced Betty and Harry.

"One of ours has gone into the drink," Harry said, delivering the news in a monotone.

All conversation ceased. Etta's stomach clutched. *Maeve is flying today.* Jumping up, she toppled her chair and made her way to Harry and Betty on leaden feet. "Is it—" she couldn't bring herself to say the name.

Betty gave a quick shake of her head. "Maeve's plane has just landed. It's Margaret Walsh."

Etta gripped Betty's hand to prevent her knees from buckling.

"And my pal, Ross," Harry said flatly. "Ross Reynolds. Their Dakota was seen to go down over the Channel and crash into the sea near Calais. They've mounted a search and are looking for the plane now."

Doreen and Dickie burst through the door. "Have you heard?" Seeing Harry's face, Dickie put his arm around his pal's shoulder and steered him off to one side, away from the others.

Louise joined the girls. "Don't lose hope. They may still find them."

The Flying Nightingales exchanged looks. They knew from their flight training that the chances were slim. Once a plane crashes into the ocean, that's usually it.

Maeve unbuckled her life jacket. She picked up the empty tea urn and stepped off the Dakota. Her boots had scarcely touched the ground when an ambulance roared up, and Graham jumped out, white coat flying. He hurried to her side.

"What in the world?"

Graham steered Maeve behind the plane, away from the curious eyes of the crew. He pulled her to him, crushing her against his chest. "Thank God you're okay." His voice was thick with emotion. "They said one of our Dakotas had gone down with a Flying Nightingale on board, and I thought it was you." His arms tightened around her. "I thought it was you," he repeated. "I thought I'd lost you."

"You didn't lose me," Maeve said, her face squashed against his chest. She turned her head so she could breathe. "I'm here. I'm fine," she soothed, stroking Graham's back. "At least I will be if you don't suffocate me to death."

Releasing his grip, Graham cupped Maeve's face in his hands. Then, eyes glistening, he gazed deeply at her and kissed her.

An extensive search was conducted for the downed Dakota in the area where the plane had been seen to crash into the sea, but no trace of the aircraft could be found.

Margaret Walsh's fellow Nightingales grieved. This was the first time they'd lost one of their own in a crash.

"I didn't really know Margaret," Maeve said, "but she seemed like a lovely, quiet girl."

Betty bobbed her head. "She was several years older than me and usually kept to herself. I'd see her in the communal hut sometimes studying those fortune-telling cards of hers."

"Me too." Doreen fastened a gaze on her fellow nursing orderlies. "One of the girls said she saw Margaret looking at her cards a few hours before she flew that day. She advised her to put the cards away, telling her it was bad luck."

Maeve crossed herself, and Betty said a silent prayer for the fallen Nightingale.

Etta released a long gust of air. "Bloody bad luck indeed, especially with the war ending any day now."

Officers and enlisted alike packed the canteen to raise a glass to the downed crew:

Pilot Officer John Ives, Flight Lieutenant Robert Southey, Flight Sergeant James Fife-Miller, Flight Sergeant Ross Reynolds, and Leading Aircraftwoman Margaret Walsh.

The Nightingales clustered together in a circle at the back where Maeve raised her glass. "To Margaret."

The girls chorused. "To Margaret."

Graham and Maeve slipped out of the canteen, the dusk providing cover as they walked hand-in-hand behind the huts. "I think our secret romance is no longer a secret," Graham said. "Not after my mad dash across the runway in an ambulance and pulling you behind the plane." He chuckled. "A tree would have offered more privacy, but I wasn't thinking clearly in the moment."

"Does it bother you that we're no longer a secret?"

"Not a jot. What are they going to do? Court-martial me? The powers-that-be have other things on their mind."

"Like wrapping up the war."

"Exactly."

"I think we should still be discreet, though," Maeve said. "No need to rock the boat."

"Discretion *is* the better part of valor. And speaking of discretion, I have news about Thelma."

"Thelma?" A guilty look crossed her face. "I'd forgotten all about Thelma."

"Most have. The war is winding down and everyone is preoccupied with that. Not to mention this latest loss. All that has pushed her death to the background."

Poor Thelma, Maeve thought. *Always priding herself on being the one in the know, now relegated to a forgotten footnote.*

Graham continued. "Apparently, while you were having your way with me at Ivy Cottage," he teased, prompting an elbow to his side, "the MPs concluded their investigation. Not finding any evidence to the contrary, they decided her death was accidental. Case closed."

Maeve frowned. "Really?" She flashed back to the sight of Thelma face down in the lily pond, remembering how later Etta had told her of the huge goose egg on the back of Thelma's head. How does one accidentally fall into a lily pond?

It was night and dark, her practical nature reminded her. *Remember how you fell in the snow when you couldn't see where you were going? If the MPs say it was an accident, then it was an accident. Time to move on.*

Maeve puffed out a sigh. "Well, that's a relief."

"For everyone, I think." Graham caressed her cheek. "And now that that's settled, if you would like to have your way with me again, I'm all yours."

"Oh, you are, are you?"

"Always."

"Well, let me see what I can do about that." She pulled Graham's head down to hers.

Chapter Thirty-Four

The next day, the BBC announced Hitler had committed suicide. The camp exploded in cheers, and that night, the canteen overflowed with revelers.

A week later, Maeve was taking care of a flight of POWs on their way back from Germany when halfway home, the pilot yelled, "Hey boys, the war is over!"

The entire plane burst into cheers. A corporal next to Maeve kissed her, his eyes bright. A private leapt from his stretcher, laughing. Grabbing Maeve, he planted a big kiss on her mouth. Another private hugged her and kissed her on the cheek. An exultant Dickie twirled the Irish Nightingale around and kissed her as well. Everyone was laughing and crying at the news.

And the kisses kept on coming.

Looking out the window of her Dakota, Betty saw explosions. *Enemy fire* now *with the war so soon to end? How can that be?* She ducked down, crouching beside an empty stretcher.

The pilot called out, "The war's over!"

Yelping, Harry flung himself across the plane. He hugged Betty and twirled her around, laughing and cheering. "The war's over!"

She gave him a disbelieving look. "It's over?" Betty cried and laughed through her tears, gazing out the window with Harry at the fireworks below.

Etta was on her way to the communal hut when everyone began streaming from the buildings, yelling and crying. "It's over! It's over. The war's over!"

Someone grabbed Etta and kissed her. Someone else swung her in a jig.

Etta whooped. Pans clanged, horns blared, and the entire camp exploded in an eruption of raucous noise. Everyone was hugging, kissing, laughing, and crying.

The canteen workers threw open the doors. "Beer for everyone!"

Motorcycles, ambulances, transport trucks, and vehicles of every shape and size raced around the perimeter of the camp, revving their engines and honking their horns in gleeful abandon.

Etta sprinted toward the hospital huts, searching for Louise. Men grabbed and kissed her, women grabbed and hugged her, and several swept her up in a dance. Matron grabbed Etta in a bear hug, her usual stern face wreathed in smiles. Moving on, the nursing supervisor hugged the Mess cook and danced a jig.

"Etta!" a familiar voice shouted.

Through the crowd, Etta caught a glimpse of a white nursing veil. "Louise." Waving, she pushed her way through the sea of bodies to her friend. At last, they found each other.

Beaming through her tears, Louise hugged Etta and whirled her around. "In the Mood" blared from a radio, and the two of them jitterbugged their hearts out.

After unloading the POWs at RAF Blakehill for processing, Maeve's plane returned to Down Ampney. Betty's Dakota followed, and both crews disembarked, laughing and shouting. Harry and Dickie slapped each other on the back, and Maeve hugged Betty tight.

"I can't believe it's really over," Betty said, tears running down her cheeks.

"Believe it, my girl. Now let's go join the celebration!"

Beer flowed freely, flasks were passed from hand to hand, and everyone sang and danced, celebrating for hours on end.

Maeve and Graham danced round and round, as did Etta and Louise, with Doreen and Will following suit.

Betty snuck off to write to Albert.

Hours later, as the music and merrymaking continued, Maeve and Etta headed to their hut, arms slung round one another and singing tipsily, "Roll Out the Barrel." Over their singing, Maeve heard something. Something odd. Tilting her head, she strained to hear. "Shh. Did you hear that?"

Etta rubbed a hand over sleepy eyes. "I hear a lot of things. Motors, music, singsongs." She yawned.

"It's something else. Sounds like weeping." Maeve followed the sound. "I think it's coming from the air raid shelter."

Suddenly alert, Etta recognized the cries of pain. Clicking on her torch, she ran toward the cross-shaped shelter dug into the ground, Maeve hard on her heels. As they approached the brick-walled trench, the cries grew louder. Etta spotted a motorcycle wheel sticking out of the ditch. She sucked her breath in through her teeth. Shining her torch into the trench, she glimpsed two forms entangled beneath the motorcycle and sidecar.

"Oh God."

The Nightingales scrambled over the side of the trench. Below, Maeve and Etta found Harry mumbling incoherently, his legs pinned beneath the heavy sidecar, a deep gash on his cheek. He was cradling the blood-soaked head of Lieutenant Blake to his chest and sobbing.

"I'll get help." Maeve turned to scramble back up.

"No!" Harry yelled.

"Harry," she soothed, "the lieutenant is badly injured, and we need to get this off you. Your legs may be broken."

"I don't care. Don't you understand? Julian's dead!" Harry wailed. "He's dead! I loved him, and now he's dead." He pressed his lips to the ginger head and wept.

Maeve froze. *Harry loves a* man. *But he's the camp Romeo....*

Etta inched over to the pilot and felt for a pulse. She shook her head at Maeve. "I'm sorry, Harry," she said, her voice gentle.

Harry's shoulders shook.

Maeve stroked his arm. "I'm sorry, too."

He groaned in pain.

"I know your heart is broken, Harry," Maeve said, "and right now, you don't care if you live or die. I know that feeling. I felt that way when my fiancé died." She placed her hand on the injured wireless operator's cheek.

He looked at her through wet eyes. Eyes full of sorrow. A sorrow so deep it pierced Maeve's heart. "But you're not alone, Harry. You have friends who care for you."

Etta squeezed his hand. "Good friends who want to help you. Would you please let Maeve and me help you?" she pleaded. "We don't want you to die. Julian wouldn't want that either."

"Julian wouldn't care," Harry said. "He never loved me the way I love him."

Harry had concussion and two broken legs. Assisted by Louise, Graham set Harry's legs. Sister Agatha was informed of the death of her fiancé and given compassionate leave. She escorted Flight Lieutenant Blake's body home to his grieving family.

The VE day revelries were dampened by the loss of the pilot. Most privately agreed they were relieved it was the lieutenant who'd died in the drunken motorcycle crash, rather than Harry. The charming wireless operator with the roguish grin was well-liked by everyone in camp, while the posh Lieutenant Blake, with his land and his title, had not endeared himself to anyone.

"Bit of an arrogant sod, if I'm being honest," one of the loadmasters muttered.

"Always acted as if he was above everyone else," his pal said.

"Lieutenant Blake thought he was God's gift to the ladies," one of the girls in the typing pool sniffed to the typist next to her.

"And he wasn't even that good-looking," the typist said. "Not like Harry." She leaned her head on her hand and sighed. "Harry's dreamy."

Harry, recovering in one of the hospital huts, asked to see Maeve and Etta.

They approached his bunk, noting the stitches on his cheek and legs encased in plaster. Maeve took Harry's hand in hers. "How are you?"

He gave her a wan smile. "Better, thanks." He waved his arm to encompass the empty hut. "Do you like my private hospital room?"

Etta winked. "I told them only the best for you."

"Too right." Harry grew serious. "I wanted to thank you for saving my life. The doc said I could have bled out if you hadn't got me to hospital when you did."

Maeve squeezed his hand. "It's a life worth saving."

He gave them a bleak look from hollow eyes. "Is it?"

"Stop that!" Etta glared at him. "You know damned good and well it is, Harry. You're the best wireless operator we have. Think of all the lads you helped save. Lads who would have died on the beaches if we hadn't gone and got them and brought them back. To hospital. Do you realize we've never lost a single soldier on any of our casualty flights?" Her eyes blazed. "I'm damn proud of that, and you should be too."

"I should have known better than to argue with a redhead."

Louise approached, carrying a glass. "I thought you might like some water."

"Thank you, Sister." Harry took a long drink. "Thanks for stitching me up, too." His familiar grin reappeared. "All I need now is a bandana and an eye patch, and I'll be a proper pirate."

"Quite rakish. You'll charm all the ladies."

His smile slipped. "Sister, could I have a few minutes alone with the girls? I'd like to thank them properly for saving my life."

"Of course." Louise smiled, flicking a glance at Etta as she departed.

"I owe you an explanation," Harry began, "and an apology."

Etta touched his hand. "You don't owe us anything."

"I do, actually. Grab a chair. You're going to want to sit down for this." Harry took a deep breath as the girls sat down, looking at them with anguished eyes. "I don't know how to say this, so I'm just going to come right out with it. Julian killed Thelma."

"What?!" His words knifed through the Nightingales, jolting them in their seats.

"Thelma was blackmailing Julian about me—about our *relationship*, such as it was," Harry said, his voice bitter. "She'd started off blackmailing Sister Agatha, but when Agatha said she didn't have any more money to give her—

her parents control the purse strings—Thelma went to Julian. She told him if he didn't pay her, she'd ruin his career, his reputation, everything."

Maeve exchanged a stunned look with Etta. *Is this all some sort of bad dream?*

Harry closed his eyes and recited in a monotone. "Julian told Thelma he'd give her the money and arranged to meet her at the lily pond. Then he sneaked up behind her in the dark and bashed her in the head with a rock. To make sure she died, he dragged her to the lily pond and held her head in the trench."

"Oh my God." Maeve felt as though she was going to be sick.

"How do you know this?" Etta asked in a voice like granite. "Were you there? Did you help Blake murder Thelma? Or did you just watch?"

Harry's eyes flew open. Sucking in a strangled gasp, he jerked back. "How can you even *think* that? I know because Julian told me afterwards. He was gloating about what he'd done and how clever he'd been, saying, 'Well, that Nightingale won't be singing to anyone.' That's when I knew he was a monster." Harry shuddered.

"So why didn't you tell someone what he'd done?" Remembering Thelma's nude body covered in filth and sludge, Etta was filled with a cold, hard fury. "Why did you let that monster murder Thelma and get away with it?"

"Because I'm a coward." Harry's face flushed with shame. "After Julian told me he'd killed Thelma, he admitted to strangling that nursing orderly over at Blakehill, too. Julian said his French letter hadn't worked, and the girl had got herself in trouble but refused to take care of it. So he took care of her instead."

He sent them a haunted took. "Then Julian looked me in the eye and calmly said, 'Nightingales aren't the only ones who can be silenced,' and I knew he wouldn't think twice about killing me too. This man who'd told me he loved me, whom I'd stupidly fallen in love with. So, I didn't say anything. *Do* anything. Because I'm a coward." Harry's voice was filled with self-loathing.

Lieutenant Blake murdered two women. Two Nightingales. And got away with it. Maeve couldn't take it in. She was struck by a sudden, terrible thought. Swallowing hard, she looked at Harry and asked in a shaking voice, "Did he kill Sally too?"

"No, Sally killed herself." Harry's face crumpled. "She had her own demons. We all do. Sally just hid them better than most. She never got over the death of her brother—Sally saw Jimmy in every one of her patients. That's why she was so good with her 'boys,' so tender, but after a while, it all became too much for her. It broke her heart to see the horrible injuries the lads endured and the terrible suffering they went through. Until one night, she just couldn't take it anymore."

"How do you know that?" Etta asked.

"Because Sally was my friend," he said simply. "The best friend I ever had. We talked all the time and confided in one another. Once, when we were both really low, talking about all the horrible things we saw and wondering how we could keep going on, we talked about offing ourselves."

Harry regarded them with sad eyes. "Sally's dalliances were no longer making things bearable for her as they had at the start." He puffed out a shaky breath. "She also knew how I felt about Julian, how much I wanted to be with him but couldn't. It was her idea to pretend she was having an affair with him. She did that as a cover for me, knowing how much I loved him..." His voice trailed off.

"Sally would sneak out at night and drink brandy Julian had got her in the Officer's Mess while he and I were together. Julian thought it was a great plan, but to make it even better he said he would brag to a couple of his pals that he and Sally were having a fling. That way, no one would ever suspect anything about us."

Harry's mouth turned down. "He said to make sure no one suspected how we felt about each other. I should really lay on the charm thick with the girls, which I'm ashamed to say I did." He rubbed his hand over his face. "I told Sally I felt bad about putting her in that position, allowing everyone to think she was Julian's bit of stuff on the side, but she didn't give a fig what people thought." His eyes filled, remembering.

"Sally replied, 'You're my friend and I care about you. I'm doing this for *you*. We've all got to grab at whatever bit of happiness we can these days." Tears streaked down Harry's face. "So, I did." He sent Maeve and Etta an imploring look. "Julian *did* make me happy. At first. He told me he was crazy about me, and I believed him. I fell hook, line, and sinker. I was crazy about *him*. Until the day I finally saw him for who he really was, and I realized I'd fallen in love with a monster. A monster who dragged my best friend's name through the mud with never a thought for her."

Harry's voice shook. "A monster who killed a young woman carrying his child, then casually killed another woman and dragged her into the muck and slime without a shred of remorse. And worse than that, he was *gleeful* about it. That's when I realized Julian hated women and wouldn't hesitate to kill again unless he was stopped." He gave the girls a tortured look. "So, I stopped him. I had to end it all."

Maeve and Etta walked around the perimeter of the camp, stunned by all they'd learned. Etta puffed on a Woodbine. "So much for the MPs investigation." She exhaled a series of smoke rings. "Let's hope they never decide to set up a detective agency."

"They're definitely no Holmes and Watson."

"More like Frick and Frack." She took a long drag of her cigarette and sent Maeve a sideways glance. "So, what do we do about these shocking revelations?"

"Nothing. We keep Harry's secrets and never breathe a word to anyone. What purpose would it serve?"

"Agreed. Julian Blake is dead, and justice has been served. Also, I don't think anyone would even believe us if we told them this story." Etta snorted. "It's like some lurid 19th-century Penny Dreadful novel."

Maeve nodded. "Besides, think how awful it would be for Thelma's parents to know that their daughter was murdered and in such an evil way." She flashed back to Thelma's face submerged in the lily pond and shuddered. "It would destroy them. If I were a parent, it would destroy me to learn my child had been subjected to such degradation."

She thought of Agnes Wilson, the first Nightingale Julian Blake had killed. Her parents already knew their daughter had been murdered, along with the child she'd been carrying. Would it make any difference if they knew the identity of the man who'd killed Agnes? A man now dead?

It might, her conscience said. Maeve wrestled with herself. Then Etta spoke, and she knew she'd made the right decision.

"Think of Harry. Imagine how his life would be destroyed if all this came to light. All because he loved the wrong person," Etta said. *"A love that dare not speak its name."*

Maeve's eyebrows rose. "Are you quoting poetry now?"

"Louise is rubbing off on me."

"She's a good influence."

"Too bad Harry had such a bad one."

Chapter Thirty-Five

June 1945

Etta strolled toward the canteen, musing about the future now the war was over. She needed to come up with a plan. She and Louise had begun discussing the ways she could go about becoming a nurse but had been interrupted by the loss of Margaret Walsh and her crew. Then, there was the chaos of VE Day and Harry's accident.

I wonder how Harry's doing, Etta thought. *I hope he's getting over Blake.* She refused to give the dead man his military rank, even in her thoughts. He didn't deserve it. *Thelma didn't deserve what Blake did to her.*

No woman deserved such violence.

Her brother's beery face leering over her filled Etta's head. She shoved the memories aside. Etta had made a new life for herself. A life she loved and was determined to continue. A life with new friends she loved. Friends who cared for her. Smiling, she quickened her steps, eager to see Louise. The senior nurse had arranged to meet her at the canteen so they could continue their discussion.

"Surprise!" Louise, Betty, and Maeve beamed at Etta beneath a string of faded bunting as she entered the canteen, a cake on the table before them. "Happy birthday!"

"Wh…how?" Etta stammered.

Betty smirked. "Sister Louise told us it was your birthday."

Etta turned astonished eyes to her mentor. "How did you know?"

"It helps to have friends in Admin."

Etta was overcome. In twenty-five years, she had never had a birthday party.

Noticing her bunkmate's emotion, Maeve suggested, "Let's have cake."

Betty's mouth turned up. "Maeve, you have the biggest sweet tooth of anyone I know."

"I won't deny it." The Irish Nightingale began to sing, "For She's a Jolly Good Fellow," and the others joined in, raising their glasses to the birthday girl.

"We'd best have that cake before Maeve devours it," Etta said. As she picked up the knife, she asked. "Is this one of the canteen's cakes?"

Maeve cut her eyes at the staff behind the counter and said in a low voice, "Actually, Louise managed to get the cook in the Officer's Mess to make it."

Etta's eyes flew to the nurse who lifted her shoulders. "She owed me. I stitched up her finger last week."

Taking a bite of the fruitcake, Betty closed her eyes in bliss. "M'mm, just like my mum's."

"The sultanas make it lovely and moist." Maeve refrained from licking her plate clean. "That's the best cake I've had in ages."

"I second that." The birthday girl licked her fingers. "Thank you, Louise."

The nursing sister smiled. "It's not every day a girl turns a quarter of a century."

Etta realized she had no idea how old Louise was. It wasn't something you usually asked a woman, and definitely not your superior officer. What did it matter anyway?

Betty clapped her hands. "Time for pressies." Grinning, she gave Etta a bulky package.

"You didn't have to do that."

"Yes, we did, silly. Birthdays mean presents."

Etta unwrapped a large jar of blackberry jam.

"I asked Mum if she could send a bit more than usual. This comes with her best wishes."

"Thanks, Betty, your mum's jam is always a right treat."

"My turn." Maeve handed Etta a flat package. "I hope you haven't already read it."

Etta unwrapped *The Picture of Dorian Gray*. "I haven't."

"Good. Oscar Wilde is one of Dublin's most famous sons. He's best known for his plays, but I didn't know if you liked plays, so I got you his only novel. According to the man at the bookshop, it's a brilliant book."

"Thanks, Irish. I look forward to reading it."

"*One can never have too many books*," Louise murmured, giving Etta a large package. Inside was a brand-new copy of *Gray's Anatomy*.

Betty released a long whistle. "Whoo, that is one big book."

"It's the most recent edition," Louise said. "Now that you're going to become a nurse, you'll need to keep up to date with the latest medical information."

Etta swallowed, at a loss for words.

"Looks like there's another book as well," Maeve prompted.

Etta lifted the second book and read aloud, "*The Collected Poems of Edna St. Vincent Millay*."

"One book for your mind, and one for your soul. You must never neglect the soul," Louise fixed her eyes on the redheaded Nightingale.

Etta felt something stir inside her. Something she'd never felt before. A look passed between the two women.

A look Maeve recognized. "Betty," she said, "why don't you and I take this last piece of cake to Doreen and leave Etta and Louise to talk nursing. You can tell me about your latest letter from Albert."

Betty's cheeks pinked. She gave Etta a playful nudge. "This one never says much about herself, so we'd have had no idea if you hadn't told us that it was her birthday, Sister Louise." She wagged a warning finger at the birthday girl. "Make sure you don't eat all that jam at once. You'll make yourself sick."

"Yes, ma'am." Etta gave Betty a mock salute.

Maeve smiled at Louise. "It was a lovely party. Etta does keep things rather close to the vest, so if not for you, we wouldn't have had this celebration." She hugged Etta. "Happy birthday, Red." She murmured in her ear, "Don't stay out too late."

Once they'd left, Etta fastened her eyes on Louise. "I've never had a birthday party before."

"I suspected that might be the case." Louise reached across the table and squeezed Etta's hand. "You're worth celebrating."

Raucous laughter from a group of loadmasters intruded. Louise removed her hand and said, "Now, let's get you sorted on your nursing career. You once said that until you made your first casualty evacuation flight to France, you'd never been out of England. Is that right?"

"I'd never even been out of *London* until my training at RAF Hendon."

"And you enjoy flying and going to different countries, correct?"

"I love it."

"There's your answer." Louise smiled. "You, my dear, need to become a full-fledged nurse in Princess Mary's Royal Air Force Nursing Service. Training usually takes four years, but since you've been a nursing orderly for well over a year, it might be shorter. As an RAF nurse, you can be posted *any*where. *Every*where. The world is your oyster."

Etta regarded Louise, scarce daring to hope. "Really?"

"Really. I'll speak to Matron and get things rolling on your behalf."

Eyes blurred and heart full to bursting, Etta said, "I don't know how to thank you."

"You can thank me by studying hard and becoming the best nurse possible. I have every confidence in you, Etta. You're going to make a wonderful nurse."

They chatted a while about what she could expect from training, with Louise regaling Etta with stories from her own training days. "I was absolute rubbish the first time I had to insert a catheter in a man," she said. "And the first time I had to give an enema to a pre-op patient, I nearly gagged." Louise lowered her voice. "I actually had to swallow my vomit."

"But you're always so calm and unruffled. Nothing seems to faze you."

"Years of practice. I was also very young at the time and had never seen anyone's nether regions apart from my own. It was quite an eye-opener for someone as sheltered as I was. With all the battlefield injuries you've seen, though, catheters and enemas will be a piece of cake."

"Perhaps not cake. I don't think that would be my favourite flavor."

Louise grinned. A grin that quickly faded. "The worst thing I encountered during my training was seeing a surgeon perform a radical mastectomy on a woman with breast cancer." She looked off in the distance. "Cora was only thirty-two. She had six children and was terrified at the prospect of surgery. She said without her breast, she'd no longer be a woman, and her husband wouldn't want her anymore." Louise took a deep breath. "Surgery was the only way to rid Cora of the cancer, though. It needed to be cut out. I told her without the surgery, she would die and leave her children without a mother."

She closed her eyes. "I convinced her to have the surgery, and Cora died on the operating table."

When Louise opened her eyes again, Etta saw the sheen of tears. "First rule of nursing. Don't make promises to patients that you can't keep."

"I'm sorry."

"So am I. So was Cora's husband. He never wanted her to have the surgery in the first place. Two months later, though, he had a brand-new wife, and eight months later, a brand-new baby," Louise said. "Out with the old and in with the new." She collected herself. "Sorry. I haven't thought about that in a while. Not the most joyful topic for a birthday celebration. Can you forgive me?"

"There's nothing to forgive."

They left the canteen a few minutes later. As they strolled together under the moonlit sky, Louise's hand brushed against Etta's.

The stirring Etta had felt in the canteen returned, and she laced her fingers through Louise's.

Chapter Thirty-Six

July 1945

Betty burst into the hut waving a piece of paper. "I'm going home!" She whooped.

"What?" Maeve stared.

"Home! I'm going home to Cherry Tree Farm. I got my demob orders!" She grabbed Maeve and twirled her around. *At last,* Betty thought, *I'll finally be reunited with Mum and Dad. And Albert. I can't wait to see him. Them.*

Maeve hugged her. "I'm so happy for you. When do you leave?"

"Tomorrow."

"Tomorrow?" Etta let out a low whistle. She regarded Betty over the top of her new *Gray's Anatomy.* "That doesn't give us much time to throw you a big party."

"I don't need a big party. Just the three of us and some cake and tea in the canteen is fine." Betty's head and heart were consumed with thoughts of home. In her mind's eye, she could see the Shropshire hills, the pasture, the barn, the paddock, and all the outbuildings. The cows, the pigs, the chickens—she couldn't wait to feed the chickens once again.

Moving on to the ancient stone farmhouse in her mind, Betty saw the thatched roof and paned windows and her small room upstairs. *Her room...* To sleep in a proper bed again. And have a bath in a tub again. A long, hot soak. She expelled a blissful sigh.

"I know what someone's thinking of," Etta teased. "A certain dairy farmer,

I expect. Mind you, don't have a roll in the hay straightaway. Make him wait a bit for it."

Betty was shocked out of her bathtub reverie. Her face flamed. "I have no intention of doing anything like that until I'm married. Nor would Albert. He's not that kind of boy. Albert's a proper churchgoing lad," she said. "Like me."

Etta lifted an eyebrow.

"I mean—you know what I mean."

"Etta's just teasing," Maeve said, "like she always does."

"Sorry, Betty, I couldn't help myself. I'm going to miss teasing you."

"I'm going to miss you too." Betty gave the girls a tremulous smile. "I'm going to miss both of you. You've become quite dear to me." She started to well up.

"Now, none of that, or you'll get me started." Maeve sat down beside her. "Have you told your parents yet, and Albert?"

"I sent them telegrams. I'll take the 8:15 from Cirencester tomorrow and arrive at the Bucknell station just before noon." She gave the girls a wondering look. "Just think, this time tomorrow, I'll be having lunch with my family again. I can scarce believe it."

And hopefully, Albert will be there too.

As Betty had requested, there was just a small do in the canteen that night to send her off. Instead of tea, though, the girls had beer for a "proper" farewell at Etta's insistence. The three nursing orderlies, as different as night and day, now friends for life, reminisced about their time together as Nightingales at Down Ampney, the good and the bad.

They talked about Sally, sharing poignant memories of the blonde Nightingale with the kind heart, jolly ways, and red lipstick. Maeve decreed that Sally's last tube of lipstick should go home with Betty, and Betty made Maeve promise she would go to All Saints periodically to put flowers on Sally's grave.

Clemmie, Doreen, Will, and Dickie stopped by their table to wish Betty *Bon Voyage*. She told them if they were ever in Herefordshire, they would be welcome to stay at Cherry Tree Farm. Graham and Louise also stopped by to say their farewells, but didn't say long, knowing the three girls needed their time together.

Back in the hut, Betty packed her case and gave the girls the last jar of her mum's blackberry jam. "Now, Etta, don't you eat all that yourself. Make sure you share it with Maeve."

"You heard Betty," Maeve said.

"I can't be held responsible if some of the other girls take it upon themselves to sneak some jam when we're not here."

Maeve rolled her eyes.

The girls exchanged addresses and promised to write to one another.

"Etta, I know you're not much for letter writing, but you'd better keep in touch," Betty said. "I want to hear all about your nursing training—what you're doing, where you're going." She shot a sly glance at Maeve. "And if you happen to meet any handsome doctors like our friend here, promise you'll tell me."

"I wouldn't hold your breath."

"You're a lovely girl, Etta," Betty said earnestly. "Look at that gorgeous red hair of yours and your pretty complexion. I know the right man is out there for you. You just haven't met him yet, but you will one day. I know it." Her cheeks pinked. "Look at me. I didn't ever expect to meet someone like Albert."

Maeve deftly changed the subject. "Will Albert be at the station to meet your train?"

"I'm not sure. The last time he wrote, he said he would, but that was a couple weeks ago. My orders came so quickly, I didn't give him much notice. He may be too busy at the farm to leave in the middle of the day. I can always see him later once he's finished working."

That's what Betty had been telling herself ever since she sent Albert the telegram notifying him of her arrival time. As a farmer's daughter, she knew full well a farmer couldn't just drop everything at a moment's notice in the middle of the day to go off gallivanting—even to the train station to meet his girl. That might happen in the films she loved, but not in real life. Betty may have been a romantic, but she was also practical and knew how things worked, and leaving work in the middle of the day was just not on.

Ludlow's only ten miles away, she told herself. Albert can borrow his dad's truck and come over tomorrow night after work. Perhaps have dinner with us. Her lips curved up in a smile, thinking of her beau in her house with her mum and dad and all of them sitting together at the table. Albert across from her so she could see his sweet face and look into his lovely blue eyes…

"Betty?" Etta waved her hand in front of Betty's face. "You still here?"

"Sorry. I was daydreaming."

"Nothing wrong with daydreaming." Etta cleared her throat. "I have an early flight tomorrow to pick up some more POWs, so I won't be here when you leave. We'll have to say our goodbyes tonight."

Betty's eyes filled and she hugged her pal tight. "Goodbye, darling Etta. Thank you for being such a good friend. I'm really going to miss you."

"I'll miss you too, kid. Be good and tell that farm boy of yours if he doesn't treat you right, he'll have to answer to me."

Maeve accompanied Betty to the train station. She had helped her friend set her hair in pin curls the night before, so Betty's stick-straight brown hair curled in waves at her shoulders.

Betty also applied a touch of Sally's red lipstick. Since she'd had to turn in her kit, she was clad in civilian clothes, a rayon blouse, and her old tweed skirt. She'd donned the blue velvet capelet Sally had gifted her to dress up her shabby outfit, though. Her hand reached up to touch the unfamiliar waves.

"You look lovely," Maeve said. "Like Ingrid Bergman in *Casablanca*." She gave Betty a fond smile. "Remember the time we were stuck in Brussels overnight, and that Belgian woman took us to have our hair shampooed and set?"

"How could I forget? That was the day after we'd had to sleep in that filthy room the Germans had just vacated. And the night before, we'd slept in the Dakota since the airfield had no facilities for women." Betty giggled. "Remember you had that big rock beside you in case any of the lads decided to pay us a nighttime visit?"

"I remember it well, and that nice sergeant major gave his soldiers what for on our behalf. I don't remember his name, though, do you?"

"I just remember he looked like Ronald Colman."

"He was a handsome man."

"Not as handsome as Doctor Moore." Betty's eyes gleamed.

The train pulled into the station then, and Betty hugged Maeve tight, the tears she'd been holding at bay escaping. "I'm going to miss you more than anyone, Maeve," she said, her voice thick with emotion. "You've always looked after me and been such a good friend to me. I don't know what I'd have done without you, especially after Sally died. I hope you know there's always a room for you at Cherry Tree Farm. Please say you'll come and visit."

"I will." Maeve's voice broke. "I promise."

Betty smiled at her through her tears. "And you don't need to come alone either. There's plenty of room for two."

The train whistled.

Maeve gave her a fierce, final hug. "Get off with you now, or you'll miss your train. I'll be watching for a letter from you with all the news of Cherry Tree Farm." As Betty boarded, Maeve added, "And Albert."

Three hours later, Betty Hall beheld the familiar scenery of her beloved Herefordshire. Her eyes misted. *Almost there now.* She didn't have butterflies in her stomach; it felt more like there was a frog jumping around in there. With shaking hands, she pulled out her compact and peered in the mirror. She fluffed her hair and reapplied her lipstick.

Not too much, though. Her dad had never much liked makeup. "No need to gild the lily," he'd always said to her mum. Betty also didn't know how Albert felt about makeup, so she didn't want to overdo it.

She felt as if she were about to jump out of her skin. Betty blew out a series of short breaths, calming herself the way she'd demonstrated countless times to the frightened casualties on her flights. *Breathe in, breathe out.* At last, the train pulled into Bucknell. Clutching her case, she descended the steps to the platform on shaking legs.

"Betty!" Her mum threw herself at her daughter and held her close. "You're home at last. Home where you belong." She wept. "Don't ever leave again my darling girl."

Betty snuffled against her mother's chest, tears running down her face. "I won't."

Then, it was her father's turn. He stared at his daughter, taking in the waved hair, rosy cheeks, reddened lips, and velvet capelet. "My little girl has become a woman," he said in wonder. "A lovely young woman." He enveloped Betty in a bear hug. "I've missed you, darlin'"

"I've missed you too, Dad. So much." Betty hugged him tight, her tears wetting the front of his shirt.

"There's someone else here too." Her father stepped aside, swiping at his eyes.

That's when she saw him.

Betty's breath caught in her throat. She had never seen Albert upright. He was a tall tree of a man.

The dairy farmer approached; his blue eyes glued on Betty. "There you are, my beautiful, brown-eyed girl." Shyly, he extended a small package with his remaining hand. "I brought you some cheese."

Graham strode through the camp, searching for Maeve. He checked the hospital huts, flight line, communal hut, canteen, and Mess, but to no avail. At last, in desperation, he approached the women's billeting hut where men were not allowed.

Standing outside the door, he called, "Maeve?"

Nothing.

"Maeve?" he said louder.

Etta poked her head out. "Hi, Doctor Moore. Are you looking for someone?" she asked innocently.

"Hello, Etta. Is Maeve here?"

"No. Sorry."

He blew out a frustrated sigh. "I've been searching everywhere for her.

Do you know where she is?"

"You might try All Saints. She goes there sometimes to put flowers on Sally's grave."

"Thanks." Graham sprinted away.

Doreen appeared beside Etta. "What in the world was that about?"

"I think the good doctor is on a mission."

Maeve laid a sprig of lavender on the headstone. "I promised Betty I'd visit you for as long as I'm still at Down Ampney, Sally. God only knows how long that will be." She sent a wry look heavenward.

"As I'm sure you know, Betty was demobbed last week and is now happily at home once again with her family. You probably also know a certain dairy farmer was meeting her at the train in Herefordshire, along with her parents. I imagine it won't be long before a letter arrives announcing when wedding bells will be ringing."

Maeve brushed a piece of dirt off the headstone. "I have news about Harry too. His casts have been removed, and he's doing well with physiotherapy. He writes that his physiotherapist at Stoke Mandeville is a good bloke and is teaching him to play chess." Closing her eyes, Maeve sent wishes for Harry's happiness winging his way.

She sat down on the grass, her fingers splaying over the velvety green. "Etta will be attending nursing school soon. Her friend, Sister Louise, is helping her with that. Etta will remain with the RAF and become a nurse with Princess Mary's Royal Air Force Nursing Service. Can you believe our girl's going to become an officer? I'm glad I won't be in the RAF by the time that happens. Imagine having to salute Etta." The corners of her mouth lifted.

"As for me, I'm proud to have served as a Flying Nightingale, but I'm ready to move on to something new." Maeve gazed off into the distance. "I'm longing to see my family, especially my little sister Briony, who's not so little anymore. I don't know whether I'll stay in Ballydavid or not, though. It all depends…." Her voice trailed off as she thought about the future. Maeve knew she'd have to make some decisions soon about what she was going to do.

Graham's voice rang out. *"There* you are. I've been looking for you everywhere."

Maeve's stomach fluttered as it always did when she saw him. Today, it fluttered even more. "Well, now you've found me." Her forehead creased. "You seem flustered. Is something wrong?"

"Something is very right. At least *I* think so, I hope you will too." Graham beamed. "I've been checking round with some of my doctor pals to see if they know of any small-town docs who might be retiring and need someone to take over their practice. I just heard from George, the friend who let us use his cottage. He said the doctor in Woolton-on-the-Water is retiring *next month.*" Excitement emanated from him in waves. "Do you know what this means?"

Woolton-on-the-Water? Our romantic hideaway? The fluttering in Maeve's stomach became a frenzied flapping. "I'm not sure."

"It means I can take over an established practice and be a family doctor once again. Only this time in a small village—a village where I fell in love with a raven-haired beauty who brought me back to life. A village with a cozy cottage the owner has said he'll sell to me." Graham dropped to his knee and reached for her hand. "Maeve Catherine Brigid Fitzgerald, I love you with all my heart, mind, body, and soul. Would you marry me and spend the rest of your life with me?"

"I thought you'd never ask." Maeve flung her arms around Graham and kissed him with everything she had. "I'm afraid you're going to have to buy a bigger cottage, though.

"One with a nursery."

Epilogue

September 2015

Maeve opened her hymnal and sang "Come Down O Love Divine" with the congregation in the small stone church. The music of the hymn "Down Ampney" was written by the village's most famous resident, celebrated composer Ralph Vaughan Williams. Maeve had returned to the familiar village with her sister Briony for the 70th anniversary of Operation Market Garden.

She glanced around All Saints Church, remembering the last time she'd been inside. Seventy years ago, at Sally's funeral. *Sally was the first of us to go. Then Thelma, Margaret.... And the rest.* Maeve closed her eyes, thinking of her friends. All the girls from her hut had now passed on. At ninety-three, she was the last one remaining.

Not the last Flying Nightingale, though. Maeve had heard there was still a handful left: Lilian Bancroft, Margaret Wilson, and Edith "Titch" (Lord) Joyce, according to accounts. Edith's Paddy, the camp jokester who'd always made everyone laugh, had died years ago, but Edith was living in Australia with her children and grandchildren where she and Paddy had moved shortly after the war.

Betty and Etta were both gone, though.

Betty Hall and Albert Martin were married at Saint Barnabas Church in Brampton Bryan in August 1945. Since Albert had three brothers at home

266

already working at the Martin Dairy Farm, he moved over to Betty's to help her father run Cherry Tree Farm. Albert and Betty had four children, three boys and a girl named Sally. Peter, the oldest boy, was a refugee they'd adopted from one of the concentration camps. The Martins had thirteen grandchildren and twenty-seven great-grandchildren. They were active members of Saint Barnabas, where Albert became a deacon and Betty embroidered kneelers for the pews and helped mind the children.

Betty became Vice-President of the local WI, inheriting her mother's Best Victoria Sponge and blackberry jam mantle after she passed. The first Saturday of each month, Albert took his film-loving wife to the cinema. On her birthday, he took her to a double feature.

Betty and Albert were happily married for sixty-three years. On their golden wedding anniversary, their children surprised them with a party at the town hall. There, Betty was delighted to see her old friends Maeve and Etta. While the three Nightingales enjoyed a reunion, Graham and Louise reminisced about their time working together as doctor and nurse.

Albert died of a heart attack at eighty-three whilst milking his beloved cows. Five years later, Betty died peacefully at home surrounded by her children, eager to rejoin her beloved.

After VE Day, a handful of Flying Nightingales, including Etta, continued repatriating POWs. Three months after the war ended, upon Matron's recommendation, Etta transferred to nursing training to become a full-fledged nurse in Princess Mary's Royal Air Force Nursing Service. She served with distinction as an RAF nurse for nearly a decade, first in Singapore, then Africa.

Although she loved her foreign postings, Etta discovered that she missed England and her dearest friend Louise. When she learned of a surgical position opening up at an Oxford hospital, Etta left the RAF to work side-by-side with Louise at the same hospital for years, doing what she'd always wanted to do.

Etta and Louise lived together in Louise's cottage inherited from her gran, where Etta gardened and read poetry aloud to her partner as Louise cooked their meals. The couple traveled extensively to Egypt, Spain, Greece, Turkey, Madagascar, Hawaii, and Iceland. They even visited Germany after the fall of the Berlin Wall.

From time to time when they weren't gadding about the world to some exotic clime, Etta and Louise would drop by Graham and Maeve's. On one such visit, Etta told Maeve about a movie they'd loved, *Roman Holiday*, and how delighted she'd been when she recognized Audrey Hepburn as the waifish teen with the big brown eyes who had sheltered Etta and her crewmates in her family's basement in the Netherlands after their Dakota crashed.

Over the years, Maeve visited Etta and Louise several times at their rose-covered cottage in Tackley. Her last visit had been three years ago when Louise was dying from a recurrence of breast cancer. After Louise eschewed chemotherapy, Etta nursed her partner at home in her final months.

"I don't know what I'm going to do without Louise," Etta told Maeve, hollow-eyed and desolate, over a cup of tea in the garden. "I can't imagine my life without her."

Three months after Louise took her final breath, Etta died of a heart attack. Maeve knew, though, that her friend had died of a broken heart.

Maeve gazed at the stained-glass RAF window with the Dakota at the top. When the service ended, with Briony at her side using her cane, she slowly made her way over to the window. Maeve mouthed the words inscribed there. "In memory of the men and women of the Royal Air Force, the 1st and 6th Airborne Divisions and Air Despatch Groups RASC who took part in Operations from Down Ampney 1944-1945."

Maeve's heart swelled with pride as she thought of all the wounded soldiers she and her fellow nursing orderlies had evacuated safely back home. The faces of the many nameless men she'd cared for on their transport back to England flashed before her eyes. The ones with bullet wounds, missing limbs, severe burns, internal injuries… The bomb-happy lads she'd held and rocked like babies.

Maeve recalled the night when their work was officially recognized. Sixty years after the war ended, the Duchess of Cornwall presented the remaining Nightingales with a medal, a lifetime achievement award, and a bronze statuette of Florence Nightingale. As the air ambulance nurses mounted the steps at the awards ceremony to receive their belated recognition, the entire audience rose as one and applauded. Maeve remembered how she and the other girls had exchanged looks of amazement as wave after wave of applause washed over them.

Her hand reached up to finger her medal.

Outside the church, Maeve stopped by the RAF Garden of Remembrance beneath the memorial window. There, several of those who had served at Down Ampney during the war had their ashes interred, including Etta and Louise. After paying her respects, she led Briony over to Sally's grave where she placed a bouquet of dahlias, rosemary, and delphiniums on the headstone.

"Maeve, is that you?" a quavering male voice asked.

She turned round to see two slim, white-haired men regarding her from the foot of Sally's grave. Maeve tilted her head and frowned, trying to remember. "Do I know you?"

The taller one approached, a familiar grin highlighting his aged features. "It's Harry."

"Harry!" Maeve hugged her old crewmate. "Oh, my goodness! It's good to see you. How long has it been?"

"Seventy years. Can you believe it?" Harry shook his head. "I never thought I'd live this long."

"Nor I."

The other white-haired man came up alongside them. Giving him a tender look, Harry lifted a hand shaking with palsy and placed it on the man's forearm. "Maeve, I'd like you to meet my partner, Bill," he said. "Bill was my physiotherapist. He helped me to walk again and regain my footing after my accident all those years ago."

Maeve's smile started in her heart and blossomed upward and outward, lighting up her whole face and erasing the years. She extended her hand. "I'm so happy to meet you, Bill."

Clasping her hand in his, Bill's warm brown eyes looked into hers. "Likewise. Harry's told me so much about you and his friends here at Down Ampney." His eyes flicked to the grave. "Including Sally."

"The best friend I ever had." Harry delivered a loving gaze to Bill. "Until you."

Maeve introduced the men to her sister. "This is my brilliant sister, Briony." She puffed up with pride. "Briony was head of the School of Mathematics at Trinity College in Dublin."

The four chatted a bit, then took their farewells. Harry hugged Maeve goodbye and murmured in her ear, "Blue skies and fair winds."

At the end of what was once the runway, Maeve bowed her head at the memorial stone honouring the aircrews that flew out on the Douglas Dakotas into Normandy, Arnhem, and the Rhine. Then she bent, arthritic knees creaking, and laid a wreath in remembrance. She looked round the barren area, remembering when it was filled with noisy Dakotas, metal Nissen huts, hospital tents, and the canteen with its ubiquitous dry cakes and fish paste sandwiches. Her eyes filled, thinking of her friends.

And Graham. Always Graham.

Maeve and Graham married in July 1945 and went to Ireland on a brief honeymoon, where Maeve introduced her handsome new husband to her Irish family. Her parents threw the bridal couple a party at the pub, complete with her mam's Guinness stew and drinks for everyone. Maeve's older brothers, Andrew and Patrick, came from Dublin to help celebrate and to tell Graham he'd better treat their sister right. After they'd closed the pub for the night, the newlyweds informed Maeve's mam and da they were going to be grandparents.

The happy couple returned to the idyllic Woolton-on-the-Water, where Graham became the town doctor, and Maeve assisted her husband in his practice. She would reassure nervous patients with a comforting word and gentle touch. Maeve was especially good with the children when they came in for shots, distracting them and giving them lollies.

The Moores lived in a three-bedroom cottage with their two children,

Molly and Rory, and a succession of border collies. Molly followed in her father's footsteps and became a doctor with a practice in London, while Rory followed his Irish roots to Dublin, where he trod the boards as an actor at the famed Abbey Theatre. Both children married eventually, providing Maeve and Graham with five adored grandchildren and eleven great-grandchildren.

After her children had grown and gone, Maeve volunteered twice a week at a nearby NHS acute hospital that provided care to returning veterans. There, she chatted quietly and sang to wounded lads and lasses back from various conflicts, including the Gulf War.

For their fiftieth wedding anniversary, Graham took Maeve to his Devon hometown of Beer, where they ate fish and chips and downed pints of Guinness. Every other year on her birthday Maeve returned to Ballydavid with her husband to see her family.

Graham served as the village doctor for sixty years. The year he retired, he was diagnosed with Alzheimer's. Maeve gave up her volunteer work and devoted herself to her husband for the next seven years, refusing to put him in care even when her children suggested she should.

There were times when Graham didn't recognize his wife and grew agitated and confused. During those times, Maeve would sing "The White Cliffs of Dover" or "I'll Be Seeing You" to him. His face would clear, and he would calm and sing or hum along with her.

Graham would gaze at Maeve, his eyes full of love and tenderness. "You have the most beautiful green eyes," he would say as he reached for her hand. "My beautiful Irish lass."

On that last day, Maeve recognized the signs that the end was near. She curled up beside her husband, held him in her arms like a baby, and crooned him to sleep with a final lullaby of "I'll Be Seeing You."

A Note from the Author

History has mostly overlooked The Flying Nightingales, who rescued an estimated 100,000 wounded soldiers from France alone in World War II. *Death of a Flying Nightingale* is my attempt to correct history's oversight. To recognize these valiant, forgotten women and pay tribute to these little-known, unsung heroes.

Thanks to their dedication, not one man died whilst in their care.

I first heard of this group of RAF women while streaming an episode of *Penelope Keith's Hidden Villages* in 2021. Penelope visited the Cotswolds village of Down Ampney in 2014 and interviewed an elderly woman named Lilian West who thought she might be the last remaining "Flying Nightingale" from World War II.

As I listened to Lilian's story, I marveled that she was only seventeen when she volunteered to become an air ambulance nursing orderly as a WAAF with the Royal Air Force. Lilian said she was given six weeks of training to care for the wounded from the D-Day beaches on evacuation flights back to England.

Six weeks.

As a former WAF (Women's Air Force) myself, I was mesmerized by Lilian's story. I couldn't believe I'd never heard of the Flying Nightingales. I turned to my husband and said, "This needs to be a book!" Then I searched for any information I could about these amazing women; to see if any books had been written about them. I found some scattered newspaper articles and newsletter accounts as well as a short non-fiction book called *A Nightingale Flew* by K.M. Neave (nee Holliday) which I promptly ordered.

As I skimmed the handful of available newspaper articles, I read about Lydia Alford, one of the first three nursing orderlies to evacuate wounded soldiers from the battlefields of Normandy one week after D-Day. Further research revealed that on 13 June 1944 three Dakotas took off from RAF Blakehill escorted by a squadron of Spitfires. The Dakotas and their crews landed in Normandy, France near Bayeux. After the supplies were unloaded the casualties were loaded on the planes. Each Dakota had one nursing orderly who tended the wounded men on the return flight.

Myra Roberts, Lydia Alford, and Edna Birkbeck became the first women to fly into an active warzone on active service by the British government. These air ambulance nurses, dubbed "The Flying Nightingales" by the media paved the way for further medical evacuations. Two hundred nursing orderlies transported over 100,000 casualties, by air, safely to England. Due to the dedication of these women, it is believed that not one man died while in their care.

In 2008, their work was officially recognized when seven Flying Nightingales were presented with a medal, a lifetime achievement award, and a statuette of Florence Nightingale by the Duchess of Cornwall.

When I received Kara Neave's book *A Nightingale Flew*, I was thrilled to learn more about these wonderful women. I was captivated by the reminiscences of Lydia, Myra, and Edna, the first three nursing orderlies sent to Normandy and nicknamed "The Flying Nightingales" by the press. Kara, a former RAF air traffic controller, who serves as a World War II reenactor, also included the recollections of five other Nightingales in her book: Elsie Beer, Edith "Titch" Lord, Florence "Rita" Marshall, Gladys Florence Batch, and Margaret Wilson.

Through The Flying Nightingales Facebook page Kara created and maintains to this day to honor these women, I was able to contact Kara and pepper her with questions about these unknown heroes of World War II. Scrolling through the Nightingales' Facebook page, I was saddened to read that Lilian West (nee Bancroft) the first Flying Nightingale I'd been introduced to via TV, and had hoped to interview, had passed away in May 2022. I also learned that Margaret Wilson, another of the nursing orderlies profiled in Kara's book, had died the previous December.

It seemed as though all the Nightingales were gone.

Imagine my joy and delight when I discovered that Edith "Titch" (Lord) Joyce was still alive! Edith's daughter, Colleen Amoretti, mentioned her mum on the Nightingales Facebook page. Immediately, I sent a private message to Colleen, who confirmed that her mother, Edith, who'd been posted at Down Ampney during the war, was 106 and now living in Australia.

One-hundred-and-six.

I asked Colleen if Edith might be willing to answer some questions for my book. Not only did Edith graciously answer my myriad questions; Colleen also sent me written reminiscences from her mother's time as a nursing orderly. What an honor and a privilege it has been to read those recollections from nearly eighty years ago. Edith kindly gave me permission to include some of her reminiscences.

The scene of her ironing uniforms and returning a pack of condoms (or French letters as they called them back then) from one of the uniform pockets to a hugely embarrassed soldier actually happened. So did the fun anecdotes of Edith's husband Paddy Joyce and his comic escapades with the VIP crucifix and the "invisible man" on the "invisible stretcher." Edith also told me about the time she and another one of the Nightingales had to mind a group of "bomb-happy" boys overnight and how many of the shell-shocked lads cried out for their mothers and girlfriends. This provided the basis for Etta and Maeve caring for the group of bomb-happy boys and a subsequent scene with Maeve and Edith doing the same. Edith shared that a couple of the men suffering from war nerves that she had ministered to, mailed her letters of thanks afterwards, addressed to "the small blonde" who'd been so kind to them in their distress.

Corresponding with Edith through Colleen has been an absolute delight. Colleen sent me photos of her mum—including one celebrating Edith's 107th birthday—and she didn't look a day over ninety. What a lovely woman.

Sadly, Edith died of cancer in November 2023 before this book was published. Thankfully, I had emailed an early version of the book to Colleen months before and she read it aloud to her mother who enjoyed the book and hearing her anecdotes relayed in its pages. I will always be grateful

Edith got to hear the story of *Death of a Flying Nightingale*.

Kara Neave also introduced me over the miles to Vincent Povey, who started the "War to Wildlife" project and created a webpage about RAF Blakehill Farm, one of the three RAF bases the Nightingales flew from in the Cotswolds area. Vince welcomes visitors to www.rafblakehillfarm.co.uk which features his research and is dedicated to RAF Blakehill and all those who served. As Vince says, "It is not an attempt at a history master's degree, it's a bloke giving a stuff about what went on over the other side of his hedge..."

Vince writes on the Blakehill website how he "stood on the exact spot where Dakota aircraft and their crews flew from, some never to return, along with countless glider infantry, as well as trying to understand the horrors that the 'flying nightingale' nursing orderlies went through. I imagined those left behind. Their grief was real, as was ours."

For purposes of the story, I chose to focus on RAF Down Ampney in my novel—where the first Nightingale I'd met via TV had been stationed—but RAF Blakehill is also featured in the book. I'm grateful to Vince for generously sharing his research about RAF Blakehill Farm and the Flying Nightingales.

Another Nightingale I discovered in my research was Anne Mettam. Her reminiscences of her time as a Flying Nightingale are included in a chapter of the 2002 book *Through Eyes of Blue (Personal Memories of the RAF from 1918)* edited by Wing Commander A.E. Ross, DFC. Anne was also stationed at RAF Down Ampney, although she didn't arrive until August 1944, two months after D-Day.

In *Through Eyes of Blue*, Anne shared a funny anecdote of how during one of her flights the contents of a urine bottle dribbled on a soldier which I adapted as happening to Maeve. Anne also told of an upsetting encounter on her plane with a German soldier, who mistakenly thought she was trying to steal his copy of *Mein Kampf* and gave her a black eye. This, along with a brief mention from another of the Nightingales about difficulties with a rude German on one of her flights, was the impetus for the scene where Betty is tripped by a German patient. Anne also wrote that she and twenty-two surviving WAAF air ambulance orderlies were invited to a Royal Garden Party at Buckingham Palace by Her Majesty, the Queen, on 15 July 1999.

There is some confusion over whether the nursing orderlies actually dispensed morphine to patients in the air. Some Nightingale reminiscences say they did, and that morphine was part of the medical supplies in their hamper. Others say the patients were administered morphine in the field before they got on the flights home and the nursing orderlies would record the time on a tag attached to each soldier—that way the nursing orderlies never had to give morphine on the flights. Since I was unable to verify this, I used poetic license by including "emergency morphine" in the Nightingales' hampers instead.

Most of the Flying Nightingales who served, demobbed from the RAF soon after the war ended and got married. Two of them died in the line of duty: Margaret Walsh and Margaret Campbell were posted missing, presumed killed, whilst on nursing duties.

On 24 October 1944, during a cargo flight from Antwerp to RAF Blakehill Farm, the plane Leading Aircraftwoman Margaret (LAC(W) Campbell was flying in strayed too close to the German garrison still holding Dunkirk. The aircraft was brought down by flak near St Pol-sur-Mer, killing all four crew members on board. Margaret is buried in the Canadian War Cemetery in Calais, France along with the rest of her crew.

On 28 April 1945 LAC(W) Margaret Walsh from Down Ampney was travelling aboard a Dakota bound for Brussels and Nivelles. The plane was seen to go down over the Channel, and crash into the sea nine miles east of Calais. Despite a thorough search of the area no trace of the aircraft could be found. Margaret and her crew mates are remembered on the memorial at Runnymede in Sussex. (The day her plane went down, some of Margaret's hutmates saw her looking at her fortune-telling cards earlier in the day. One of them, Elsie Beer, warned Margaret it was bad luck to do so.)

In the section with the flying missions to the Netherlands after Operation Market Garden, I included an Easter egg when Etta and her aircrew are hiding out from the Germans after their plane crash. The young Dutch girl who discovers the crew in the forest and helps them is based on the true story of fifteen-year-old Audrey Hepburn, who was part of the Dutch Resistance. According to various accounts, Audrey, who spoke English fluently after having been educated in the UK, apparently brought food to downed Allied pilots occasionally. Some accounts say she and her family hid one of those pilots in their cellar for several days, but all accounts agree that the young Audrey was starving and malnourished, reduced to eating grass, endive, and tulips to stay alive.

After the war, RAF Blakehill, RAF Broadwell and RAF Down Ampney repatriated hundreds of POWs from France and Germany. Down Ampney closed its gates in 1946, but RAF Blakehill and RAF Broadwell lasted until 1947.

Today, few indications remain of the former airfields.

RAF Broadwell has returned to farmland and now has a large solar farm covering it.

RAF Blakehill is now a wildlife restoration area and nature reserve.

As for Down Ampney, the only trace of the RAF airfield that remains is a memorial plaque in a field at the southern end of the former main runway that reads:

"From this airfield in 1944-5 Douglas Dakotas from 48 and 271 Squadrons RAF Transport Command carried the 1st and 6th Airborne Divisions, units of the air despatch regiment and Horsa gliders flown by the glider pilots regiment to Normandy–Arnhem and on the crossing the Rhine operations. We will remember them."

Indeed, we will.

Acknowledgements

This book was one of the most difficult ones I've written. As a former journalist and member of the U.S. Air Force I felt it was my duty and responsibility to honor these courageous women by being as accurate as possible in telling their story. To ensure I had all the historical details right.

As an Anglophile formerly stationed in Oxfordshire who loves World War II stories set in England, it was a joy to do the research. I dove deep, reading newspaper articles, books, and various accounts, and asking questions of those in the know. I learned so much about the Flying Nightingales and that time period in British history and felt compelled to include as much of that research in my book as I could. Unfortunately, that resulted in an early version reading like non-fiction, rather than a novel. My dear friend and longtime editor Lonnie Hull DuPont kindly pointed this out when she edited the book, then called *The Nightingale Girls*. "This is a novel," Lonnie said, "and in a novel, story is king. This isn't a history lesson."

Back to the drawing board I went, cutting and slicing.

Several trusted friends read early drafts and provided helpful feedback: Cheryl, Kim, Betty Jo, Sandy, Susan, Dave, Ruth, Jennifer, Jan, and George and Doni. (A salute to fellow Air Force vet Cheryl Harris, who read first draft chapters as fast as I wrote them and eagerly asked for more.)

Special thanks to the erudite George Foxworth, a voracious reader and dear friend I greatly respect, who made some invaluable suggestions after reading an early version.

My gratitude to Annette Smith, Susan Johnson, and Sue Gaston for answering my myriad medical questions and for reading specific medical sections of the book for accuracy. Any mistakes are mine.

A shout-out to John Eichenberg, my retired USAF loadmaster brother,

who answered my questions about plane tires (or as the Brits spell it, "tyres") bursting on landing and vetted Etta's Dakota crash scene. Thanks, John-boy.

Sincere gratitude to fellow Anglophile author Connie Berry who read a later draft and kindly provided helpful suggestions.

Many thanks to my friend Patricia in England who answered my periodic questions, "Would Brits in 1940s England have said this, or called this that?"

I owe a huge debt of gratitude to Catriona McPherson who read early chapters and scrutinized them for appropriate Britishisms. Thanks for also reading a later version, Catriona, and catching candy (sweets), Scotch (whisky), dating (courting), and gotten (got.) Any Americanisms in this story of English women set in Britain that slipped through are this Californian's mistakes.

I couldn't have written this book without the insight and invaluable knowledge of the Flying Nightingales provided by Kara Neave and Vince Povey in England and Colleen Amoretti, and Edith "Titch" Joyce in Australia.

Thanks so much Kara, for kindly answering my barrage of questions about the Nightingales, from what they wore to what they ate and drank to what I might find in their billeting huts on Down Ampney, and so much more! Thanks also for generously taking the time to research my questions on your end, and for kindly providing photos and details I wasn't privy to. (I especially love the great photo of you in Nightingales garb as a WWII reenactor.)

Thanks, Vince, for sending me helpful, hard-to-find details of the Dakota flights and aircrews, information about RAF Blakehill and RAF Down Ampney, and the Flying Nightingales. I appreciate your research and prompt responses to my endless questions.

My deepest gratitude goes to Colleen Amoretti and her mum, Edith Joyce, the last living Flying Nightingale (as far as we know) for answering my myriad questions about life as a nursing orderly at Down Ampney during the war. Edith's recollections of her time as a Nightingale added a depth and richness to this story it wouldn't have had otherwise. I'm forever in her debt and only wished she'd lived long enough to hold a copy of the book in her hands. Thank you, Colleen, for being the conduit between your mother

279

and me, and for sending me Edith's reminiscences of the war you'd written down over the years.

Thank you to Verena Main Rose and Shawn Reilly Simmons at Level Best Books for believing in this book, and for Verena asking, "Have you thought of making this into a series?" The answer was a resounding yes—a spinoff series set after the war. Stay tuned for the next Nightingale mystery in 2025. Special thanks to Shawn, for that drop-dead gorgeous cover.

My bibliophile sister, Lisa Jensen Cook, who has read all my books over the years, read the final version of *Death of a Flying Nightingale*, and brought tears to my eyes when she said, "This is the best book you've ever written. I loved it!" Thanks, Lee. That means the world.

Last, but not least, thanks as always to Michael for being the wind beneath my wings both in life and my writing endeavors. Without your love and support (and delicious meals) I couldn't do what I do. Thank you for always encouraging my writing and for listening as I read aloud sentences. Paragraphs. Scenes. Chapters. And offering your insights and suggestions— many of which I followed. (Smiles.)

About the Author

Laura Jensen Walker is the award-winning author of more than 20 books including the #1 Amazon bestselling, Agatha-nominated *Murder Most Sweet*. She flew a typewriter across Europe in the Air Force and fell in love with all things English at an RAF base in the UK. Captivated by the tales of an overlooked group of WWII RAF women—the Flying Nightingales—she knew she had to tell their story. Laura lives in Northern California in a wannabe-English cottage with her Renaissance-man husband and their two rescue terriers.

SOCIAL MEDIA HANDLES:
  Facebook: Laura Jensen Walker
  Twitter/X: LauraJensenWal1
  Instagram: @laurajensenwalker

AUTHOR WEBSITE:
  www.laurajensenwalker.com

Also by Laura Jensen Walker

Non-Fiction:

Dated Jekyll, Married Hyde

Thanks for the Mammogram

Mentalpause and Other Midlife Laughs

God Rest Ye Grumpy Scroogeymen (coauthored with Michael Walker)

Good Girl: A Memoir of Overcoming Rape, Breast Cancer & Fundamentalism

Fiction:

Dreaming in Black & White

Dreaming in Technicolor

Reconstructing Natalie

Miss Invisible

Daring Chloe

Turning the Paige

Becca by the Book

Murder Most Sweet (Agatha nominee for Best Debut)

Hope, Faith & a Corpse

Deadly Delights